Sq

Enjoy the story!

Brian W Peterson

Wager of Death

Brian W. Peterson

To my family.

ACKNOWLEDGEMENTS

As counter-intuitive as it may sound, having a third novel published is just as exciting as the first two. First, it means I didn't die in the interim. That's a good thing. Second, there's that nervous energy during the lull between the novel's completion and actual publication. It's like a person afraid of thunderstorms who just saw the lightning flash, waiting for the thunder to crash – except in this case, the crash is a relief. Third, it's a pleasure to work with the people who help make the book go from idea to reality.

In the context of the third point, I wish to thank my cover artist, webmaster, and, "hey, can you help me with... (whatever I'm freaking out about at the moment)?", Melinda Patrick. She is a professional painter, web designer, and the artist for all three of my covers. She also maintains my website, making me appear to be a legitimate member of the twenty-first century.

The tedious but dedicated work performed by Dan Knaus made my novel sound better than I deserved. His editing skills and helpful suggestions were insightful.

Special thanks to my cousins Mick and Jamie Buttress, who have been immeasurably helpful at Kansas City-area comicons, helping me to promote my novels. They've put in a lot of time helping me and all they've gotten in return was a lousy t-shirt – well, a funny t-shirt, but still. I've also bounced ideas off them for future novels, and just being around these two men, who have been like brothers to me my entire life, has been uplifting.

The encouragement and support I have received from friends and family mean more to me than the English language was meant to convey in fewer than four or five paragraphs, but I can sum it up with, "thank you." Your encouragement keeps me going. The same applies to my readers. The positive feedback I've received, including at shows, about my first two novels has been nothing short of exhilarating. To have people say, "I read your first book; I'll take your second one," is quite a rewarding feeling.

And to the woman who puts up with me sequestering myself in a room to write, bouncing strange ideas off her, and serving as my pre-editor and Chief Encourager: aren't you glad your husband isn't normal? How boring would that be?

To all referenced above: thank you. Thanks to you, I have completed Book #3. God willing and the computer don't crash, there will be more.

Brian W. Peterson
Somewhere on the edge of the Great Plains

Chapter 1

The moist chill in the air left a fleeting fog on the lenses of the man's glasses as he stepped out of the doorway. Before he could reach up to remove them, the glasses cleared. *Gil's Guitars* no longer served as respite from the late-autumn night air. The five-foot, seven-inch gentleman of Korean descent walked the deserted city block to his car. Only forty minutes prior, parking close to the store proved impossible. Now, he walked alone – or so he believed.

Behind him, Won Yoo heard footsteps. They belonged to a taller man who took longer strides. No other shop remained open at this late hour, and the feeling of being alone clawed at his mind. The thought caused him to quicken his pace.

The doors to his Toyota unlocked. Yoo gripped the keyless entry control and ignition key like a frightened child. Only steps away from entering the Camry, he heard the voice.

"Don't get in that car or you'll regret it." The voice resounded with firmness. Confidence.

Yoo turned to face his pursuer. "What do you want?" His strong Korean accent filled the street.

The pursuer was not large, yet he appeared to outweigh his prey by at least 70 pounds. "Get away from the car."

The lack of emotion in the voice added to Yoo's discomfort. With a nervousness that showed in his trembling hands, he obeyed the command. He stared at the face of the pursuer in an attempt to see detail. The darkness, the shadows cast by the angles of the nearby streetlight, and the occasional huff of breath, made visible by the ocean breeze which drifted in from the southwest, all combined to give the approaching figure a menacing appearance. The navy-blue trench coat, which held back the coolness of the night, provided another layer of visual captivation for the frightened man.

And that flat, strong voice did not help.

Yoo panicked. With fingertips inches from the door handle, he instead allowed the pursuer's words to direct his next decision. Rather than seize the best chance for safety – inside his car – he allowed the chaos which enveloped his brain to overtake him.

He ran.

Yoo ran down the sidewalk, toward a busy intersection two blocks away. He could hear a bus cross the intersection. A car horn let out a passing shriek. A small hill kept him from seeing what he knew populated the area: cafes; a coffee house; people.

The pain from the pursuer's hand – clasping like a robotic arm, then closing with a vise-like grip – caused him to forget the cafes, the coffee house, the people. His head crashed into the concrete wall of a store front. The fierce grip spun him, forcing him to face the man who had become his attacker.

A hand clamped onto his throat. His eyes began to dim, as though a power outage drained away his existence. The next sensation he felt came when his back hit the ground. The *thud* sounded distant, as though someone else's body smashed into asphalt, but far away. He landed in a small opening between two buildings. The two men disappeared from street view.

"Are you Won Yoo?"

Looking up at his attacker, Yoo responded weakly. "Yes." After a delay of only one second, he added, "Please don't hurt my family." His voice regained some of its strength to plead for his loved ones.

The attacker ignored him. He opened his trench coat and pulled a wooden club from his waistband. Tapered at the bottom to provide a better grip, it looked like a half-sized baseball bat.

Yoo did not see the club until the attacker's arm raised. He saw the silhouette of the weapon, backlit by a streetlight just a few feet away and around the corner of the building to his right. Lying prone, he struggled as best he could while in such a disadvantaged position.

The first blow struck his left knee. The *crack* echoed between the buildings, which rested only four feet apart from each other. Yoo let out a yelp. He had a high pain tolerance, but the club delivered more than he could bear.

Mercy accompanied the second blow. It struck on top of his head, just above the forehead. Black hair turned brilliant red. The blood flowed onto the asphalt, but Yoo lacked awareness of the sticky substance – or the next blow. Or the next 25 blows.

The attacker reached again into his trench coat – which shielded the man from the night's damp coolness from neck to just above his knees – this time for a rag. He wrapped the club in an effort to avoid transferring the dead man's blood onto his clothing, unaware of the splatter that littered his pants and the bottom of his coat.

Oblivious to the small drops of blood, he walked onto the sidewalk with a relaxed stride, past *Gil's Guitars*, and around a corner. This area of town did not have street cameras, so he walked with a casual certitude, comfortable in the belief the death of Won Yoo would remain unsolved.

Three hours later, a group of high school boys discovered the gruesome scene quite by accident. They explained to the police they were playing 'keep-away' with a friend's baseball cap when it was inadvertently thrown into the opening between the buildings. The young owner of the hat saw the bloody mess and the authorities were summoned.

They failed to mention the selfies with the body for which they all posed, which the officers would later see on several different social media sites.

The kids would be celebrities at school in just a few hours.

Chapter 2

"When's the last time Bill's been late?" The bearded man seemed impatient. After asking the question, he resumed his search through the large, plate-glass windows, as though staring outside could conjure up their friend's appearance.

"For breakfast?" The clean-cut blond man obviously had been disturbed from some deep thought. His head jerked as though he had been physically pushed. His suit – he only wore dark blue – clung to his body with such a tight hold, Walt always wondered how his entire wardrobe did not rip at the seams.

"For anything." Walter Musgrave stroked his beard – something he did when he was nervous, impatient, unhappy, angry, or otherwise emotional in a negative way about something – anything. His light-blue eyes looked heavy from lack of sleep. His brown hair and beard, with thin streaks of gray scattered about, gave him the look of a college professor.

"Never." Unlike his business partner, Alexander Heil uttered few words. Bright blue eyes highlighted his Nordic face. He looked as though he had stepped straight out of a 1930s Aryan comic book. His quiet nature only added to the mystique many felt about him. His wiry build distracted others, allowing him to let loose with subtle remarks and a calm but sharp wit.

"This isn't like him. I hope he's all right." Jacket unbuttoned, Walt looked the part of a businessman in the gray suit which highlighted his light-blue eyes.

"He's fine." Alex wished to communicate he was finished with the subject. His square jaw drew taut whenever something annoyed him.

"I'm not so sure, Alex. This isn't like him."

Alex pulled his cell phone from his suit jacket pocket. "It's six forty-five. He's fifteen minutes late."

"I know. Fifteen minutes."

"Come on, Walt. Relax." Despite his words, the nervousness seemed contagious. Before he could drop his cell phone into the inside pocket of his jacket, Alex stopped and looked again at the time on the front of the phone. He could have seen the time on his iPad, but Walt's anxiety seemed to give Alex the need to move.

"I've just got a bad feeling about this." Walt took a break from scanning the window and observed his immediate surroundings inside the small restaurant. All 20-or-so tables displayed the activities of a weekday morning. At some, men and women enjoyed their meals in tranquility, sipping coffee in their attempt to mentally and physically accept the new day. Other tables bustled with pre-work discussions; friends and co-workers – alive, energetic, like horses at the starting gate, about to race off in a thunderous cloud of dust.

"You always have a bad feeling about things," Alex shot back, his tension level rising. "Come on. Relax. Besides, you're making me nervous now." With his back to the front window of the restaurant, he no longer read the news story on his iPad as his focus disappeared into the pit of anxiety dug out by Walt.

"Sorry. It's just Bill Yoo's the most prompt guy I've ever known."

"Yeah, I don't think that's correct grammar. But you're right." Alex gave his article another attempt.

Before Walt could respond, he saw the hurried flash of their other business partner as he passed by the glass and then entered the eating establishment. He surveyed the room even after he

12

spotted his partners. The expression on Walt's face broadcast that he witnessed the odd behavior. The frantic man made his way to the table, glancing in every direction as he walked.

Walt spoke first. "Bill, you okay? You look like hell."

"No! I'm not okay." Of Korean descent, Bill spoke nearly perfect English. His few struggles with the language included indefinite articles, occasionally forgetting to say such words as "a" and "the." The minor imperfections of his English were masked by a slight Texas drawl, which was more noticeable than the slight Korean accent.

Alex glanced at Walt; the worrying had been warranted. "Don't pause. Tell us." A rare moment of impatience, fueled by curiosity, from the quiet Alex.

"At about five o'clock this morning, my phone started blowing up." His eyes darted to nearby tables, as though cause for suspicion lay with every patron. "My nephew is the rookie in Sheriff's Department and he was contacted about me being murdered last night. By the time he figured out it wasn't me, the rumors blew up." Bill used his hands to imitate an explosion as sound effects burst from his mouth.

Walt looked horrified, but Alex merely squinted, waiting for the story to continue.

"I've known for years there's another Won Yoo in the area. Won Sun Yoo. They found his body last night."

"And you're...?" Walt asked, not wishing to interrupt, but overcome with curiosity.

"Won *Yi* Yoo."

"Okay, so I understand the confusion," Alex began with a slow, thoughtful pronouncement. "But why are you acting so freaked out? You're a mess. You're all sweaty. You're looking everywhere when you talk. What's the matter?"

"The murder appears random." Bill delivered the statement as though the entire matter should be clear.

"Yeah. So? I mean, where was it?" Walt asked. "There are a lot of bad areas in SoCal." For the first time, Walt ceased to feed off Bill's negative energy.

"You have to understand, Won Yoo and I were the only Won Yoos in Ventura County."

"That's understandable," Walt joked, in a failed attempt to lighten the mood.

"He was in Camarillo. He lives – lived – in Thousand Oaks, just couple miles from me. I only saw him once. He-"

"Okay, wait a minute." Alex made a habit of speaking only when he desired to make an important point. "What's that? Fifteen miles from your house? I can see if it were close to you, but Camarillo's two cities over. It was random, Bill. Don't worry."

"He's right," Walt added. "If someone was after you, why would they look for you in Camarillo?"

"Besides, who'd want to kill you?" Alex framed his logic as a question.

"I don't know," Bill replied. "I just know there were two Won Yoos and now there's one." Again, the words filled the air with authority, as though his convoluted logic was the only conclusion to be reached.

"Did you look alike?" Walt asked.

Bill stopped his fidgeting and fixed his gaze on his business partner. After a pause, he burst into laughter. With that, Walt and Alex laughed. The laughs turned into hearty, loud sounds of relief.

"All the jokes you've made and you ask me that?" Bill could not respond with a straight face.

"Hey! You joke about it just as much as I do!" Walt defended himself in a jovial tone. "You're the one who said all white people look alike." They all laughed again.

Bill took a deep breath and resumed his serious tone. "Won Yoo had kind of a thick accent. I could tell the one time I met him he came here when he was fourteen, maybe sixteen years old. You can just tell by how people talk."

"You were how old?" Alex tried to piece together Bill's point.

"When I came to America? Ten. The other Yoo owned a grocery store in Encino. He opened a second one in Thousand Oaks just a few years ago when his business kept doing better and better." Bill looked behind him, just in case. "He kept to himself. He didn't associate with the other Koreans, which is not uncommon. A lot of Koreans I know are like that. That's why I don't know many Koreans."

Walt and Alex exchanged glances as they attempted to follow Bill's crazy train of thought.

"Well some Koreans don't go to community events – Korean community events. Things like that," he explained. "Of course, I don't go to many, either." He chuckled in a way that signaled his discomfort.

"You have a lot about which you can be happy," Alex injected in his typical style of grammar. "The company is growing, we have the DOD contract pending, and we're on our way upward." Also typical of his style, his words conveyed an emotion that his tone lacked.

"We're gonna be rolling in the dough," Walt added, almost as if to translate the stale language of his partner and friend.

"We already are," Bill responded, his tone telling the others that his emotions were leveling off.

Alex's blatant attempt to change the subject to all that was good in Bill's life worked. Walt continued with the positive talk. "Now if we can just get these bureaucrats to move in and out quickly we'll be okay."

"Ten years," Alex reflected.

"Twelve for us," Walt reminded Alex that he was the final businessman to join the leadership team that became Triumvirate Technologies.

Smiles replaced frowns as contentment pushed aside paranoia.

"Are you ready to order?" Walt asked his nervous friend.

"No. You guys go ahead. I'll watch you eat. I lost my appetite after all those calls and texts." He started to look at a nearby table, then snapped his head back as he caught himself repeating his acts of paranoia. "I'll grab a snack in the break room at the office."

Walt wasted no time in signaling for service – air filled his coffee mug and he felt hunger pangs. Alex perked up at the thought of food. He failed to understand Bill's concern in the first place. The others knew what Alex thought: it was sad a man had died, but this was no concern of his. Life was for the living, and there was work to be done, a company to grow.

Alex and Walt ate their breakfasts, the morning drama having drifted out of focus. In a more deliberate fashion than earlier, Bill slowly looked around the room every minute or so. The nervousness never departed.

Chapter 3

The Fire Captain barked commands over his radio, his red helmet bouncing with every emphasized word. He directed his crew where to go, where to aim their hoses, and how to address the hazards he saw. Firefighters in yellow helmets carried out his orders.

The long "ladder company" truck sported a bright yellow paint job on the body of the truck and a bright white ladder on top. At the moment, the ladder extended upward and outward at a thirty-degree angle. Water rocketed out of a nozzle, aimed by one of the firefighters, toward its target. The words "Ventura County Fire Department" were emblazoned in bold blue letters on the ladder, and the name was also found on the door of the cab. The two-toned cab – yellow on the bottom half and white on the top – briefly served as an office for the captain as he struggled to hear over the noisy scene.

Nearby, two much shorter "engine company" trucks provided the equipment as firefighters stretched out hoses while still other firefighters coaxed yet more hoses to life.

Overhead, a nearly invisible yellow helicopter with blue trim shined its spotlight onto the burning building, helping firefighters avoid pitfalls which could cost lives.

"Higher! Higher!" The captain shouted into his radio at the operator of the ladder as he exited the cab of the ladder truck.

With a calm demeanor, a gray-haired man exited a yellow and blue SUV and put on his white helmet as he strode toward the captain. "Any threats of more explosions, Captain?"

"Not from this building, Chief. We've contained the fire to diminish the threat. My crew got the information we needed while we rolled. We set up accordingly when we arrived."

The Chief nodded his approval, then stepped away from the chaos and took in the full scene. Where a corner of a building once sat, charred black debris remained. Flames shot into the night, but the darkness hid the thick, black smoke. He spotted a young man wearing a black helmet and motioned for him. When the man came close enough to hear, the chief asked, "Cadet, do you know what this company does?"

"Yes, sir. It's a tech company. I'm not exactly sure what they make, but I know they have a software division. I'm pretty sure they don't use volatile chemicals or explosives, though."

"'Pretty sure' won't cut it, son. Find out if you want to make it past cadet."

"Yes, Chief." With that, he headed to a fire engine to access an electronic tablet.

A blue Lexus GS 300 slid to a halt twenty yards behind the chief. In one motion, Walt shut off the engine, leaped from the car, and began his run toward the fiery mess. Upon spotting the white helmet of the Fire Chief, he changed his path.

"Excuse me, I'm Walter Musgrave, one of the owners of Triumvirate. What happened?"

"I'd like to ask you the very same question, Mr. Musgrave."

• • •

With the fire extinguished, embers still glowed and small mountains of debris smoldered in dozens of spots. Wisps of smoke floated upward in neat columns for several stories before spreading in the gentle breeze. Walt explained – first to the Fire Chief, then to the Fire Investigator, then to the first police officer on the scene,

18

then to the detective who arrived – about the placement of security cameras and how they, unfortunately, were wired locally and did not broadcast to any other buildings. He explained the lack of flammable materials in the building and every relevant point which came to mind.

He assured the authorities and then Alex and Bill after their arrivals that security would be beefed up.

The timing bothered Bill; only the result bothered Alex and Walt. The murder of Won Sun Yoo and now this explosion were two separate events, the others assured Bill. Nevertheless, he failed to find comfort in such assurances.

Despite the positive talk, one fact could not be denied: Triumvirate Technologies was under attack. Either the Ventura County Fire Department or a Cause and Origin expert would find out what caused the explosion, but without doubt an intentional act caused the conflagration.

• • •

When the Sun began its climb above the horizon, the amount of damage remained hidden by the debris. The real damage could be found inside the walls. The fire started in the wrong place – or right place, if malice was at work – for the company's chip business to continue to operate at optimum performance.

Despite Alex and Walt's assurances, Bill remained a skeptic. What gave all appearances of arson came 24 hours after the murder of someone who shared his name – or at least a name close enough by Western standards.

Twenty-four hours after the fire, Bill Yoo had a dream about what appeared to be an arson, the murder of Won Sun Yoo, and the end of his own life. The brilliant man who was born north of Seoul, near the Demilitarized Zone, now lived in danger of being consumed by recent events. He needed a break – emotional and physical – to allow him to get back to the focus and acuity which made his business partners and associates marvel.

Chapter 4

The company party roared with laughter as beer and hard liquor flowed. Loud, vibrant music dominated the rear deck in the back yard while an almost dainty flow of quiet conversation, classical music, and the smell of wine – with a few glasses of mixed drinks here and there – drifted out of the den and living room of Walt's over-sized house.

His staff called the house "Musgrave's Mansion," though, in reality, it was nowhere near the size of the estates found farther east down the 101 Freeway, particularly in Bel Air, Pacific Palisades, and other such mega-rich locations for which Walt held no interest. The house was too big for him, but with a maid service he endured "too big" for moments like these; the company parties were a source of great pride.

This particular evening had a purpose beyond the usual company profits news or celebrating Christmas or Independence Day. Their newest executive, Dennis Fry, was the toast of the evening. The 27-year-old Vice President of Business Operations became a hit after only one month in the position and four months with the company. His golden-brown hair and brilliant green eyes, along with his square jaw, gave him the look of a movie FBI agent, or the early days of a U.S. Senator-to-be. Upon seeing his tan, his good looks, and his thick-chested build, people were surprised to learn he was not one of the many local surfers.

Word spread throughout the house the time for brief speeches had arrived. A game of billiards paused in the game room; the rear deck music stopped; the volume to the Lakers' game on a large, flat-screen TV was muted; and all 112 employees plus spouses and significant others crammed into the Great Room and surrounding rooms to hear the owner of the house, who leaned against a railing, perched halfway up a curved staircase.

The crowd struggled to find comfortable places to stand free of others' elbows and shoulders. No one seemed to mind; everything was free, including the transportation to the house. A few minutes of discomfort could be excused.

Behind Walt, above him on the staircase, stood the new executive, whose expression showed the crowd his amazement at the mass of bodies.

"Ladies and gentlemen of Triumvirate," Walt bellowed, to quiet the crowd. A pause reinforced his message desiring full attention. "Are we having fun yet?" His broad smile grew broader as loud laughter and cries of "yeah!" and other happy exclamations carried throughout every room of the mini-mansion.

"We hadn't planned another party until right before Christmas, but promoting Dennis Fry has allowed Bill, Alex, and me to focus on growing the business in different ways – ways we only dreamed about just a few years ago. Now, the three of us are working on deals in seven countries for our non-military software and microchips, our battery technology is taking the technology world by storm, and – as you all know – we're hammering out the final stages of a very large contract with the U.S. military."

The crowd cheered, including the many in the kitchen, the entry to the den, and those lined up in a hallway that led to bedrooms.

"So, enough of all that. In just his first month in his new position, Dennis has learned his job quickly and he's made a number of proposals for efficiency improvements. We think this young man is going to make Triumvirate an even better company and a better place to work!"

Cheers again. The temperature in the house rocketed upward due to the number of bodies, and the steaminess made it feel like July in Oklahoma, but no one seemed to notice. They understood that, in all probability, the coming Christmas bonus would be higher than the prior year's. Minor inconveniences could be excused. The cheers faded, but with reluctance. They were present to enjoy the moment and celebrate their successes.

"Of course, all this means one thing." Walt paused. He had the attention of every occupant of the house. "Alex just might take a vacation next year." Walt laughed as the employees howled with laughter and delight. At the top of the stairs, Alex simply smiled and shook his head.

"He's told me he doesn't want to say much, but without further ado, please give an official Triumvirate welcome to the VP of Business Operations, Dennis Fry!"

Only the drinks in the hands of the partygoers limited clapping, but the guests managed to fill the void with boisterous, throaty yells of appreciation and approval. A few chanted, "Dennis, Den-nis," as though at a sporting event.

Dennis stepped down to the stair above Walt. The older man looked up, decided to give up the limelight, and walked to the bottom of the staircase. This was Dennis' moment.

"Thank you, everyone," Dennis called out to the group, his loud voice carrying throughout the house. His brilliant green eyes radiated a confidence everyone could see. "You are too kind. I've only been out of college for five years, so I know I have a lot to learn." He surveyed the room with a quick but wide glance. "But I'm proud to be part of Triumvirate Technologies." Dennis held up his glass for everyone to see. "I'm drinking *Crown*. Why is the rum always gone? Thank you."

Without hesitating, Dennis walked to the bottom of the steps to join Walt. Several people in the crowd laughed as someone shouted *"Pirates of the Caribbean,"* but most missed the movie reference in his parting words. The young executive shrugged as he looked at his boss. "Sorry. Didn't have much to say."

Walt chuckled, then turned to the still-assembled group. Barely visible to most, despite his 6'2" height, he let out a booming message. "Party on!"

The crowd laughed and cheered as they dispersed. Back to billiards and foosball and ping pong and the televised Lakers' game and music and cigars and drinking they went. The closest moment to unhappiness for anyone came when a mild disagreement broke out at halftime about checking the Clippers' game. Finally, the man in the minority agreed to find another television in the expansive house.

The employees of Triumvirate Technologies enjoyed their evening of partying.

• • •

The party neared its end when Dennis approached Walt. For the first time in an hour, Heidi was not on the new-hire's arm. "Hey, Boss. Got a second?"

"Sure. What's up?"

"I'm sure you've noticed me with Heidi tonight."

Walt did not respond with words. Instead, a narrowing of eyes and an ever-so-slight smile did the talking.

"Well, I'd like your permission to date her."

"She's a grown woman, Dennis. There's not much I can do about that."

"Yes, but there's the whole employee thing."

24

Walt nodded his understanding. "If she was a permanent employee the answer would be 'no.' But she's just weighing out some options. She's thinking about going to New York, she's got some opportunities in L.A., and she's got an offer on the table in Dallas. But I'm sure she told you all that."

"She did."

"That's why the answer is 'yes.' Again, if she was a full-time employee, then no. But you're fine. Just remember, I'm a boss and a father, and that can – and *should* – be a scary combination for any young man." He smiled when he said it, but Walt's enunciation of 'should' got his point across.

Dennis grimaced. "I understand. I'll be a good boy." His grimace turned into a grin, followed by a huge smile.

"One word of advice, Dennis."

"What's that?"

"She doesn't like to be told what to do," Walt explained.

"A man doesn't tell a woman what to do. She tells herself," Dennis replied. When Walt stared back, unsure how to respond, Dennis added, "Cary Grant in *Notorious*. Great movie." The huge smile returned.

Walt smiled back, but as Dennis walked away, the smile evaporated.

As Bill approached, he studied his business partner's face. "I can see those wheels turning, Walter."

Walt smiled.

"Alex is coming. He had a question for you and evidently, he wanted to talk about it with you and me. He didn't mention Dennis." Bill scanned the Great Room. There were still over 20 people present. "There he is."

Within seconds, Alex joined the pair. His no-nonsense style extended to after-hour parties. "What's the latest on security at our facilities?"

Neither Walt nor Bill minded Alex's ultra-serious approach to life, and neither viewed the timing as inappropriate. Alex, after all, oversaw business development. Bill was the technology expert and Walt the sales guru. While only Bill lacked business school training, they all had their areas of specialization. They trusted one another. They recognized each other's strengths.

Alex's strength lay in providing the focus the business needed. As the only pure businessman – Walt considered himself salesman as much as businessman – Alex's instincts were rarely questioned by his partners. While Walt could sell canned snowballs to a golf course and Bill could envision the technology needed to build a roller coaster to the Moon, Alex was walking, talking business theory in action.

The subject at hand was one in which none of the partners possessed expertise. Their trusted staff attorney roamed somewhere in the crowd, but absent his immediate presence, Alex led the conversation.

"Re-doing our security systems for better monitoring? Guards? Maybe armed?" Alex's words left his mouth phrased as questions, but Walt knew him well enough to recognize orders, despite the equality of the partnership.

"I talked to Tony earlier tonight," Walt explained. "I didn't get real specific 'cause I didn't want people overhearing – didn't want people concerned – but yeah, he's on top of it. He said it'll cost a chunk of change to re-do the camera systems, but I didn't ask how much. I just told him to get it done."

Alex nodded his approval, but Bill looked as though he were in deep thought.

"The insurance guy will be out Monday," Walt continued. "He's already told Torres repairs can start after he's been out."

"What if," Bill began, trailing the second word as the thoughts behind his eyeballs continued to race. "What if." Alex and Walt waited for Bill's mouth to catch up with his fast-moving brain – a common occurrence. "We build a security headquarters in the open lot east of Building C? We're growing, guys. Privatize our own security. Taller fencing. Cameras." He stopped and looked at the others. "We've been derelict with security."

"Whatever you want, Bill. Just coordinate it with Tony. I don't know how much security we need, but we are growing, I know that." Alex nodded as he spoke, as though still pondering Bill's words.

When Heidi walked up to Walt, he was happy for a reason that differed from the young men in the company. He was happy his daughter spoke to him – not because she had ever stopped talking, but because he always feared such a time could arrive. Father and daughter had never connected, and their relationship remained stuck in "tenuous" mode. They were like a highway built from opposite directions, with the intent of meeting in the middle. Somehow, somewhere, the connection was never made – two roads, ending miles apart.

At five-feet-five, Heidi's thin frame made her seem taller. Like her father, her light-blue eyes could cut or mesmerize. Her full-bodied, light brown hair danced to and fro every time she turned her head, brushing the tops of her shoulders with each movement.

"Dad," she began. His heart beat faster when she called him 'Dad.' Usually she addressed him without using a name or nickname. "I'll be out late, just so you know." Even at 23, she retained a high-pitched, girlie voice.

Walt grinned. "Just make sure you take good care of my new executive."

Heidi laughed at the unexpected comment. "See ya tomorrow." She spun and walked away, keeping hidden from her father the look of bewilderment on her face. "Worry Wart Walter" she had called him – to his face – just last week. Now he did not even ask what time she would come home.

Walt watched her go, his thoughts betrayed by his eyes, wandering from Heidi to Alex and Bill, then to Dennis, who stood across the room, chatting with coworkers. The eye-darting ended when interrupted by the presence of the company attorney.

"Hello, gentlemen! Just who I need to see. Helluva party you guys throw. Every time." Tony Harris was the lone legal counsel on the company's payroll. On occasion, a team of lawyers would have to be hired, but that team received Tony's oversight. To "all things legal," he was about to add "security expert" to his resume.

"There you are!" Walt blurted, as though he had searched the entire house for the man.

"Like you can't find me with this red rug on," he said with a laugh, pointing at his red, curly hair. The hair was his, but he liked to tell people it was a bad toupee. "Besides, you coulda texted me." He paused for effect. "Oh! That's right. You don't read your texts."

"I read your texts. You know that." Walt fought off the embarrassment of being the only member of the team to not fully utilize his cell phone's capabilities. "I just don't respond."

"We were talking about security," Alex brought them back to the subject at hand.

Tony was not ready for business. Two large glasses of wine, two margaritas, and four beers out-voted the need for a business discussion. To Tony, "security" only meant everyone would make it home safely from the waning party.

"Hey, where's Dennis?" the redhead asked. "I haven't seen anyone receive that much praise since Jack Bauer stopped a nuclear bomb from going off."

The joke was met by Alex's sobriety. "Remember, two nukes went off with Jack around."

Though buzzed from the alcohol, Tony's expression came through without room for misinterpretation as a *what just happened?!* look covered his face. He glanced at his business associates before saying in a loud whisper to Walt, "He just critiqued a fictional character."

"Right now's not the best time to be joking about bombs going off." Bill's smile attempted to lessen the severity of his own words and defuse Alex's annoyance at Tony's tipsiness.

The normally professional Tony stood motionless, a blank, stupid smile glued to his face. After five seconds of surveying the expressions on his friends' faces, he responded – smile intact. "Okay. Nothing nuclear happening. What do you need from me?"

"Security." They all knew Alex could open a 'Calvin Coolidge School of Brevity' if he wished, but the one-word response caught Walt and Bill off guard.

"Just looking for an update," Walt expanded on Alex's answer.

"Well I'm sorry, guys, but my update to Walt yesterday is the answer today. I'm bringing in people to give me bids, I'm listening to ideas. I mean, I'm on board guys, but it's been three days. The debris hasn't even been hauled off yet." The alcohol's grip on Tony's brain loosened noticeably.

"All right." Alex understood. He would not say so unless he meant it.

"Thank you." Annoyance in full view, the good-natured lawyer fell silent.

Walt studied the attorney until Tony looked his way.

"Am I the only one who drank tonight?" Tony seemed incredulous at the others' seriousness.

Bill – 'Mr. Personality' of the group – smiled. "Not as much as you did."

As Tony threw up his hands, Bill laughed. The last week had witnessed a shortage of laughs among the top men, so it helped to ease the burden, if only for a brief moment.

"Look, I was in the Marines. I could drink you all under the table!" Tony's comment drew laughter again as Walt nodded his agreement.

"I have no doubt," Alex volunteered.

"I'd never challenge you," Bill said with a wry smile.

"Hey. What time is it?" Walt acted as though he had a hot date.

Tony pulled up the sleeve on his sweater and looked at his gold wristwatch. "Eleven twenty-two," he replied.

"Okay, thanks," Walt answered.

"Got somewhere to go?" Bill asked.

"No. No. You're not old enough to worry about this yet, but the doctor has me on some stupid heart medicine and I have to take it in the evening."

Alex watched as Walt made his way toward the kitchen. The expression on his face gave away his thoughts.

"Don't worry about his heart, Alex," Tony said, without looking at him.

"What? Oh. No." Alex acted as though he had been shaken out of a deep sleep. "No, I'm just thinking about Bill's idea of a security center.

Tony and Bill exchanged glances as they chuckled.

Chapter 5

"Let's lay it out there. What does everyone think?" Alex took control of the impromptu early-morning meeting. He sat behind his desk while the other leaders of the company spread out in the fourth-floor office. Although there were enough chairs for everyone, Tony stood, Bill paced and Dennis and Walt sat. The arrangement gave the look of a lack of order, but with Alex's presence, order always existed.

"Peter Simms comes to mind," Walt volunteered.

"Who's that?" Dennis asked.

"He sabotaged the battery line two years ago," Walt answered.

"Not just a brief stoppage," Tony added. "He destroyed production equipment. Shut us down for weeks."

"What was his beef?" Dennis asked.

"He came up with some idea we used," Walt explained. "And he didn't think he was paid enough."

"Unbelievable," Tony shook his head. "We paid him a ten-thousand-dollar bonus."

"Not enough, huh?" Dennis said as he looked around the room.

"We saved probably thirty-thousand-dollars a year off his idea, so he thought he deserved more," Bill chimed in.

"So, we fired him. It was fun." Tony smiled.

"Fun?" Bill asked in amazement.

"Yeah. It wasn't the usual routine, everyday boring stuff. It was fun," Tony explained.

Walt shook his head in disagreement.

Alex laughed. "Okay, who else?"

"I saw a G&S Systems car the night before the fire," Dennis said.

The others reacted with surprise and shock. "Did you tell the authorities?" Bill asked, his amazement apparent.

"We did the talking, remember," Walt reminded Bill.

"Who did you tell?" Tony wanted to know.

"I can't prove anything. I don't have anything," Dennis explained.

"Cut him some slack," Walt interjected as the energy level in the room soared. "He just saw a car. You just saw a car, right?"

"Yeah. Turning into a hotel in the Westlake Village area."

"They have cars?" Bill asked no one in particular.

"Apparently so," Tony answered.

"What are they doing around here?" Walt stated with concern. "There's no reason for them to be around here."

"Where exactly did you see him?" Alex asked, getting back to the point.

"I was on the 101 near Westlake Village," Dennis answered. "We got off at the same exit and he went into that Hyatt over there."

"Hyatt?! Damn!" Tony whistled after his minor outburst.

"Company cars, high-dollar hotels." Bill shook his head and looked at Tony.

"Unbelievable!" Walt added.

The men responded further according to their personalities: Walt with anger and suspicion; Tony with skepticism toward any explanation why a G&S Systems representative would be in the area, for any reason; and Bill with bewilderment at illogical data – namely, why G&S Systems would have a company car in the area. Alex took control of the deteriorating conversation and overlapping comments and got to the point.

"Tony, contact the Ventura County Sheriff's office and see if they can use this information," Alex ordered. "Walt, see if you can figure out why their guy was here. There's no industry for them here."

All the men understood the significance of the unstated accusation. G&S Systems held a special, sour taste in the mouths of the executives. What started as a small microchip company based in Silicon Valley morphed into a national player in all things technology once they signed a contract with the federal government. Their programmers worked alongside various federal agencies, and they were even seen from time to time in Washington, D.C., working with the staff of House and Senate members on computer systems.

They branched out further once they secured a missile guidance system contract with the Department of Defense. Their employee count – and revenues – grew exponentially for five straight years and their profit margin remained above the 20% threshold. They were a "happenin' place," as Tony had put it.

Various industry sources claimed G&S Systems felt threatened by the multi-pronged growth of Triumvirate Technologies. Chip design and manufacturing helped propel Triumvirate's profit margins, but the battery division drove the sector into a frenzy – and caused the executives at G&S Systems to have sleepless nights.

"It's not enough they're turning into a giant," Walt complained. "Now they want to take us down?"

"They've had it good for how many years?" Tony asked.

"They're a gorilla, no question," Bill added.

"What do we do if it is G&S?" Dennis asked.

34

"We stop them. We find a way to stop them." Walt's emphatic response caught everyone's attention.

"We don't know it's them yet. Let's see what we find out." Alex returned balance to the conversation which again spiraled downward. "Who else?"

"What if-?" Bill began, then in his typical manner, he stopped, his brain whirling like a carnival ride. "What if you talk to that CEO lady you know, Walt?"

"Oh," was all Walt could manage.

Tony laughed. "Rose Bakkeby. That's all Walt needs – to see his old girlfriend."

"She's your –" Bill started to pursue the matter before Alex interrupted.

"That's a great idea. I like it." Alex looked at Walt. "She's connected. She's CEO of a company bigger than ours, so she can find out information if she doesn't know. She'll be a perfect source."

"If she knows anything." Walt stated the obvious.

"Great idea, whoever she is," Dennis said.

"Oh, just a great idea," Tony laughed.

"Thanks a lot, Bill," Walt said as he shook his head.

"Have fun, Walt," Tony mocked.

"You want to come along with me, Red Mop?"

"Why don't you just call her?" Dennis asked.

"That'll never work with her," Tony answered. "Never work. This is gonna have to be face to face."

Walt sighed. "Okay. Whatever."

"I'm leaving for the day. I've got a meeting after lunch in downtown L.A.," Alex announced.

"I've got a tech meeting in Orange County tonight," Bill added. "I'll be back late tomorrow morning."

"You leaving now?" Tony asked.

"As soon as we're done. Off to the Newport Beach," Bill replied.

"And I get to meet the Department of Labor team in twenty minutes," Dennis announced.

"Have fun with that," Bill laughed.

"I think I'll go home and hide," Tony joked.

"Probably not a bad idea," Walt added.

The meeting broke up. While nothing of substance had been accomplished, they all recognized that perhaps – just perhaps – they had laid the groundwork for solving the mystery of who attacked their business.

• • •

Triumvirate Technologies had grown from sharing an office building with other small businesses and law firms to its current location, which amounted to a small campus. The four buildings were labeled alphabetically. Building B contained the battery manufacturing operation. Building C, which suffered the mysterious fire and explosion, contained the chip manufacturing portion of the business. Building D, a small, 40-by-40 building, served as a way station for shipped items, both incoming and outgoing. The small dock on one side of the building represented the first step in a grand plan lodged somewhere in Bill's cranium.

Buildings B and C looked like small airport hangars, containing enough space for operation growth, and enough room to store needed materials.

Building A was a typical-looking concrete and steel office building. Four stories tall, sections remained empty, prepared for growth. The founding gentlemen of Triumvirate had no intentions of moving. Alex had his doubts; Walt just shook his head; but Bill had the vision to ensure the present location would be permanent. They even owned ten undeveloped acres, which could be sold, if necessary, for a nice profit as land zoned for commercial use.

It was in Building A – simply known as "the offices" – where the triumvirate and the business staff spent their days. The software division was also housed here. Only Alex had a top-floor office at this stage in the building's evolution.

Walt's third-floor office, with its historical décor and impersonal feel, did not appear to be that of a man on the rise. Behind his head hung a portrait of George Washington. To his left was a reproduction of Charles Henry Granger's painting depicting Patrick Henry arguing against the Stamp Act in the House of Burgesses. A photo of the raising of the American flag at Iwo Jima draped the wall next to the door. No one who entered Walt's office doubted his patriotic fervor.

"Fervor" was not quite the correct term to describe his emotions at the moment. He knew federal bureaucrats were in the building, and he knew their presence signaled the beginning of the equivalence of a corporate rectal exam. Negotiations for a federal contract had commenced, and the Department of Labor automatically became involved.

The young executive entered Walt's office with the head bureaucrat in tow. "Mister Novak, this is Walt Musgrave." Dennis extended a hand toward Walt as the Labor official entered the room.

"Ah, Mr. Musgrave. I'm pleased to meet you." Che Novak reached out his right hand as a broad smile enveloped his face. The small man with small arms and legs and thick, black hair seemed to glare at the businessman from behind the smile.

Walt stood and grabbed his hand in greeting.

"Such a small office for a head of a growing company."

"Yeah." Walt chuckled. "We're not terribly worried about appearances like that around here. I assume you just got here?" Walt's nervousness could not be missed.

"Che Novak is the gentleman who will be overseeing the review of our books. He's from the OFCCP" Fry explained.

"Che?" Walt fought to hide his disdain for the man's name. Before he could think of another subject and drive out the silence, Novak smiled again.

"My mother adored Che Guevara and Trotsky, so she named me 'Ernesto Leon Novak' and nicknamed me 'Che.' It stuck."

"Ah," was all Walt could manage. He dropped his head and sat. When he returned his gaze to the bureaucrat, he discovered Novak watching him as though studying an adversary.

"But if you don't like Che Guevara, that's okay with me." Novak allowed his smile to remain.

"I'm not worried about anyone's politics right now." Walt's grumpy tone put the lie to his words.

Novak surveyed the office décor. "Who's that guy?" He singled out a painting.

"That's Patrick Henry."

"Ah, yes. The 'give me liberty or give me death' speech."

"Actually," Walt began as he struggled with his tone. "That's from when he argued against the Stamp Act. Henry argued that too much government interference is bad for a country. Bad for liberty."

Novak laughed. "I see. Then I'm sure Mister Patrick Henry wouldn't like me very much."

"Uh, Mister Novak. Let's you and I resume our tour. Then we'll clean your car. Wax on, wax off. Come on." Dennis laughed. He wanted to lower the temperature in the room.

Novak looked at Dennis, unsure whether he should feel insulted.

"It's a joke – a movie line," Dennis reassured him. "I like movies."

"Do you know how long you'll be here, Che?" Walt let the last word hang in the air, emphasized with a slow pronunciation of the short, three-lettered name.

"I was telling Dennis I think we'll be done in about three months. So, get used to seeing me."

"Three – three months?! What could possibly take three months?!" Walt felt on the verge of losing control of his sudden gush of anger. "We can give you two people for half a day for a few weeks. That oughta speed things up."

"Actually, I was thinking something like four people, full-time – for the duration, of course." Novak kept the smile, but his brown eyes turned to steel. "The entire three months. Plus, I'll have some of my own assistants with me."

"Mister Novak," Walt began, a slow boil evident beneath the surface of his face, which turned red. "With all due respect, we're running a company here, and we're not exactly large, you know. We're about to become bigger, but I don't see how I can afford to assign four – let alone two – people to you full-time."

"Trust me. You can afford it. Or, think of it this way: you can't afford not to. Think of all the profits you'll be making when you get a DOD contract."

Walt took a quick breath through his nostrils. The conversation was going to have to end soon for him to maintain control. "What are you saying, Che?" His words came out as a slow, calm, harmless question.

"I'm saying it would be very beneficial for you if I were able to finish my job in the shortest time possible," Novak said, his incessant smile never leaving. "The sooner we get this done, the happier DOD will be, as well."

Walt looked to his reproduction of the George Washington portrait – the one Washington himself hated, by Gilbert Stuart. He took a quiet breath before answering. "Okay. Dennis will get you four people, full-time."

"Don't hate me, Mr. Musgrave." Novak could not let his smile go. "I'm here on a job, just as you have your job."

"Oh yeah, what's your job?"

"My job is to protect taxpayers."

Walt resisted the urge to give a comeback. He knew Tony would be proud of him.

"Now, Mister Fry," Novak sucked in a large breath, like a victor after battle, chest expanding. "Wouldn't you like to buy me lunch?" He exhaled and allowed his smile to grow larger still.

"Sure. No problem." Dennis replied, happy the subject changed.

"We can have a couple of rounds and then get settled in."

Dennis frowned. "I can't drink during business hours."

Novak slapped the younger man on the back. "I'm sure Mister Musgrave will understand if you bend the rules a little." He turned back to Walt as he half-pushed Dennis through the doorway. "Nice to meet you, Mister Musgrave. I'm sure we'll be seeing plenty more of each other." The young executive and the bureaucrat disappeared.

Walt stared at the empty doorway for several seconds before he finally spoke to the empty room. "What's the penalty for murder?"

Chapter 6

"I don't want you overdoing it with this Che Guevara guy."
Walt had not allowed the passage of three hours to calm him any.
With Alex gone for a day of meetings in downtown Los Angeles
and Bill off to one of his creativity seminars – this time about
expanding technology beyond common thinking, Walt was told –
the eldest member of the triumvirate had not managed to vent his
frustrations to anyone yet.

Dennis recognized Walt's irritation level. "I understand, but
this guy has the force of the entire Department of Labor – the entire
Executive Branch of the U.S. government – behind him."

The pair stood in a hallway, across from the entrance to a
men's restroom. Walt spoke quickly, seeming to understand his
time alone with the young executive was limited. "I want you to
come up with excuses why you can't take him to lunch every day,
and pull your people away when you can so this ship doesn't grind
to a halt." Walt seemed unaware of the mixed metaphors.

"Mister Musgrave, I-"

"'Walt.' I told you, call me 'Walt.'"

"Okay. Look. Walt. I don't think you get it." Dennis'
frustration shined through. "This guy will make our lives miserable.
That's why he was acting so over-the-top. He was sending you a
message this morning. Just cool off and let it go. I'll take care of
this guy."

"I'm not asking."

"And I'm not making up consequences here. This guy is the
Devil with a federal name tag." Dennis took a breath to calm his
tone. "Walt. Listen. Some people exist to live; some people exist to
drain life from others. This guy wants nothing more than to drain

away your life – the company's life. Don't let him do that to you," Dennis pleaded.

Teeth clenched, hands formed into fists, Walt turned and stormed away. When he reached his office, his red face and angry stride broadcast his emotions better than a neon sign flashing above his head.

Tony was the unlucky one who arrived at the doorway seconds after Walt entered. The lawyer looked back in time to see Dennis and Novak enter the elevator down the hallway. When he turned his attention back to Walt, he saw a wildfire in a business suit.

"Uh oh. Somebody met the bureaucrat," Tony half-sang.

"I've already had enough!" Before he could focus all his energy into a rant, the telephone interrupted. He picked up the receiver and masked his emotions. "Walter Musgrave."

Walt dropped his head as he listened to the voice. "Yeah." The caller had more to say before Walt responded again with a "yes," followed by another pause and a "why thank you, sir."

Tony stepped all the way into the office and shut the door. As he eased into one of two chairs in front of the desk, Walt worked on ending the call.

"He's a good young man. He definitely climbed quickly, but we have a lot of confidence in him." Walt's final pause allowed the caller to say his parting words. "I appreciate that, sir. You have a good day, too. Thank you for calling."

Walt set the phone onto its base with a gentle touch, looked at Tony with a wild look, and picked up a thick Defense Department report. Before Tony could speak, Walt lifted it higher, then smashed the 160-page document onto his desk, sending a loud *slap* reverberating through the room. The angry businessman clenched his teeth and glared at Tony.

Tony did not speak, but did not appear to be startled, either. Instead, he fought off a laugh. After several seconds of examining the fuming man, he could not resist: "You all right?"

"That was Fitzmorris at DOD. He called to tell me he heard about Fry's promotion."

"And that makes you angry?" Tony sounded more like a psychologist than a lawyer.

"No. I'm pissed because I want that Che Guevara guy to go away, and I want Fry to quit being his chauffeur!"

"You realize this is just Day One?" It was only a half-question.

"Yes! That's why I'm so pissed!"

"I'm looking at this from the opposite direction." Tony let out a slight chuckle as he spoke, amused by his friend's anger. "I'm looking at this as Day One, as in, 'big deal.' Doesn't mean it's gonna happen every day."

Musgrave took in a slow, deep breath before responding. "It's Day One as in, this is going to go on and on and on." His voice rose as he spoke. "I want that guy outta here!"

"What did he do that caused you to call him 'Che Guevara?'"

"That's his name. It's 'Ernesto Tolstoy Novak.' His nickname's 'Che.' His momma loved the murderous thug, Che Guevara."

Tony laughed heartily. "You're kidding?! She named her kid after a South American communist and a great Russian writer? That's odd."

"No! No! Not Tolstoy. Trotsky. The Russian communist. That's what I meant. Forget his name! The guy's a loon. He's here to hurt us. His department's even called the 'CCCP' or something like that."

Tony laughed again. It was obvious to both men that Tony enjoyed this moment more than he should – and at Walt's expense. "He's with the OFCCP – The Office of Federal Contract Compliance Programs. It's an arm of the Department of Labor."

"Whatever! I've been told. Yes." Walt was not in the mood for facts at the moment.

"Listen, Dennis can't help it. He's gonna be stuck with these guys for a while. He's between a rock and a hard place."

"He can do what I told him to do, which is dodge the guy!" Walt bristled.

Walt had calmed down a little, but now the emotions taxed Tony. "Walt. Listen. I did research on these guys. They fine companies for non-existent offenses, then they inflate the amount of the fine when they report it publicly."

"Why?"

"They get raises and promotions – well, they used to, I don't know if they still do – based on how much they stick it to companies. They work out deals where they blackmail companies to go along with the exaggerations. It's how they operate."

"That's insane."

"Hey, it's the federal government. What do you expect? They convince the public they uncover all this imaginary discrimination based on numbers. They're gonna nail us, Walt, so just expect it. We have a lot of Hispanics in the area and we don't employ many, so it's gonna happen."

45

"What?!" This news did not assuage Walt's anger or high blood pressure. "We go by who applies and their qualifications! We-"

"Walter, Walter!" Tony threw up both hands, as though he could physically calm and silence his boss. "Walter, *listen*. I'm just trying to prepare you. Get over it now. I didn't say they're fair, I said that's what they do."

Walter allowed the scolding to dull the sharp points off his anger. "Okay, so can we work out a plan?"

"Do you know how many businesses – great businesses – have experienced this? If they didn't figure it out, we're not gonna. That's just the naked truth right there."

"I gotta explain all this to Alex and Bill." Walt stroked his beard as he thought about the matter.

"I bet ya Alex already knows. He knows everything. I'll talk to them, but if you talk to them first, explain it this way." Tony became demonstrative with his hands and arms, as though he could not speak if he sat on his hands. "The Department of Defense wants to award somebody a contract. We want that contract. The OFCCP wants to punish whoever wins the contract. They use statistics – remember the Mark Twain quote about statistics? – and they'll give the appearance that we discriminate. The public eats it up. The government rode in on a white horse and saved the little guy from another big, bad business. That's it. Your whole explanation. They OFCCP will fleece us for a million dollars or so and-"

"A million dollars!"

"That sounds about right." Tony continued. "We'll have essentially paid a tax for the right to receive some bad publicity, then everyone moves on and forgets it ever happened. Boom.

That's it." Tony became his nonchalant self again. "It's wrong. It's crazy. But the public eats it up. This stuff happens all the time."

Walt shook his head, half in anger and half in an attempt to process all the information he just received. "I just want them gone."

"All we can do is brace ourselves and ride out the storm. That's it." Tony shifted in his chair, as though he were uncomfortable with his own words. "We'll get a couple of bad news stories on the L.A. TV stations and one article per newspaper, and that's it. If we do something stupid and really make 'em mad, then they'll drag out the process and encourage more stories about us."

"You're a good, tough lawyer, but now listen to you. You're backing down pretty easy." Walt's words stung like a scorpion.

After several seconds, Tony shrugged off the sting. "It's the Department of Labor, Walter. They have a few dollars more than we do. Trust me." No returned fire, just a calm assessment.

Walt let out a loud sigh. He looked at George Washington as he responded to the lawyer. "All right, but I don't know how long my patience will last."

Tony climbed to his feet as he glanced at his gold watch. "You're the one who loves the exhilaration of a good battle."

"This is blackmail, not a battle."

"True, but you'll still find it exhilarating." With a laugh, Tony opened the door and left, leaving Walt alone to stew in his calming yet still hot anger.

Chapter 7

The construction crew had not worked on resurfacing and curb repair for the past several hours. Equipment had been locked up for the night and tranquility dominated the air, although the cones and yellow tape remained. The lingering, biting smell of fresh asphalt floated over the empty parking lot. Movie-goers forced to park in a nearby darkened lot were left with a taped-off path through which they navigated the half-paved, half-destroyed lot as they fought to ignore the pungent odor.

A small crowd exited from a side door of the large building and fragmented as they separated from what they had in common for a brief two hours. A few made their way through the yellow tape maze to the makeshift parking area behind the theater. Two stragglers – a man and a woman – walked arm-in-arm toward their car. Before they reached it, the last car of the small band of strangers pulled away. The couple walked the final steps alone.

So they thought.

As Kim Yoo climbed into the passenger seat of their Mercedes, she heard a strange sound from the other side of the car. The driver's side door swung open, but she did not see anyone. "Bill?" She called out. Another strange sound. A *thud*. Wood on bone – wood on skull, to be exact.

She leaned toward the driver's door, and in the car's interior light – faintly though it glowed onto the ground, several feet from the car – she saw bright red blood on top of Bill's head. The *thuds* continued. She could see his body move with each strike, as though their eldest son were jumping up and down on his back.

Kim Yoo did not remember screaming. She did not remember the struggle to climb over the center console or the fall to the ground outside the door. She did remember seeing a dark figure disappear just as she looked up, milliseconds after her tumble to the ground.

As she cradled her husband's lifeless torso and head, she gained the awareness she was screaming a long, continuous scream. And she gained the awareness she was now a widow and her two sons would grow up without their father.

• • •

"I'm Detective Robert Encarnacion. People call me 'Detective Rob.'" The tall, lean, dark-haired man of Hispanic descent reached out a hand. Alex noted the long fingers and rough feel to his hand.

"I'm Alexander Heil, and this is my business partner, Walt Musgrave." Alex let go of the handshake to motion toward Walt. "I've been told you're aware of Kim's wishes, so please, keep us in the loop on things."

"Yeah, sure. I can do that." The detective motioned for the men to follow him. He led them into an office and closed the door behind them. He leaned against his captain's desk as he waved for the men to sit down. "My number one question for the two of you is, is there anything you can give me? Anything you can throw out that may point me in the right direction?" As he waited for an answer, Encarnacion walked to the blinds to shut out the rising sun.

Alex and Walt exchanged glances, as if to decide who would do the talking. Alex drew the unseen short straw.

"A few days ago," Alex began.

"Friday. No, Thursday night," Walt interjected.

"The other Won Yoo in town was murdered," Alex completed the sentence.

Encarnacion snapped his head around. "I didn't draw that case. I was off that day, but I heard about it." He returned to leaning against the large, wooden desk.

"On Friday morning, we met Bill –" Alex stopped and looked at Walt. "Won Sun Yoo, right?"

"That's the other guy," Walt said.

"The other guy was Won Sun Yoo. Our friend is – was – Won Yi Yoo." Alex slowed at the weight of the small word: *Was.* "So, Bill was really uptight about this other Won Yoo's murder, and he thought it meant something. It freaked him out."

"Did he think somebody was after him?" Encarnacion inquired.

"He acted that way. Walt?"

"He did. He acted that way," Walt repeated Alex's words. "He said no one had anything against him, but I think it was just the name thing. That's what did it."

"Or maybe," the detective mused. "He had reasons to be fearful and he just didn't tell you guys."

The businessmen chuckled, though their level of discomfort rose.

"You'd have to know Bill," Walt was the first to explain. "He had a problem with telling too much." He turned to Alex. "It's weird talking about him like this." He then returned his focus to the detective. "I used to have to explain to him about limits about personal matters. He had no filter. His wife was always embarrassed by the stuff he said. It was hilarious sometimes."

"All right. I'll look into the other Won Yoo's case. This makes a lot of sense, too." Detective Encarnacion squinted, almost concealing his brown eyes, as he thought and spoke, bringing pieces together. "The murder of Mister Yoo appears to be a crime of passion. He was beaten savagely – pretty quickly – then stabbed with some sort of long knife. I won't know 'til we get full results back from the coroner, but that's the preliminary information. But it was all so, so brutal. It was like the guy had something against him. Nothing was missing – stolen. Now maybe–" He stopped, his plunge into deep thought obvious. "Maybe nothing was stolen because his wife was there, and he got scared off. This looks like a crime of passion, but you guys and his wife don't seem to think he had any enemies."

• • •

The meeting lasted another ten minutes before the two businessmen left the police station together. Walt pointed his blue Lexus on a heading back to their office.

"You buy that about a crime of passion?" Walt asked.

"No. Not at all. It doesn't make sense." Alex spoke with a slow, methodical cadence as he thought through the situation. "I get it. I know crimes of passion happen a lot. But I think Bill wasn't freaked out just because a guy with the same name was murdered last week. I think it was because it was a guy with the same name who kept to himself."

Walt looked away from the road to take a quick glance at his business partner. "You mean, you think Bill thought he was the target because no one had a reason to kill the other Won Yoo?"

"Yeah. I do. I mean, you could say that about either guy. Both were in business. But then we had the fire and that just cinched it in his mind. He was nervous right up 'til the end."

"Okay. That makes sense," Walt volunteered. "But why park in that dark lot?"

"Maybe he didn't want Kim to know how rattled he really was," Alex said.

"Or maybe he didn't have a choice. Maybe that's just the way it ended up. The front lot was probably full."

Neither spoke as Walt navigated the roadways. Both sat in their comfort zones: in their thoughts. Neither excelled at exploring – let alone sharing – feelings with others. Neither wished to feel at this moment for fear of what it was they would feel.

Walt gave away one of his thoughts with a question. "If there's a God, why do people die so young?"

"Because this isn't a final destination," Alex responded and returned to his private world. Typical of his way of handling matters – any matter – the subject of death closed without further discussion.

The pair drove the rest of the way to the office in silence. They both had to mentally prepare for their interactions with the Departments of Defense and Labor. They also understood not only was the 'triumvirate' in Triumvirate Technologies gone, but they had lost their creative genius and the personality of the leadership trio. And they lost their close friend.

In the quiet of the drive, they both wondered what was next – but they did not speak their thoughts.

Chapter 8

The long, torturous week of shock, anger, and sorrow gave way to a week of depression as the employees of Triumvirate Technologies struggled to accept the horrific murder of the charismatic member of their leadership. The genius was gone.

Twelve days after the bloody attack on Bill Yoo, normalcy made an attempt at a return. Inside a small Oxnard café just yards from the beach, the young executive with perfect hair eyed his date as an alien taking its first look at a human being. His jeans and loose pull-over shirt hid his solid frame, but his eyes could not hide his thoughts. Finally, Dennis blurted them out, interrupting the excitable Miss Musgrave.

"I think you're far more nervous than you need to be!" He laughed, in part to ease the terseness of his words, but also to convey his genuine amusement.

The interjection startled Heidi. "What? Do I sound nervous?" Her light-brown hair danced on her shoulders as she spoke. "Am I making an idiot out of myself?"

Dennis laughed again. "No." He laughed more, which only served to confuse his date. "You're a bright woman, but I've never seen you so, so, *energetic* before." He stressed "energetic" in a way that conveyed it was a euphemism for a much harsher adjective.

"I'm sorry." Heidi's face burst into a bright red orb.

"No. Don't be sorry. I just don't want you mad at yourself later. It's just me. Dennis. That's it."

Her face returned to its normal pink complexion; Dennis studied it for a moment. Her light-blue eyes and full, thick hair gave her an appealing look, but she did not possess striking beauty. Attractive, yet almost average, her high-pitched, girlish voice reflected her cute disposition, although she knew such a voice was not ideal in her father's world.

For his part, Dennis' square jaw line gave him the look of a businessman. The conservative haircut, bright green eyes, and authoritative voice mesmerized the young woman. Though four years his junior, Heidi was not easily impressed. Because of her father's line of work, she had encountered numerous Dennis Frys over the past few years. Now out of college and with over a full year of work as a foundation, she was ready for almost anything – anyone – she believed. Still, her fascination with Dennis was not difficult to spot.

"I'm sorry if I was babbling."

"It's all right," he reassured her. "You were just going on about your plans a little. I'm happy for you, but just be patient."

A nervous silence set in before Dennis broke it. "So, tell me about your dad."

"Well." She ended the word with an abrupt jerk of her head. "He's not one of my favorite subjects. I love him, but I don't always like him. He sometimes forgets I'm not thirteen any more. He's had a hard time coming to grips with me being twenty-three, that's for sure."

"I guess that's what happens when you're raised by a single father – a single businessman father."

"Yeah. I guess." She stared into space, over Dennis' shoulder, and did not seem to notice the handful of other customers scattered throughout the small café. "I guess," she repeated. She turned her attention back to Dennis and looked him in the eyes. "You're not one of these guys who wants to date me because my dad's your boss, are you?" She asked in a way that showed she did not believe he was such a person.

Dennis chuckled. His warm laughs drew her in further, as though he put a gentle arm around her and snuggled her to his side. "No. I'm not one of 'those guys.' In fact, I'm very confident in who I am. Remember, I just got a big promotion. It's good to be king. I'm good at what I do."

"I bet you are," she teased, missing another of his many movie references. "Otherwise, you wouldn't have climbed the ladder other places to get such a plum job here."

"You're very perceptive." His smile eased the tension even further. The earlier nervousness dissipated into the air above the table and out the door of the out-of-the-way café.

"You never told me how you came up with this place."

"Oh. Well. Nothing special." Dennis looked around the room. A middle-aged woman in a white outfit hurried down the length of the dining area, on her way to get orders for the other customers. Enough customers to warrant the café's existence patronized the establishment. He noticed none of it. "I just heard somewhere it was a great place, so I thought I'd bring you here. Besides, if we went the other way on the '101' we'd be in crowds. I don't like crowds."

"Me neither!" Her smile lit up her face and warmed his heart.

They both chuckled, more relaxed than ever.

"You don't have to tell me about your father if you don't want," Dennis sounded as though he were attempting reverse psychology. After a pause, and what both understood to be a redaction of the prior statement, Dennis changed tack. "Tell me about anything. Whatever you want."

"Tell me about yourself."

"Nope." He spoke with a firmness wrapped with a cheerful, yet charming, tone. "You'll learn plenty about me over time, but I'm more interested in you. You've told me a little about where you're going — a couple weeks ago, at the party, and tonight — so tell me where you've been. What made you? Tell me about your life."

Heidi tried to resist but could only smile. He had charmed her into answering. She was now an open book.

• • •

It seemed like an ideal place to meet — until he arrived. Walt stood outside, on the sidewalk, waiting for his "date." He did not wish to refer to her as such because she was both an old flame and a rival. As he watched her approach, no setting seemed ideal, and he anticipated the pain and frustration he was about to encounter.

How Rose Bakkeby became his rival was not as far-fetched a story as how she became his college girlfriend. When she arrived at the exclusive, members-only Los Angeles restaurant and club, to which they both held memberships, he suffered no illusions about why he never missed her.

After a brief greeting, they made their way into the restaurant with a view of the L.A. Basin. Lights from buildings, cars, and streetlights covered the ground as far as they could see. Bright dots in the sky moved east to west, dropping one at a time with precise regularity into Los Angeles International Airport.

He ordered a club sandwich, which was reasonably priced for an exclusive restaurant. She requested the chicken soup with kale. Another memory he would like to forget: the way she ate.

"I'm sorry about Bill." With the waiter on his way to place their orders, the conversation could begin. Both faces carried the expressions of apprehension, like a divorced couple ten years hence.

"Yeah, it's just –" He broke off his sentence and allowed his gaze to focus out the window, at the controlled chaos of lights below and above. "I don't know how to put it into words."

"Everybody liked him. He was brilliant, and he had a personality to make up for you and Alex – oh. I didn't mean that as bad as it sounded." Embarrassment almost shrouded Rose's blonde hair and brown eyes.

"How are you fifty years old and you still don't have to color your hair yet?" His soft smile signaled his good intentions.

"Don't even try. I put my foot in my mouth." She smiled before adding, "and you could cover those gray streaks if you wanted."

"I don't." Walt responded.

"Yes, you're a man. You get to be 'distinguished looking' as you age. Don't rub it in."

Before Walt could celebrate the positive direction of the conversation, she reminded him why they were never destined to be a couple.

"You're here because of the fire, aren't you?"

Walt's back stiffened, causing him to sit up involuntarily. "Yes. I am, as a matter of fact," he confessed.

"And you suspect my company."

"I suspect a lot of people."

"You never did appreciate intelligent women, Walt. You're so transparent." Her emphasis of "transparent" rendered the sting two-hundred degrees hotter than it should have felt.

"I admire intelligent women. You just couldn't accept that it was you I clashed with, not all smart women." His deliberate, even delivery triggered a response.

"Okay, if you wanna go down this path, then I suggest –"

"I don't!" He ducked his head, as though hoping no one would hear him in the quiet dining area. A few people glanced their way, then resumed their own conversations.

"Rose. Listen. This isn't about me and you. This is me trying to figure out who's attacking my company. We're under attack. There've been three incidents so far."

"Three?"

"Yeah. I'm counting the murder of the other Won Yoo. That was a misfire."

"I saw that name in a news story and it took me a minute to realize it wasn't Bill. I forgot about that."

Walt looked out the large window again. "Do you know who's been attacking my company?" He could not look her in the eye when he asked because they both knew it was an accusation.

"Now how would I know?" Her voice indicated any trace of prior good will left with that question.

"Look. You're the CEO of my closest competitor. You –"

"Closest geographically! Not closest financially. Lifecom is way closer to your company in target market. We're closing in on becoming a Fortune 500 company. I don't need to worry about little ol' Triumvirate Technologies." She succeeded in keeping her voice down, though not her tone.

Walt's expression told her that he was stewing in his own frustration and anger. "Then tell me what you do know."

She let loose a loud, obnoxious cackle of a laugh. "So first you accuse me of murder and arson, then you wanna pump me for information, as though I'll just forget the accusation!"

"It was not an accusation," he lied. "It was a question. I had to ask."

"Oh." She cackled again, with a pitch similar to that of a peacock. "You *had* to ask." Another cackle.

Walt grit his teeth, then pursed his lips in an effort to hide the pressure he put on his front teeth.

"Don't grind your teeth, Walt. It's not good for them." She flatlined the command.

"When's the last time we had a civil conversation?" Walt asked.

"I think it was 1990-something." She managed half of a smile; one half of her mouth remained straight.

"That long ago, huh?" Walt responded, the wistful tone in his voice betraying where his mind had traveled.

"Dennis Fry."

Walt jerked his head. "What?"

"You asked me to tell you what I know. Dennis Fry. I'd be very wary of that guy."

"You know he's our new executive."

"Of course I know that, Walter. I also know that I'm friends with his previous boss, Cliff Wendleton. Cliff told me about Fry when he found out you hired him." It was her turn to look out the window, into the darkness. She could see a police car, lights flashing, race down a nearby street. "He said the man is devious, has a bad, bad temper, and talked about Triumvirate a lot."

An uncomfortable chuckle escaped Walt's throat. "We vetted him well, I thought."

"Did you speak with Cliff personally?"

"No. We talked to his people, though."

"Well, just maybe," Rose started, then stopped.

"Just maybe what?"

Rose considered her words. "I know Cliff pretty well. I can see him unloading Fry on you. I can see him thinking, 'yeah, let's get rid of that guy' if he didn't like Fry. I'm not saying he did; I don't know."

"You're saying you think Wendleton had his people say only good things?" Walt asked.

"Well, you know nobody gives bad references anymore. Everybody's afraid of getting sued."

"That's true. But still," Walt continued. "We checked him out pretty good."

"Okay. Okay. But that's all I got for you."

Silence reigned. Only the quiet conversations at nearby tables and background noises of the restaurant filled the air as other patrons received a respite from the aggressive conversation between college sweethearts turned rivals – more personal than business rivals.

"I'm sorry, Walt. Sometimes I don't do very well with forgetting why we split up." Her face and tone matched her words.

Disarmed, Walt continued in the same vein. "It's been twenty-nine years, but we always fight like it's been twenty-nine days." His warm smile was returned by his long-ago girlfriend.

"We're probably better off not to examine why that is." She laughed at the memories which raced through her mind.

"I can tell you're remembering the good times," he said.

"Yeah," she responded, a softness in her voice could not be missed.

With the unspoken truce in effect, neither brought up the nasty subjects of murder and arson for the rest of the evening. Instead, they talked about old times and spent the evening repairing damaged bridges, which had separated them for nearly three decades.

Chapter 9

First came the text message, which gave her a surprise – almost a shock. A day later came the ring of the doorbell. As Heidi opened the door, she remained uncertain whether she had made the correct decision. He was a "former" boyfriend for a reason, yet there he stood before her, like a recurring dream. She took a deep breath, which could not be missed, before beginning her greeting.

"Hi, Troy. What brought you back?"

"Ya need me." The flat response from the large man could have bowled her over, he spoke with such force and certitude. Troy Gustafson carried little Scandinavian blood, despite his name. His dark brown – almost black – eyes over-powered his medium-brown hair. His deep tan hinted of being in the California sun every day while his thick arms, neck, and chest signaled long hours in the gym.

"Uh, why's that?" Heidi fought off multiple queries which came to mind and stuck with the basic question.

"I know what happened to Bill and the arson attack." Troy's piercing eyes seemed to penetrate the eyes of his former love interest.

"I'm doing okay," she protested. With a sudden awareness of her surroundings, she asked, "Do you want to come in?"

The six-feet-four-inch stack of muscle marched his supplement-induced 245-pound frame through the doorway and followed Heidi into the nearby living room. A response to her question seemed unnecessary.

Ignoring her hand motion to sit on a chair, he instead maneuvered around a coffee table and planted himself next to her. Heidi found herself falling onto the couch with him before she could protest. "You're just waltzing right back like nothing ever happened." She seemed unable to determine whether she meant that as a question or an accusation.

"I'm back. For you." His gaze burned as hot as ever.

"I'm not back," she deadpanned.

He let slip a smile. "Heidi. Let's be honest. I know you. You're a mess right now. You're going through a mess. I know how much you liked Bill."

"*Loved. Loved* Bill." She returned the hot gaze.

"I saw it on the TV news and I thought, 'Hey, Heidi needs me.' So yeah, I'm 'waltzing back,' as ya say." He rocked his shoulders back and forth at 'waltzing back,' as though her word choice ignited a silliness he could not control.

"I have a boyfriend," she lied.

His eyebrows shot up, as though the words contained an impossible message to accept. "Really?" A tone of utter disbelief dominated the two syllables.

"Really," she retorted.

"You're too career-focused to have a boyfriend. And picky."

"Think again."

"Is he as wonderful as me?" Troy grinned.

"Well, let's see. He doesn't look at other women when we're walking down the street. He doesn't constantly refer to other women as 'gorgeous babes,' at least not in front of me." She glared as she spoke, her blue eyes lighting up brighter and brighter. "And he actually listens when I talk. So, I think he's got a good start on 'wonderful.'"

"Good start, huh?" Troy indeed listened, and he found an opening. "So, ya haven't been together long. Well, now." He let his last two words extend out as long syllables that hung in the air until Troy was ready to continue his display of arrogance. "I'm sure he doesn't know ya well enough yet, and what ya need, so maybe you should put off seeing him for a while."

Flabbergasted, Heidi looked at him, mouth agape, before laughing. "You are out of your mind!" She flung her hair back, as though it reached far past her shoulders. "What is it with you?"

Troy laughed. "Ya miss me. I'm just having fun." He laughed more. "I know ya think I'm arrogant, so I'm just giving ya what ya expect of me; but, my words are accurate. Ya do miss me. Ya need me." He slid closer to her. "And I need you."

Heidi let out a sigh but did not bother to push away from him. "You just never change."

"Of course not. Then I'd be boring. Like your dad."

They both laughed.

"Who's your boyfriend? Anybody I know?"

"No. He's not from around here, and just so you know, we're probably going to get married sometime next year," Heidi lied again.

"Huh. Is that so? Well, what's his name?" Undeterred by the proclamation of marriage plans, Troy seemed anxious to find out the identity of his competition.

"Dennis Fry. He works for my father."

"Is he the janitor?" Troy snickered.

"He happens to be the top junior executive at the office," Heidi harrumphed. Before she could gloat further, Troy wrecked her plans.

"Junior, huh? Is that what ya call him, 'Junior?'"

"Why don't you just leave?" That Heidi was tired of Troy's clowning could not be missed.

"Dennis Fry." Troy paused in reflection. "Dennis Fry. I know that name."

"Sure you do."

Troy snapped his fingers. "That's the name of the cook at that seafood shack on PCH, headed toward Oxnard." He laughed as though he had just told the funniest joke ever.

"Troy, we're not getting back together."

"Heidi," Troy smiled as he responded, his mocking tone so ridiculous he could not keep a straight face. "You're too independent and driven to need a boyfriend. Except ya need me. Don't forget that."

"You haven't told me what you're doing, you haven't told me where you've been," Heidi protested. "You just text me one day and show up the next to announce that I need you."

"Yeah. Pretty much." Troy laughed. "All right, all right. The next time I see ya, I'll tell ya a few things. Nothing major or anything, just catch up."

"Even you can't handle too much of yourself for long," Heidi quipped.

"Yeah, well." Troy laughed again. "I'm here for ya, babe. That's all. No hidden motives. I got no problems right now. Things are going well. I just came back for you. For you." He emphasized his final point before continuing. "Remember that."

Troy lifted his large frame off the couch, walked out of the living room, and headed toward the front door. Heidi followed; her duty as the hostess seemed to pull her. When he reached the front door, he turned to give his departing remarks. Heidi stopped as he reached out his large arms and rested them on her shoulders.

With his nose two inches from her forehead, he said in a quiet voice, "I'll be back for you."

"Troy."

"Heidi, forget all about that Dennis guy. I'll take care of you." He kissed her forehead, then looked into her eyes as he slid his arms until his hands rested on her shoulders. He saw uncertain, troubled blue eyes looking back. "It'll be okay."

Troy released her shoulders and let himself out the door.

Heidi closed the door and locked it. "Ya. You. Ya. You." She rolled her eyes as she mocked Troy's terrible speech habits. With hands pressing on the sides of her head, she walked up the stairs, in dismay at the reintroduction of Troy Gustafson into her life.

• • •

Security cameras had not been installed with sufficient precision on the grounds of Triumvirate Technologies to account for vandals, arsonists, or other actors with criminal intent; they were set up for monitoring delivery vehicles and for the appearance of security to potential interlopers. With the recent fire in Building C, camera coverage was worse than ever.

The attacker knew he held the advantage. He dressed in dark clothing and wore a dark mask, but his approach toward Building B was at a pace approaching a stroll. With one stroke, the small sledgehammer broke the glass. The man set the hammer and a plastic five-gallon gasoline can on the ground. He pulled a cigarette lighter from his pants pocket and lit a rag stuffed into the can's opening. Within seconds, the container hit the floor inside the building and burning gasoline spread a few feet.

The amount of gasoline was not significant, but the location was. Chemicals used in the manufacturing of cell phone and computer batteries occupied the entire corner of the affected area.

Fire spread without hindrance to the chemicals. In a matter of minutes, the fire would be raging.

The arsonist disappeared. The guard at the front gate would learn there was an intruder when the explosion roared through the night air.

Chapter 10

"Good morning, Alex." Walt attempted to feign cheeriness to cover his depressed mood as he walked into his partner's office.

"You should've called me – immediately!" Alex showed no interest in hiding or pretending anything.

"Look, Alex. You were handling the end of the business you handle. I handled this end of the business." Walt's face showed he was willing to engage in battle, if necessary.

"We're not talking about a low-level business decision, Walt. The company is under attack. We've got some damned nut job or something running around. Maybe if Bill hadn't been murdered it wouldn't be such a big deal. But it *is* a big deal." When he stressed "is," he nearly yelled. Alex never yelled.

As Walt sat in a chair across the desk from Alex, Tony entered the room. He did not bring his large personality and mental drawer full of one-liners. The serious subjects they were facing did not allow for Tony's frivolity.

"Gentlemen." The sober tone in his greeting caught the attention of Alex and Walt.

"If anything else happens, I need to be notified right away." Alex repeated his message for Tony's benefit.

"Alex, we did what was right at the moment," Tony explained as he sat in the only other open chair, next to Walt. "Building B wouldn't be any less destroyed if we called you. The ashes look the same today as they did in the middle of the night Saturday."

With an angry expression on his face, Alex grudgingly nodded. "All right. So, what do we know?"

"The attacker was on foot – at least they didn't drive onto the grounds," Walt answered.

"The fire was perfectly placed. Workers had a little storage area and that's where the fire started. It was a gas can doubling as a giant Molotov cocktail, sort of." Tony gave the rest of the information they possessed.

Alex shook his head. "And, of course, you know those batteries were a large part of our DOD contract."

Walt tried to be positive. "We'll be all right. The formulas for the long-life batteries aren't lost, just the materials. We'll buy more, build more. Insurance will pay for a lot of this, and we'll just let DOD know we'll be delayed."

"And we're beefing up security," Tony added.

"When?!" Alex snarled.

"Today. I've already got the security firm on its way. That's what I dealt with yesterday," Tony answered. "I had a helluva time getting a hold of someone on a Sunday, but I pulled it off."

"Where's Dennis? He should be in here." Alex lacked his usual focus. His head twitched. His hands moved constantly. He was a nervous wreck for all to see.

"I can grab him," Tony offered.

"Just make sure he's up to speed. You have the security stuff under control, right?" Alex looked at Tony.

"Yup."

"And what about our other junior executives?" Alex half-demanded. "We have two other young, aspiring Rockefellers around here somewhere. I never see them."

"Bill was in charge of both of them, so they're kinda running the day-to-day of technology in Bill's place right now," Tony answered. "I mean, I can bring them in if you want." The pained expression on Tony's face made it clear he struggled to decipher exactly what Alex wanted.

Alex shook his head as he looked down at the calendar on his desk. Tony understood the head shake to mean the two junior executives would be left to handle their daily routines. Dennis continued to be the only one of the young business partners who mattered.

"Walt, stick around. I want to hear how it went with Rose Bakkeby." Alex looked at Tony, giving him a cue to leave.

Without a word, Tony exited Alex's office. He closed the door behind him, which allowed Walt to freely recount the business side of the conversation of two nights ago. When he had fully briefed his business partner, Walt wrapped up with a question. "So, what do you think?"

"Obviously, we can rule out Fry. It sounds like somebody didn't like him for some reason, but he's knocked the ball out of the park for us."

"Agreed." Walt's affirmation closed the case on Dennis Fry.

"What does that leave us?" Alex's intensity showed no signs of abating.

"I have Donna preparing a list of ex-employees. I've got a couple in mind."

"Oh?"

"Yeah, I'll give you one example," Walt said as he searched his memory. "Peter Simms is one guy who comes to mind. You remember when he sabotaged the line?"

"Sounds familiar." Alex squinted again, trying to remember. "You mentioned him the other day, I think."

70

"Naturally, I'm looking at competitors. That's why I had dinner with Rose. Nothing there. I'll keep you posted."

"Thanks."

Walt considered his words before continuing. "I'm inclined to lean toward a jealousy angle. Payback. Who feels like we screwed 'em? Who feels cheated? Or who just feels like they'd be a notch higher if we weren't around?"

A knock at the door interrupted the discussion. Before Alex could respond, it opened, allowing Tony and Dennis to enter.

"What do you have?" Alex asked.

"Just Fry. Dennis was in a hallway, downstairs," Tony responded as he returned to the chair he previously occupied. "We have to move forward without Bill, so I assume you guys are gonna keep Fry's plate full."

"Right now, it's full enough with the CCCP," Walt interjected.

"I think he's a little young to know what those letters stand for," Tony said, a wry smile breaking out.

"Nope. No idea," Dennis volunteered.

"It's the Russian letters for 'USSR,'" Walt explained.

"Ah. So, you're still not happy with the OFCCP, are ya?" Dennis asked, knowing the answer to the question. "They're like SPECTRE to you, huh?"

"I'm not happy with them." Walt ignored the reference to James Bond movies. He did not smile, although a quick glance at Tony informed him the lawyer found the 'Che' and bureaucracy situations amusing.

"So, Dennis has his hands full with the Department of Labor," Alex said, eyes squinting while in thought. "Tony, you're on this security situation. I want full camera coverage as soon as

71

possible. Walt, I know you've got the DOD, so I'll handle getting us more material for manufacturing, and I'll also stay on top of getting bids for a new Building B."

"No, I got that," Walt replied. "There are lots of materials to be replaced, so I'll deal with the contractors."

"Okay. Sounds good." But Alex was not done. "Now regarding this OFCCP, I've been doing some research."

Tony flashed a knowing smile.

"They find statistical variances and use the data as a basis for claiming racial and ethnic discrimination. So, for us, we have an inordinate number of East Indians and Chinese working here compared to the local population." He looked at the three men, who all nodded. "You know this?"

"Yeah, I did a bunch of research myself," Tony replied. "I told Walt all about it, and I told Fry about some of it, too."

"Yeah, well, I still don't like it," Walt said in a quiet voice. "I get really mad about these things."

Tony laughed. "It didn't help the head guy's name is 'Che,' as in 'Che Guevara.'"

"You're kidding?!" Alex laughed. "Who would do that to a kid?"

"It's a nickname, but he loves it." Walt's lack of a smile made it clear he saw no humor in the matter. "I've told Fry to spend as little time with them as possible."

"Sorry, guys, but we want them outta here quick, right?" Dennis presented his question more as a statement.

"Yes. Just keep doing what you're doing." Alex did not like the situation any better than Walt but controlled his emotions better. "Walt's way more political than I am. Just get rid of them as soon as possible. We've gone from a well-oiled machine to a company teetering out of control. The sooner we get this part of it behind us the better." He looked at Walt to drive home his point. "We're going to get fined and we're going to get bad press. They're going to justify their own existence by claiming civil rights violations. We can't fight city hall. Just get this over with, take the hit, and pay the fine."

"Agreed. Bend over and smile," Tony chuckled.

"Agreed." Dennis was next to chime in.

Walt took a deep breath and let it out loudly. "I hate arrogant bureaucrats. Bureaucrats are necessary, but I hate the arrogant ones." He turned to look at Dennis. "Whatever you have to do, I guess."

"Just be glad they're not looking into our personal lives," Tony laughed.

"Yeah, can you imagine if they found out I used to drink like a fish and I love a good bet what they'd do?" Walt's wistful expression gave him the appearance of a man who would rather be drinking and gambling at the moment.

"Well, we don't have to worry about that," Alex concluded. "Let's just get this over with so we can finalize with the Defense Department."

"Sounds good," Tony declared with enough energy to propel him from his seat. "Come on, kid. We've got a lot of work to do."

Dennis stood up, followed by Walt.

"Yeah, I hear that," Walt said.

Alex stared out his window as the men left his office. He should be able to see Building B from this vantage point. Instead, he could see a golden hillside beyond the company property, normally obscured by the building. Had he chosen to stand, he would have seen the charred debris of the building. He chose not to observe the depressing sight.

• • •

"Why?" Heidi understood that perhaps a passerby could hear her, but the fact remained inconsequential as she repeated, "Why?" The farther she walked from her car the deeper the realization cut: she had agreed to meet with Troy; she had consented to seeing him again. At least it was in public, she told herself multiple times. "Why? Why?!" A woman old enough to be Heidi's mother flashed an odd expression as she caught a glimpse of the younger woman's actions and mutterings.

"Of course," she grumbled as she entered the small café. Troy, ever the prompt one, sat at a table, waiting. "Don't you work?" She asked her question with a sharp note, but Tony's laugh rounded off the edge.

Heidi took a seat with her back to a window. Troy's face seemed to glow from the California sunshine which flooded the dining area. His brown hair appeared almost golden and his dark eyes lit up his face.

"Happy lunchtime to you," Troy beamed.

"I'm happy to see you're so happy," Heidi responded.

"Being with you, every day is a good day."

"Oh, please," Heidi replied with a polite mixture of laughter and disgust. "Glad to see you can still BS with the best of them."

"What?" He feigned insult. "My happiest days were with you." He maintained the smile, despite his next words. "Then ya dumped me, of course."

"Let's not do that, okay?" She meant the question as a demand.

"Okay, okay. Listen," Troy stared into her eyes. "I have to admit, once I saw that on the news about Bill, I started thinking about you. Then I just kept thinking about you."

Heidi rolled her eyes.

"Really. I'm being serious," Troy pleaded. "Ya have to believe me. We had our problems before, and I'm here to amend my ways."

"Make amends," she corrected. "Listen, I know you're gonna tell me how you've changed your ways and how I should forget about what you used to be, so –"

"Wait, wait, wait." He smiled. "Heidi, I haven't changed a bit. I'm still me. I'm still that wonderful guy ya miss." He picked up a menu and used it as a pointer. "I'm not here to plead with ya or beg ya or anything like that." He noticed Heidi's eyes following the menu, so he placed it back onto the table. "I'm here for you." He leaned forward. The sunshine seemed to radiate off his face, back at Heidi, as though off a mirror. "I'm here for us."

Heidi sat in silence. She looked around – a nervous movement in her neck kept her head in motion. After absorbing his statement, she looked into the glowing brown eyes. "I'm fine, Troy. Really."

"I'm checking up on your boyfriend. I'll see how fine ya really are."

"Troy, you're making me uncomfortable."

Troy laughed as though she had just told him a knee-slapping, hilarious joke. "I'm sure I've made ya more uncomfortable than this before."

"That you have."

"You'll be fine, once I'm taking care of you," he added.

"You've always had a way with words, you know it?" Her words flowed from an acid bottle.

"Thank you," he laughed.

Heidi again rolled her eyes. "Can we just order?"

• • •

To Heidi's surprise, the meal proceeded with pleasant dialogue and sprinklings of fond memories mixed in with many laughs. Her Reuben sandwich and diet soda went down well with his stories and explanations and their small talk. She learned that indeed he was correct: he was the same old Troy. He did not wish to change; he would not change.

"How do you like running a business," she asked.

"Ya think running a surf and sports shop is running a business?" Troy seemed incredulous.

"Yes, dummy, that's running a business," Heidi lectured. "It doesn't matter if it's one little shop. You have responsibilities. Payroll. Utilities. Codes."

"Well, not codes," Troy responded. "My buddy, Cory Durrell, has been the inspector the last year, so I'm good."

"Always some shortcut with you." Heidi shook her head. "Let's put it this way. If you blow your dad's money, you're screwed."

Troy shrugged. "Yeah. Probably."

Heidi shook her head again.

"Don't shake your head, ya still miss me."

Heidi eyed him, as though she could spot his arrogance before it materialized. "There are times I miss us. Moments. But I think we had to break up."

"Baaaa." Troy sounded like a child with a bad taste in his mouth. "We were great together. I know you've focused on the bad and just remember that, but we were a great couple."

Sentimentality finally caught up to Heidi. A small, contented smile covered her face as she looked down at the empty plate in front of her.

"I know ya gotta go, so take off," Troy ordered. "I've got the bill. And keep in mind, we're going dancing soon. We'll hit a few clubs." He moved his shoulders back and forth, up and down as he spoke. "I can't this weekend. I gotta take a run up to Half Moon Bay, but the next weekend, we're hitting the floor." His head moved to an unheard rhythm.

Heidi laughed. "We'll see. No promises yet."

"Ya will. You'll go. Now ya better get back to work."

Before her emotions could catch up, she said 'goodbye' and left the small café. Her walk down the sidewalk was not replete with "whys;" rather, one thought summed up her entire situation: "Oh boy."

• • •

Concentration proved elusive for Walt. He wanted the Department of Labor out of the building. He was tired of their sniffing around and all the stories he had heard about their methods. As he prepared to make another call to a contractor about debris removal and subsequent rebuilding of Building B, Dennis poked his head into Walt's office.

"I've got a plan to get rid of these guys," Dennis said.

"Oh yeah, what is it?" Walt perked up.

"Can't tell ya."

"Oh, come on! Don't be ridiculous!" Walt's blood pressure leaped.

"Trust me," was all Dennis would volunteer.

"No bribes."

"No bribes. That'd cause us lots of trouble," Dennis admitted.

"Then how?" The skepticism in Walt's voice tumbled out.

"Trust me."

Walt's frustration grew. An angry expression dominated his face.

Dennis stepped into the office. "Two weeks. They'll be gone. They'll still have a final report to do, but they'll be gone. Back to D.C."

"You're blowing smoke."

"Nope."

"I smell a bet coming on." Walt allowed a wry smile to break out.

"That's right. You lost those Fiesta Bowl tickets to Tony last year, and the Orange Bowl tickets this year." Dennis smiled.

"How'd you know about that?" Walt laughed.

"I'm a quick learner."

"Dennis, I'm not in the mood to play games right now. What do you wanna bet?"

"The-" Dennis could not complete his answer before Walt had a thought strike him, which he had to blurt out.

"BUT, you have to tell me your method."

"No can do on the method," Dennis maintained his smile, wide as ever.

"All right." Walt gave in. "What's the bet?"

"The company." Dennis kept the smile.

"What company?" The statement did not make sense to the elder man.

"Your stake in Triumvirate, signed over to me." The smile left, underscoring the seriousness of the statement.

"Get out of here!" Walt grabbed a paperweight – a small replica of the Declaration of Independence – and feigned a forthcoming assault.

Dennis strode away. His casual stride indicated nothing was wrong in his world.

Walt picked up his phone. "Donna, I think I'm out of my blood pressure medication. Can you set up an appointment with my doctor, please?" When he hung up the phone, he stared at the empty doorway. After a few seconds, he turned his attention back to his list of contractor phone numbers, shaking his head.

• • •

"I've never sat down for an FBI interview before. Is there anything I should know?"

"Just let me know all you know and we'll be fine," Agent Boles answered, his white shirt and solid, dark-blue tie exposed by his open jacket.

"Okay, but I'm a bit nervous."

"No need to be nervous, Mister Fry," Boles said in an effort to comfort the younger man. "We're videoing this for our records, but just remember what I said. No need to embellish anything. It's just a matter of what you saw. Nothing more or less."

Dennis looked around the small examination room and found it to be the definition of 'Spartan.' No decorations covered the dull, beige paint. The 24-inch-square pieces of carpet formed a design of its own; its dark, dull color scheme could lure even the most hardened criminal to boredom. The most interesting aspect of the room sat a few feet away: the video and audio recording equipment.

"No pressure, no worries," Agent Boles reassured the young executive.

"Okay. Fire away." Dennis thought he was ready for the rapid-fire questioning, which would define his statement.

"Where were you going the night of November third?"

"I was westbound on the 101 Freeway," Dennis responded.

"Yes, but where were you going?"

"Does it matter?"

Agent Boles could not hide his struggle with patience. His deep voice developed a rough edge. "Mister Fry, these are just introductory questions. Routine questions. If you're ever deposed – have you been deposed before?"

"No."

"Okay, trust me on this," Boles began. His eyes closed and reopened in what amounted to a slow blink. "This is normal. In deposition, you'll be asked questions like your Social Security number and home address. I'm not even doing that. This is a routine, normal question that will help set the scene." Boles' frustration did not allow him to hear the level of repetition he had reached.

"Okay."

"Okay. So where were you going on November third?"

"I was returning home."

"From where?" Boles' voice signaled his unhappiness.

"From a dinner with some friends."

"Okay. Dinner with friends. Then what did you see?" Boles surrendered. The information would suffice for now.

"Well," Dennis looked around the small room. "Not much. I just was fascinated when I passed a G&S Systems car on the 101.

I know they're out here on business sometimes, but never in a company car."

"Then what happened?" Boles paused before realizing the gaping hole he left. It was apparent Fry was the wrong person for whom he should open such a hole. "After you saw the car on the 101 Freeway?"

"I backed off and followed the car to the Hyatt in Westlake Village."

"What exit did you take?"

"I don't recall," Dennis answered. "I just know it's the one by the Hyatt."

"Did you do anything else, Mister Fry?" Boles inquired.

"No. That was it. I just kept driving."

"I see." Boles compressed his lips together into a tight line. "So," he hesitated before speaking. "Did you touch the car?"

"No."

"Did you get in the car?"

"No."

Agent Boles' eyes narrowed. His law training kicked in. "Did you in any way interact with the car or with the driver of the car?"

"No. Not at all." Dennis studied his questioner's face. "What's this about, Agent Boles?"

"Have you told this to anyone else?"

"Yeah, I have," Dennis answered. "I told Alex, Walt, Bill, Tony, and the Sheriff's Department. I didn't give my bosses as much detail as I'm telling you, but I told them about it."

"Is there anything else we need to know about the event or events you just described?"

Dennis hesitated. He glared into Boles' eyes. "No. Nothing else you need to know."

Chapter 11

"You're out of your mind, Dennis," Walt said as he took another drink of his draft beer. He held the glass mug up, as though examining the beer inside it. "Helluva microbrewery they got here."

The establishment started the evening with an even spread of saw dust on the floor, but clear walkways and paths had developed over the hours.

"*Sonny's* is a good little joint. You've never been here?" Dennis studied the older man as he waited for the answer.

"Nah. Haven't had a drink in three years."

"Really?" Dennis allowed his eyes to widen and his face to show surprise. "You mean, you don't drink anymore?"

"Not in three years. But I just needed to unwind tonight, what with Bill, the arson attacks, the CCCP, the Department of Defense, and all this crap." Walt looked around the bar. The table he and Dennis occupied sat only a few feet from the main bar. He briefly eyed all the bottles behind the bartender, in case he wanted to switch to another brand.

"Do you guys know anything about a party here tonight?" Dennis stared beyond Walt as he uttered the line.

Walt cocked his head, confused by the question.
"Oh. Just a line from a movie I've watched a dozen times. Never mind. I'm a big movie buff." Dennis caught a waitress' eye.

"So I've noticed."

Dennis watched the waitress until she took the cue and approached the table. "Can I help ya, hon'?" the pretty brunette asked.

"I'll have another margarita, please." Dennis lifted his glass to demonstrate only one more gulp remained.

"Sure thing. And you?" She looked at Walt.

"I'm fine. Two beers are enough, I guess." Beer filled more than half of his large mug.

Once the waitress was far enough away, Walt asked the question that concerned him the most. "What's this you were talking about, betting the company?"

"Oh, just blowing smoke, I guess," Dennis responded with a laugh.

"You said you could get 'em out in two weeks."

"Yeah. I could. But let's forget about it." Dennis emptied his glass.

Walt watched the younger man; Dennis returned the stare.

"What did you –"

"Forget it," Dennis said with more force, but added a laugh to push aside the building tension.

"You think I'd just walk away from my baby?" Walt's voice signaled his determination.

"Yep." Dennis pushed the empty glass to the edge of the table.

"You're out of your mind."

Before Dennis could respond, the pretty brunette returned. Dennis looked her in the eyes and smiled.

"Here you go, hon'." Her cheery voice contrasted with the men's conversation. She turned and walked away.

Dennis watched her walk, then turned his attention back to Walt, only to discover the elder man's gaze remained zeroed in on him.

"You're out of your mind," Walt repeated his last words.

Dennis laughed a big, hearty laugh that filled *Sonny's* bar. He lowered the volume when he spoke. "Oh, the things people say

84

when they're drinking. Walt, old man, I was just trying to lighten the mood at the office. Things are stressful. You can feel it everywhere."

Walt neither relaxed nor smiled. "Uh huh," was all he mustered.

"You couldn't walk away from your 'baby,' could you?" Dennis' tone dripped with sarcasm.

Walt glared at the younger man but would not answer. He took another drink, then narrowed his eyes and zeroed in on Dennis' green eyes. "Alex would go berserk."

"I'm not worried about Alex," Dennis deadpanned.

"What?" Walt laughed. "Not worried about Alex?" Walt roared with laughter. "That quiet German will rip your head off if he has to." Walt reached his pinnacle of laughter. "Not worried about Alex!" He continued his laugh.

"You heard me," was all Dennis volunteered, his tone flat.

"Ya know, you're an amazing creature," Walt finally said with a laugh. "You date the boss' daughter, you ingratiate yourself to the bosses." His thought cut off midway. "You think a boss isn't that important. You think it's all a joke? We get fined a million bucks and that's a million bucks not dedicated to hiring more people or purchasing more capital." He looked aside, disgust on his face. He seemed unaware his conversation bounced around, from subject to subject. "Somebody has to make the products we buy. Manufacture it. So, if we aren't buying capital, that affects someone else's job."

"You know I know all this. I take it serious," Dennis countered. "You know it was all a joke. So relax."

"When can you get rid of them, Dennis?"

"Two weeks."

"How?"

"We've been through that," Dennis answered, then took his first sip of the newest margarita.

Walt's level of agitation increased. His head jerked back and forth, looking at other tables. His hands could not remain stationary. He fidgeted with the handle of his beer mug. "Get rid of them."

"I'm sure they'll be gone in a month or so, even with my best efforts," Dennis teased.

Walt picked up on the tone. "Two weeks. You can do it!" He shot back.

"Wanna bet?" Dennis grinned with a slight curl of his lips.

"You're out of your mind."

"You sure?" Dennis' smile grew, until it could be seen from across the bar.

"Let me give you a movie quote, Dennis. 'Make my day.' Get rid of those people." Walt returned to staring into Dennis' eyes.

"You sure? Money won is twice as sweet as money earned." The wide smile remained.

"*The Color of Money*. You're not the only one who sees movies. Now make them go away, dammit." Walt did not show a hint of humor.

Dennis laughed again. "The things people say when they're drinking."

• • •

An hour after Dennis' departure, and one additional house beer later, Walt had tired of a basketball game on one of the TVs and the occasional chit chat with the waitress. He stepped into the cool night air, where the unseen Pacific Ocean spread its influence over the area by ushering in a moist breeze. The taxi should arrive any minute, but he wanted to suck in some of that night air. After three years of temperance, three beers made their presence known inside Walt's skull.

Walt had assured Dennis that a taxi ride home, while expensive, was not a big deal. His conversation with the young executive left him uneasy, so sticking to the original plan was reasonable, in Walt's mind – he did not wish to ride with Dennis again. *Something's off about that Dennis Fry*. His thoughts came to him in slow, broken pieces. *I don't trust him*.

At almost midnight, the streets held a firm grip on silence, disrupted by the occasional car rolling by. Only *Sonny's* remained open in this part of town on a weeknight. The soft breeze, though gentle, still managed to cut through the exhausted and now half-inebriated businessman. In an attempt to convince himself that he was impervious to the cold, he threw up his arms as though he were Rocky Balboa celebrating victory.

Having failed at fooling himself, Walt paced, looking around as he did so. The figure he saw approaching appeared as a distant speck, at first. He soon made out a blurry image walking down a slight hill. As the figure approached, the fact that it was a man became apparent – a man heading toward him.

Closer yet, and Walt felt a twinge of nervousness in his limbs. He had a bad feeling. From the opposite direction, he heard – but could not see – an approaching car.

When the man came to within forty feet, Walt felt sweat under his armpits and on his forehead. Before his impaired mind could think, a baby-blue Chevy Malibu pulled to a stop at the curb in front of him. Walt did not bother to read the logo on the side. He opened the back door and jumped in. "Go! Do not pick that guy up!" He enunciated every word at a volume loud enough to awaken anyone within two blocks. "Just *go!*"

As he closed the door and the startled taxi driver screeched the tires pulling away from the curb, Walt peered out his window with great curiosity and alarm. Who was that man? Instead of a face, he saw only a blur. He saw a long trench coat and the man's head looking down and away from the car.

The rush of adrenaline brought him out of his alcohol-induced fog and he gave his home address to the driver. The farther the taxi got from *Sonny's*, the better the bar's former patron utilized his brain. By the time they reached his driveway, Walt Musgrave had convinced himself the man in the trench coat was just a passerby. He felt foolish for fearing a man who simply walked down the street.

No matter. The incident was over. Walt paid the man and entered his house, intent on getting into bed. The shadowy figure who had advanced toward him was not his problem – Dennis was his problem. Something odd was occurring inside the young executive's brain. Walt aimed to figure out the enigma that was Dennis Fry.

• • •

The backyard was large in square feet by southern California standards, but most of the ground sloped downward at a steep angle, toward the neighborhood below, allowing for only a small, flat, useable area. The yellow-white light from the streetlight below cut into the darkness of the houses on either side of the house in the hills; the house below blocked the light to his house, allowing the man to stand in his yard in darkness. His trees gave the man a feeling of even greater seclusion. He was but a figure – a slight bit of occasional dark movement to the careful observer.

Unbeknownst to the dark figure, such a careful observer waited, with great patience, at the bottom of the yard, on the slope of the hill.

The height of the wood fence proved visually meaningless to the neighbors on lower ground. Anytime the owner of the house on the hill walked into his back yard during the day, they could see him. Perhaps that was one of the reasons why the homeowner enjoyed his nighttime forays into the darkness.

The owner of the house on the hill stood outside, in the black of night, on his concrete porch. He could see the houses on either side of his own, which also sat obscured from streetlights. At this late hour, on this work night, their inhabitants had been in bed for hours.

The serenity of the silence, broken only by the sounds of the distant, unseen freeway, and privacy provided by the darkness gave the owner of the house on the hill respite from his normal routine. That he remained clothed in his workday attire; that he often stood for ten minutes at a time in one spot; that he ignored the stars above and the sounds of raccoons in a clump of trees near one fence – all were unknown to his neighbors because they never had been told of his years of relaxation late at night, standing in the back yard.

The careful observer at the bottom of the property made his way up the hill – unseen but not unheard. The owner of the house failed to look in the direction of the muffled sounds – surely another raccoon, maybe an opossum. They liked the fruit trees in neighboring yards and wandered over the fence on occasion.

Over the course of five minutes, the careful observer closed the distance to the owner of the house on the hill, until at long last they became one dark figure. Only the raccoons, maybe an opossum, heard the crushing blows. The owner of the house on the hill enjoyed the darkness no more. The careful observer navigated the steep hillside with a patience which suggested he had made a simple detour from a walking path or had completed an ordinary task.

Except this task would involve wiping blood off a club.

Chapter 12

The house phone never rang; he never gave out the number. He did not know why he even continued to pay for the line. It probably had something to do with his internet service – 'bundling,' they called it. But right now, the house phone rang. At 4:14 a.m.

Walt rolled over and looked at the clock. The inside of his head felt as though someone had stuffed a firecracker in one ear and lit it. The ringing stopped as the voicemail system took over. *Must be a wrong number*, he thought. He could not put together two consecutive thoughts without one being how much his head hurt.

The phone rang again. After two rings, it stopped. He let out a groan peppered with so much pain he did not recognize the sound was his own – it sounded more bear than human.

Within seconds, knocking – more like pounding – on his bedroom door assured him this was all real. An hour from now, when the alarm sounded, he would not be able to chalk this up to a bad dream. Walt sat up in bed.

A muffled voice from the other side of the door shouted a command. "Get on the phone!" It was Heidi. He should heed her words.

"Okay, okay." Walt reached over for the phone, lifted it off the cradle, and struggled to find the "Talk" button. Once he attained the small victory, the next challenges lay ahead: speaking and comprehending. "Hello?"

A look of horror enveloped his face. *How can this be happening?* He thought back to the man in the trench coat. To Bill. To the arson attacks. "Oh, God in Heaven, I'm so, so sorry! Please tell Christy I'll do whatever I can for her."

He found the button to end the call. He did not have a plan of action. He did not know what came next. He felt confused. His head ached. His heart ached. His life, his company – everything was flying apart. Alex was dead. Murdered.

With Heidi on the other side of the door, asking what was going on, Walt sat and stared into the darkness. An empty man. He lacked direction, strength, or understanding of the situation. His head roared like ocean waves crashing onto rocks. He did not know what to do, what to think. He wanted to sleep, but that was now impossible. Right now, everything seemed impossible.

• • •

Tony climbed into the passenger seat of Walt's car. As soon as the door closed, Walt gunned the engine and they drove away.

"What do you know?"

"Almost nothing. Brent called me and said he was robbed. He didn't say how he died."

Little conversation occurred during the rest of the drive until they reached Alex's house. The Heils had resided here, in an upscale area above Lake Sherwood, directly south of Thousand Oaks, with the houses too close together for such pricey homes, the entire time Walt and Tony knew them.

Once inside the house and hugs and tears were shared, Detective Robert Encarnacion was able to resume his duties. Christy Heil gave the police the same permission the Yoo family gave – Walt and Tony could know and have access to everything; Walt and Tony were family. They would put it in writing if the police required it.

"We meet again," Detective Encarnacion said in a sober tone.

"Yeah," Walt responded, his voice quiet.

"What happened?" Tony blurted out.

"He was beat to death with a club. Savagely. He wasn't stabbed like Mister Yoo was. But unlike Mister Yoo, he was robbed. The attacker took cash from his wallet. His wife," Encarnacion swept his hand toward the new widow, "estimates he carried a thousand dollars with him most of the time."

"Yeah, that's about right. He told me that before," Walt interjected. "I always told him, with credit cards, that much wasn't needed."

Brent Heil plopped onto a couch, exhausted. As the brother of the deceased, he already felt a heavy load on his shoulders. "Isn't there something that can be done?! Two murders and two arson attacks! Something has to be done!" He was on the verge of losing control of his emotions.

A woman whom Walt and Tony did not know coaxed Brent out of the room. She turned to Christy as they prepared to go to another part of the house. "We'll take the kids in a few minutes. I've got to get Brent calm first."

Walt felt relief. Their situation was bad enough without someone stirring up more emotions.

"Look, Detective Rob, there's something I've gotta tell you." Walt looked at Tony, knowing his friend was not going to be happy. "Last night I was at a bar with Dennis Fry until around midnight."

"Walter!" Tony sounded like he was playing the role of mother.

"I was standing out front of *Sonny's*, in Agoura Hills, and this guy wearing a trench coat was walking at me. I jumped in a cab and got out of there." Walt shot a glance back at Tony, who held his perplexed expression. "Maybe it's not related, but nothing usually bothers me. This did."

"What time was it," Encarnacion asked.

"A few minutes before midnight."

"We have the time of death for Mister Heil as one o'clock, give or take," Encarnacion explained. From here to Agoura Hills – that's entirely possible."

"So where was Alex found?" Tony asked.

"In the back yard." Christy's voice cracked as she spoke.

"What happened?" Walt was amazed and frightened their friend had been murdered in his own yard.

"He was doing his usual. Standing in the darkness. Unwinding." Christy paused to wipe her tears. Her brown irises were difficult to see through the tears and the red which dominated her eyes. "He was outside and after a few minutes I heard some thuds. I went out when he didn't answer my calls, and I –" She stopped. She could not speak any longer.

Tony had a quizzical look on his face. "You mean he went outside with his wallet on him?"

"You know Alex," Christy managed to blurt through her tears. "He was dressed. Always was right up until bedtime. He was real formal, he didn't like to put on more comfortable clothes."

Walt smiled at the memories of Alex and his stoic, almost Spartan approach to life.

"So," Tony began, then stopped, still thinking. "It looks to me like the person who murdered Bill learned his lesson when he killed Alex." Confused looks filled the room. Tony continued before anyone could speak. "Make it look like a robbery."

"Could be," Detective Encarnacion nodded as he spoke. "Could be. The problem is, right now it looks like a robbery, so that's how it'll get recorded."

"Tony." A thought hit Walt. "We gotta get to the office and call another meeting. We need to tell our people before word leaks out."

Tony looked at his watch. "Yeah. We better go." He looked at the detective. "Detective Rob, if you come up with anything else, please let us know. Let Christy know, but let us know, too."

"Will do."

With that, both businessmen stopped to hug the widow and say a few tender niceties, then they left. They had to inform their fellow employees another member of the triumvirate was gone.

• • •

During the entire drive to the office, Walt struggled to think. Despair clouded his mind as though it were a wool blanket covering him on a hot summer's day. When he thought about what to say to his employees, that anguish dragged him down. When he thought about his friendship with Alex – or with Bill, for that matter – the blanket of despair became a concrete block. Over and over, every thought was interrupted by another. He fought a battle to sustain every – any – thought to completion.

He did not speak to Tony, and the lawyer returned the courtesy. There was nothing to say. No words could heal the wounds in his heart or put the business back on course. There was nothing – except despair. At one point, he contemplated pulling the car over and puking his guts out onto the side of the road, but his stomach was empty.

By the time he pulled into the parking lot of the now-misnamed Triumvirate Technologies, he felt as though he weighed 500 pounds, so heavy was the emotional pain. Over time, anguish subsided, but despair would never leave him when his memories returned to Bill and Alex. He might not always notice it, but it remained with him, a part of him. He felt it in his chest and inside his skull. It invaded his dreams and his conscious thoughts. It manifested itself in a variety of ways, but right now it was present in every way: physically, emotionally, spiritually, and psychologically.

The despair gripped him. Heavy. Pressing.

Chapter 13

This is absurd! Walt thought, his anger rising. "Sure, I understand," he said into the phone. He paused to let the person respond further. "Okay." He paused again before repeating, "Okay."

Tony walked into Walt's office, just in time to see Walt return the phone's receiver to its base to end the call. After doing so, Walt lifted it with a slow, deliberate movement before slamming it down.

"Does that make you feel better?" Tony asked, chuckling at the little routine he had witnessed scores of times over the years.

"Yes, it does!" Walt shot back, no humor in his voice.

"Look, man," Tony began. His eyes and head movements told Walt a vigorous search for the correct words had been launched. "You've got to make sure you don't drive yourself into the ground. Maybe you need a few days off."

In other circumstances, Walt would have reacted with anger or perhaps derision. Now, with so much happening, he could only laugh.

"Well, I tried." Tony shook his head, a doleful expression overcoming his face. When Walt did not fill the ensuing silence, Tony remembered the banging of the phone. "Who was that on the phone?"

"DOD. They're looking into a five-year-old incident." Walt's anger, and thus his volume, began to rise with each word. "I mean, how crazy is that?! They're looking at the time when Peter Simms sabotaged the chip production line."

"Yeah," Tony became animated. "That was a fun one. We talked about it a while back in Alex's office." He laughed, as though the incident evoked exciting memories.

"What is wrong with you? That was a hassle."

"Yeah, but it was different," Tony explained. "Not the same old boring crap I usually get around here. I actually got to do something." Tony's happiness appeared genuine.

"Only you thought it was fun."

"Don't get me wrong," Tony defended himself, happy demeanor intact. "The guy did damage, cost the company money, but it was fun dealing with the police and firing him and dealing with that side of things. I don't like to fire people, but they're new adventures for me."

Walt planted his elbows onto the top of his desk and dropped his face into his hands. To him, Tony was not making any sense.

Tony's blissful demeanor evaporated. "Look, man, the funeral was Saturday – what, two days ago. Can't some of this wait?"

Walt lifted his head in a deliberate manner so he could look straight at his friend and lawyer. "We have battery inventory to replace, I have to make a final decision on a contractor to rebuild Building B; Building C is just about done; I'm moving forward with Bill's idea about a security center; there's – are you catching on yet?" His sharp tone did not bother the recipient – they had known each other for too long to let something as minor as attitude get in the way of their relationship.

"I get it. I get it. But you're gonna have to delegate better. I know it's early, but you're also gonna have to hire some good people to replace –" He caught himself. "To take on the jobs Bill and Alex used to do." Tony paused to check Walt's reaction. "And it's a no-brainer you're gonna have to give Fry and those other two junior executives — I always forget their names — more work than ever."

"Fry!" Walt snarled. His head fell backward in disgust until he looked at the ceiling.

"Oh, boy. What now?"

"Oh, I'll go into it later. Besides, I still think Peter Simms has got to be a suspect in all this crap." That he jumped subjects with the rapidity of a river current blasting over boulders did not occur to Walt. "And those freakin' bureaucrats. Che!"

"Are we talking about the Dodgers?"

Walt looked startled. "What? Be serious, dammit!"

"I'm just making a point — the way I make points — that you're bouncing around, incoherently, and you're getting tough to follow. Why? Because you need a day off."

Walt groaned before he could find the proper words for a response. "Lay off, man. I've got enough on my mind without you acting like my ex-wife."

"Speaking of, I'm surprised *she's* not a suspect, too." Tony emphasized 'she's' in order to make his point. When Walt only grimaced, Tony saw his opening. "I mean, after all, you haven't heard from her in a while — you always hated each other. She's the perfect suspect."

"I considered her."

Tony roared with laughter. "Of course you did!" More laughter rushed up from his gut, like a geyser at Yellowstone. "Of course you did!" Tony collected himself before continuing. "You never heard from her again, did you?"

"Nope. Paying her off was the smartest thing I ever did. That was more than twenty-five years ago." Walt cocked his head as he tried to remember.

"Well, ol' Stacey is probably somewhere in the Caribbean, loving life." Tony laughed, but Walt failed to see the humor. "If she's still alive."

"Oh, I'm sure she's still alive. She didn't do drugs and she wasn't a heavy drinker, so that's in her favor," Walt explained. "Besides, she has a mission in life, so that keeps a person young."

"Oh, yeah? What's that?"

"Making men's lives miserable. She was an ace at that." Walt finally cracked a smile. Tony, already in the mood to laugh, launched another belly-blaster into the air.

"You can laugh all you want," Walt half-scolded. "But that's what she did. She makes people – and she seems to hate men, I learned – she makes them miserable. But she's not sophisticated enough to pull all this off." He paused to think before voicing the most recent thought. "Besides, she's not capable of murder." Another thought brought his entire body to life. "In fact!" He almost shouted. "She'd never do the arsons, either. She'd be afraid to get her nails dirty!"

At this point, another laugh from Tony was only natural. "If some of the ladies around here could hear us, we'd be off to 'sensitivity training.'"

"Yeah, bull. They're worse than we are about other women." Walt's pronouncement was matter-of-fact.

"Well, you got me there, old buddy."

The phone rang. Walt exhaled with a loud snort and shook his head. "Walt Musgrave." His terse response could not be missed. It became apparent to Tony that Walt had interrupted the caller.

"Hang on. Hey, can you hang on just a second? I have Tony in the room. He'll want to hear this."

Walt reached down and pushed the 'speaker' button.

"Tony, I have Agent Bauml on the line. Go ahead."

"Hi, Tony," the disembodied voice filled the room. "I'm calling on behalf of Special Agent Bretz. He wanted me to call and give you guys an update."

"Okay. And 'hi' back at ya." Tony changed his focus to Walt and whispered, "I told them to call you if they couldn't reach me."

"This is what I have so far," Agent Bauml said. "We're working with the Ventura County Sheriff's Department. We have full confidence in their office and in Detective Encarnacion, but we have more resources."

Tony looked at Walt and whispered, "Makes sense."

"There was a G&S Systems representative in the area, at a Westlake Village hotel, just as your Dennis Fry told us. That was a marvelous coincidence he saw them. This same representative was at another local hotel for another conference when the second arson occurred."

Both Walt's and Tony's eyebrows shot up.

"The G&S representative," Agent Bauml continued, "allowed us access to his car. The trunk was empty, but tests showed residue of explosives in it. I'm not at liberty to tell you at the moment what kind of explosives."

By his expression, Tony could see Walt did not like the lack of transparency. "Don't worry about it. I'll explain later," Tony whispered.

"The representative has been arrested, and we are pushing for no bail due to the possibility that he is also responsible for the murders."

"Who is this guy?" Walt asked.

"His name is Edward Petrosian," Agent Bauml responded.

"Never heard of the guy," Walt said.

"Me neither," Tony chimed in.

"He has no criminal history, but he's the only one who drives that car," Bauml answered.

"I guess we have to figure out what this all means," Tony said as he looked at the wall with the Patrick Henry painting. "I'm at a loss."

"Just remember Special Agent Bretz is doing this for you as a favor." Bauml's voice gained a notch of seriousness. "This information is not to be shared with anyone."

"Got it," Walt responded.

"Yup," Tony added.

"That's all I have. We'll be in touch later."

"Okay, Agent Bauml. Thank you." Walt ended the call, then looked up at the attorney. "Now we have to feel around and find out who at G&S put this guy up to this."

Tony nodded. "I think there's a lot more to this. You're right. I know where you're going. This guy wouldn't do this on his own."

Before Tony could utter another sentence, Dennis walked in. His casual attitude and calm demeanor masked the tensions between Walt and him. He spotted the lawyer and reacted with natural ease. "Hey, Tony. How goes it?"

"Hi, Dennis." Tony's cheery response kept the conversation relaxed.

"I've got some papers." Dennis held them up, as if to justify his presence. "And then I ran into Donna and she asked me to have you sign some things, too, Walt." He maneuvered past Tony and stopped next to Walt's desk. "Here I just need your initials – it's a place you missed on a DOD form." He set the form down for Walt to see, his finger pointing to the exact spot.

Pen in hand, Walt put his initials on the sheet.

"These next three – four – documents are from Donna. I have no idea what they are. Sign each one at the bottom."

Walt dutifully signed the documents without a concern about the contents of each page.

"Two more things from me." Dennis flipped through the pages in his hand. "This is the McHenry deal for some battery compounds. I don't know much about it. I came in on the tail end of this. I just know we really need it since the attack at Building B."

Walt kept a careful eye on his subordinate, then took the papers and signed multiple times.

"Oh. You missed one." Dennis pointed, which caused Walt to add his signature to yet another line.

"And one last document. Please sign on the final two pages. It's a huge shipment for circuitry. They don't know where they're gonna store it, but they know they'll figure it out before the shipment arrives. At least that's what Singh told me." He handed the final set of documents to Walt.

With signatures everywhere needed, Dennis stepped back from the desk.

"Walt was telling me," Tony started. "All the work he has to do."

"I have to pull some of that slack," Dennis chimed in.

"Yes, that would be good, Fry," Tony agreed. "Walt's got the DOD, the OFCCP, the FBI."

"The IRS," Walt added.

"Oh. The In-depth Rectal Surveyors," Dennis said with a laugh.

"Yikes! That's about right," Tony laughed.

"Actually, I've been taking care of the OFCCP people," Dennis interjected.

"Good," Tony answered.

"We've got some alphabet soup going on." Walt finally warmed up to the conversation.

"And I'm gonna get rid of the DOL – do they call the Department of Labor by their initials?" Dennis interrupted himself with a question. "I'm gonna get rid of them ASAP." The three laughed.

"I think we're close to record territory for letters," Tony chuckled.

"At least for Triumvirate," Walt laughed. I'm sure the government's used to it.

"Well, I gotta get." He then tried out his best Arnold Schwarzenegger voice. "Hasta la vista, baby." With that, Dennis turned and headed out the door.

Tony looked toward the empty doorway and waited several seconds. "Well, he didn't seem too bad, other than the lousy 'Ahnuld' impersonation."

"Yeah, you never know about that guy. I wonder if he's manic depressive or something," Walt said, mental wheels turning behind his eyes.

• • •

In the hallway, several yards from Walt's office, Dennis stopped. He looked around, his guilty disposition evident by the furtive glances he took in multiple directions. He thumbed through the sheaf of papers until he reached the one-page document he wanted. With more stealthy glances in all directions, he pulled the paper from his small stack. He looked at it with care, then focused on the signature at the bottom: *Walter E. Musgrave.* "Now I'm gonna drive you crazy," he mumbled. A smile leaped across his face and reached his cheekbones.

With one more look around, Dennis walked, with a broad smile, back to his office. A little more bounce in his step was detectable to the careful observer.

Chapter 14

"Well, don't you look like a twenty-million-dollar portfolio!" Dennis said with a laugh.

"Oh, thanks. That sounds like something my dad would say." Heidi wore a pair of jeans and a bright blue, buttoned-down blouse. She stepped back to let him into the Musgrave house.

"I know, I know," Dennis laughed again as he defended himself. "That's why I said it. I was gonna ask if that's what your dad would say."

She led him to a small room, down the hall from her father's den, which resembled a sitting room. The Musgraves referred to it as 'the second living room.' They sat together on the couch as she continued the conversation. "Oh, it's something he'd say, all right." Heidi relaxed. Dennis could see it in her shoulders and eyes. Her face now lit up, eyes beaming like lighthouse beacons.

A coy grin crossed his mouth as he observed Heidi's reaction to his mere presence – particularly now that he was not acting like her father. "I guess I could've said, 'you look like a hundred-million-dollar government contract.'"

They both laughed as she hit him in the ribs with the back of her hand.

"I deserved that." He smiled as he studied her face as though it were a road map. "But I'm learning your dad, so you gotta give me some points for that."

"Yeah, that's true. Everything's about sales and marketing and business. He's an expert marketer, but since Triumvirate, he's learned a lot about finance and all that." Her glowing smile diminished to one of contentment, as though she could stay in the moment, no matter the subject of conversation.

"I like your dad," Dennis allowed his voice to trail off, to convey a major change of direction which was not far behind.

"But?" Heidi took the bait.

"He – oh. He, he's fine. Never mind."

"But what?

"I didn't say 'but.' You did," Dennis pointed out.

"There's something you obviously don't like. What is it?" The hook dug deeper into Heidi's curiosity.

"I don't know. I don't mean to rag on your dad or anything. Us getting to know each other is about us, not your dad or my position with the company." He eyed her with a look of pained hesitance.

"No. It's all right. Really." She, too, had much more to say but held back.

"Nah. I didn't mean anything by it."

"Dennis. My dad and I don't have the best of relationships. It's okay. That's the way it is." Her tone dissolved into an earnest begging.

"Well, I just." He stopped as if rethinking his words. "I just think he's a little off his rocker."

"What?" Her physical reaction moved her away from her guest.

"I'm sorry," Dennis responded. His quick response conveyed his regret.

"No, no. It's okay. I've just never heard anybody say that before. My dad's a lot of things, I've just never heard anyone say he's crazy."

"Well, not crazy, exactly," Dennis tried to explain. "He's just – he just believes a lot of stuff." He shifted his body on the couch to face Heidi as he opened up. "He just thinks everything's a conspiracy and everyone's against him and everybody's trying to hurt him, you know?"

Heidi allowed her shoulders to droop a little. "Well, yeah. That's true. He does see enemies behind every rock. I'd agree with you there."

"I find him tough to like because, well." Dennis signaled his discomfort by way of facial expression. "Because he just seems prone to exaggeration."

Heidi did not hide her surprise. "He's always been honest. I don't know if I've seen him exaggerate stuff."

"He just gets carried away with things and – look, I'm not totally comfortable with this conversation. Let's get going. I'm hungry for some Chinese food."

Heidi hesitated before climbing off the couch. "Okay."

As she reached her feet, Dennis stepped close to her. "Look. I'm sorry. He's my boss and your dad, and I shouldn't complain about him." He dropped his head in a sign of his pursuit of forgiveness.

The ring of the doorbell seemed to blast through the house – down the halls, into every room. To Heidi, the ring sounded louder than normal. Startled, she flinched.

"Expecting someone?" Dennis asked, a playful tone signaled he noticed her jumpiness.

"No. Not at all," came the response. "I'll be back."

Within seconds, Dennis heard a booming male voice. He could not hear the entire conversation, but did hear 'why are you here?' twice and 'boyfriend' once. He stood in the doorway as Heidi and Troy headed toward him.

Heidi's embarrassment could not be missed. She extended a hand in Dennis' direction as she reached him. "Dennis, this is my former boyfriend, Troy. He dropped by recently and now he's dropped by again."

Troy reached out his large hand. "Hi, Dennis. I'm Troy. Good to meet you."

"'Ex' boyfriend, I heard?" Dennis did not attempt to hide his contempt for the larger man.

"Those things do happen," Troy smiled, undeterred by the cutting words.

"Sometimes they do," Dennis responded dryly, his eyes focused on Troy's every move. "So, what do you do?"

"I'm a small businessman, a workout expert, and a surfer."

"Oh," Dennis held out the syllable with feigned respect. "A 'workout expert.' That's quite a degree. What is it? PE?"

Troy laughed as though the joke was harmless fun. "I'm PE and you're BS. Awesome." The laughter stopped, punctuating an insult of his own.

"Only my Bachelor of Science actually means something," Dennis sneered.

"Okay, guys. This really isn't necessary," Heidi protested. "I'm not some damsel who needs fighting over."

"That's a good thing for him," Troy got in a second shot, his smile as large as the hallway where he stood.

Dennis raised his eyebrows but elected not to respond with words.

"I'll tell ya what," Troy changed his tone with a sudden idea and pulled his phone from his pocket. "I'll be the first to call for a truce right now. Let me get a pic of the two of you." Within seconds, he held his cell phone at the ready.

Troy's plan worked to perfection. Wanting nothing more than peace to break out, Heidi gurgled with glee at the thought of good will. Before Dennis could react, she stood at his side, arm around his waist, ready to pose.

For his part, Dennis seemed less enthusiastic, but in an effort to please Heidi, he put his arm around her shoulder and radiated his best fake smile.

Troy clicked off four photos before announcing, "Okay, smile." He pushed the button three more times. "Anyone else's phone?" While Heidi felt her pockets and then rushed down the hallway to her purse, Troy slid his phone back into his jeans pocket.

"What are you doing, man?" Dennis asked, as though speaking to a teenager.

"I stopped by to visit Heidi. I didn't know she had company."

"What? Were you raised in a barn? Didn't you think to call first? You just drop in on people?" Dennis was not in a mood to cut the surfer any slack.

"What? Are you related to Walt? 'Raised in a barn?' Who talks like that unless they're 80 years old?" Troy mocked. "Dude, hang loose. I'm just visiting."

"Dude? Hang loose?" Incredulity dripped from each syllable. "Who talks like *that*?"

"People who see the Sun shine every day and the Moon rise every night," Troy laughed. "You're within a few miles of the beach, man. Act like it." He laughed more.

The laugh ushered more anger into Dennis' veins. "Sounds more like 'moonshine' for you, Neanderthal."

Heidi returned, phone in hand. "Here you go." She handed her phone to Troy, who took multiple photos for her.

"More pics," he announced, proud of his idea.

110

"That's way cool, man," Dennis said, a flat voice carrying the intended message of being unimpressed.

"Way cool," Troy repeated, deflecting any intended sting. He turned his attention to Heidi. "Where ya headed?"

"Out," Dennis' curt response interrupted whatever Heidi might reveal.

"I step aside," Troy mocked. "I'm sure ya know how to show a girl a good time." He returned his attention to Heidi. "Okay, I'll go. Ya can walk me to the door."

"I'll be right back," Heidi told Dennis.

The two walked the short distance to the front door. Dennis retreated out of sight, back into the second living room.

Once alone, Troy dropped the subservient demeanor. "I can see you've got a pompous donkey of a winner there, Heidi. Where'd ya find him, 'Snobs Are Us'?"

Heidi failed at her attempt not to laugh. "Stop it, Troy. He's a great guy."

Troy's famous smile filled the entryway. "Listen, I can spot a scentless manure manufacturer a mile away." Heidi's quizzical look caused him to add, "An uncle of mine from the Midwest visited last month. He said all kinds of things like 'madder than a wet hen,' and 'if the creek don't rise,' and 'full as a tick' and all this crazy stuff."

Heidi laughed. Despite their differences, she always managed to laugh at Troy's humor – almost always.

"This guy's for real? I mean, this guy's a piece of work."

"Troy," Heidi pleaded.

"All right, all right. I'll go." He caved in to Heidi's wishes. "I'll shut up about him, but I'm telling ya, this guy's a bad guy. I don't know why, but I know it."

111

Heidi smiled, warmth permeating her being. "Thanks, Troy, for watching out for me. In a sick sort of way, I'm almost glad you're back."

Troy laughed. That Dennis could hear it down the hall was unmistakable. "Okay. As long as it's in a sick sort of way, I guess it's okay with me." He leaned forward and kissed her on the forehead, then the check. "I'm going now."

Heidi's smile told them both she did not want him to go, yet she could not wait until he walked away. She closed the door behind him, looked in Dennis' general direction, and took a deep breath.

Heidi burst into the room, in body and words. "What was that all about?" She hid her accusation in the form of a question.

"What?" Dennis played dumb.

"You were like two high-school boys fighting over a girl."

"If you want to go to dinner with him instead of me, you can," Dennis responded, no hint of feeling in his voice.

"Stop it." She could not manage a stronger response.

"He's a big, strong guy. I'm sure he could rip me into pieces if he wanted," Dennis continued with his flat tone.

"Yeah. So?"

"So, if you have an old boyfriend back in town and you need some time," Dennis said, anger and self-doubt detectable. "I understand."

They eyed each other, sleuths looking for clues.

"I was never that big," Dennis persisted from his emotionally detached position. "No matter how much I worked out, I was never that bulky."

Heidi's sigh filled the room. She threw back her head, allowing her hair to reach the middle of her back, then thrust her head upright again. "Let's go eat dinner, all right?"

112

"Okay." Dennis did not sound like a man who felt wanted. "Let's go."

The happiness of the evening seemed to exit through the front door with Troy. Without another word, the couple walked the short distance down the hallway and out the front door. As she locked the door behind her, Heidi grumbled in a low voice, "Why now? Why?" She climbed into Dennis' Audi and the car backed out of the driveway and disappeared down the darkened street.

• • •

High on a bluff, on the back porch of a darkened house, two former lovers had found each other again. Neither fully trusted the other. Neither made the other's Most Desirable list. Each thought the other a fool. But somehow, they both needed each other. His world included only one friend, many business associates, and a daughter, but Walt was alone in the world all the same. Rose felt the need to 'be there' for him and to revisit the nostalgia.

I wonder what she's thinking, Walt said to himself as he sat on the wooden swing, next to the woman he never forgot, after all the years. *She's probably thinking 'what's he thinking?'* The thought made him smile, but inside the enclosed porch, ambient light struggled to penetrate their cozy little world.

"How are you?" Both recognized the low self-esteem which seeped out of each word.

"Baby, I am doing fine." Walt brushed his hand on Rose's thigh with a caring touch as he spoke. He took in deep breath and sighed a loud, contented sigh. "Marvelous view you have here."

"Yeah, it's too dark to really see the ocean now," she laughed. Her words caused the couple to look down, toward the cars passing by below. The dark void which spread into the distance marked the edge of the Pacific Ocean. On this clear night, faint dots to the left marked cargo ships waiting their turn, on approach to Los Angeles and Long Beach Harbors. Also to the left, the bright lights in the sky denoted airliners dropping into and jetting out of Los Angeles International Airport. Streetlights were visible near the coast and on hillsides.

"Are you here enough to enjoy it?" Walt already knew the answer to the question.

"Oh, no. Not even close. I'm probably home as much as you. Maybe less 'cause I have a board of directors. Stockholders always looking over my shoulder – it's the Information Age, you know." Rose reached over and grabbed her glass of wine from a small, bamboo table which she could not quite see. "While I'm digesting the numbers, somebody's writing me an email 'cause they saw the info or heard the rumors on CNBC or Fox Business or Twitter. Yeah, it's constant."

"Thanks for all that listening you did earlier. Thank you."

"I can't see you," Rose began, although a smile was evident in her voice. "But I can tell your eyes are twinkling. I'll never forget the way your eyes twinkle."

Walt could not shake one sentence she had uttered – twice – during the evening. He knew Rose had a certain intuition which always amazed him. Her words stood in opposition to what he, Alex, and Tony believed; nevertheless, those words reverberated through the silence more than her prior sweet comments and excitable exclamations. *Keep your eye on that Dennis Fry – I'm tellin' you.*

After a couple of seconds, their hands found each other's. No additional words were cast into the night.

Chapter 15

Walt hung up the phone; an unusual calmness permeated his body. He grinned as he looked at the phone – not because the conversation went well – it did not – but because he had made a silent, conscious effort to calm himself. To control his anger. To lower his blood pressure. A lot had happened in the short time since they moved forward with a contract with the Department of Defense. And it was all bad. While Bill and Alex had met violent deaths, Walt did not have the sensation or fear he was next. Instead, he feared a stroke or heart attack. So, he was going to calm himself.

Then Dennis Fry entered his office.

Walt grit his teeth in a last-ditch effort at calmness, but the smug look on Dennis' face was too much. Walt's tiny smile disappeared.

"Hey, Boss." Dennis' chipper mood seemed fake to both men.

"Yeah, what is it?"

"You didn't see the piece of paper I was carrying when I walked in?" Dennis held up the one-page document in front of his face, temporarily obscuring Walt's view of Dennis' face, suit, and tie.

Walt grabbed the paper and read it without speaking. "What?!" was all he managed before getting halfway through it. "I never –"

"Ah, but you did. There's your little signature at the bottom. *Walter E. Musgrave.*" Dennis' mocking tone contained a harsh edge. "Does the 'E' stand for 'exacta'?"

Without hesitating, Walt wadded up the paper and threw it into the nearby trash can.

Dennis laughed. "You didn't think that was the original, did you?" He laughed again, for good measure. "Walt, you wanted the bet. You have a history of gambling, so it only makes sense you signed it. Now we have a bet. I'll get rid of the OFCCP in two weeks, and I get your share of the company. You walk away. Right now, it looks to me like the whole company's yours, so guess what? The whole company will be mine."

Like a human volcano, Walt erupted. Before Dennis could finish his last two words, Walt leaped to his feet and lunged toward the younger man. Dennis retreated to the door. Words attempted to leave Walt's mouth, but only unintelligible gurgles and roars mixed together to produce sound.

"You signed it!" Dennis left the office as fast as possible without running. He looked back in time to see Walt reach the doorway.

"You're fff-" A thought hit Walt with a force of a car hitting a block wall at high speed. *I can't fire him. Then I'll have to explain everything to the DOD.* He gripped the door casing. His trembling hands betraying his blood pressure. *Then if the FBI finds out, that'll really sink us. Oh God! I can't fire the little bastard!*

Down the hall, the elevator door opened. Dennis looked in the direction of his enraged boss. "I'll be back," he yelled with his second-rate Schwarzenegger impression. He stepped into the elevator as Walt shot a glance his way.

Walt returned to his desk, his mind racing. 'You have a history of gambling,' he had said. *How did he know that?! Who told him?!* Walt could not accept that Dennis somehow, some way, could have the upper hand. The bet – or non-bet – aside, it alarmed him as he considered how much research Dennis must have performed. He never remembered he himself had handed the tidbit to his young adversary in a meeting in Alex's office.

• • •

"Walt, he's got nothing. Nothing at all." Walt heard the words yet did not feel consoled.

"You're sure? Even with my signature?"

"First of all," Tony began. "No judge in the state of California is going to consider that a legal document. Second, you sign documents all the time sight-unseen." Tony paused to think through his answer. "That could be a tough sell to a jury, but it'd never make it that far. A judge would understand that it's easy how your signature would end up on such a document."

"Hell, I've signed documents just for him probably a dozen times just in the short time he's been here." Walt tried to make himself feel better, but failed.

"Look, we'll confront him later, and we'll –"

"Let's confront him now!" Walt demanded.

"We can't. On my way up, he was leaving the building with that DOD guy," Tony explained, a reassuring calmness in his voice.

"DOD guy? Here? Why didn't I know about it?"

"I don't know, Walt. The guy had business up at Edwards Air Force Base, so he decided to drop down and get an update on some minor change." Tony paused. His efforts to relax his friend seemed to be failing. "We had a twenty-minute meeting, then he met with our software people, then he went out to lunch with Fry. You know these people seem to like Dennis for some reason."

"Yeah, that's what worries me." Walt was not prepared to be calmed, especially when someone from the Department of Defense was in town, he was not informed, and one of his own employees was out to cause him harm. "I think this puts the murders and arson in a new light."

"Dennis?" Tony laughed.

"Yes. Dennis. Fry suddenly wants to take over the company and he's not a suspect? Come on!" The force of Walt's words communicated in a crisp, clear tone that he did not doubt himself.

"You really think Dennis could kill Bill and Alex?"

Walt took a deep breath. "I don't know what to believe, but what he just pulled was pretty extreme."

Tony held up the crumpled piece of paper. "I'll keep this, but there's no reason for you to give it a second thought. He's messing with you, Walter. I don't know to what end, but he's messing with you." Tony folded the paper in half and put it inside his suit jacket pocket. "I have a full afternoon, but tomorrow we'll sit down with him and I'll be tough on him. It'll be the three of us."

Walt nodded. He was out of words.

"Get your paperwork done and get out of here," Tony ordered, sounding like Walt's mother again. "There's been enough crap going on around here; no reason to stick around."

Again, Walt nodded.

Tony stared at Walt for a brief moment before turning to leave the office.

Alone, Walt allowed his thoughts to run free. One thought, however, repeated itself over and over: *Dennis Fry is going to pay for this. He will pay.*

Chapter 16

He feared this moment. He feared every aspect of his relationship with Heidi when he knew she might disagree with him. Walt understood he was not the best father – distant, detached; whatever the word, he was it.

Heidi Christina Musgrave had grown up without a mother, and her father lived a life devoid of emotion. Walt studied up enough on the subject to know her odds of either bulimia or anorexia increased, as did the chances of having a damaged self-esteem. While he knew it, understood it, and theoretically fought against it, in reality Walt failed to do enough to show his daughter she was more important to him than his work.

Heidi knew Triumvirate Technologies was Number One in his life while she was a distant Number Two. She knew he could not help himself. It was the way he was wired, she reasoned. The excuse did not make her feel better about him or herself, but it did help her have a small degree of understanding.

She managed to avoid the pitfalls of an emotionally distant father, including eating disorders, but what remained was a kind of cynicism toward the man. He was her father, but he was, in a way, just another man – a man who happened to reside in the same house and paid for things for her. He told her he loved her – on occasion – and he looked out for her best interests, but at times she looked at him as more of a mature roommate.

She could always tell when he was nervous about dealing with a specific subject with her, and this was one of those times.

Walt was not in the habit of watching television, but at the moment, as he waited for her arrival, he did just that. As a routine, he tried to keep up with the news – usually business news – on his

119

smart phone, but on this night, he was sitting in front of the television in his front living room when Heidi entered the house through the garage.

"You? Watching TV? What's wrong with this picture?" Heidi teased, her high-pitched voice climbed higher than normal.

"Yeah. Oh. Hi, honey." He stood to face her.

"So, what's up?" She walked to a nearby chair and sat.

"I was just waiting for you to get home. I just wanted to chat with you about something." Walt's forceful, commanding voice weakened. This was not Walt the Businessman, full of fire and drive.

"Okay." She dragged out both syllables, as if still studying his words.

"I have to ask you a question." No query about her day. No consideration of how she was feeling or asking how her life was going. Straight to the point.

"Okay." Again, she dragged out both syllables of her reply as trepidation crept across her face.

"Dennis is trying to con me into an insane bet. Did he mention anything about it to you?" There was a thread of hope in his voice – a hope Heidi could explain everything away and the incident would be over, as though it could be put in a box, wrapped like a Christmas present, and sealed shut. Forever. But it was not to be.

"What are you talking about?"

"Oh." Walt could not hide his dejection. "So, he didn't say anything, huh?" *What was she supposed to do about it, anyway?* Reason returned to his thoughts. *Even if she knew, what would it matter?*

"No. He's never mentioned any bet to me. Are you still betting the horses?"

He saw an opening to change the subject but chose to ignore it. "Forget the horses. This is different." Walt hesitated before explaining further. "Fry came up with this crazy scheme to bet the company."

"Bet the – what?!"

"He's messing with me, but I don't know why."

"Dad." It was uncommon for her to refer to him by any name, let alone a name of affection, but this time it was more exclamation than endearment.

"He came up with a bet about getting rid of these stupid government bureaucrats, and if he wins he gets the company."

"And if he loses?" Skepticism colored her voice.

"He leaves. Quits."

Heidi stood with an abrupt lurch, staring, mouth agape, as though she had just spotted a five-armed purple alien.

"I'm not kidding," Walt added, in hopes of convincing his skeptical daughter.

"I – I don't know what to say. That just –" She interrupted herself to think. "That just makes no sense."

"Tell me about it!" Walt thought, at last, he had found an ally.

"No. It makes no sense as in, I'm wondering if you're okay."

This was not the response the elder Musgrave wanted to hear. His eyes bulged. *If I'm okay?! Are you kidding me?!* He fought to avoid giving voice to his thoughts. "Look," Walt managed to fight off his anger – to a small degree. "I *know* it doesn't make sense – at least to a rational person – but I'm not evaluating it, I'm just trying to find out if he said anything to you about a joke or anything."

"No. He didn't mention this to me."

Walt studied his daughter's face and concluded she was telling the truth.

"I don't know about your boyfriend. He –"

"He's not my boyfriend." Her curt response left no room for doubt.

"Okay, okay. Good. Glad to hear it, 'cause I'm starting to wonder about him." As he continued to study Heidi's face, he gathered she wondered about him.

"I need to know something," Heidi began, her words came out in a slow cadence. "Are you okay?"

"Well, I admit, I'm a little bothered by this, but yeah, I'm all right."

"No. That's not what I mean." She paused, searching for a delicate way to state her concern. "You've lost two friends lately and now you're acting a little strange. I'm a little worried –"

"A little strange?" Walt could not conceal even an ounce of his displeasure. "You think I'm acting strangely? Dennis Fry just conned me into signing a document that's for a bet and you think I'm acting –" Each emphasis of 'I'm' made his point, at least to Walt, but Heidi focused on the document.

"You signed a bet with him?!"

"He conned me! It was mixed in with a bunch of papers. I mean, I don't know for sure when I signed it, but it's the only time it could've happened that makes sense." Walt's impatience rose to rival his anger at Dennis.

"Have you been drinking?" She had never before leveled such an accusation against her father, even when he was at his worst, during his troubled days after Tina's death.

Anger rose like oil in a newly struck well. "What?! Do you not hear what I'm saying?! Fry conned me! Don't you get it?!"

"No! I don't!"

That they both were yelling disturbed Walt. *This is not going like I thought it would*, he yelled at himself. "Heidi! Listen! Please!" He paused to lower his heart rate. "Listen, honey. Dennis Fry is not a good man. I haven't figured it out yet, but he's – there's something about him. There's something wrong with him. I just haven't put my finger on it yet."

The young woman shook her head, unconvinced. "No. I think you're being –" She fought for the right word. "You're being, you're just, over-dramatic."

Walt threw up his arms in disgust. "Oh, yeah! Sure!"

"You think we're dating, so you're being over-protective or something."

"I'm asking you whether you knew about this. That's it." He fought off the urge to yell.

"Why would I know and not tell you?!" She yelled with new vigor.

"I'm not accusing you of anything. I was just asking!" He surrendered to the urge to let loose his anger. He always tried not to not raise his voice to her, but the conversation had become maddening.

"You're out of your mind!" With that, Heidi stormed away.

While Walt could not see where she went, he knew she was headed to her bedroom. He knew it would be wise of him not to follow her. He also knew he had completely blown it with his daughter. Whatever trust she had in him was gone, and she would now side with Dennis during any upcoming skirmishes between the two men.

The conversation was a complete and total failure.

Chapter 17

"Why was your car wiped down?"

"What? What does that mean?"

"Come on," Agent Boles made no attempt to hide his disdain. "Get with the twenty-first century, Slick. I'm sure you watch *NCIS* or *CSI*-Whichever City and some cop shows. You know what it means to wipe something down."

"Oh. That kind of wipe down?" Chris Staley trembled like a seal on a small ice floe, encircled by a pod of killer whales. "I – I – I don't watch much of that stuff. I mean, I've seen some of it, yeah, but yeah. Not much."

Before Staley entered the room and took his seat, Boles had moved the camera in as close as possible. Staley's curly dishwater-blond hair and light-brown eyes shuddered along with the rest of his body at the intensity of the moment. Between the brightness of light in the small room, the pressure from the FBI agent, the extra layer of claustrophobia added by the camera and fill-light just a few feet from his face, and the circumstances themselves, Staley sweated and squirmed.

"I looked through your records. You have no criminal record, but –"

"That's right."

"You seem to have a thing for gunpowder and swords." Boles' eyes bored into Staley's, causing the recipient of the questions to look away from the agent every time he looked up.

"I told that other FBI guy about that. It's no big deal. I –"

"Tell me!" Boles bellowed. The thick-chested agent towered over the seated suspect. His dark-blue windbreaker with 'FBI' emblazoned on the back hid his muscular frame, although his deep voice provided sufficient intimidation. With his dark, menacing eyes he intentionally gave the appearance of a man willing to use violence when necessary.

"Me and my friends were trying to make flash-bang things. I don't know what you call it. Just flash explosion things like in *Batman*. Christopher Nolan's *Batman*. You know the scene where they use different ways to distract people from –"

"Who's Christopher Nolan?" Boles asked.

"He's a movie producer. He made the best *Batman* movies. Didn't you see *Batman Begins* and *The Dark Knight*?" Staley trembled with each word, sounding more like a man with a gun to his head.

"Who are you trying to kid, Staley?" Boles' harsh tone served to frighten Staley further. "*Batman* doesn't use swords."

"Yeah, but that's for the comic-cons. That's for when I dress up like a Viking warrior – Ragnar. I like to –"

Boles sighed. "Does Ragnar wipe down the inside of his car?"

"No. No. Listen. I didn't wipe down my car," Staley begged for understanding. "I didn't even know you guys used that expression. I thought that was just Hollywood." He sounded as though he could burst into tears at any moment. "I don't know how to wipe down a car."

"Tell me about your experiences with C-4."

"The explosive?!" Shocked, Staley struggled to sit upright. "I don't know anything about explosives!" A wave of panic crossed his face. "The other guy didn't ask me about explosives. What are you talking about?!"

Boles folded his lips inward as he attempted to fight off a smile. "Yet you have containers of gunpowder and you experiment with your friends with –"

"I told you, that was Batman stuff. It was just for fun!"

"Mister Staley," Boles' mocked his adversary. "I'm starting to see why the judge didn't grant you bail. You don't know about explosives, but you experiment with them. You don't know what it means to wipe down something, but you do." The agent laughed. "You're just full of contradictions, aren't you?"

"No. No." Staley's denials quieted, his panic subsided. The fear that overcame him weakened his frame.

"You told Agent Bauml you hung out in the bar all night – the night we've been talking about."

"Yes, all evening," Staley replied.

"You expect me to believe you just hung out in the bar – let me guess, you were sober all night. Oh, I believe you were there." Boles stood and stepped away from the table. He stretched his neck out before returning to the table so the microphone could pick up his question. "I just find it interesting that you have so many witnesses of you at the bar, but not at the time you need witnesses. It's like you wanted witnesses in case you were ever in this situation, before you went off and played with your explosives."

"But I didn't play with explosives that day," Staley pleaded. "That's just in preparation for comic-cons. That's it. Not *real* explosives. Just flashy stuff." He stressed 'real' to convey the nature of his experimentations.

"So, gunpowder isn't a *real* explosive?" Boles repeated the emphasis of 'real.' "Is dynamite *real*? Is pentaerythritol tetranitrate *real*?"

"Penta–riddle what? I can't even say that," Staley sobbed.

"PETN. You know what it is," Boles snarled.

"No! I don't. I don't!" Staley cried as he teetered on the edge of emotional control.

"What do you know about other kinds of explosives, other than kiddie stuff like gunpowder?" Boles demanded.

"I just used it for fun stuff."

"Did you have any in your car?" Boles asked.

"No."

"In your company car?"

"No. It's the only car I have," Staley sounded spent.

"Are you afraid of me?" Boles asked the suspect.

"Yes," the man answered, sounding like an exhausted quarry, hunted down and waiting to be killed. "You look like what the Black Panther should have looked like."

"The what?"

"The Black Panther. The superhero," Staley quaked as he answered.

Agent Boles looked at the suspect and fought off a smile. "You should be afraid of me, especially if you're lying to me."

"I'm not lying!" Staley came to life.

Earlier in the day, Agent Bauml had asked questions about Staley's knowledge of Triumvirate Technologies and its leadership. Witnesses had confirmed Staley's story: as with every other time they had seen him at a conference, the *G&S Systems* representative made a habit of plopping down at the hotel bar and keeping the seat warm for hours on end. A slow drinker he spoke to anyone who spoke to him first, but otherwise kept to himself.

At comic-cons, he dressed as Batman on Saturdays and a Viking on Sundays, without fail. He carried a plastic sword with his Viking outfit because of rules against real swords at most of the comic-cons, but had one real, inexpensive sword for events where swords were permissible. He and other like-minded friends thought it was cool to carry as many props as the 'real' Batman, which explained the containers full of gunpowder at his house.

Agent Boles walked away from the videotaped interview with the understanding Chris Staley was no more likely to be the arsonist and murderer targeting Triumvirate Technologies than Christian Bale was likely to walk into federal prison dressed as Batman.

Boles ordered Staley returned to his cell, then left the corrections facility. He knew as he left the facility he would begin the paperwork to release this man. The investigation into the crimes at Triumvirate Technologies remained opened and active. They lacked credible leads or a credible suspect.

Later, Boles enjoyed showing the video to Agent Bauml, particularly when it reached the part where Staley referenced the Black Panther comic book character. The agents shared a good laugh as they assessed their now-former suspect.

Chapter 18

The immaculate conference room contained the plush settings prescribed by the late Alexander Heil. The large, marble table with rounded ends and leather, wheeled chairs could seat 18 meeting participants. The 'sailing' theme of the room was reflected by the light-blue paint and the three separate paintings of sailboats. What should have been an exterior wall was instead a plate-glass window, though the view only opened up to the back lot. Alex had wanted a room in which important guests could be met with dignity.

Che Novak's black hair seemed a fraction taller, pushed up by his cheeks, which were in turn forced upward by his broad, happy smile. He sat at the head of the table, which spanned most of the length of the room. Seated at his left was a forty-year-old assistant who was even smaller than Novak. His brown hair much lighter than Novak's, John McRae looked like a bookworm. His small, wire-framed glasses, thin mustache, and pale, white skin gave him the look of someone who never saw the Sun or performed outdoor activities.

Seated to Novak's right was Paul Leonard, a middle-aged investigator who shared none of McRae's physical qualities. Tall, heavy-set, and bald, his build completely offset his smaller peer's.

When Walt entered the room, Dennis and Tony were already seated across from each other, both avoiding the open chairs next to the bureaucrats. The surviving member of the triumvirate walked to the nearest chair, next to Dennis, but on the opposite side from the government workers, leaving the chair open between Dennis and McRae.

Walt, in all of his robust, blunt glory blurted out, "Dennis told me you're done. How can you be done?!" He sat next to Dennis as he finished his point, dressed up as a question.

Novak's smile grew so large his little face could barely contain it. "Gentlemen, thank you for being here." He took the time to look at every man in the room, including his lieutenants. "I thought you'd want to hear the preliminary findings."

Walt took a deep breath, which everyone in the room heard. It served more as a statement than a means to obtain oxygen.

"Gentlemen, so as I'm sure you're aware, we found widespread, shall we say, 'irregularities' in your hiring practices, but your books looked very good. We don't do a financial audit, but we do look at the books as they pertain to your hiring and firing practices, how raises are administered, and how you discipline your employees." Novak paused for effect, as though hosting a game show, on the verge of announcing the winner.

Novak droned on for five minutes of what would be a preface if he were reading a document. The leaders of Triumvirate Technologies were lulled to near slumber until Novak uttered the words, "and now to our findings."

Walt looked around the room. The others stared at the speaker, their focus pinpointed on his every word. Something did not feel right. *Why are we doing this? Why are there findings unless they're done? He said 'preliminary findings,' so are they done or not?*

"We've completed our investigation and we'll be out of here by the end of the day."

Novak's words crashed hard inside Walt's mind. *Fry! They were supposed to be around for weeks. Months. Almost forever!* He could not remember at the moment how long they were threatening to disrupt the operation; too much had happened. Deaths. Arson. *Fry. Yes, Fry! He said he'd get rid of them and now they're going.*

Lost in thought, Walt missed a couple of Novak's points, but was jolted out of his own little world by the words: "In a minute I'll give you each a copy of our preliminary report."

"There are only six pages here," Novak continued. "I've tried to keep everything short and sweet. The bottom line is the fine levied against Triumvirate Technologies for a variety of violations is $5,247,119.12."

Walt's palms slapped the table, causing all eyes to turn to him. He closed his eyes and crinkled his face, as though attempting to peer into the Sun.

Undeterred, Novak proceeded, increasing Walt's blood pressure. "If everyone will turn to page five, you'll see the summary of the violations, beginning with gender, race, and sexual-orientation discrimination." He paused to glance at Walt. "A severe age discrepancy exists in this company, as well."

I can't believe this- "What? No religious discrimination?" He interrupted his own thought for a caustic remark. "I've made jokes about Hindus before. Or was it Sikhs? I don't see that in the report."

"Mister Musgrave, I had hoped you would take these issues seriously by now." Novak's condescension echoed through the room and was visible on his face.

"Novak," Tony intoned, anger not far off. "Keep your mouth and attitude in check. If you wish to expound on your report, please proceed." He was in full attorney mode. "If you intend to merely lecture us, we will see to it that you are escorted out of the building. Now, please proceed in a professional manner."

132

Despite flashing an angry glare, a quick gulp betrayed Novak's true feelings.

Walt was not ready to allow the two seconds of quiet make it to a third. "There's no racial discrimination here. I wouldn't put up with it, Alex wouldn't't've put up with it, and Won Yi Yoo wouldn't't've put up with it."

Tony chose not to return Walt's glance and was successful at fighting off a small smile. He understood why Walt did not use Yoo's American name.

Before Novak could respond, Walt continued with his point. "So, what's the catch? You want something from us?"

It was Novak's turn to express his indignation. "I resent the implication, Mister Musgrave."

Self-control failed. Walt leaped to his feet, sending his wheeled chair into the window behind him. "Well, I resent you coming into *my* building and making patently false accusations!" He yelled every word, but his emphasis on "my" was meant to remind the man from Washington, D.C., where he was sitting.

Undeterred, Novak coolly responded. "I can easily demonstrate the existence of discrimination."

"I have no idea what the hell you're talking about! We do *not* discriminate at Triumvirate!" Walt closed his eyes and took a deep breath. When he opened them, he looked straight at Dennis. *What? Does he think he's a spectator?!*

The younger man did not see the daggers flying out of his boss' eyes straight at him. His gaze was fixed on a folder Novak pulled from a pile of folders.

Walt sat. His red face and clenched fists advertised his thoughts and feelings.

"According to our statistics, this city is 22% Hispanic and 10% Asian. Your company is 60% white, 21% from India, 17% Asian, and approximately 1% Hispanic. That's over-representation of Indians and Asians at the expense of Hispanics." Novak looked around the room with a slow, careful gaze intended to show he was in charge of this meeting. "We also went through your hiring records. I see no evidence that African-Americans applied. You refused four out of five applications submitted by Hispanics, but at the same time you accepted two out of five applications submitted by whites." His emphasis on "accepted" carried an ominous tone.

Tony saw a different result. "Based on your numbers, we're hiring at approximately the same percentage as the local population of Hispanics, it's just that we have a high number of Indians and Asians because of the sector of the economy we're in. So, based on what you just said, if we're only hiring 40% of the whites we interview, then we're actually discriminating against white people." A sly grin lit up Tony's face.

For the first time, one of the lieutenants spoke. Paul Leonard, the heavy-set one, offered his rebuttal to Tony's reasoning. "The Department won't see it that way, Mister Harris. We're looking for discrimination against African-Americans, Hispanics, women, and other protected classes."

"Not whites?" Fry spoke up for the first time.

"They're not a protected class." Leonard's answer defined the limits of the government's battlefield.

"As I was saying," Novak said, regaining control of the meeting. "This summary only gives the bare bones. For greater details, we'll be releasing our comprehensive report to you and the media in about two months. However, until that time —"

The shockwave unleashed by an instantaneous explosion of movement enveloped the entire room. It took a fraction of a second for Walt to leap up, sending the chair flying into the large window behind him again, and release at the top of his lungs his displeasure with the entire process. "Media! Two months! What are you trying to do?!" He answered his own question before anyone else could respond. "Destroy us! That's what you're trying to do!" Every word was a shout. Every word was amplified in volume by the nearby walls. Every word projected pure anger. "Alex and Bill and I built this company and now you wanna destroy it?!" It was half question and half accusation.

John McRae picked the wrong time to pass out the six-page report. 'The summary only gives the bare bones' had been his cue. By the time Walt finished his explosion, a copy of the preliminary report rested in front of the angry businessman. Within seconds it lay in pieces, spread out in front of him on the table.

Tony stood to calm his friend. "Come on, Walter. Forget the report and let's go." From the opposite side of the table, his efforts provided no results.

"No. Walt's right. I have a stake in this company, too." Dennis sounded aggrieved. "Why go to the media? And how will this affect us with DOD?"

"I'm not at liberty to speak for DOD," Novak responded.

"Interesting choice of words: 'liberty.'" Walt was not finished. "What happened to my liberties, Che?" He glared at the bureaucrat as he stated his name in a mocking tone. "What happened to America? I used to be free to run my own business. To hire the most qualified people. I got blacks – although you failed to point that out; you only looked at applications from the last few years, I guess. I got whites. I got women. Hell, I think I got a couple of queers down in Quality Control. I don't have a bigoted bone in my body. Then you waltz in here and, and, judge my business based on numbers you want to see?!" Exhausted, Walt plopped into his chair.

"Mister Musgrave," Novak began, but Tony's extended hand made it clear: he should shut up.

"This used to be America," Walt resumed his tirade, except now in a quiet voice. Recent events seemed to have pushed down on his shoulders as he sat in his chair, and now it robbed him of his strength to yell. "Where the little guy could become a big guy. A guy could be free to live as he saw fit, go into business, be his own boss, obey the laws but do what he wanted within those laws." He took a deep breath. The room fell silent as he continued. "A guy just had to treat people like he wanted to be treated. That was it. That was America. You guys are tyrants. At least lackeys for the tyrants. That's all you are."

"Now who's lecturing whom, Mister Musgrave?" came the terse response, with a haughty tone to match, from Novak.

The glare from Tony seemed to frighten Novak into silence. "You're in his chair in his conference room in his building on his land on the First Amendment. You *will* listen." Tony emphasized 'will' and did not receive an argument.

"You guys come here and trash me for nothing," Walt said in a calm voice. "Nothing!" he suddenly yelled. "What have I done wrong?" He was back to being calm, at least in voice. "What have I done? You ask any black, any Hispanic, any woman, any PERSON – ANYBODY – if they're mistreated here! If they feel discriminated against here!" The calm now alternated with yelling. He was running out of gas, emotionally and physically. "Ask 'em. Go ASK! We care about people here, not groups."

Walt stood and walked to the plate-glass window. He picked up an extra chair and heaved it with all his might into the window. The laminate in the glass prevented it from shattering, but the point of impact suffered irreparable damage and several spider web cracks zigged and zagged away from the impact point.

Everyone in the room gasped, except Walt. He turned to the bureaucrats and pointed toward the door. "Che, it's time you leave. Get out of my building."

"Excuse me, sir. We have not finished reviewing–"

"Get out!" Walt's volume increased dozens of decibels from his first order.

Novak stared at the businessman. A defiant expression dominated his face.

Walt picked up the telephone which rested on the table, in front of Dennis. "Get security in the Sailboat Conference Room right away. Usher these federal leeches off the premises immediately." A calmness washed over his face and through his chest. Deep down, he knew he had not handled the situation well, but at the moment, form and ceremony were not relevant to him. He hung up the phone. "Che, I believe you and your non-diverse group of bureaucrats should leave now."

When Walt walked to the exit, Tony followed. Dennis took the cue and also followed, but stopped in the doorway. "I believe you know your way out of the building. Our security has been cranky lately, so you best hurry."

The bureaucrats looked at each other, stunned. The meeting was over – permanently.

• • •

As two security guards passed them in the hallway – half of Triumvirate's daytime complement of professional protection –

Dennis called out for Tony, whose fast-paced strides made it difficult for the younger man to catch. The attorney did not hide his annoyance.

"I was trying to catch Walt."

"What was he thinking in there?"

"What do you mean?"

"You heard what he said in there. You can't go on about 'queers' these days. It's the twenty-first century. Those government guys are gonna use that against him."

"Look, Dennis," Tony's level of unhappiness, not having abated since the conclusion of the meeting, began to rise again. "Don't worry about what he can and can't say. That's above your pay grade."

"He came across as a bigot."

"Did you listen to anything he said? He came across as anything but."

"He has to stop and think before he speaks," Dennis admonished the lawyer. "You know that."

"Look, Dennis. In case you haven't figured it out, Walter has his flaws. He's not perfect. I know that's shocking. But he also lets everybody live their lives. He doesn't care who you sleep with or what you look like." Tony glared at the junior executive. "He just doesn't care, Dennis, so get over it. If you don't like that he said this word or that word, too bad. If you don't like that he says things the way he wants to, too bad."

Before Dennis could respond, Tony spun and marched away. The attorney's opportunity to calm Walt would have to wait – he now needed to be calmed, himself. Tony turned and shot a wicked glance back at the haughty younger man, never breaking stride in the meantime. Between the bothersome bureaucrats and the meddlesome up-and-comer, Tony exuded disgust. His hasty pace and the side-to-side shaking of his head signaled his revulsion about the developments of the last few minutes.

Dennis leaned against the wall and watched Tony's emotion-laced departure before watching the next indignant exit – this time, government officials being escorted in silence toward the main lobby, on their way out the front door.

Chapter 19

"Can I ask you a question?"

"Of course."

"Did you try to force some crazy bet with my father?"

Dennis threw his head back. He had just finished the story of the entire meeting with the OFCCP officials, so the bet was a new subject. "A bet?"

"Yeah, my dad said something about you tricking him into signing some document." Heidi's high-pitched voice made her sound vulnerable and her eyes amplified the effect.

"A document? Heidi, what are you talking about?" A convincing puzzlement wrapped Dennis' questions. "Ya know, I'm not feeling a whole lot of love lately. You're old boyfriend's back and now this."

She caught his eyes dart down to catch the rise and fall of her breasts as she inhaled and then let loose a deep, frustrated sigh. "You know what? Never mind. I don't even wanna talk about my father. He's – he's maddening. He's – I think he's starting to lose it or something. All this pressure from the murders of Bill and Alex are starting to get to him." Her light-brown hair fell to the front of her shoulders as she dropped her head forward. "I don't know what to do about him."

"When all else fails – fresh tactics."

She looked up, her eyes signaled the confusion in her mind.

"Don't you people watch movies? Hardly anyone gets my movie references. It's *Face/Off* with John Travolta and Nicholas Cage."

"Yeah. I think I saw it." She was not impressed with his timing for lightheartedness.

Dennis reached forward and put a hand on her shoulder. "Get up. Let's take a walk." His demeanor changed from that of tenderness to a man in control.

Heidi followed orders and rose to her feet. The backyard wood swing creaked as the couple removed its burden. The robins on the lawn scampered away, refusing to take flight.

"Listen, Heidi," Dennis started, tenderness returning to his tone. "Right now, for better or worse, I'm content with our friendship. I want it to stay like this. I do want you to know you can talk to me any time you want." He stopped when a Steller's jay squawked its shrill call of anger. "I'm worried about your dad. He hasn't handled the stress well. I get it, I get it, but he's just wearing down. If he wasn't so stressed, that meeting today could've gone a lot better, too."

Heidi frowned, which caused Dennis to smile. "What?" she asked as a brief smile crossed her face.

"Oh. Nothing." He laughed. "Just admiring you. Your frown made you look so sweet."

Her eyes welled up with tears and she abandoned her caution. She threw her arms around Dennis' chest and squeezed as tight as she could manage. Dennis patted the back of her head with one hand while he rubbed her lower back with the other. The brief embrace ended when she pulled away, but not before she snuck a quick kiss onto his cheek. Lips pursed, she smiled through her tears. "Thank you. I needed that."

"You're okay," he whispered.

She pulled away and looked him in the eyes. "And no more worrying about Troy, right?"

The tenderness in his eyes, the concern for her which radiated from his face, the caring attitude – all evaporated at that moment.

"That guy."

"Dennis, I bring him up to tell you, forget him. Put him out of your mind." Heidi led him through a wooden gate and out of the back yard.

Dennis laughed. "If you wanted me to forget him, then why bring him up?"

"I just – I just mean, don't seem so insecure about him, that's all." Heidi tried not to beg. She closed the gate behind them as they walked on the perfectly cropped lawn on the side of the house.

Dennis could not hide his anger – even his sigh sounded on the edge of rage.

"Thank you for your kindness, Dennis." They stopped walking as she spoke.

"I'm sorry, but I've gotta go. Got some business to tend to. But like I said, any time you need to talk, let me know." With an abrupt turn, he continued across the lawn, into the front yard, and to the driveway.

As Dennis climbed into his car and drove away, Heidi stood on the front lawn and watched him go. She waved as she spoke words she knew he could not hear: "I can't figure you out, Dennis Fry. I just can't figure you out."

• • •

"Can I ask you a question?"

"Of course."

142

"If you knew Fry was a bad guy, why didn't you tell me?" Walt covered his words with the gentlest voice he could muster at the moment, but in his gut, he cringed. His face showed no emotion.

"I hope that doesn't mean you blame me." Rose's words were half pointed statement, half pointed question.

"No. Just a legitimate question I don't know how to word any other way."

Rose sat up, lifting her head from his lap. The wood swing with the great view groaned as her weight shifted. For the first time in several minutes, Walt took his eyes off the Pacific Ocean, which disappeared into the glare of the setting Sun and the off-shore clouds. "By 'legitimate' you're blaming me, right?" Her terse tone shattered the mutual affection and spoiled the sunset.

Walt frowned – a facial expression which had become a constant companion over the last few weeks. "No," he sighed, a softness in his voice she did not recognize.

Rose stared at him, her eyes never leaving her college boyfriend.

"Please believe me."

"I do. I believe you." Neither spoke as she studied him. She examined his eyes; his nose; his lips. His face remained frozen – rock-solid, yet with pain visible. "I do believe you, Walt, and I want you to know I've never hated you. I've been *mad* at you." She laughed as she emphasized 'mad.' "But I've never hated you. I only would've let Fry go to your company if I hated you. Unfortunately, I only heard about you hiring him later."

Walt nodded. His expression did not change. The pain was obvious, but they both knew it was caused by far more than the struggles with Dennis Fry. "Baby, listen." Rose smiled and Walt knew why. "Baby," he began again, recalling that she liked it when he called her that. "I can talk to Tony – you know that – but there's something," he paused. "Special. There's something special about reconnecting with you and now being able to talk to you."

"How many times have we seen each other over the last ten – fifteen years?" she teased.

"I know. You know the difference." He laughed.

"I know. I'm just teasing."

"When I had dinner with you the other night, I just wanted to – to." He stopped, trying to think of the right word.

"Interrogate?"

"Yeah. Interrogate you." He laughed again. "I wanted to interrogate you about that little dirtbag Fry."

"But you still love me." Her eyes narrowed as she waited for his response.

"I know." Short. Not sweet. But simple.

"So, what are we gonna do?"

"Well, the bet isn't really legal, so –"

"I mean about us!" Rose tried not to show her irritation as she emphasized each word stronger than the prior one.

"Oh." He tore his eyes away from the spot on the horizon where the Sun had viewed the southern California coast for the final time that day. He looked into her eyes. "Well, let's get this situation out of the danger zone first."

Her exhalation was more of a *harrumph*. She looked out to sea and folded her arms with a purpose.

With little emotion in his voice he responded to her actions. "I'm sorry, but I'm exhausted right now. It's been a helluva day. A helluva month."

She nodded as a sadness enveloped her – both for him and herself.

"I'll make it up to you," he said, staring into the fleeting daylight. "I just have to prepare for a battle – a different battle, or another battle – whatever – than I thought I'd be fighting."

"What do you think this guy wants?"

Walt knew the question was impossible to answer, but he responded with the theories which resonated in his mind. "He wants a shortcut to running the company. Once Bill and Alex died, he –"

Like a zombie from the movies, Walt stood up: slow; disjointed; awkward. He reached forward and grabbed the railing, steadying himself.

Puzzled, Rose climbed to her feet. She brought her face close to his to see his facial features in the fading light.

"I can't believe it." The slowness of his words came out like ketchup seeping out of a bottle. "I cannot believe it." Walt turned and faced Rose. "He joins the company, then the owners start dying. He tries to position himself to be the heir to the firm. Then he'll kill me."

His mind raced faster than his pounding heart. Shock dulled his anger. The realization made perfect sense. Other possibilities *could* exist, but this one made too much sense.

"What are you saying?" In her mind, she knew the answer to her question. In her heart, she failed to understand how a human being could commit such acts.

Visions of Bill's and Alex's bodies – images he never physically viewed – came to mind. Death. Blood. Murder. He did not realize the tightness of his grip on the metal railing caused pain in his hands – his brain could only process the thoughts of horror and shock.

"Walt? You okay?" She could no longer see him now that daylight had retreated, but she did not want to leave his side to go turn on the deck lights.

"And he's dating my daughter."

Chapter 20

Walt looked around "Richie G's." It was the first time he had set foot in the popular downtown restaurant since the morning Bill Yoo arrived late, panicked about the death of the 'other' Won Yoo – the last time the Triumvirate sat down together to share a meal. Walt forced a smile when he recalled Bill had refused to eat, his appetite taken away by nerves.

The breakfast-and-lunch eatery was a popular place, so he had arrived early to get a table. Only a few miles from the office, the mom-and-pop joint was a perfect pre-work meeting location. As for this morning, Walt had no idea why Tony had sent a cryptic text at eleven o'clock the previous night, but as his attorney wished, Walt arrived at the requested meeting spot and found a table.

Within minutes, Tony arrived, but not alone. The short, thin, bald man accompanying him wore slacks and a casual, pull-over shirt with a collar. His high voice at first startled Walt, but his steel grip of a handshake diverted attention from the voice.

Tony performed the introductions. Curtis Bretz. FBI – the Los Angeles office. They had crossed paths in law school, became friends, and maintained occasional contact to this day. Once niceties were out of the way, the business at hand became apparent.

"I want Bretz to check some things out, on the sly," Tony explained.

"How does that work?" Walt asked. "I mean, don't you have to have a case open or something?"

"I do, and I will," Bretz responded. His voice sounded as though he had traces of helium in his lungs. "Harris here told me who the detective is. I've known Rob Encarnacion for over ten years."

"Bretz isn't gonna actually investigate the murders and arson so much as just monitor the situation and keep me in the loop." Tony stopped when the waitress walked to the table.

After quick orders of coffee, orange juice, and food, the conversation resumed. During the chatter, Walt caught his mind wandering on multiple occasions, remembering Bill and how he acted on that morning in this very restaurant.

"We have more resources than any police department or sheriff's department," Bretz explained. "So, if we do get invited in, or need to get in, we'll figure it out."

"Are you going to use a profiler?" Walt asked with eagerness.

"No," Bretz replied with authority. "No need. Some of those guys are good, but it's part art. They partially go with their gut. Hell, I got a gut." Bretz laughed. "I've been doing this forever." He laughed again. "But I prefer science. Facts. Evidence. We don't need a profiler. We'll catch our guy – or guys – with evidence."

"You don't believe in them?" Walt seemed incredulous.

"It's not that I don't believe in them, it's just it depends on who it is." Bretz telegraphed he was not interested in pursuing the conversation by waving his hand with a flick of his wrist. "There are some good ones." He paused just long enough to signal a change of subjects. "We were invited to interview the G&S rep, but he was clean. That guy couldn't explode an egg in a microwave."

"You're kidding me?" Walt did not hide his skepticism.

"We turned that guy every which way," Bretz explained. "Let's just say, especially since I shouldn't be talking about this, that he's not the guy. No doubt in our minds. The evidence supports our conclusion, and if you met this guy, you'd see what I'm talking about."

148

"Where do you go from here?" Walt asked.

"We're back to monitoring. If something comes up that requires our abilities, we'll be there," the agent explained. "If G&S had been involved, because they have federal contracts we'd be investigating. But that's not the case."

"If you do poke around some, we'd certainly appreciate it." Tony looked at Walt for affirmation.

Before Walt could agree, Bretz responded. "Sure thing. Anytime we can catch bad guys, it makes the job rewarding."

"Can you check up on Troy Gustafson for me?" Walt asked.

"Who's that?" Bretz questioned, the name new to him.

"My daughter's old boyfriend, who just started coming around again."

"Sure. Write down his name on this card." He passed a business card to Walt. "I'll see what I can find out about the guy. If there's something to check out, we will." Bretz paused. "Just remember, I can't talk to people about open investigations. I'm doing this because of my friendship with Tony, so anything said here stays between us."

Tony and Walt nodded their understanding.

The conversation turned to trivial matters of local events before devolving into Tony telling stories about Bretz to Walt and about Walt to Bretz. By the time the men finished their breakfasts, Tony was out of stories and full of eggs and pancakes.

"Don't worry, Walt," Bretz spoke with a forceful, reassuring tone despite the odd voice. "We'll catch whoever this is. But in the meantime, you might wanna think about hiring a bodyguard."

• • •

He shut the door behind him before turning to speak. "Tell me how you did it!" Walt growled. Dennis watched his boss shut the door and turn to face him. Walt's face burned a fiery red. He leaned over Dennis' desk to put his angry face closer to the young executive.

"We just had a chat." Dennis' smile seemed to reach the walls to the sides of his desk.

At the moment, Walt just wanted the toothy grin to go away. "You're insane!" he blurted, unable to launch a structured, logical attack.

"We all go a little mad sometimes."

Walt missed the reference to the movie *Psycho*, but he would have agreed with the film choice, had he known.

"I said, 'Che, if you don't hurry up and get this done, you'll have to deal with the wrath of Dennis Fry. Now trust me, Che. You don't want that.' That's what I said." Dennis smiled with his mouth closed, his expression amplifying in every way possible the mockery that matched his sarcastic words.

Walt slapped the desk with his hand.

"You're an idiot, Fry!" He spun around, completing a full turn to face him again. Adrenaline surged through his body but he lacked a physical outlet for it.

"Ya know, if you shaved off that beard I'd *really* see how red your face is." The emphasis of the word "really" added to Dennis' derisive attitude.

"If you don't tell me, I *will* fire you." Walt emphasized "will" to make the point clear.

"You fire me and the DOD will see a collapsing company. A man out of control. Lost because of the murder of his partners. Mad. Maybe even the murderer himself. You'll lose it all, Walt."

The words seemed to scrape out of Dennis' throat, the delivery adding to the desired intense feel.

Walt's features tightened. *He could be right*, was Walt's only unbroken thought. All other thoughts jumbled as they collided with one another.

"But hey, you have something to be happy about." A fake smile emerged from Dennis. "I'm your future son-in-law."

"Like hell you are!" Walt's earlier growl morphed into a roar. He turned and stormed toward the door, flipping a chair out of his way in the process.

"Hey, Boss." The irony of the term was certainly intentional.

Walt stopped in the doorway to listen, though he did not know why.

"I'm kidding about the 'future son-in-law' thing. You won't ever be my father-in-law because the bet's changed." Dennis paused for dramatic effect. "Now, I know what you're thinking." Dennis' tone reached the highest point of mockery he had ever attained when dealing with Walt. "You're thinking it's rude to change a deal after the fact, but I'm not reneging. Nope. Now it's 'loser commits suicide.' And you lost. So, now I have –"

His fury unleashed, Walt slammed the door. He did not hear the rest of Dennis' last sentence. Several employees in both directions of the hallway turned to see what caused the crash. As he marched away, rage invading every part of his body, his skin feeling like it was going to burn off, he fought to wipe from his memory the last image he saw of Dennis Fry: a wide, arrogant smile.

• • •

While Walt, Tony, and Special Agent Bretz had been eating their breakfasts, two young hikers had started their day-long journey up the Santa Susanna Mountains above Chatsworth. They did not get far before spotting a pair of legs sticking out onto the trail. Before long, a Los Angeles County Sheriff's Deputy was at the scene, followed by a coroner. Noted on the body were knife piercings to the neck, below both ears – the mark of the *Devonshire Street Crips*.

Because the murder victim was a known drug dealer, the Sheriff's Department made a series of assumptions, all based on the fact the *Devonshire Street Crips* were prolific in the drug trade. These assumptions would be investigated, but the death of a drug dealer at the hands of a local gang would not be on the top of a detective's pile for long; the manpower did not exist for turf wars or for a dealer who owed the *DSC* money.

During the course of the day, the case of the murder victim took an interesting turn. By the time Walt's blood pressure lowered after his encounter with Dennis, the Sheriff's Department had made a fascinating discovery: inside the victim's apartment were photographs – spread out on the kitchen table – of Won Yi "Bill" Yoo, Alexander Heil, Tony Harris, and Walter Musgrave. Traces of explosive materials were also discovered. They searched but did not find a cell phone or any type of paper evidence which would assist the investigation. Nevertheless, the photographs provided stunning evidence of the victim's possible involvement in the appalling events surrounding Triumvirate Technologies.

When Special Agent Curtis Bretz was made aware of the developments, he volunteered to be involved in the FBI's next case. He now had his solid "in" to the investigation: a gang-related murder had occurred. He wanted the case because of the identity of

152

the victims. Now he could fully assist his friend, Tony. He could also bring together the Los Angeles County Sheriff's Department's investigation of their new murder victim and the Ventura County Sheriff's Department's cases of murder and arson at Triumvirate Technologies. Add multiple counts of terroristic bombings and Bretz had himself a big case that would be closed in near-record time. He was confident he could have the matter resolved, minus all the paperwork, within weeks – maybe less.

Investigations were not supposed to be this easy.

Special Agent Bretz only needed to establish evidence that put this drug dealer at the scenes of murder and mayhem. The photographs of the leaders of Triumvirate Technologies went a long way toward solving the cases. Once the FBI inspected the dealer's apartment, enough evidence would be found – perhaps something missed by the LA County Sheriff's Department – and the case would be closed: nice and neat.

The entire matter looked simple enough.

Chapter 21

"Well, this isn't what I had hoped for." Bretz began the conversation as he sat. "I have good news, just not as complete as I wanted."

Walt and Tony exchanged bewildered glances as they took their seats at the same time, leather groaning as their bodies landed in the chairs. The conference room was the most luxurious room in the building, with a permanent coffee maker, a water cooler, and a large wood cabinet built to hold kitchen accessories and to accommodate snacks. The plush, rich carpet and painted walls suggested the owners of the building wished to exude class when entertaining important guests.

"What's going on?" Walt's demand was softened only because it was phrased as a question.

"Don't look at me," Tony blurted. "I just let him into the facility." He turned to the FBI agent as he flashed a playful smile. "Curtis, what's going on?"

"I was going to buy you breakfast and give you all the good news, but – wait." He saw the expression on Tony's face and heard the grunt that was about to become a sentence from Walt. "We got 'em. We got the guy who killed Won Yoo and Alexander Heil. We just don't have the motive wrapped up yet."

The businessmen smiled. Walt's smile grew into one bigger than he had managed in weeks. "So, what's the bad news?" he asked.

"There is no bad news," Bretz continued. "I just wanted to be able to tell you I had the whole thing wrapped up. I don't. I knew the case wouldn't be closed completely, but I thought I'd at least be able to answer the 'why' of it all. Why he was obsessed with your company."

The businessmen nodded. Walt thought knowing 'why' would have been comforting, but for now, the very fact the murderer had been caught was incredible news. He breathed an audible sigh of relief. The exhalation filled the large conference room.

"Who is he?" Tony beat Walt to the obvious question.

"Who *was* he?" Bretz emphasized the second word.

"Ah. I see," Tony responded, his body movements animated. "Shootout with the cops?"

"Nope. His name was Bruce Ellis Desmond. Locally, he went by 'Norman DeWinter.'" Bretz paused.

"How many aliases did he have?" Tony asked.

"Forget the alias. It's a long story," Bretz responded, sounding as though he was still mulling over his answer. "All indications pointed to him being named 'DeWinter' until we ran him. In the system, we found his real name and his history."

Tony and Walt exchanged glances, their own thoughts driving their expressions, but both displayed awe in how events unfolded.

"Anyway," Bretz brought the conversation back on track. "We found Desmond murdered. Up in the Santa Susannas. On a hiking trail." Bretz's staccato approach signaled he wanted to get all the facts in with as little chit-chat as possible. "Two hikers found him. Had indications it was a gang killing, which got the FBI in on the case."

"Gang? This whole time this has been a gang thing?" Walt was incredulous.

155

"No, no. I said a gang got *him*. We're still investigating his history, looking deeper, but it looks like he was kicked out of the Army in the nineties. We're not sure why, but he did three years in Leavenworth. Still looking into the details. All I know is he struck a superior officer. When the Army caught on that he was a bad dude, they ejected the trash. But in the meantime, he learned explosives."

"Triumvirate's military hires have been great, but I guess every organization's gonna have some go bad." Tony looked as though he continued to chew on his last thought. "Even the military."

"He was a bad actor, no doubt," Bretz continued. "When he got kicked out of the Army he became a hitman for the Mob in New York and later Chicago. In Southern Cal, he was a drug dealer and part-time hit man." He surveyed his audience. "L.A. Sheriffs knew him as a drug dealer. I'm betting his killing days were behind him, until recently. Things are still sketchy – we're still waiting on info – but he was a bad dude. His 'M.O.' with the mafia was he knocked off people, but he didn't use a gun. He liked explosives, so he blew things up for them. The no-gun thing probably has to do with not having traceable evidence on him when he was arrested – numerous times."

"And Bill and Alex weren't killed with guns."

"And neither was the other Won Yoo." Bretz looked at the other men for effect. "I'll have all his background info pretty soon, I'd imagine, but at least I had enough to update you."

"So, it wasn't the movie-quoting maniac," Walt said to no one in particular.

"Pardon me?" Special Agent Bretz did not understand the reference.

156

Tony chuckled. "Walt here hates our newest young executive and had fancies that he was the murderer. Dennis Fry. He's seen every movie ever made, it seems."

"No. Not him," Bretz confirmed.

"Okay, so why us?" Walt's thoughts culminated into this one question, which he rephrased. "Why Triumvirate?"

"I told you, we're trying to finish the puzzle. We have all of the center, just not some of the edge pieces."

"Yeah," Walt continued with his line of thinking. "I understand that, but to us it's a big piece of the puzzle."

"And was it just this guy?" Tony added.

"That's what I've been checking out," Bretz added, his high voice attempted to reassure. "So far, we've been unable to find DNA evidence, but street security camera footage we've obtained does put him at least near the scenes. Each time he appears to have been alone."

"So, no chance anyone else was involved?" Walt zeroed in on the subject.

"We haven't gotten to his financials or all of his history yet, and so far, we don't have enough information to answer that." Bretz looked at the two men, which caused Tony and Walt to fall silent. "I want you to understand something. I have no doubt – zero doubt – that this is the guy for the arsons. We have evidence from the guy's apartment. But right now, I don't have anything for the murders. It's him, but nothing concrete yet. Just so you know."

Tony was the first to speak. "But you're confident."

Bretz nodded with firmness.

Walt and Tony exchanged glances – this time comforted, satisfied glances.

"Okay," Tony exclaimed. "This is great! Nothing concrete yet, but this sounds like the guy." His broad smile caused the others to respond in kind. "We're gonna celebrate tonight," he said as he looked at Walt. He turned to his FBI friend. "Anything else we need to know?"

"Not at the moment," Bretz answered. "But, of course, I'll keep you informed."

"Wow. Well, this is great news." The words should have had a verbal exclamation point after them, but exhaustion clung to Walt.

"I do have one little, tiny question," Tony ventured. His wry smile made it clear he was about to open a topic which Bretz would regret. "Who killed this guy?"

"That," Bretz's voice trailed off for a moment. "We don't know definitively. That's another reason why this case isn't closed. Was it made to look like a gang killing, or was it really a gang killing? I'm ninety-nine percent it's a gang thing, but I want to be one-hundred percent."

• • •

Walt and Tony sat in the conference room, hashing out their feelings, their memories, their concerns for the future. Special Agent Bretz's had departed twenty minutes prior, but the men decided that now, in the middle of the workday, was a good time to talk – deep, philosophical talk.

"It's been eleven days since Alex was murdered," Walt said. The somber note in his voice would have been obvious to a deaf person.

"I know. It's sick. It's unreal. I can't believe it."

The pair fell silent for the first time since Bretz left. Twenty minutes of heart wrenching was enough for Walt. "I don't like to talk about my feelings, so thanks, man. I guess I needed it."

"Hey, it's why we've been best friends for so long."

"Yeah, that's true." Walt laughed. "And we're making money."

"Unlike when we were in college and we'd drive around half the night," Tony finished Walt's thought.

Walt smiled and shook his head. "It drives me crazy when you do that."

"What? Know what you're gonna say? What do you expect, old man?"

Walt fell silent as he smiled. His gazed drifted to the bright, disorganized colors of paint which littered the walls. "How much did we pay to do this room?"

"What? This is high-class, man. This is–" He stopped mid-sentence.

"Hey, guys." Dennis waltzed in.

"I'm sorry, are we using your room? You have a meeting scheduled?" Tony looked at his gold watch.

"No, no. I just heard you guys were in here so I thought I'd check things out."

He always acts so innocent when there are other people around, Walt thought. *How's he do that?*

Dennis walked to the table and stood, looking down at the two men. "Anything I need to know?"

"Nope." Walt's tone matched his laconic response.

"Actually, there is something you'd like to know," Tony turned to look at Walt as he finished his sentence.

Walt glared at Tony, making it clear explanations should end before they started.

Undeterred, Tony continued. "We got some great news. The guy who murdered Bill and Alex was caught. Apparently, it's the same guy who also bombed us."

"Yeah, that's great news!" Dennis beamed. "I saw it online, at the *Star's* website."

"They had it?" Tony's shock could not be hidden.

"Yeah, they quoted anonymous sources."

"And you didn't think it was big enough news to tell us?" Indignant, Walt glared at the younger man.

"Guys, this is the first time I've seen you all day," Dennis said, innocence dripping from his throat, as though a water hose dangled from his mouth.

"Wanna bet?" Tony half-asked, half-accused Dennis.

The two glared at each other for a long three seconds before Dennis broke the silence. "I've got work to do." He turned and left the conference room without looking back.

Walt's smile remained small enough to be obscured by his beard, which showed an outbreak of a few more rogue gray hairs outside of the streaks of gray. "What was that about?"

"You know," Tony answered. "The bet, plus, he was in my office earlier this morning. I called him out on it." Tony smiled. "He just makes things up as he goes along, I guess."

"No, he's usually more calculating than that." Walt thought about the manner in which his signature was obtained. "Way more calculating."

"Anybody who thinks *you'd* bet your company is off his rocker," Tony laughed. "Anybody. Who'd make that bet?"

"Yep," Walt nodded. *That's right. I haven't told him about the latest. I can't tell him now. He's gonna flip. Let's let him enjoy the good news. I'll tell him later.*

"Keep your eye on that guy," Tony added for good measure.

"Of course." Walt slipped away, into his thoughts, about the young man who vexed him. "Of course," Walt repeated, although he had already forgotten the context. *Time to surprise Dennis so I can be free to make my next moves.*

• • •

"I don't understand." The last time she saw Troy, she could feel embers, though faint and barely warm, reigniting in her heart. But now, Troy behaved like a hiker breaking camp, stomping out the coals lest a full-scale fire break out.

"We need to go, now," he responded.

"I need to grab my purse." As she turned to run up the stairs, he grabbed one of her arms with his large hand – by her biceps, and around to her triceps and back again.

Troy shook his head. His expression and eyes obviated the need for words.

"What's wrong?" The fear which overtook her could not be missed. "I've never seen you so serious."

"Trust me. We need to go, now."

"But my –"

"Now."

• • •

The Jeep 4x4 raced eastward on Interstate 10, keeping pace with the other cars which sped along the wide freeway.

"You're kidnapping me."

"I'm rescuing you," Troy retorted. "I've explained it all to you. I wanted ya out of there to give ya time to think."

"Take me home," Heidi said, an unmistakable resolve in her voice.

"No. Ya need time away. Ya need to think about everything I just told you."

"If you won't take me home, then you're kidnapping me," Heidi shot back.

"Heidi, please," he begged. "You've gotta take this more seriously."

"You said you wanted me to think, and I did. I think I want you to take me home."

Troy took his eyes off the road and the surrounding cars long enough to glare at his ex-girlfriend.

"How's your cousin so sure?"

"Heidi, dammit! I've explained this to you."

"You're telling me that's why you took our picture that night?" Heidi wanted Troy to understand she did not believe him.

"Listen carefully. I'll tell ya again. As soon as I saw the guy, I knew I'd seen him before, in a picture," Troy explained. "While I talked to him and listened how he was toward me, I remembered it was in the Bay Area, with my cousin." Troy stopped speaking long enough to change lanes to pass a slower car. "I got the idea of the picture of the two of you, and I sent him the pic. He saw it and said, 'That's the guy. That's the guy who we think killed those guys in college.'"

"He thinks."

"Yes, Heidi. But it doesn't matter." Troy shook his head. "Ya don't wanna listen, that's all there is to it. My cousin knew him

162

as 'Dennis Cooper.' Cooper got into it with some of my cousin's friends and two of them turned up dead."

"Was he even arrested?"

"Heidi, he's a bad guy. Everyone can see that. Everyone who interacts with this guy knows he's a bad guy. My cousin kept a picture of him all these years because the guy freaked him out so much."

Heidi stared straight ahead, unwilling to discuss the matter further. Troy was not done.

"He's charming, he's dependable. Women seem to love him. But he's got a dark side that just won't quit. I don't wanna see ya hurt."

"Are you sure this isn't about you being hurt?" Heidi designed the question for maximum infliction of pain.

"Oh!" Troy pounded the steering wheel. "Stop! You're hurting my head. Ya think if I thought he wasn't dangerous – if he wasn't psycho – I wouldn't just take him on fair and square? That I wouldn't just come back for ya and sweep you away?"

"This isn't your way of 'sweeping me away'?"

Troy closed his eyes in frustration for several long seconds. "Heidi, I looked ya up out of concern for ya after Bill was murdered. Who do ya think probably murdered Bill?"

Heidi laughed. "Now I know you've gone off the deep end."

"I'm telling ya, the guy's nuts."

"No, you're nuts!" Heidi lost her composure. "Take me home, damn you! Take me home now!"

"What are ya gonna do when the guy snaps? Ya think ya can defend yourself against him?" Troy yelled back. "Ya think ya can stop him? I'm telling ya, this is a guy who's murdered people!"

"And I'm telling you, you've got the wrong guy!" Heidi lurched away from Troy as much as possible while seat-belted in place. She folded her arms and shook her head for over a minute.

• • •

Heidi's best chance to escape came in the little mountain town of Running Springs. When traffic backed up due to a car waiting to turn left into a parking lot, she looked at Troy and sighed. They both understood the moment: No matter how misguided Troy's efforts, this entire ordeal would end soon; no need to create a scene and perhaps involve law enforcement. She stayed in her seat.

Heidi stayed in her seat until they arrived at their destination: just shy of Big Bear Lake, Troy turned his Jeep off Highway 18 and up a narrow dirt road. Near the top of the road, he turned again, into a dirt driveway, which gave way to an asphalt driveway. Though it had been plowed off the highway, deep snow covered the ground and ancillary roads, thus the dirt road and long, winding driveway proved more challenging to navigate.

Heidi took note of her surroundings. They had passed two other driveways during the ascent, and up the mountain from their destination sat at least one house. She looked at her captor/rescuer. "What now?"

"There are clothes, toiletries, beddings. Everything. We'll be fine." Troy exited his Jeep and walked to the passenger's side. When Heidi refused his gentlemanly help, he laughed.

They climbed exterior, wooden stairs. Off to the east, Big Bear Lake sprawled away from them and out of sight, but no boats were visible. The trees stood with a blanket of snow covering every branch. The bright Sun had no effect on the winter scene, which appeared to have been painted onto the landscape only hours before their arrival. Troy knew, off in the distance and unseen from this vantage point, skiers raced down the mountainsides of the area's resorts. This early in the season the base was low, but between snow-making machines and the recent storm, most of the runs were open for the business of cold, fast, downhill fun.

Heidi did not look around and wonder about boats on the lake or skiers and snowboarders racing down mountains. She wanted to go home. She wanted away from the crazy stories originating from the man she used to love. From the moment Heidi stepped into the house, she began plotting her escape. In her mind, she was a prisoner – kidnapped by a jealous ex-boyfriend. She did not have a plan, but she vowed to take advantage of opportunity when it appeared.

Chapter 22

"I'm stepping down. The company will be yours. You won the bet."

Dennis had not even planted himself in his chair when Walt made the announcement. He looked at the older man and smiled, but before he could respond, a young waitress bounced up to the table. "What would you like to drink?" It was clear she felt an instant attraction to Dennis.

"Unsweetened tea. I'll go boring tonight."

"Okay." She gave an extra-long smile to Dennis before she turned to fetch his drink.

The restaurant was loud enough to allow the two to have a conversation free from prying ears. Incessant chatter emanated from the nearby bar, while the dining section, where Walt and Dennis sat, witnessed enough laughter and noise to make the establishment the wrong place for an intimate evening with a date.

"Already hitting the bottle, I see." The words cut into Walt, as designed.

"I said, you win. The company will be yours."

"You're right on both counts. I didn't need confirmation from you." Dennis smirked. The small, devilish grin made his eyes narrow. His face glowed.

To Walt, the grin was a look of utter evil. Instead of responding with anger, he chose to return the grin, complete with narrowed eyes.

"You know it wasn't a legal bet, Fry, but I decided to step down and turn the company over to you."

"Not good enough."

"Say again?" Walt shifted in his chair, his legs and back feeling a sudden discomfort not present only two seconds prior.

"Not good enough." Dennis seemed to enjoy repeating the cold yet flippant pronouncement.

Walt caught himself. Instead of letting out a shout, allowing anger to overtake him, he kept the words in by clamping his teeth. He could not hide the fury. His red face, his clenched fists, his quick breaths through his nose betrayed every emotion which washed over him. The raging torrent of words, however, were dammed up by the taut jaws.

A broad grin replaced the small, vile one. "You're always a step behind me, old man."

"I'm offering you a –"

"Frankly, my dear. I don't –"

"I said, I'm offering you –" Walt returned the favor of being cut off, only to be cut off again, himself.

"You're not offering me anything!" It was Dennis' turn to allow rage to overcome him, although his voice remained low, steady.

Before either could continue, the young waitress, who looked to be perhaps 19 years old, returned with a glass of tea.

"Would you like a straw?" She seemed to fall into a trance as she delivered the words.

"Please." Dennis returned the smile. Warmth oozed from his throat and eyes.

She froze for a long second, then left the table with an abruptness Dennis found amusing.

When she was out of earshot, his faux warmth froze over, his gaze returned to Walt. "I'm taking, Walt. Do you understand? I'm taking. You are not offering."

"You listen to me, kid." Walt wagged a finger at the young executive. "The only reason I didn't fire you is because of all the crap going on with the CCCP and the DOD. Pretty soon it'll be the IRS. It's because of all those alphabet soup agencies I didn't fire you already. So, I suggest you quit your –"

"And I suggest you don't suggest anything to me. I'm telling you, old man, I don't care about your offer to step down. It's irrelevant."

"What do you mean 'it's irrelevant?' Are you leaving?"

"No. I told you at the office. Loser commits suicide. By a week from Friday." The grin returned.

Walt's eyes widened. His scalp tingled. Dennis had said the words with such conviction. *He's out of his mind.* "You're out of your mind." Walt knew his words sounded weak, defeated.

"Do you see what a nice guy I am, Walter? I'm giving you time to get your affairs in order. To say goodbye to people. To get your will drawn up, if you don't have one already." The warped grin grew. "I'm a compassionate guy, Walter."

Walt could not speak. He had so many responses he wanted to utter, to shout, to scream at the top of his lungs – his mind and tongue froze from the excessive amount of information to communicate. He could only tremble.

"That's right, Walt. You should shake. You should be scared. Very scared of what I'll do to you, what I'll do to your relationship with Heidi, if you don't honor your end of the bet." The words punched the air with a quiet gusto, a calm frenzy. No one at the surrounding tables could hear. The two incensed businessmen were in public, for the whole world to listen, yet no one else heard.

"I will kill you if I have to." Walt fought off the urge to shout his words.

"You can dream. You can imagine, but it's just your brain's way of relieving your stress. That's all. In the end, you're gonna kill yourself." The way Dennis stressed the final word exuded confidence.

"I'm gonna have Tony put an end to this. He's gonna take care of this legally." Walt knew what he meant, but he could not find the words to turn his threat into a muscular weapon.

"Not gonna happen." The confidence Dennis projected was like a thick, dry blanket that covered him during a snowstorm.

"He'll put your ass in a sling that you'll –"

"Tony is not a threat to me." Dennis only seemed to grow calmer as the rage in his boss soared.

The waitress returned to the table, a girlish anticipation on her face. "Are you two gentlemen ready to order?"

Dennis looked at her with a pleasant, calm smile. "Sweetie, I'm leaving. This gentleman isn't hungry, but he could use another beer." He rose from the table and with a gentle grip clutched her arm. "Now tell me about your steaks so the next time I'm here I can order one." He ushered the young lady away from the table, leaving Walt alone.

Walt watched the pair walk away. With every thought, he seethed with a level of wrath higher than the last. *I'll kill him! I will kill him!* No other thought occupied his mind. *I'll kill him!* was all he could manage. He knew he could not fire him. The Department of Defense must certainly be questioning the status of the business after the deaths of Bill and Alex. To fire Dennis now would be another sign of chaos. Besides, Defense officials liked Dennis. *No, he has to stay.* His mind calmed, but only enough to assemble the thought that murdering Dennis was not the wisest of ideas.

Walt sat at his table for another hour. True to Dennis' assessment, he felt no pangs of hunger; he only downed beers. It was a weeknight. He should be home. When he walked to the parking lot and climbed into his car, he did not realize he was being watched.

• • •

Walt stumbled from the garage and into his house. He had downed enough beers to be legally drunk but not enough to prevent him from keeping between the lines, most of the time, during his drive home. He had not found himself in this state in several years.

Heidi's little Mazda sat in the three-car garage; the blacked-out house clued Walt that he should be quiet – he did not wish to awaken her at this late hour. As always, he had lost track of her schedule. Her part-time status at Triumvirate could mean an early morning alarm or sleeping until mid-morning.

Walt did everything but tiptoe as he walked up the stairs and to his bedroom, although "walked" was a charitable description of his struggles. He fell asleep before he could complete the act of undressing, confident he had managed to avoid waking his daughter, whose bedroom was down the hallway.

• • •

Heidi crawled along the floor in an effort to avoid the bright backdrop created from outside – the moonlight and its reflection off the snow. Clad only in panties and a pajama top that made it to her mid-thigh, she searched in the darkness. She found her target. Inside a pocket of Troy's pants, which hung on the back of a recliner, his keys were her salvation. The ring of keys included the one which would start the Jeep.

Keys in hand, she crawled back to her bed, slipped on her pants, and moved toward the bedroom door.

Troy snored like a poorly oiled piece of machinery. She stepped around him in her bare feet, ready to escape her captor's mountainside hideaway. Two steps from the door, the snoring stopped. Before she could decide what to do, she felt a familiar grip – around her ankle.

"What are ya doing?" Troy asked.

"I'm – I'm going to the bathroom," Heidi lied.

"There's a bathroom in this room," Troy pointed out as he released her ankle. "Turn on the light."

She complied with the order. The light flooded the room and blinded them both.

"Ya would've frozen to death out there," Troy scolded.

"I was only going to your Jeep," she replied. She held up the keys for him to see.

Troy sat up, shedding the top of the sleeping bag. Wearing only his underwear, the would-be rescuer held up a hand. "Give them to me."

Heidi slapped the keys into his hand.

"Get back to bed."

"Why are you doing this to me?" Heidi demanded.

"If ya do anything like this again, I'll sleep in bed with you," Troy threatened.

"No!" Heidi shouted. "No. I've had it with this."

"I don't do that whole voting thing," Troy said. "It's only good for certain things, certain people. No voting means ya do what I say, so get back in bed."

His deep voice added authority to the command, and she complied. Troy struggled to his feet and walked to the switch on

171

the wall. The large master bedroom was built for comfort; the floor was not. "It's five-damned-thirty, Heidi. Can we not do this again, please?"

"What do you expect me to do?"

"I expect you'd trust me and we'll get along fine, that's what I expect." Troy seemed to realize he wasted his time with his logic.

"How long is this going to go on?" she asked.

"I don't know."

Heidi could hear him adjust the sleeping bag as he climbed back into its warmth.

"I hadn't thought that out," he added. "I just knew I had to protect you."

Troy could not see Heidi's thin smile. In a strange way, the words comforted her, yet she could not shake her feelings – the smile was a mix of comfort and frustration. "I wish you'd found a more sane way to protect me."

"Sane?!" Troy shouted into the darkness. "I'm protecting you from insanity." He enunciated every word – something he rarely did – to help express his resolve.

"There's something I want you to know." Heidi added to Troy's anger. "I work at Triumvirate, and I've seen his resume and college information. He didn't go to UC Davis as Dennis Cooper. He went to UC Santa Barbara under his own name, Dennis Fry. You got the wrong guy." She did not admit to him that she only remembered this fact as she lay awake in bed.

"I don't care what ya say," Troy responded, unaffected by her supposed trump card. "My cousin recognizes that guy from UC Davis, and he knows exactly who he is."

Neither had additional responses for the other. Troy had communicated the main message: 'Don't do that again.' Heidi

172

knew him well enough to have a slight fear of the muscle-bound man. Rather than plot her escape, she faded off to sleep, certain now was not the time for additional plans.

Chapter 23

Walt read the latest news on his iPhone as he sat at the kitchen table. Overnight financial news from Europe and simultaneous terrorist attacks in Munich and Bonn engrossed his mind. Quick glances at his English muffin provided the only distractions from his news gathering. The gloomy morning outside the window would soon give way to sunshine; residents knew the weather routine.

Something gnawed at him. This did not feel like any other day. Halfway through his third business story about the European Central Bank, an odd thought struck him: *Where is Heidi?* Not every morning brought the father and daughter together for breakfast, yet this morning had a different feel. He had a sense she *should* be there, downing a protein drink or a bowl of fruit. He set his phone on the table and leaned back in his chair as he chewed the final bite of the muffin. *Something's not right.*

Walt squinted as he dragged his mind into thought. Shy of 7:00 a.m., thought processes were only warming up, like an athlete stretching out his muscles before an event. *Maybe she's here, but I haven't heard a sound. No water running; no footsteps; nothing.*

He picked up his phone and brought up Heidi's name in his contacts. Within seconds, Heidi's voice announced he had reached her voicemail system. *It didn't even ring.* With concern in his eyes, he made his way to the stairs and up to her bedroom. Knocking on her bedroom door proved fruitless.

Dennis. As Walt pulled up 'Dennis Fry' in his contacts list, the thought struck him that Dennis came to mind without triggering a twinge of anger or frustration. Within seconds, Dennis answered.

"Dennis, it's Walt." Dennis attempted to respond, but Walt cut him off. "Listen, this is important. Have you seen Heidi?" For the first time, Walt's blood pressure rocketed. The negative response was not the answer he sought. "Did you see here at all last night?" Again, the negative response brought physical suffering to the father. "Okay, thanks. I'll keep you informed." With that, Walt ended the call. In the depths of his mind, he knew Dennis was angered by the abrupt termination of the call.

An idea struck him. Walt again called Heidi's phone. This time, in the hallway in front of her bedroom door, he listened for the ringer. Instead, the call again transferred directly to voice mail. "Oh yeah," he muttered. Now he remembered.

Walt removed a small knife from his pants pocket. He inserted the tip of the three-inch blade into the lock and jiggled it. Within seconds, the lock clicked and Walt burst into the room. No Heidi. Purse on the dresser. Phone next to the purse.

With a deep breath and the thrust of his hands behind his head, Walt attempted to deal with the revelation. He interlocked his fingers and drove the back of his head into his hands. He looked up at the ceiling, where he found no answers. Heidi, it seemed, had vanished.

• • •

Troy stood in the kitchen, his back to Heidi. She obeyed his order to stay close to him, even though she would have preferred the living room couch.

"How do ya like your eggs?"

"Scrambled."

"Scrambled, like Fry's head," Troy laughed.

"You've got him all wrong, Troy." She paused for effect. "I get that you're jealous, but he's not a bad guy." She leaned her

175

elbows on the bar in front of her, shifting her weight on the bar stool.

"My cousin worked an on-campus job with him at UC Davis," Troy pleaded his case. "Some dumb thing like maintenance or something for the football stadium. Anyway, they had some little office there and this guy Fry had pictures of people he hated. There were like five or six or something." He turned to look at Heidi.

"I told you, he went to UC Santa Barbara, not UC Davis," Heidi smiled with a look of triumph, as though she had played the final card which ended the game and handed her victory.

He wagged a spatula in her direction. "I told ya, he was 'Dennis Cooper' at the time."

"Eggs."

Troy turned to see the eggs needed attention. "Anyway," he continued. "One day there was a picture missing and my cousin says, 'hey, there's a picture missing.' Dennis says, 'he's been taken care of.'" Again, he neglected the eggs to face Heidi. "The guy's body was found in a shallow grave a week later."

Heidi rolled her eyes. "Weak. And wrong guy."

"He didn't go to UC Davis, I know." Troy shook his head.

"So, because of that little comment and because your cousin thinks he's got the right guy from the photo you took, you've kidnapped me and brought me up here!" What started as a question ended in anger.

Troy turned, plate in hand. "Here's your eggs, scrambled, and bacon and toast. Look at that. I've got skills ya didn't know about."

Heidi tried to smile, but being aggravated made it difficult.

"Look, I'm here to protect you. My cousin is a big guy, kinda like me," Troy returned to pleading. "He's not as strong as

176

me, but back then he was solid. And he was afraid of the guy." He turned back to the stove to start his eggs. "As soon as he saw my text he called me. I heard his voice. He was shook up."

A long silence ensued as Heidi consumed her breakfast. After eating half the plate's contents, she was ready to resume the conversation. "Why didn't he go to the police?"

"He did." Troy faced her again. "But the police saw it as one witness and Dennis told the cops they hated each other, so they chalked it up to my cousin trying to pin it on him out of hatred. And – and he got rid of the photos of the other guys he hated before the cops visited. Smart guy."

"Eggs."

He turned to see his eggs cooked beyond the over-easy he desired. "Aw crap, I ruined them!"

Heidi laughed. "You were doing okay until you kept looking at me."

Troy took the pan off the hot burner before turning to look at her again. "It's always a pleasure to look at you." He stared for just a moment before returning to his overcooked eggs.

"This is all based on one picture you took, huh?"

"Ya gotta remember, Heidi," Troy continued with his story as he sat at the bar next to her. "He saw him a couple of times a week, at least for a semester. After that guy was murdered, Dennis Cooper left UC Davis. My cousin, Matt, never saw him again. Until I showed him those pictures I took of the two of ya and him by himself."

"By himself?" She continued eating her breakfast as she eyed her former boyfriend with a look of disdain.

"Ya know how easy it is to take a lot of photos and to change the zoom without anyone knowing. Yeah, I knocked off several. Six or seven or so."

Heidi shook her head. "I can't believe how jealous you are."

"Believe what ya want," Troy said between bites. "But I only sent him the photos as a conversation piece. I had no idea this was gonna happen. I just knew the guy looked familiar and I knew I saw him in one of my cousin's pics last year when I was in the Bay Area, visiting him."

"Uh huh." Heidi's eyes narrowed.

Troy stuffed his mouth with another bite. "I swear to you." His words were garbled.

"I want you to take me home today," Heidi ordered, her voice resolute.

"No can do. I've gotta talk to my cousin today, see if he has anything on that old murder first. Anything he can tell the cops which will mean more to them now." Troy's wistful expression conveyed his lack of a true plan.

Heidi sighed. "How long is this going to go on?"

"I don't know. We'll figure it out. Just trust me." The words sounded hollow; they both knew it.

• • •

"Come on, Walt. You're smarter than this."

Walt hung his head. Seated behind his desk, his level of determination was such that no matter what Tony said, he could not be swayed. "Tony, you can call me a moron, you can threaten to quit, you can call the media – it doesn't matter. I'm not budging."

"You said you have a plan but you won't tell me what it is." Tony glared at his friend from his chair across the desk.

178

"I told you, you're part of that plan. That's good enough for now." Walt's eyes seemed to plead with the lawyer.

"Why won't you tell me the plan right now?" It was more demand than question.

Walt looked at the closed door. Before he could speak, Tony reacted to Walt's glance.

"What? You don't trust I can keep a secret?"

"Tony! Calm down, please." They both understood that was usually Tony's line to Walt.

"I can't calm down. My best friend is keeping a plan – that could change his life – secret from me, which means it's a *stupid* plan and I don't like it." His emphasis on 'stupid' underscored his growing ire. This was a side of Tony which no one in the office ever saw; Walt had only seen such indignation from the lawyer a couple of times over the decades.

"Tony, Tony, listen. I'm a mess right now. Heidi's missing. My other two business partners have been murdered. We've suffered arson attacks against us. I have an employee – an executive, no less – who wants me dead. Hell, I thought worst-case scenario it was some guys on the dock who were destroying this company. It's one of my executives!"

"Heidi's missing?"

"Yeah." The steam of anger seemed to ease. The opportunity to talk about the matter calmed Walt to a small degree. "I've called the police, but right now, they say it's not a big deal. Hasn't been long enough."

"Does Dennis know anything?"

"No. I called him this morning." Walt dropped his head. "It's a little tough to concentrate." He raised his head with new energy. "And now you're not helping by not trusting me."

179

"Anybody hurts Heidi and I'll have them taken care of," Tony said, the bravado evident. "I know some people."

Walt gave a quizzical look to his friend.

"You mentioned the murders," Tony began, as he sought to change the subject. Thinking as he spoke, the lawyer continued. "Dennis didn't commit the murders. This is a separate issue. Bill and Alex's murders are different from Dennis wanting you dead. You're confusing the two."

"Yeah, yeah. Whatever." Walt shook his head, then thrust his face into his hands. "You know some people? What does that mean?"

Tony ignored the question and proceeded with the original subject. "Why do you think I'm just supposed to accept the plans of a worn out, emotionally drained guy? Walt. Listen to me. You can't think straight. Whatever your plan is for Dennis, let me help." It was Tony's turn to plead.

"Here's what I'll tell you." Walt's face remained buried in his hands, elbows planted on his desk. "I've got a private detective lined up. I haven't hired him yet, but I'm gonna. Then I'm gonna spend my days researching this with the PI, trying to figure this out. That's why I need to step away. I need to devote time to stopping Dennis. I can always come back later." He let out a sigh that filled the room as he lifted his head. "As it is, I've been through his personnel file over and over, looking for any clue. I practically have it memorized." He pawed at a file on his desk. "In the meantime, Triumvirate will continue to operate." He lifted his head and tightened his face as he looked at his skeptical friend. "You're gonna help investigate, too. Bretz can do his FBI thing, but he's not part of the plan. You and me, we're gonna take different portions of Dennis' life and figure this stuff out."

"Okay."

"The PI is gonna look through his history – better than we did. We only looked for crimes and fiduciary problems," Walt continued. "You're gonna look at his personal history and look closely at what the PI comes up with. Besides working with the investigator, I'm gonna spend a lot of time pushing him out of Heidi's life."

Tony realized the plan did not make sense – it was not a true plan. "Good luck with Heidi, but you're not stepping down."

"Oh, yes I am." Walt spoke with a firmness which signaled Tony would either have to back down or fight like a cornered mountain lion. Tony chose the latter.

"Oh, no you're not. This company needs you." Tony's firmness equaled Walt's.

"Tony, I can get more done. For Triumvirate Techno-"

"There *is no triumvirate*, Walter!" Tony was almost shouting now. "Don't you get it?! The triumvirate died with Bill! It was buried with Alex! I'm sorry, but that's the way it is!"

"No! I can keep it going! But I've got to step away first."

"You can keep the *company* going! Don't you see? The *company*! It depends on you. There is no triumvirate, but there's the company, and there's you. Only you can keep the company going." Tony's voice morphed into a raspy, airy, plea for sanity. "But if you step down, this company can't survive. It needs you."

"I'm stepping down." Direct and to the point, Walt glared at his long-time friend.

"And you need to go to the police."

"No! Absolutely not. No way. If I go to the police, eventually the Feds show up. If they do, our DOD contract is over. That contract is huge."

181

"Walt, you're not thinking right. You have to look at –"

"I'm not going to the police – or the FBI!" Walt now resided on the brink of shouting.

"He's committed a crime. It's illegal to try to force someone to commit suicide. I realize you don't have much to give the authorities, but you have to knock him off balance somehow."

Walt clasped both hands on top of his head. "I am not going to the police." His staccato response needed repeating, he believed. "I am not – repeat, 'not' – going to the police or any other authorities. Got it?"

The last, brief sentence cut into Tony's thick skin. "Thanks, Walt, for caring about how much I look after you."

For the first time over the decades, Walt felt their friendship strain. A tree branch bending, creaking. "Get over it, Tony." No humor could be found in Walt's tone. No friendly smile or look eased the fierceness of his opinion or determination.

Tony looked around the room before responding, eyes not focused on any one object. Walt could see the wheels turning, measuring. When his gaze reached Walt's eyes, Tony resumed the heated conversation. "What do you expect to find? You don't know. Why? Because you haven't considered all possibilities. What about Stacy? What about former employees?" Tony's eyes cut into Walt's. "Hell, what about Troy Gustafson? The guy comes around right after all this started. You know how many criminals like to revisit the scene of the crime, or start showing up around the victims to see the harm they've caused? To admire the damage they've caused? Of course you don't. You don't know anything about that kind of thing."

Walt started to interject, but Tony waved him off.

"Criminals, whether it's for revenge or perverted pleasure, sometimes they make up believable stories on why they're back, and they dance on the misery of others." Tony paused just long enough to get his point across. "So, what about Troy? You've only toyed with ideas in your mind. You haven't given deep thought about the murders. You haven't given anything serious thought. It's all shallow thinking, like it's a done deal. Like you know. Like you don't have to think this through. You think about it a little in passing and that's that." He paused, but the anger would not subside. "What do you expect to learn about Dennis?" Tony answered his own question. "You don't know. You haven't considered that maybe he's just a nutcase, but non-violent. Or maybe, God forbid, he's a psycho who will kill you if you mess with him. Maybe you should just talk to people in his past beyond business references. But, you know why you don't tell me specifics about your plan, other than that nonsense you just gave me? Because either you don't have specifics or it's a stupid plan and you don't want me to know."

Walt laughed. While he heard every word, not one penetrated his brain. "Now who's babbling?"

Tony all but flew from his chair. Breathing heavily and seething with a greater level of anger, the lawyer reached the door and gripped hard on the knob. Though his voice remained under control, an unmistakable hissing sound escaped his throat. "When you investigate, you investigate every possible angle, methodically. Carefully. Quietly. When you're being chased by a lion, you don't wander into the open and announce yourself so it can rip out your throat. You're an idiot, Walter. A damned freakin' idiot."

Tony opened the door as he uttered his final words to his best friend. As he slammed the door behind him, he looked up to see several employees stop in their tracks. They stared at their company's lawyer as he stormed down the hall and eventually out of the building. Within minutes, those same workers relayed to other coworkers what they had seen. Little time would pass before most of the employees in Building A would know of the incident.

Chapter 24

At his desk, Walt caught himself repeatedly looking at the same document on his computer monitor – he was unsure exactly how many times. He expected a call at any moment from the only person he knew well enough at the Sheriff's Department who had clout. In the last hour, since his stormy discussion with Tony, Dennis had dropped by the office twice. That was not helping.

The moment he began another attempt to digest a report about lengthening battery life for hand-held electronic devices, the phone rang. He saw the name on the phone's readout.

"Detective Rob, thank you for calling me. What do you have?" Walt listened without patience to the brief answer. "I don't care whether she's officially missing or not. If I always hear the first forty-eight hours are the most important, why are you waiting twenty-four hours to see if she's missing?"

Walt listened to a much longer answer as he grabbed his computer mouse and shut down programs. *It's obvious I gotta do this myself.* To his chagrin, the answer continued. *But where do I start? She could be anywhere.* "I understand all that," Walt interrupted, even though he only listened to half of the explanation. "But her purse and cell phone are still in her room. Think about that. What woman – no woman goes anywhere without her purse or cell phone." Another long answer. Another bout of shutting down programs, followed by shuffling reports and loose papers on his desk.

"Thanks a lot. We'll talk later." Walt ended the call without the detective's consent. Once the call terminated, Walt fought off the meltdown people who knew him expected from him. "Damn you! Damn you all! You and you're stupid rules! My little girl's out there somewhere and –"

A knock at the door truncated his mini-tirade, which was calm by Walter Musgrave standards.

"Yeah," he snapped.

Dennis opened the door and walked to Walt's desk. "I heard you yelling, so I take it no progress with the cops?"

"No. None." Walt failed to change his mood, even though Dennis entered his office as an ally.

"What's your plan?" Dennis asked.

"I mean, we can't just drive around. What will that accomplish?"

"Then we need to sit down and brainstorm," Dennis said, eyes narrowed, face clouded with rage. "We need to figure out where she last was and work from there."

Walt looked up at his employee and nemesis and let out a loud sigh. He nodded and stroked his beard as he responded. "Good idea. The cops won't help us yet. The detective said they get so many missing persons reports they can't review them all and most people show up on their own, when they're ready."

"Yeah, the ones not found in a ditch or buried under a serial killer's house." Dennis saw the pained expression on his boss' face. "Sorry. I'm just as mad as you. We don't wanna think that way."

"I understand. It's something we'll have to consider if we don't figure this out soon." Walt hung his head. The heavy emotions of losing Heidi hovered above him, circling like hungry vultures waiting to pluck the heart out of his chest. "Let's give it a little more time. Let's chat after lunch and we'll go to a conference room and start piecing things back together, okay?" *I don't want to talk to this guy! I want nothing to do with him.*

Dennis nodded. With locked jaw and reddened face helping to conceal his fear, Dennis turned and left Walt's office. Both fists clenched, he turned back to Walt and growled, "If someone hurts Heidi, they're gonna have to deal with me."

"And me." Walt left his chair, and then his office, in search of a distraction.

●　●　●

Thanks to the recent storm, local ski resorts sported a snow base ranging from 25-44 inches of natural powder – not bad for this time of year. On the drive up, Heidi's awareness only extended to the roads, which remained clear and open. Her plan to cut across properties to get to the nearest house was in the process of failing as she fought the snow, which measured up to three feet deep around her. Dressed for a sunny day a few miles inland from the beach rather than the mountains encompassing Big Bear Lake, Heidi shivered. Her jeans and blouse wet; her tennis shoes useless; her skin numb yet filled with pain; she realized her foolish decision had put her life at risk. The icy, biting wind cut into her, seemingly to her bones. The overcast sky reflected her gloomy chances.

She remembered the long, winding driveway from when the pair had arrived at the house the day before and feared her captor could track her down with ease by car. Now, after a mere twenty minutes, she allowed her thoughts to stray. Her fight against the snow and uneven ground slowed.

When Troy had entered the bathroom and it had become obvious his absence would last more than a few seconds, she had grabbed her chance. She knew the car keys had remained in his pants pocket, so she had set out on foot. Her head start, though brief, provided physical separation. She had hoped the first minute of his realization of her absence would bring denial. She had hoped such a delay, before he discovered she had bolted out the door, would bring enough confusion to buy more precious seconds. She had hoped.

The wind gusts diminished the distance she could hear. Twice she thought she heard Troy calling to her. Twice she pressed forward, harder than ever. Now, after twenty long, painful, cold minutes – her adrenaline depleted and will to escape faded – she longed to return to her kidnapper.

She no longer knew which direction would take her back to the house Troy's family owned. She could follow her footsteps, but the wind grinded away at the path and her vision. Her watery eyes and the powdery snow whirling in the wind added additional misery to the unbearable trek. Thoughts of turning around persisted until she rounded a small hill and caught sight of a nearby house, forty yards below her.

• • •

Troy understood how the situation appeared; getting Heidi back to his house was the number one goal in the young man's mind. Failing to see Heidi's tracks far down the driveway, where she entered the woods and hillside, Troy drove the curvy roads, expecting to see her around the next bend or the bend thereafter. Bellowing into the wind proved futile, so driving around seemed like the best option.

Finding Heidi changed from a rescue mission to one of self-preservation. His skin was now on the line. Law enforcement would not understand his definition of "savior."

• • •

Heidi struggled to stay on her feet. Down the steep hill she climbed and slid and fell. She reached a 10-foot rocky drop, unaware the snow covered an easier route just a few yards away. Her heart pounded. Her brain sent the rest of her body into survival mode. Like her skin, her thoughts went numb.

But she knew the house below drew ever closer. Ill-prepared for the environment, exhausted, nearly out of time, and at the edge of defeat, Heidi slipped downward, toward warmth and rescue.

Chapter 25

"I think it's that guy – Troy." Hatred welled up from within Dennis. Walt could not miss it.

"Troy Gustafson? What makes you say that?"

"When I met him at your house, he had an ego the size of your neighborhood," Dennis deadpanned, anger too great to see any irony or humor in the statement.

Walt laughed. "I've known Troy a long time. I can't see him hurting Heidi." When Dennis had pulled Walt into the conference room, the latter wanted nothing to do with the former. Earlier in the day, he had acquiesced to Dennis' idea of brainstorming by suggesting they get together after lunch, but to Walt, it was a throw-away line meant to appease the contemptible young man. He did not trust Dennis; he had come to despise him; yet he was driven less by loathing and more by concern for his daughter. He knew Dennis could not find Heidi from the office, but the young man's intelligence could aid in the process. While logic told him to stay away from Dennis, Walt's heart relented. Heidi's safety was more important to him than his building hatred of Dennis.

"I don't have anything to go on," Dennis said, his focus unrelenting. "But I've thought it through." His hands gesticulated more as his passion rose. "He's the one. I don't know where she's been lately, but I can tell you he's the one." His blood pressure boiled. "I haven't liked that guy since the night I met him."

"How long ago was this?" Walt asked.

Before Dennis could respond, Tony opened the door of the conference room. "There you are. I was coming by to find out the latest on Heidi."

"We haven't found her yet," Walt answered.

"I think it's Troy Gustafson," Dennis interjected, emotions still at a high level.

"What makes you say that?" Tony asked.

"I met him," Dennis snorted, no humor in his voice.

Tony lifted his cell phone. "I've got my FBI agent friend on the phone, Curtis. Hang on." He lifted the phone to his ear. "Can you check out Troy Gustafson?" After a pause, he spelled the last name for him.

"Dennis," Walt began, skepticism in his voice. "I don't buy that Troy would hurt Heidi. I don't see it."

"Okay, thanks." Tony ended his call and closed the door behind him. "Look," he said as he took a seat next to Walt. "We all care about Heidi. We all want to rip apart anyone who hurts her; but, let's not assume she's been hurt. Let's assume she went somewhere. To get away. To unwind. Where would she go?"

"She wouldn't do that," Walt said. "She's not wired like me. She's low-keyed enough she doesn't have a need to get away. She doesn't need to escape reality or go into the backyard and sit in the dark or anything like that."

"And she's been pretty relaxed lately, I'd say, at least until Troy came around," Dennis added, his anger still not subsided.

For another 30 minutes, they bantered about Heidi's demeanor, attitude, and possible whereabouts. They all agreed on one thing: God help the person who brought harm to her.

• • •

The doorbell did not summon help. Pounding on the front door yielded the same lack of a result. Heidi trudged to a large, multi-paned window separating the warm indoors from the frosty outdoors. A feeble punch from her fist failed to change her condition.

The small house sat far enough away from the hillside to give the illusion of safety from a future landslide. On a flat area large enough to hold a house and small yard, the original owners had built the house up on a raised section of dirt many years prior. The front porch and house rose six feet above the surrounding land, giving the house respite from the moisture of melting snows or heavy rains. The covered porch provided shelter from the mountain sunshine, when the area was so blessed.

Heidi observed her surroundings, but not for the beauty. Because of clouds and blowing snow, she could not have seen the distant lake and surrounding mountains if she had so desired. She needed a way into the house before her assailant could locate her – that was her only concern. That her assailant happened to be her former boyfriend did not factor into the equation. With sweat on her face and scalp – defying the cold – her pounding heart failed to distract her from the mission at hand. Taut muscles in her arms and legs reflected the intensity which flooded her body.

Under the covered porch, she noticed a small rock garden, which stretched the length of the front elevation of the house. Filled with small rocks and pebbles, snow missed covering much of the decorative rock, leaving brown and red earthen materials visible. Heidi searched for a larger rock until she found one the size of her fist. With a feeling of victory in her chest and brain, she returned to the porch; she stood and faced down the window before her.

The loudness of the crash proved irrelevant – no one could hear the sound unless Troy had parked the car and embarked on a walking search. She mustered the courage to navigate the jagged glass shards which remained attached to the pane. A hurried yet delicate set of maneuvers brought her through the window without a hitch until she let out a yelp. She looked down to see blood dripping from her left arm. Getting her legs through proved tougher than she thought as a piece of glass ripped her jeans at the calf and more of her blood dripped onto the carpet.

In the house at last, she limped toward the kitchen, where she spied a telephone. She dialed 911 as she surveyed the damage: small cuts on both hands from putting her hands on the glass-littered carpet; the cuts to her left forearm; and a deeper cut into her right calf. The cut to the leg hurt the most.

"What's Troy gonna do if he beats the cops here?" she muttered aloud.

• • •

In his office, Walt had given up on work. *Maybe I should go home, just wait there.* He stared at the ceiling. *Maybe she's already home by now.* He stared at the desk calendar in front of him. *This is driving me nuts!*

Tony burst into the office, cell phone in hand. "Okay, got it," he said, excitement in his voice as he ended the call.

Before he could explain, Walt leaped to his feet. "What is it? Is it Heidi? Is she okay? What do you know? Tell me?"

Tony knew his best friend well enough to let the questions flow until Walt figured out it was time to shut up. "A little over a half hour ago, she called the police up in Big Bear."

"Big Bear?!"

"She's fine, but she had to break into someone's house to call the police."

"What happened? What the hell happened?!" Walt demanded.

Tony paused before answering. He waited for the suspicious look he knew would be thrown his way before announcing, "Troy

193

Gustafson has been picked up for kidnapping her. They triangulated his phone. He was out looking for her because she escaped."

"Troy Gust– Are you kidding me?! Troy Gustafson?" Walt plopped into his chair. "But she's okay?"

"They're patching up some cuts now and then they're –"

"He cut her?! Are you kidding me?!" Walt leaped to his feet to return to his incensed state.

"I don't know, Walt. I don't know what happened. We'll find out soon enough." Tony eyed Walt like a boxer in the ring, standing before his opponent as the opening bell rings. "I'm happy she's okay. That's all that matters. I'll text you the address where you need to go in San Bernardino to pick her up."

Tony spun on his heel and marched out the door, his duty complete.

Happy about Heidi, but sick about his recent argument with Tony, Walt packed up his computer and a few paper files before embarking on the drive through Los Angeles and out to San Bernardino, a city nestled at the foot of the mountain range by the same name. The 220-mile round-trip drive would take over two hours going and likely another hour longer coming back in southern California traffic.

He had plenty of time to think. Joy and sorrow; happiness and sadness – all crammed into the same space at the same time. Life, which had been such a pleasure just months prior had grown so painful, so infuriating, so confusing.

Heidi's alive! He repeated the mantra in his mind as he drove the freeways in an attempt to push away every other emotion and memory. Yet there was the business. Tony. Dennis. Everything.

Heidi's alive!

195

Chapter 26

The traffic mounted on I-10 as Walt headed west in his blue Lexus. He took frequent glances at the worsening eastbound traffic in repeated attempts to remind himself he could be going much slower than 40 miles per hour.

"Sorry about my bedroom door, but I told you before it keeps locking by itself and you need to fix it." Heidi gently admonished her father. "I keep a key on a table in the hall for when it does that."

Walt grunted.

"Thank you for stopping and buying me these clothes," Heidi said, her voice soft, grateful, her desire to manufacture conversation obvious.

"Of course, honey. Anything for you, you know that." Walt's gentle words represented a rare moment of displayed compassion.

"It's so funny how you never seem to worry, yet here you are," Heidi struggled with her words.

"What do you mean?" Walt's voice and head movement betrayed his lack of understanding.

"Well, I don't mean to be critical or anything, it's just – it's just I thought you'd send somebody else out here to get me." Heidi examined her father's face. "I know you care, but it's times like this when I appreciate seeing it."

Because of the traffic, Walt could only glance at his passenger. "Heidi, I always care, one-hundred percent of the time. Always. I've never had a moment when I didn't care about you. I – I'm just not good at –" He stopped. Words escaped him.

"Showing it?"

"Yeah. I'm just not comfortable that way." He glanced in his driver's side mirror and then turned the wheel to change lanes. "I just feel like others see me as fake when I do show I care."

"Were you this way with Mom?"

"Oh, no. No, not at all." He looked her way again. "But your mother understood me completely. Your mother – I mean, don't get me wrong, I wasn't a basket of emotions around her." Walt laughed, causing Heidi to laugh. "But Tina – your mom was the only woman I've loved that deeply. I love you, but that's a different kind of love, you know, so –"

"Dad," Heidi interjected. "I understand. It doesn't make me feel unloved when you say that about Mom. You don't have to explain yourself." She chuckled as she continued her study of the right side of his face.

"Not to change the subject," Walt changed the subject. "But now we're away from everyone, I need to understand this better. What happened with Troy?"

Heidi's eyes narrowed. She could not hide that she noticed the switch from Gooey Dad to Serious Businessman Dad. "He just flipped out. I think it all started when he met Dennis. He got jealous."

Walt's mind switched to that thorn in his side. He grabbed his phone and took a quick peek at the readout.

Missed Call: Dennis Fry (6)

He can wait, the little punk. He can wait 'til Heidi calls him.
With the knowledge that his phone was set to 'Do Not Disturb,' Walt directed his attention back to his daughter. "Did Dennis do or say something to him?"

"No. It wasn't Dennis' fault." Her defensive tone marked the first crack in the veneer of the loving truce between father and daughter.

He turned to Heidi with a quick smile before returning his eyes to the traffic. "I had to ask. I know them both, remember?"

"Well, anyway," Heidi's sharp tone cut just deep enough to not be missed. "Troy never grew up. I think he has some since we broke up, but not enough. He just couldn't stand the thought that he lost. That's how he looked at it." Heidi stared at the traffic ahead of her. "It's like a sport to him. You win or lose, only he doesn't understand there's a lot of losing in life, so it's about how you deal with it, not that you won or lost."

Walt grinned. "You've always been more philosophical than me."

"Getting kidnapped and having to escape makes me even more philosophical, I guess." She touched her hand to her bandaged forearm, hidden by the long-sleeved sweater Walt purchased for her at a San Bernardino department store.

"What did he say? You had lots of time to talk. How did he approach this?" Walt's fascination was more than curiosity. "I mean, you're my daughter. I need to understand this."

"He just talked a lot about how we belonged together," Heidi said as she watched the other cars.

She's choosing her words carefully. What isn't she telling me?

"He talked a lot about how much he missed me," Heidi continued.

She's forcing her words. She's hiding something. The thoughts nagged at Walt. "And?" He attempted to prime the pump of words in her mind.

"And that's it, I mean…" Her words trailed off. She looked at her surroundings, then back at Walt. "He babbled and repeated himself a lot. He made the case – repeatedly – that I don't belong with Dennis. I think he overplayed our relationship in his mind. He seemed to think we were a couple, Dennis and me, which we're not. So, yeah, there just wasn't a whole lot."

Walt frowned. "He kidnapped you to keep you away from Dennis or to keep you for himself?"

Heidi waited a beat to answer. Her answer told Walt that her approach was to be careful and rehearsed. "Troy kidnapped me because he never grew up and he wanted to possess me. So, it was about him, no one else." Her gaze drifted to the cars out the passenger window.

"Does he know Dennis?"

"No."

No hesitation there. Walt fought off the urge to laugh, to ridicule his daughter's thin layer of obfuscation. *If I push her too hard, she'll never tell me anything.* "This just all seems odd," he verbalized. "This is unlike the Troy I've always known."

"What are you saying?" Heidi's tone jabbed deeper this time.

"I'm just saying this seems odd. That's all."

"Let go of Dennis. I don't understand why you're trying to make this out to be about Dennis." Heidi's jab into Walt's heart deepened.

"Troy made this about Dennis, not me." Walt maintained an even emotional keel.

"No, I said he made it about himself. Dennis just happened to be at the house and they met." Her irritation rose. Her face flushed. Her breathing quickened.

"Look, Heidi. I'm just trying to figure this out, all right?" Walt's voice grew louder with each word.

"You're obsessed with Dennis."

The traffic. Dennis. Heidi's emotional turn. It was Walt's turn to feel his face redden and pulse increase. "I'm obsessed with keeping you safe. I thought I lost you. Don't forget that."

The silence gave Walt the hope that Heidi weighed his words. Another lane change gave him time to lower his blood pressure.

"Let's just change the subject," Heidi broke the verbal silence. "You don't like Dennis. I know that. I'm safe. Let's forget all that. There are other things in the world to talk about."

"You're such a cross of me and your mother it's funny." Walt allowed a smile to break out. "You're serious and bossy like me but always letting your emotions brim at the top like your mom." He laughed.

"Did you drive Mom crazy like this?" Heidi could not manage to make the question sound harmless.

"Yeah," he nodded. "Sure, I did. That's what happens when you're married to somebody. You drive each other crazy but love every minute of it because you love each other."

Heidi rolled her eyes. "Mom must've been a bigger saint than I realized." She tried not to laugh but failed.

"Oh, like she didn't have any faults," Walt chuckled.

"I don't see how she put up with you," Heidi deadpanned.

"She loved me." Walt knew his answer beat any response she could conjure up.

"Just remember, please, I can't figure you out the way Mom did."

"Oh, please. You're not that much of a saint." Walt laughed.

Heidi let go, allowing herself to laugh.

Walt enjoyed the moment, but he knew the mere mention of Dennis Fry's name would turn this two-and-a-half-hour drive into what would feel like a 10-hour detour through Hades.

• • •

With Dennis on his way over to the house, Walt decided the time had arrived to repair his wounded relationship with his best friend. After agreeing by text, Walt headed out in his mid-life crisis, an orange BMW Z4 Roadster. He would rather argue with Tony than see or hear Dennis.

The Sun completed its journey, taking its daily leave beyond the waters of the great ocean as Walt pulled into Tony's driveway. As the driver stepped from his car he heard a familiar voice. "Get up here or you're gonna miss the ocean."

Walt made a hasty attempt to race the light, arriving on Tony's second-floor back deck with only minutes of light remaining.

"It's too breezy to smoke cigars out here tonight," Tony announced, the disappointment evident.

"There's always the porch," Walt said, holding out hope.

"Yeah, that'll work."

• • •

With the house's only view of the ocean nullified by the darkness, the two friends sat in a screened, covered porch – "sorta outside," Tony always called it.

Despite its big-house price, Tony's place was not large at all. Built in the 1960s, the 2,400 square-foot house was too big for the single man but reasonable in size if he ever decided to settle down and marry. At this moment, marriage remained far from his mind. With apologies for their recent behavior out of the way, Tony changed the subject to his upgrades of the property.

"You like the paved driveway?" Tony squirmed to get comfortable in the patio furniture.

"Yeah, I noticed that." Walt took another puff of his Hoyo de Monterrey.

"It only took me three years to get to it," Tony said with a laugh. "Damned tired of the dirt all the time, 'specially on windy days." He eyed his Romeo y Julieta Maduro. "Ya know, who needs Cuba? These Dominicans got it down."

"What do you have, a Robusto?" Walt asked.

"Yep." Tony nodded, then changed subjects. "I got my security system offline. That old crap needs replacement. You can do homes really cheap these days. I've got it all figured out, right down to a dummy DVR in case thieves ever try to steal the recording." He took a slow draw from the cigar.

"Thanks for the Honduran," Walt motioned with his Hoyo de Monterrey.

"You and those cheap Hondurans." Tony shook his head.

"Cheap?! I'll have you know my Hondurans are only a little less expensive than your Dominicans."

"I'm telling ya, the Dominicans got it down. I've had Cuban cigars and they didn't impress me none."

"But you were in Canada," Walt scolded. "They may have been knock-offs."

"What's Canada got to do with it?" Tony demanded.

"I don't know. I just know if it's hand-rolled, it's probably good stuff." The final reaches of Walt's argument eased Tony's mind.

"Good point." He paused for effect. "But they're still cheap."

Walt shook his head. "When are you getting your security system back up and running?"

"Oh, probably not for another week or two," Tony responded. "What are the odds of me needing it those exact two weeks or so?"

"You better get it done," Walt chided. "Murphy's Law."

"I know. You're right." Tony took another puff from his cigar. "I'm doing this myself; it's just a matter of getting to it in a couple weeks." He spotted Walt's faux-ivory-handled knife on the small table next to his chair. "You still cut your cigars with a pocketknife, huh?"

Walt shrugged.

"I told you, a shell from a .38 works best – not a .380, but a .38 revolver. Perfect size." Tony was not about to entertain an opposing viewpoint.

"I always have one of my pocketknives on me. I have a bunch. They work if you do it just right."

Tony rolled his eyes.

"It's an art," Walt grinned. He knew the impossibility of convincing Tony.

"You and your pocketknives." Tony laughed. "What do you have, forty?"

Walt ignored the question and considered that, after what Heidi had just been through and the previous angry exchange he had with Tony, sitting around laughing, smoking a premium cigar, and enjoying life were all good things.

"You ready for some news?" Tony teased.

"Oh boy. I know that look. What?" Walt's relaxation ended with the abrupt question.

"I wanted to wait until you got partway into your cig," Tony explained. "Gustafson's already out on bail."

"What?!" A crash of furniture knocked about accompanied the verbal and physical explosions. "What are you talking about?" Walt erupted. On his feet, he continued with his outburst. "How the hell can that happen?" He looked at his grinning friend. "You're kidding, right?"

"No. I'm not kidding," Tony confessed. "I'm smiling because I knew what was going to happen, although I'm impressed you held on to your cigar."

"What happened?!" Walt yelled.

"Put my chair back and sit down," Tony ordered, though his calm demeanor did serve to lower Walt's temperature a few degrees. "I don't want my tile floor damaged." As Walt did as requested, Tony continued. "Craziest thing I ever heard. The man was out in hours. I mean, that happens, but I just figured Troy would be in overnight. But a family attorney showed up. He posted bail. He was gone. Crazy."

Walt plopped into the patio chair. "I don't get it. How can this happen. How?!" His last word could have been heard by a deaf man.

"Seems Troy's uncle up in Frisco owns a law firm – real estate law, I hear – but they've got this criminal defense friend." Tony stopped, as though he had completed his explanation.

"So, the guy just walks?!" Walt again shouted.

"Hey, hey. You're gonna bust my eardrums and ruin the whole cigar experience. Take it easy," Tony counseled. "Take it easy. He's not walking by a long way. He'll lie low. He's been directed to stay away from Heidi. It'll be fine. Besides, I love Heidi like she's my own daughter. I'm not gonna let anything happen to her just like you aren't." As Walt fumed, Tony shook his head. "That's the way the system works."

"How can we have a system that lets kidnappers go? That's nuts!" Walt held no interest in hearing an explanation about 'the system.'

"That's the way it is sometimes."

"That's absurd!" Walt attempted to calm himself. He took another draw off his cigar and thrust his lower jaw into his free hand. Stroking his beard provided little respite from his anger. "How long have you known?"

"I found out while you were on your drive down," Tony answered. "I decided I'd tell you after we got you chilled out. You need at least a few minutes a day of not being on the edge of a heart attack."

"Yeah, screw heart attacks. I want that guy to pay." Humor did not color his words.

"He'll pay. Mark my words," Tony tried to reassure his friend and boss. "We'll see to it. He'll pay, but this is how it works."

"Damn!" Walt fought off another eruption.

"If you wanna go on a cussing tirade, I don't care," Tony chuckled. "You've slid backward on the drinking, so why not the cussing."

Walt bit into his bottom lip. Cursing would not accomplish what he wished to accomplish. "Words are not enough," Walt growled.

"I know," Tony empathized. "I know."

Walt reached into his front pocket for his cell phone and began looking for information.

"What are you doing?" Tony asked.

"I better let Heidi know about Troy," Walt answered.

"Don't worry about it. I called her immediately."

Surprised, Walt looked at his friend. "How did she take it."

"She seemed all right. I told her if she sees him anywhere – anywhere at all – to call 911, and then you, and then me. She said 'okay.'" Tony stared at the ceiling for a moment before turning his focus to Walt. "He won't come around."

"How can you be so certain?" Walt asked.

"First, don't forget, I know Troy, too. I was around him some when they dated. Also, it seems he thought he was protecting Heidi," Tony said. "From what, no one's told me yet. I guess I'll get an answer from the police tomorrow morning when I talk to them." Tony sighed. "This is a weird deal, Walt. Troy thought he was protecting Heidi from someone or something, and whatever he said convinced a judge he's not going to harm her."

"I just don't get how they could let a dangerous person like that out." Walt returned to his rant, although at a lower volume. "How can someone who did something so bad be let out on bail?"

"It's our system, man. It's our system," came the predictable reply.

Chapter 27

Wearing a pair of shorts and a t-shirt which featured a surfer on the front, friends would not have mistaken the figure for anyone other than Troy; but friends were not around. Instead, as he exited the bar, quiet permeated the ocean air. Cars lined the street a block from Pacific Coast Highway, but the absence of human life added to the stillness – except for a shadow which popped up in front of Troy's car.

Troy saw the figure when it reached arm's length. The first attempt at a question – or was it a greeting? – ended with an abrupt movement from the shadow and an explosion emanating from the top of Troy's head, cascading downward through his neck, to his shoulders, and into his chest. Thrust into unconsciousness, he did not feel the inevitable pain which followed.

Troy's next sense of awareness dwelled on the intense throbbing in his head. Agony. Foggy thoughts log-jammed; questions abounded, but only the intense pain from the crushing blows he received mattered. His focus on the pain left him unaware of his surroundings. As the minutes passed and the fog eased enough to allow thoughts to flow again, he attempted to reach up to feel the source – the top of his forehead, above the outside of his left eye – but a new thought entered the haze: he could not move. His hands and feet were tied.

The severity of the pain prohibited cogent thoughts from reaching maturity. Had he maintained the ability to reason, he would have explained to anyone who would listen he felt as though his head had been crushed in a vice while set on fire. Throbbing, combined with an ache, made him wish he could detach his head.

A loud ringing in his ears made the pain worse. The act of thinking remained impossible, as though part of his brain had been shut down for repairs. The impenetrable darkness added to the confusion. He could not ascertain his location, and his lack of mobility added to the feeling of being lost – of hopelessness. And that unremitting, piercing ringing!

Time passed – how much he did not know, but parts of the brain seemed to open for business. His left eye was closed; his hearing was limited by the ringing; he lacked memory of how he found himself in such a predicament. The fierce pain distracting his thoughts led him to divert extra energy toward thought – just the simple act of assembling a thought produced additional suffering. As the seconds gave way to minutes, his senses slowly regained their powers. He detected the sensation of motion. He was in a vehicle; probably a trunk. A man – a mere figure in the darkness – had struck him with a heavy object on the front of his head.

Troy had a brief flash of a memory, a voice – whose voice he could not be sure – telling him if he ever found himself locked in a trunk by a kidnapper he should kick out the taillights so a police officer would spot the vehicle. He dwelled on that thought for what felt like an hour – ten seconds in reality – before reaching the conclusion he was tied to part of the car. He could not roll over to kick out a taillight. He could not roll over. He could not kick. He could only move his fingers and his head – and moving his head proved a painful mistake.

• • •

Troy lacked the ability to track time. For all he knew, he could have been in the car for ten hours. It seemed like days. He only knew the vehicle had stopped and had not resumed moving. No voices, which meant no police officer or other person to come to his rescue. Only incredible pain. Unbearable throbbing pounded his skull.

The trunk opened. The darkness shielded the identity of his assailant. The sadistic villain picked up an object near Troy's feet and lifted it at an awkward angle. With a sidearm stroke designed to avoid hitting the car, the attacker struck Troy in the ribs. Metal cracked multiple ribs. Troy's scream was truncated by a devastating blow to his jaw.

• • •

Troy heard himself groan. Consciousness did not remain steady. He felt as though a knife had been jammed through his skull, from his forehead to his jaw, not realizing it was the result of the original blow to his head – or was it the strike to the jaw? Wrists tied together. Labored breathing, punctuated by gasps. A stabbing pain in his left side. Ankles tied together. Lying on a hard, wood surface. Blood in his left eye.

"Fight me fair," Troy's gruff voiced called out. He felt as though he did not utter the words – that someone standing next to him spoke on his behalf – yet he meant every word with great conviction. Troy had never experienced distress to this level – his head felt as though it would explode at any moment – yet somewhere deep within himself, he felt the urge to fight.

He also knew more pain was about to be delivered – mercilessly.

"You're about to die," the voice responded, as though the words were meant to be comforting.

Troy could not recognize the voice. The ringing in his ears – throughout his entire head – masked the sound. A man. He could not perceive the calmness, the lack of emotion. Troy could only hear a man in control of his life – his frail, beaten, bloody life.

Consciousness left Troy, but returned in intervals until he awakened to realize the hard wood on which he found his injured body was a boat. A small boat. The attacker moved in a rhythmic dance, as though to music drowned out by the ringing in Troy's ears.

A rowboat. The attacker's movements put oars to water.

"You're gonna drown me." Troy did not realize his voice was difficult to hear. His slurred speech made understanding him even more difficult.

"Maybe. I've thought about killing you before you go under, but I've ruled that out."

Troy again focused as much energy as possible to his brain, yet he could not recognize the voice. Oars hitting the water sounded muffled. The only sounds he heard well were his tortuous breathing and the incessant ringing.

"Who are you?" Troy slurred.

"I'm the last person you'll ever see."

The Moon seemed to separate the clouds, allowing its night shine to penetrate the darkened scene. Troy lifted his hands to see the zip ties which bound his wrists together. Like a drunk, he moved his arms and lifted his head to see zip ties around his ankles, wrapped by a chain. He attempted to register a thought which could explain the presence of the chain but failed. He also failed to see the three 45-pound barbell weights attached to the chain.

The assailant stood, legs spread apart for balance. Troy rolled his head and looked up at the figure, backlit by the Moon. Before Troy's brain could engage further, a downward blur brought crushing pain to the outside of his left knee. Troy propelled himself up – a reflex to the strike – but endured a blow to his left elbow.

In a rowboat, in the middle of the night, in a quiet lake, Troy's shrieks and cries for mercy went unheeded.

Troy opened his eyes, unaware of the time which had passed during his state of unconsciousness. The Moon seemed to be in the same position, but he could not be sure. He could not be sure of anything except excruciating pain, although he did notice he was positioned on his left side. He lacked the mental acuity or physical strength to roll off his side, to take weight off his broken knee and elbow.

"It took you long enough to wake up again." The Voice was not finished with his subject. He stood up, arms above his head. This time, Troy caught a glimpse of the crowbar a mere second before it crashed down into his right knee. He barely moved. The second blow missed his elbow, striking his humerus. Troy's large triceps muscle was not enough to cushion the blow. Before his brain could tell him what to do, another strike met its target, shattering the elbow.

• • •

"We've been out here an hour," the Voice announced. "You ready to die?"

"Yes! Yes!" Troy thought he screamed, but what came out of his mouth sputtered in blood and pain.

Once again, the Moon hid itself behind clouds. Two coyotes yipped only fifty yards from shore. A Great Horned Owl hooted into the night, responding to a distant bird of the same species. His battered body at the stern of the small boat, Troy was unaware of the coyotes or the owls or any other surroundings. He only knew of unrelenting misery.

"Please kill me," Troy attempted to beg.

"You're pitiful," the man responded.

211

Troy struggled to see movement in the darkness, the Moon again obscured. He saw the man step toward him. The figure bent over and scooped Troy into his arms, pressing the prisoner against the transom of the tiny boat. Troy felt the sensation of rising up, scraping against the edge of the boat until his body reached the top of the transom. Seconds later, cold water rushed over his body, within seconds helping to numb some of the pain – not enough, but Troy happily accepted any easing of the agony.

An unseen hand grabbed Troy by the hair and held his head above the water. He was not in command of his senses enough to notice his assailant had rowed only 75 yards from the lake's shore. The hair grab amplified the pain from the first debilitating blow he had received earlier in the night, sending shocks of pain throughout his frame. For a brief moment, the Moon peeked through thin clouds. With attacker's and victim's faces close together, through the pain and darkness Troy saw the face of the man about to become his killer. Before he could contort his mouth to speak the man's name, the sadist spoke.

"During the next drought, they'll find your decayed body. The fish will eat your flesh."

The hand released Troy's hair. The victim lacked the strength to fight the zip ties or the effects of the assaults from the night's barrage. With what little mental awareness which remained, Troy had a sensation of being inverted, head near the lake's surface. The side of the boat pressed into his ribs. He felt the pulse of water rush against his body after the weights entered the lake. Instantly, the 135 pounds of gym equipment dragged him downward, feet first.

Troy Gustafson was too weak to fight for the surface as his body plunged the 20 feet to the lake's bottom.

Chapter 28

Heidi chewed on the last bites of her fruit as Walt entered the kitchen. Dressed in a long-sleeved top and slacks, she did not wish to show off her minor wounds. Walt, in his suit, gave every indication of being rushed.

"Honey, you're going to work?"

"Yeah," she answered, her voice melancholy, strained. "I need the distraction. I'm fine. I just wanna get it out of my mind."

Walt stood a few feet from her, looking down at his daughter. She looked up from her chair, a quizzical look replaced words.

"I'm just concerned, wondering whether you should just stay home," he offered. "Maybe you should relax. Unwind."

"I appreciate the concern, but I need to occupy my brain," the brunette said as she stood. "I'm limping a little, but I'll be fine. I thought about reading a book or something, but I'd be too distracted by my thoughts, so I'm going in."

Walt's frown turned into a look of anger as he thought about the gall Troy Gustafson possessed to kidnap his daughter. *What is wrong with that guy?* he asked himself, as though the question had an answer. "Okay," he responded. "If that's what you want. But if the leg gets to be too much, come home. Agreed?"

Heidi smiled, then rose from her chair to physically greet her father. She wrapped an arm around him and squeezed before releasing him. The brief hug reflected the short bursts of affection they showed for one another. "Thanks. I'm only scheduled for six hours today, then I'll come home and rest some more."

Before Walt could respond, the doorbell chimes caused his head to snap around. *Probably Dennis. He's always got the worst timing.* Walt did not possess a capacity for positive thoughts about the young man.

Heidi followed her father out of the kitchen to the front door. Neither expected to see Detective Encarnacion standing on the front porch.

"Detective Rob," Walt exclaimed. "Come on in." He motioned with his hand for Encarnacion to follow as he continued speaking. "I assume you're here with information about why Troy was released yesterday."

"Where were you last night at around eleven o'clock?" The detective's stern manner startled the Musgraves.

"Well, I guess by eleven I was here, I'd think." Walt looked at Heidi for support.

"I don't know," she said, offering no help. "I didn't hear you come in."

"What's the problem?" Walt asked like a man who did not wish to hear the answer.

"Troy Gustafson is missing."

"Oh, good grief!" Walt exclaimed. "The man has family in the Bay Area and over half of Oregon. He probably took off."

"A witness says she saw someone matching Gustafson's description get thrown into a trunk of a car and driven away late last night." Encarnacion's harsh attitude did not abate.

"Where?" Walt inquired.

"Where were you last night at eleven o'clock?" the detective demanded.

"I told you. Here," Walt answered, patience wearing thin.

"No, you told me you 'guess' you were here." The detective ratcheted up his accusatory tone. "Do you guess or do you know?"

215

"We've got to work on your bedside manners. You come into my house and you –"

"Mister Musgrave," Encarnacion sighed. "We had a deputy watching him in Malibu and Santa Monica last night when he left the bar. Before our guy could get outside, Gustafson was gone, but his car was still there."

"So, you came here to accuse me."

"I'm not accusing you of anything, Mister Musgrave," the detective snarled. "But you need to come clean with me."

"My daughter was missing overnight and you said it wasn't long enough to worry about. Now your people lose a guy and – oh. I get it." Walt smiled as he looked first at Heidi, then at Encarnacion. "A little ass-covering, huh? You lost a guy, so you gotta point the finger." Walt laughed as he hid his anger.

Encarnacion looked around the entryway as he carried the appearance of a kid trying to explain to his mother how he lost his good coat while at school. "I've probably told you too much, but you've told me too little."

"I'm about ready to throw you out." Walt remained calm but meant every word.

"This is the last time I'm asking here. Next time will be at the station." With his eyes narrowed, Encarnacion looked tough enough to back up whatever he uttered.

Walt studied his new-found adversary. Encarnacion's unrelenting approach worked. "If I left Tony's at around ten o'clock, that puts me here well before eleven, so yeah, I was home."

"If?" Encarnacion glared at Walt. "You speak in scenarios, Mister Musgrave."

"I was here." Walt returned the icy stare.

216

"I agree with my dad," Heidi interjected. "Troy's got a ton of family all over the place. He's probably fine."

"The witness went to her car last night to get away from somebody in the bar," Encarnacion replied. "She was being bothered by some guy. She saw somebody park a car and sit for a while. Then the driver got out and approached who she was sure was Gustafson coming out of the bar. A few seconds later the trunk opened and the car drove off. She got out and looked but Gustafson wasn't around." He eyed both Musgraves. "It's only logical the person was thrown in the trunk. Gustafson is missing this morning."

"And you thought I had a lot of gaps for not knowing exactly what time I got home," Walt let loose a shot of venom.

"Ms. Musgrave." Encarnacion turned his attention to Heidi. "Could you excuse us for a moment, please?"

She looked at her father, who nodded.

Encarnacion watched her exit and waited until he felt certain she was out of earshot. He stepped forward, toward Walt. "Listen to me, Musgrave. I know you're upset about what Gustafson did, and I don't blame you, but don't take the law into your own hands." He wagged a finger in Walt's direction. "Don't try to fix this. Let the legal system do that."

"Oh, yeah." Acid dripped from every word of Walt's response. "The legal system. The same legal system that let this idiot go in the first place. Bail. What a joke."

"The DA's office couldn't stop that."

"Exactly. All these judges and lawyers and do-gooders broke the system, and then when someone disappears you look at an innocent guy like me." Walt kept his voice low, but not his attitude. "Quit worrying about the innocent and start worrying about the guilty. This dirtbag could be out there, ready to spring on Heidi again, and you're here, threatening me because you lost him."

"You just let us handle the legal matters, Mister Musgrave." Encarnacion again wagged a finger at Walt.

"Then handle them. That would be nice."

"I'm warning you, Mister Musgrave –"

"I'm late for work, officer. Perhaps you should –"

"Detective," Encarnacion corrected him.

"Perhaps you should go find something to do," Walt snarled. "You've got a missing kidnapper, it looks like to me."

The detective turned and walked out the door. As Walt closed the door behind him, Heidi reentered the room, a look of concern on her face.

"Troy could be on the loose again?" she asked.

Walt turned to face her. As he spun, he put on his best 'happy face' with a large smile. "It's all right. Either it's true about Troy being stuffed in a car or he's split town. One or the other."

"He could be lurking," a quiet Heidi said, the pain in her voice and fear which reverberated through her body apparent.

Walt reached out and brought Heidi to him. Her head rested on his shoulder. "I'm not gonna let anything happen to you." He squeezed her. "It'll be fine. I'll watch out for you."

Heidi stepped back and looked at him. "Okay." She took a deep breath. "Okay," she repeated.

Chapter 29

"You sure have seemed relaxed this past week," Heidi chuckled.

Dennis looked around; a playful attitude overcame him. "Don't I always seem relaxed?"

"Yeah, but since I was kidnapped, you've been – different. Relaxed." Heidi eyed her date as she waited for a response.

"I'm happy you're okay," Dennis smiled as he answered.

She studied his face, as she learned to do with her father. "You know, so many times, I can't get a straight answer from my dad, so I learned to read his face." She spoke with a slow cadence, still studying. "It helped me to learn to read others."

"Oh?"

"And I'm wondering if you're just more relaxed because Troy disappeared."

Dennis fidgeted in his seat. "Has it already been a week?" With a slight pause, he let the subject pass. "Do you notice that all we ever do is eat? We need to go dancing or something."

"And the way people change the subject," Heidi added.

Dennis erupted with a loud, hearty laugh that filled the small restaurant. "I met Troy one time. I never considered that bozo a threat. Believe me. I knew I'd never have to worry about him."

Heidi's wry smile broadcast her doubt in his last statement. "Okay. If you say so."

"You don't believe me?" It was half question, half observation.

"Of course I don't." Heidi's answer left no room for tact.

"All I can tell you is, I'm glad he's gone, I'm glad you're okay, but I was never worried about Troy Gunnerson."

"Gustafson."

"Whatever."

Heidi held her wry smile until the server arrived at the table.

"Our food's here," Dennis announced, sounding like an excited little boy.

• • •

Orion the Hunter continued his pursuit of the Pleaides, only hindered by Taurus the Bull. Behind the trees, out of Walt's sight, Orion's faithful dog, Sirius, stayed at his master's heels. Walt could not see the dog, but he knew it would rise above the trees within the hour. At the moment, Walt felt like the bull. He knew he was stronger, yet somehow the hunter held an intangible advantage. The bull protected the Seven Sisters while Walt protected his baby: his company. Unlike the hunter, Dennis did not seem to have a sidekick. *He's a lone nut*, he thought.

Walt knew enough about the myths of the stars to understand the various accounts of the constellations and their ancient stories, but on this night, he felt a certain kinship to the characters and this version of the myth, which he preferred over other renderings of the tales.

He stared off into space again, but this time into the light pollution, which kept him from seeing celestial objects. After a full two minutes, he felt a surge of emotion fill his chest and throat.

"I'm sorry, Tina." He again fell silent. He glanced back at Taurus before continuing. "Bill's dead. Alex is dead. I'm losing Heidi, although things are a little better. It's all falling apart, Love." He dropped his head before making his way the few feet to the wood swing, where he sat, into his dejection. In his favorite spot for solitude, Walt peered into the darkness of his back yard. The Japanese Pittosporum hedges, which his gardener shaped and molded for him, provided a ten-foot-tall barrier that blocked light from neighbors on both sides of his property. The hill behind him provided assurance a house could not be constructed in that location.

"Tony's been pissed at me a lot lately – I don't really blame him. I haven't been myself. Fortunately, we're better now." He wished he could melt into the wood grain of the swing. "I gotta figure out what drives this Dennis guy. He's out with our Heidi right now. I can't stop it – she won't listen to me. She's a grown woman. What am I supposed to do?"

He paused to look again at the sky. "I'm sorry, Tina. I've made a mess out of everything. I'm a lousy father, and she and I know it." He shook his head at the thought of his only child. "She and I know it."

At the sound of a car pulling into the driveway in front of the house, Walt discontinued the monologue as he sat on the swing. Within two minutes – and a hundred more thoughts by Walt – Heidi set foot into the darkness, unsure of herself.

A week had passed since Heidi's adventure with Troy and his subsequent disappearance. Each day had seen a mild deterioration in the father/daughter relationship until it reached the point where it had been for years. The lack of trust and the cold interactions had slowly returned.

"You here?"

"I'm here."

"I thought so." She turned to close the door behind her. "I saw the light on in the bathroom off the living room. You only turn that on when you come out here."

"I use that so there's a little light for me to see when I come back in."

"That makes sense." Heidi approached her father in the darkness. "Talking to Mom again?"

He nodded until he realized that she could not see him. "Yeah."

"You okay?"

"Yeah."

"You don't sound it." Her words were caring, but absent a gentle, empathetic tone.

"I'm fine." *You can tell where she got her lovey-dovey side,* he thought. *Too bad she didn't take after her mother for that. Cold-hearted like her old man.*

"Okay. If you say so." The flat quality to her voice did not change.

"Where's Dennis?" He took the edge out of his voice for her benefit.

"He said he had some business to attend to – some personal business, apparently. He'll be back in an hour or so, he said."

"Did you have a fun night?"

Heidi paused before answering. "Yeah. We did."

Walt wished he could see her face, to read the pause in her response. No such luck.

"We went to a Mexican restaurant in Woodland Hills," Heidi continued. "One I haven't been to before."

"A Mexican restaurant you haven't been to?" Walt was incredulous, but said it in a mocking tone.

"Yeah," she laughed. "Hard to believe, isn't it?"

Walt again climbed to his feet. "Well, I guess I'm ready to go in."

"Okay. When Dennis comes back, we're going to some club. I think we're going dancing."

222

"Okay. I'll be in the den."

The lack of an emotional connection was apparent to father and daughter, but together they entered the house. She went to her bedroom while Walt made his way to the den, where he planted himself in front of his desk. He continued his silent lament that his daughter had little love for him, yet knew it was his own fault.

• • •

Walt tried to read a book he had picked up not long before the company's troubles began. The intensity of the psychological thriller had proven too much for his injured soul once life began to disintegrate. The storyline involved dreams, and he feared his slumber could become as tumultuous as his waking hours, so he put the book down.

Young Orion crossed his mind. The old Bull, protecting. The deception which led to one of the Seven Sisters riding on the back of the bull. Orion's trusty sidekick. Chasing. Protecting forever. Deception. His sidekick.

Walt sat up straight in his chair, as though startled. He pushed himself back from his desk. The wheels on the chair squeaked as he rolled. *A sidekick. How obvious! How obvious can you get?!*

Walt reached forward and snatched his cell phone from the desk. *A partner! A freakin' 'partner! How could I have not thought of it?!* The call did not connect. He tried again. Nothing. One more time – he could not understand why a ring would not sound from the piece of small yet powerful technology.

Walt fumbled with the phone until he found an old text from Tony. He spoke his words as he typed – one finger at a time – sounding like a child learning to read. "Call. Me." He did not bother with punctuation. "I. Have. A. New. Angle." Walt found the slow delivery – and the verbal confirmation of the lethargic method – maddening. "I. Think. Dennis. Had. An Accomplice."

His words were typed in lower case, but spoken in the broken cadence reserved for someone recovering from a traumatic brain injury. "This. Is. Important."

Only seconds after hitting "Send," his heart leaped. His old friend was responding. He could see the three dots moving at the bottom of the page. *What will he say? What will he think when I tell him what I think might've happened?* His excitement overcame his melancholy mood.

The indication Tony was typing stopped. This must be it. His response was imminent. Together they would solve this sick, mysterious chapter in their lives.

No response.

"What's he writing? A book?" Walt's level of anticipation climbed further.

The three dots moved again. Typing again. *Finally!*

Nothing.

Walt stared at his phone as though he could command a response to materialize. For the next five minutes, Walt stared. Unable to accept the lack of a response, Walt plugged in his phone, despite the fact he could see a battery strength of 77%. Over the next ten minutes, he checked the electrical connection two more times and called Tony's phone three times. Every time, the call would not connect to get a ring.

He scooped up the novel and hurled it across the den. "Dead everything! Everybody! Everybody's dying on me!" His shout seemed to bounce off the walls and return to the tired, frightened man's heart. His eyes, red from a lack of meaningful sleep, puffy from the stress and non-stop schedule, made him look ten years older than the half century he had lived. "Tony better be all right!" He shouted again, and again the words reverberated off the walls as though trapped in the room with him.

Heidi did not run down the stairs, from her bedroom, which confirmed to the outer reaches of his mind he was alone with his phone, his shouts, and his misery. "Tony better be all right," he repeated, although this time the fiery energy faded.

• • •

After another 30 minutes, Walt settled down enough to read. This time, the book he held was a non-fiction tome written by a former FBI agent, who chronicled his career and cases as a profiler, when he tunneled inside the minds of psychopathic and sociopathic killers. Walt wanted to know what made Bruce Ellis Desmond tick – to understand how he could demonstrate such brutality, let alone direct it toward Bill and Alex. He lacked a true reason to comprehend, yet he felt a need. He thought, somehow, an explanation would help his psyche heal.

As he read, a thought locked deep within a secret compartment of his brain seeped into a conscious, obtainable area. While he dared not speak the thought which had crept forward, he sought to understand Dennis. The more he read, the more he pondered. The more he pondered, the more he wondered whether he was missing clues about his subordinate. The more he wondered whether he was missing clues, the more he feared Dennis was a psychopath, capable of fooling everyone, including the sharp eye and mind of Alex Heil.

Is Dennis Fry a killer? It's occurred to me before that he killed Bill and Alex. It makes sense. This guy is a –

The doorbell rang. Walt leaped out of his chair – it felt as though his heart collided with his rib cage. He took a deep breath.

It's only Dennis, he reminded himself. *He wouldn't hurt me in my own home.* He attempted to continue reading until another thought invaded his mind: *Would he?*

Distracted from his reading, he heard the door open, followed by Heidi's sweetest of sweet voices. Within seconds, he heard the sounds of feet racing up the stairs, followed by the faint sounds of footsteps in the entryway. Although the double-doors to his den were open, he was situated at too great of a distance to know exactly what was transpiring.

The house grew quiet.

Thoughts of *Dennis Fry – Psychopath* raced between Walt's ears. He sat and rotated his chair to see if and when someone entered the room. He mustered the strength and focus to continue his reading.

Five more minutes of quiet reading was interrupted by hurried feet on the stairway and a barely audible apology from Heidi to the guest. Within seconds, the footsteps grew louder. Walt stopped reading, but stared at the book, creating the illusion he desired.

"Dennis and I are headed out in a second." As was typical, she did not address her father by a title. She stopped in the doorway, with Dennis in tow, to await Walt's response.

Walt presented the two with a look of surprise, as though he heard noises and voices in the house for the first time. "Oh. Okay."

"Mister Musgrave." Dennis stepped forward, into the room.

He never calls me that anymore. What's this about? "What's up?"

"I just wanted to talk business for a second." The younger man advanced toward the desk. He turned his head to address Heidi. "I'll be right there. Just wanna have a quick chat with your dad."

He bent down to talk to Walt, who elected to remain in the inferior position of being seated. Dennis' voice lowered. "I just wanted you to know that everything is running on time. All the projections are as expected."

"Oh?" Walt stood in a conscious effort to alter the dominant/submissive dynamic, which caused Dennis to stand up straight. "What timing is that, Dennis?" Walt's attitude dripped with scorn. Both glanced back at Heidi, who had missed Dennis' hint and remained in the doorway.

"*All* of our timing." By stressing the first word, Dennis communicated with the clarity he desired.

"I see." Walt's stone-cold glare fixed on the young executive's eyes. His jaw locked. His eyes narrowed.

Dennis flashed teeth, putting so much effort into his fake smile his face almost squeaked. "No matter what happens next, I just want you to know I'm here for you." Without delay, Dennis turned away, to rejoin his date.

Oblivious to the drama unfolding before her, Heidi reacted with an unpredictable response. "Hey Dennis, you have a different shirt on."

He looked down and chuckled. "Yeah, I was near my place on my way back from my errand and I thought, well, my other shirt was too tight for dancing."

"Oh." She nodded, then forgot about the matter. "You ready to go?"

"All right, ramblers, let's get ramblin'." Dennis uttered another of his movie lines. Neither of the Musgraves caught the quote, but as he reached Heidi, Dennis turned to address his boss. "Remember what I said. I'm here. Always." The final word was drawn out, to underscore the hidden message.

"Oh, hey. I found your cell phone in my purse when I was changing purses." Heidi held up the smartphone for Dennis to see, then handed it to him. The L.A. Chargers cover made the phone distinct.

"There it is. I was wondering what happened to it." With a light touch, he grabbed Heidi's arm and they walked together toward the front door.

The last words heard by Walt were from his daughter. "That was so nice of you, Dennis. I appreciate you looking out for my father like that."

Walt stared at his phone after a brief search for a response from Tony. One additional call produced a result identical to previous attempts. He was now certain, more than ever, Dennis Fry was a bad and evil man, capable of the mayhem that had occurred at his company.

Proving such fears would be difficult – he had no doubt of that.

• • •

Not a sound could be heard in the house. A light on the second-floor patio penetrated the night air for only a few yards beyond the house, its glow dim enough not to be spotted by random boats passing near the shoreline three miles down the hillside. Set far enough off the main road and obscured by small hills, the light did not reach a single person at this moment.

Inside the house, in the enclosed patio, a smattering of blood adorned the furniture – drops spread about as though sprayed in a mist. A red pool congealed on the tile floor, at the doorway. An overturned lamp lay in a thin layer of blood which formed a brief path – the path of a bleeding man who had dragged himself across the floor. That path ended in a heap of a carcass – one arm twisted underneath the body, the other spread outward, hand resting on the floor.

A cigar had burned a black splotch onto the ceramic tile before extinguishing due to lack of attention. An end table, resting on its side, sat near the head of the corpse. The skull of the dead man caved inward where the nose, upper jaw, and cheekbones used to be. Blood covered the opening to one ear; the other ear remained invisible with the head turned 45 degrees to one side. The bloody mess of an indistinguishable face told the story of brutal post-mortem strikes. Other injuries were not obvious without closer examination.

On the floor, ten feet from where the man had struggled for his final breath, in the path he had crawled as he expired – as indicated by the blood stains – a cell phone lay in the 'stand-by' position. The blackened screen hid the dead man's attempt at a final text exchange – and evidence the killer manipulated the dying man's finger to erase the text which had been on the verge of being sent.

• • •

The dream was forgettable, irrelevant. It made little sense. But that pounding! And the doorbell. Walt opened his eyes to hear the doorbell again – it was not part of the dream, rather what had awakened him.

Groggy, slow, experiencing pain in several joints that had not been used in several hours, the tired businessman climbed out of bed and reached into the darkness for his robe. By the time he reached the front door, turning on lights along the way, Heidi had reached the top of the stairs. He opened the front door to see a police officer.

The Ventura County Sheriff's Deputy possessed a young face and a grim expression. "Mister Musgrave?"

"Yes."

"I'm officer Steve Bell. Detective Rob told me to speak to you in person. I didn't have your phone number, I apologize."

"Damn, kid. What time is it?"

The deputy pulled a cell phone from his front pocket. "It's three-forty a.m., sir. I have some terrible news."

Walt stepped backward, away from the doorway, as though putting distance between the messenger and himself would lessen the severity of the tragedy which was about to hit. A cop at the door. The middle of the night. Here to see him. Heidi was safe, so it could only mean one thing.

"My understanding is he had no family, so I am here to inform you that Mister Tony Harris has been found dead. I'm sorry, sir."

Walt's knees buckled. He grabbed the door with both hands for support. Somehow, he managed to stay on his feet. While part of his brain raced with fond thoughts and memories of his best friend, another thought screamed out – a menacing, hideous thought. A thought he could not shake from his head: *Dennis!*

"What happened?" Walt knew it was his voice, but he did not recall forming the thought or deciding to speak. He did not feel as though the words left his own mouth. His stomach wanted to eject everything in it but his mind felt too numb to give the command.

"I can't discuss that right now other than to say we're investigating the matter."

Cop Speak, and Walt knew it. He could not bear another death, particularly Tony's. Still conscious, he dropped to the floor, as though dozens of bags of concrete were dropped onto his shoulders. He landed on his butt and stared straight ahead, past the deputy's knees. The deputy gave a few instructions concerning when to go to the police station and whom to see, but Walt heard none of it. His limbs were numb, though he could see they were still attached to his torso. His chest felt crushed, as though the bags of concrete had him trapped. His head ached; a fog had set in and hampered his mind from operating with proper efficiency. Sound did not penetrate his eardrums. He could feel Heidi's arms around him, but despite her nearness, a feeling of detachment prevailed.

"Dennis," he whispered. Heidi could not hear the quiet remark through her sobs. She could not remember a time in her life when Tony was not a part of it.

Walt did not know how long he sat on the floor and shook, or at what time Heidi let go of him. He only knew he had to visit the police station. This was happening – for the third time.

Chapter 30

"I've got a guy here who says he knows who's been killing all those people on your Triumvirate case." The sheriff's deputy poked his head inside the doorway as he spoke.

"Yeah, yeah. I'm expecting him. Thanks. Send him back." Detective Encarnacion nodded, with only a brief glance thrown at his coworker.

"There's a woman with him, too."

"Oh. Really? I don't know who that is. Send her back, too. I haven't had my coffee yet and I'm pulling crazy long shifts and these people time their days by the Sun rising." It was obvious the man everyone called 'Detective Rob' was too tired to be intrigued.

Within seconds, Dennis and Heidi entered. Both seemed hesitant.

Detective Rob held out a hand, indicating the pair should sit. The metal-framed chairs were old and covered with a thick fabric. By the looks of them, the chairs had been in the station for longer than either of the guests had been alive.

As they sat, the detective spoke first. "Mister Fry, I presume?"

"Yes. Dennis Fry." He thrust his hand forward and the men shook on the introductions.

"And you are?" Before his question could be answered, it hit him. "You're Walter Musgrave's daughter!"

"Heidi." It did not take a police detective to see her embarrassment and hesitancy to speak – let alone be present – at this meeting.

"And what do you have for me?" To the point, Encarnacion wanted – needed – information.

"My bo – Walt Musgrave has been acting strangely, very strangely lately. I've just been doing the math and I think –" He stopped speaking to look at Heidi. Her countenance broadcast her feelings.

Encarnacion could not keep his eyes off Heidi. If faces could display words, his would read: *What is she doing here?!* Her presence was a distraction. First kidnapped, then the kidnapper goes missing, now she's here with concerns about her father. Through his tired eyes and countenance, he could not conceal the shock. "You think what, Mister Fry?" He tried to refocus onto the subject at hand.

Tears pooled in Heidi's eyes.

"I think Walter Musgrave is a madman and he's killed my coworkers."

"The FBI disagrees with you."

The tears could not be held back. Heidi reached for her purse and pulled out a tissue.

"That's what we think."

"Musgrave? Are you kidding me?!" Encarnacion's look came across stronger than his words of shock. "I hassled the guy to make sure he doesn't take revenge on Gustafson for the kidnapping, but, but killing his business partners?"

"Yes, sir, I am- I mean, no sir, I'm not kidding. I'm dead serious." Solemn and dejected, Dennis sounded as though he had just given the order to drop a nuclear bomb on his hometown.

"I've been around Walt Musgrave and, well, I just don't see how –" The detective sucked in a deep breath. "I gotta be neutral, so I'll certainly listen to what you have to say." His sense of incredulity did not diminish.

"Look, I know Walt's been somewhat active in the community, and I know Alex and Bill were involved – more so, even – and I know he's not the prototypical crazy guy, but there's just some indicators, that's all." Dennis held to his somber mood.

"He's just been different," Heidi tried to explain. "He's been paranoid. He's been, just –" She broke down. Tears flowed without ceasing. A creek overflowing its banks after a storm. She tried to wipe her eyes but lacked enough tissue to keep up with the torrent. She hid her head, in sorrow and in shame – shame of what her father had done.

"Here's the weird part." Dennis changed his voice to an airy, desperate concern. "He's lost. He's turned paranoid. I don't think he even knows he's done these things. I believe he's separated his actions to the point he doesn't even remember what he's done."

"Are you a mental health professional, Mister Fry?"

"No. I'm not."

"You're not, but you're making these pronouncements, that maybe you read on the Internet or something, and you've determined he's committed these crimes and he has a cognitive dissonance about these crimes. Is that it, Mister Fry?" Detective Rob studied Dennis' face for a long five seconds before continuing. "I can appreciate what you're saying – you both obviously believe it – but can I have some evidence? Evidence would be good."

"We don't have any, but I do think I have something for you. When did Tony die, a week ago?"

"Five days ago." Encarnacion did not need to look at notes for the answer.

"I just know the night he was murdered, I was over at his house and Walt was acting pretty weird." Dennis paused as he waited for the inevitable hard look from Heidi, which she provided.

"You didn't tell me about anything else." Heidi's voice did not sound its normal, sweet self. She sounded as though she had smoked a carton of cigarettes in thirty seconds.

"I didn't want to shake you up, hon. At the time, I thought it was probably nothing." Dennis put his hand on her shoulder, his empathy rising by the second.

"So, what happened that night?" Patience flowed out of Detective Rob.

"Well, he stashed something in his drawer. I couldn't see what it was." Dennis paused before continuing. "He just acted real guilty, ya know? Like a kid would act if he's caught doing something."

Encarnacion leaned back in his chair. "That's all you got? A movement? A guilty looking movement?"

"And a flash of gold. I saw something gold. I don't know what it was." Dennis did not change his expression. He bore the look of a man who had just left a funeral.

The detective leaned forward in a slow, deliberate motion.

"He has these crazy ideas about Dennis," Heidi added. "He's always been a tad paranoid, but it's just little stuff. Now he's just, I don't know, like –" She searched for the exact word, but failing to find it, settled on, "Different. He's just – paranoid. Nervous. Almost crazed."

"His three best friends have all been murdered."

"Yeah, but," Heidi struggled. "But. I don't know how to put it."

"You said something gold. Do you know what it was?" The tired-looking detective turned to Dennis, seemingly interested in the conversation for the first time.

235

"No. I just saw something – a flash of something – he was putting it in his desk." Dennis stared at the man across the desk.

"With all due respect, you two have a *feeling*. You think – you fear – something. You saw him put something in a drawer." Being the man of reason was the detective's job. "If you come up with anything else, let me know." He stood to signify the meeting was over. "But I don't want you to follow him or spy on him, is that clear?"

Heidi stood, but Dennis did not. Encarnacion stepped toward his office door.

"There's more." Dennis' flat statement caused the detective to stop. Encarnacion appeared annoyed.

"I started looking back, and I've figured out when Bill and Alex were murdered, he was alone." Heidi started to protest, but Dennis lifted a hand to cut her off. He continued with his explanation. "Not when he finds out about the murders, but the approximate times they've occurred. I know with Bill and Alex and Tony he was by himself. I think he was in on it with that other guy you think committed the murders. I think he was involved."

The detective returned to his chair. "Still no evidence, but you do bring up some interesting points, assuming you're right."

"And she can give you supporting information about his behavior changes," Dennis added.

"Yeah," Heidi said, soft resignation ruling her voice.

"Three best friends murdered, people." Encarnacion's annoyance was clear.

"Is there a way you can check his house – his house is huge, there's gotta be a million hiding places – so you can look for evidence?" Dennis' mood changed. A livelier, more energetic man now sat across from Detective Rob. "You'd think you could find

236

something. I mean, this is a guy who's always wanted to run the company his way. He has motive."

"Dennis, are you sure?" Heidi expressed the first indication of doubt. Her observations conflicted with her heart, even though she lacked heartfelt feelings for her father.

"Yes, and you are, too." Dennis turned and put his arm around her, despite the obstacle presented by the chairs.

"So, after all these years, he's just going to kill everyone in his company, especially when they're on the cusp of a large contract – yes, I've heard all about it – and he's going to risk it all to *kill* to take over." Encarnacion shook his head. "I feel like I'm in the Twilight Zone right now."

Dennis ignored the detective. "I know it's tough to think your dad's a madman, but we know what we've seen." He paused, allowing the others to take in the words. "It's hard to accept, but it all makes sense now."

"It makes no sense, and I don't have enough for a warrant if it did, Mister Fry. You'll have to jog your memory. You, too, Ms. Musgrave." Behind his eyes, Encarnacion's wheels turned, in contradiction to his words. One did not have to be a mind reader to see the mental struggles. "Where is Mister Musgrave now?"

"He said he needed to get away," Heidi answered. "A couple of weeks ago, he didn't come home one night but he looked fresh the next day, so I guess he's seeing someone or he's staying in a hotel. But sometimes 'getting away' just means taking a drive for hours up PCH. He loves Pacific Coast Highway."

"I have an idea. There's no way I can get a warrant right now, but you live in the house, ma'am, so you can help."

• • •

237

Heidi and Dennis exited the police station as the sheriff's deputy who had escorted the couple into the station approached Encarnacion. "What was that all about?"

"Craziness, really. But I've got a guy who's losing his mind and I'm gonna send him a message. He pissed me off earlier, so it gave me an idea. I think I know a judge who'll give me a warrant," Encarnacion said with a smile.

"You're not the vengeful type."

"Yeah." The detective paused. "True, it's not really about vengeance," he said, truthfully. "But if I don't send this guy Musgrave a message, just to scare him, he'll wind up killing somebody or screwing up my case so we never catch the killer."

"You gonna arrest him?" The deputy grinned, curious.

"No. Just get a warrant. If I write it up right, I can get it and search his house. Shake him up. Then have a chat with him from a stronger position, make him chill out a little." Detective Rob Encarnacion grinned at the thought of his own brilliance.

• • •

Birds scurried to and fro in the back yard, searching for their last meals of the day. The two empty feeders added confusion to this important time of day for the goldfinches, nuthatches, and various sparrows that dominated the yard. Scurrying and confusion in the front yard resulted from the number of sheriff's deputies carrying items out of Walt's house and then reentering.

Walt's Lexus pulled into his driveway and stopped short of the garage. He exited his car, bewildered.

"Mister Musgrave, I'm Officer Bell. You remember me." Officer Bell did not ask a question.

"I do. What's going on here?!" Walt responded with a harsh tone. From his driveway, he looked at the chaotic scene. "Has my house been broken in to?"

"Can you turn around, Mister Musgrave? You're under arrest for the murder of Tony Harris."

Chapter 31

Walt's head hung like that of a tired, defeated man. After ten minutes, he requested to speak with his lawyer, only to recall his lawyer was dead – and he himself was the lone suspect in his death. After frenzied, disjointed thoughts cobbled together to form a coherent message, he informed Detective Encarnacion he needed to contact Mel Harvey.

The conversations were blurs – kaleidoscopes of sounds, thoughts, accusations. They were accompanied by emotions he did not wish to recall. He faced accusations of killing Tony. Evidence had been discovered in his house. If he murdered Tony, then he had participated, in some form or another, in the murders of Bill and Alex. There were other felonies. And that DeWinter/Desmond guy.

Thoughts scraped their way through his head, as though brain tissue lay mangled and dangling in the wake of each transmission of nerve impulses.

He heard Encarnacion say something about a "ridiculous theory" and "are you a psychologist?" He had a vague understanding Encarnacion stated, "Fry said the same thing." Like lights reflecting off fog, diffusing the intensity of the brightness, words spread, floated, maneuvered around the room in ways Walt could not quite understand.

His brain struggled to remain in one piece, it seemed. The thick mental fog did not lessen when a brief spat arose about Dissociative Identity Disorder, whatever that was. A full mental breakdown seemed imminent.

Bail hearing, tomorrow. Jail, overnight. An officer escorted him away. He later thought he remembered a brief conversation alone with Mel Harvey. "Don't talk to *anyone*." And, "You're in no condition to talk to me right now."

The fog squeezed his brain until the pain robbed him of his mental focus and destroyed his comprehension skills. He behaved like a well-dressed zombie. No matter his behavior, murder was the charge.

• • •

Before the bail hearing, Walt's senses returned. He understood the charges and the peril facing his freedom – his very existence. Despite evidence found in his house – Tony's gold watch, Gustafson's car keys, and a small club – the judge granted bail, albeit a high one. Set at $1,000,000, the one-tenth Walt had to pay was immaterial compared to the loss of life. The prosecutor made no attempt to hide her disgust at the allowance of bail. The hearing itself ensued as a quick yet painful procedure, but at least it ended. His nightmare had only begun.

• • •

On the sidewalk with his attorney, Walt digested the proceedings. "Mel, we gotta talk. This is all some kind of mistake."

"No," Harvey replied. "It's not a mistake. Let's go to my office so we can hash this out."

Walt's face contorted into a look of uncontrollable rage, a man not ready to accept what was about to be said to and about him. "Mel, I just told you, it's a mistake." He stressed every word, as though enunciation would decide his case.

"We'll chat in my office." Despite glares from the businessman, the attorney would not acknowledge his client during the brief walk.

• • •

The moment the door to Harvey's office suite closed, Walt erupted. "What the hell's the matter with you, Mel? You don't believe me? You don't friggin' believe I'm innocent?! Is that it?!" The pair stood in the lobby of Harvey's small law office. The receptionist sat behind a counter, mouth agape. Harvey surveyed the scene – no other clients.

"You're gonna listen to me, Walt, and you're not gonna argue with me." Harvey walked to the door that led to his private office. "We should talk in my office."

"I'm staying right here," Walt growled.

Harvey stopped in his tracks. He let go of the door and turned to face his enraged client. "I said it's not a mistake. This isn't mistaken identity. Listen to my words, Walt. If you wanna avoid spending the rest of your days in a situation like you spent last night, it's time you shut up for once in your life."

Walt froze. His attention – his life – rested on his attorney's mercy. This was not the way he knew Mel Harvey. Harvey was a mild-mannered, odd, almost buffoonish figure who seemed as though he bumbled and stumbled his way through life. Now, when the stage was his, the man took charge – a prima donna actor in front of thousands on Broadway.

"I know what you babbled about yesterday, but if it wasn't for the fact we pulled one of the most liberal judges in the county when it comes to law and order, you'd be in prison until your trial." Harvey walked toward his client as he poked holes in the air with his index finger, his gray comb-over bounced as he stepped. "If your fingerprints had been on the watch or car keys you'd be a goner. Locked up for good." He surveyed his client's eyes. "I don't know if you're guilty or not. Maybe you can explain it away, but you – either somebody left powerful evidence in your house or

242

you're guilty as they come. There's not a jury in the world – well, except maybe O.J.'s – that wouldn't convict you on that alone."

Walt frowned. He did not understand how the objects found their way into his house, but he did understand the appearance of guilt.

"But there's an opening, Walt. The police were told some theory about multiple personalities. They call it 'Dissociative Identity Disorder' these days. Well, if the lead detective on the case has even the tiniest of doubts about your sanity, then we've got an opening to keep you off death row."

"That's crazy."

"I don't care, Walt. If *they* think you're crazy, that's all we need. I can neutralize the detective on examination. Boom! We win. No death row. That's the goal."

The shudder which manifested in Walt's face and hands began in his gut before working out to his limbs. He still did not know all the details of the accusations, yet he understood the severity of his predicament.

"We're gonna get you a psych eval. The prosecution will do the same. People are gonna peer into your mind, Walt. Get used to it."

At the moment, Walt felt unsure whether he could peer into his own mind, let alone allow someone else in. After a brief conversation, the attorney made the request, and Walt agreed, to take a walk. Sitting would not do for the accused – he needed to move. He needed to expend energy that might otherwise consume him. Walt's soul raged, like a California wildfire headed for a population center, out of control, heat growing, flames roaring. His anger, his frustration, his pain – all needed to be extinguished in order for him to return to his normal life as a respected businessman.

Instead, he found himself walking in a nearby park, alone with his criminal defense attorney, explaining his side of a convoluted, disjointed story, including every last detail about Dennis Fry.

The problem was, Walt began to think of himself as crazy.

Chapter 32

"You haven't told me one solid thing you have."

"Tony Harris' watch, Troy Gustafson's car keys, and a club – the murder weapon in several of the cases."

"And how many people have access to that house?"

"Oh, and Musgrave's pocket knife in Harris' house, which is probably how he got in the house, by jimmying the door, if Harris didn't simply let him in."

The conversation had turned into an argument just minutes after Special Agent Bretz shook hands with Detective Encarnacion. Bretz's brown eyes looked as though they could catch fire. Encarnacion signaled he would not back down.

"Listen, I've heard Tony Harris was a friend of yours and I'm sorry. But I've got a guy dead to rights and you're fighting me. I don't get it." Encarnacion's voice ventured to the edge of pleading for understanding.

"I've been looking into Dennis Fry, and I'm trying to tell you he's a bad guy. Bad things happen around him." It was Bretz's turn to approach the threshold of pleading.

"Give me something," Encarnacion challenged, turning the tables from the point where the argument began.

"Circumstantial. All of it," Bretz admitted. "He went to UC Santa Barbara and a Business professor he clashed with allegedly committed suicide. He jumped off a cliff. My people are looking into reports that he went to UC Davis as 'Dennis Cooper.' I'm not sure about that, but a Dennis Cooper was investigated for murder up there."

"I remember the suicide," the detective nodded. "But it wasn't 'alleged' – there was no doubt. The professor had a suicide

245

note in his pocket. With UC Davis, let me know if you get anything, but that had to be a different guy." Encarnacion paused to change subjects. "Cooper. How are Dennis Cooper and Dennis Fry related?" Encarnacion relaxed his tone yet maintained the challenge to Bretz's points.

"He did. He had a suicide note. And Cooper and Fry are one in the same. We're double-checking our proof now," Bretz retorted in a measured tone. "He went to UC Davis as Dennis Cooper and a guy Fry had a run-in with was found murdered there. There was also a fellow college student of Fry's murdered, but that angle was never really checked out at the time. We're on that one now, too."

"You're right, circumstantial," Encarnacion seemed to mock the agent.

"Yeah, but the note was scribbled, like it was rushed," Bretz returned to the subject of the UC Santa Barbara professor. "The whole thing just never made sense."

"You got nothing there." Encarnacion smiled, allowing the comment to poke Bretz.

"His first job was in the Bay Area – San Mateo. A middle manager he didn't get along with was mugged and beat to death." Bretz paused as he prepared to recount more.

"It's the Bay Area. Come on." Encarnacion was not moved. "Lots of crime up there."

"His next job was down here, in Woodland Hills. He was CFO for a biomedical company," the FBI agent plodded through his memory. "They ran him out after six months. That job wasn't on his resume when he hired on with Musgrave. There's a non-disclosure, so we'll only find out about that if there's cause and we go to a judge."

"Cause? Curtis, we got our guy." The detective looked at Bretz as though he were astonished at the lack of understanding. "And why do you know so much about Fry, anyway?"

"Because Tony and Musgrave thought this guy was up to no good."

Encarnacion did not have a tart riposte; rather, he stood for the first time since the conversation commenced ten minutes prior. With a slow, deliberate sweep of the room, his eyes met the agent's eyes. "And you're acting as though I'm basing everything on what Fry's told me."

"Exactly." Bretz studied his long-time counterpart and temporary adversary, who seemed to be considering perhaps his source held a certain bias against Walt.

"But," Encarnacion came alive with a sudden burst of energy. "Fry was right. He saw a flash of gold at Musgrave's desk and the watch *was* in his desk." Encarnacion paused to allow his words to twist, like a knife in a deep wound. "Don't forget his daughter," he added. "You're not saying she was with him in San Mateo or at UCSB, are you?"

"No. But his daughter's involvement doesn't impress me any." Bretz's cold response left little room for guessing where he found blame for Tony's death.

"Well, just so you know," the detective signaled his intention to give out unsolicited advice. "I think you've got nothing, and I've got evidence. I think you're on a case you shouldn't be on because a friend of yours has been murdered. I'd like to work with you again, Curtis, I really would, but you've got to bring something to the table."

"Fine. Then let me sum up what I think." The federal agent glared at the county detective. "You've got a suspect who fits the profile of a guy who'd vehemently argue a speeding ticket from the CHP." Bretz paused. He wanted every word to sink in. "The suspect's fingerprints aren't on the watch or on Gustafson's keys, even though they're in his possession. There was no reason to keep those keys – or to keep the watch, for that matter."

Encarnacion's eyes narrowed.

"The pocket knife at Harris' house is no big deal. The two went to each other's houses all the time."

Encarnacion looked away.

Bretz continued. He could see the detective mulling over what had been said. "And he's rich, so he doesn't need the watch." Another pause. "The evidence shows the murder weapon had been cleaned off except at the very end. Why? Why would you clean off the weapon but not clean it one-hundred percent?" Another pause, during which Encarnacion remained silent, gave Bretz more confidence. "Your source is talking about split personalities but has no education in the field of psychology. Did you know Dennis Fry's a movie buff?"

"So?"

"So, if he can remember a lot of movie quotes, he's seen a lot of movies, gotten a lot of ideas. Hell, I've gotten a lot of ideas from movies." Bretz laughed. "You think the bad guys don't? I've seen movies about Dissociated – split personality. You think this guy hasn't? Have you run Walt's phone yet?"

"We're in the middle of that, yeah."

"When you get the results, I bet you Musgrave's phone will show it was in his house when Tony was murdered, just like he said. You wanna know why?" Bretz's low-key personality increased its liveliness as he spoke. His energy level could not be missed. "I'll tell you why. Because Musgrave wasn't at Tony's house at the time of the murder. Fry gets his knowledge from movies. In the movies, except some of the newer ones, they don't ping cell phones. They didn't have cell phones until recently. Being alone used to be brutal on an alibi, especially in the older movies. But not anymore. Not with cell phone towers and technology." For the first time during the entire meeting, Curtis Bretz smiled. "Some of the newer movies have it right, but there are a lot more that don't. Fry's knowledge of the world, including criminology, comes from movies."

"If you're right about Musgrave's phone, we'll talk." Encarnacion's mood, now a somber shadow of the cockiness from just minutes prior, struggled to avoid slipping into utter dejection.

"Oh, I'm right. I have no doubt. There's too many red flags in this guy Fry's life. Too many. He's a bad character and everyone who has dealings with him sees it." Bretz stood in front of his chair. "The movie guy is eventually gonna get his own phone traced. When the pendulum swings and we get a warrant on this guy, then he'll be done. Cooked. Fried."

Bretz walked to the door, opened it, and stopped. He looked at the floor for a moment, as though he would find the proper words on the carpet. "Robert, please don't ever tell me what case I should or shouldn't be on. I'd appreciate that." Before Encarnacion could respond, Bretz walked through the doorway.

• • •

"You're not coming in."

"Oh, Walter. You're so paranoid." The mocking tone was a tool Dennis used to slice into people, but this time, the blade felt dull.

"I don't care what you say, Dennis." Walt's tone was wrapped in an armor colored by plenty of experiences with the young man. "I'm comfortable in this doorway. Not on the porch. Not inside my house."

Dennis sighed. After a brief hesitation, he delivered his statement. "DOD is fine at the moment. I've explained this is a mixup, some strange confusion, and you'll be running things again in a month or two. The office is fine. They're all concerned about you, but fine. No one knew you came in and sat at the back of the church during the funeral, so telling them that made them all happy. But I'm taking care of everything. There's nothing to worry about with me at the helm. I've got it all under control."

"And I sent an email a few minutes ago." Walt studied the younger man's face as he spoke.

"Oh? And?"

"You'll read it." Walt brushed him off.

Dennis pulled his cell phone from his pocket.

"You can read it later. You don't need to read it right this second," Walt ordered. "It just explains my innocence and says I'll be back and that I look forward to things returning to normal. That's it."

Dennis nodded.

"You drove all the way over here to tell me what you could've told me in a text or email?" Walt could no longer suspend his disbelief.

Arrogance flooded Dennis' countenance. "I wanted to see how pathetic you looked."

"You wanted to see if I was shriveling up and falling over, about to die," Walt said, his confidence matching that of his adversary's.

"That, too."

"That, primarily."

"Listen, old man. You're not done losing yet." Anger replaced arrogance. Dennis had the look of someone ready to engage in a fistfight.

"I haven't lost yet. It's just been everyone around me." A cold, calm anger rose from Walt's stomach and settled in his face, where his eyes narrowed and his eyebrows furrowed. "You have a sick way of attacking, I'll give you that."

"None of it matters, old man. You're gonna be dead." A slow smile crawled across the young executive's face. "And I can't wait to read your suicide note. It's gonna be epic!" He laughed an exaggerated, deranged laugh. "Because I'm gonna help you write it."

Walt knew he had heard that laugh before. *Probably one of those damned movies of his.*

Dennis walked down the sidewalk, to his car, which was parked at the curb in front of the house. He laughed loudly enough for Walt to hear as he climbed into his car.

Walt watched the car disappear down the street before he shut his front door. He walked backward, away from the door, as a man stepped out of what had been a shadow created by the opened front door. The short, slender, bald man shook his head.

"That's the first time anyone's heard it but me," Walt said.

"It's just a matter of time." Special Agent Bretz looked Walt in the eye. "We'll get him." Bretz pulled a digital recorder from his pocket, looked at it to ensure it recorded properly, and turned it off. "Just a matter of time."

Chapter 33

Walt could walk with energy because he blocked out the pain – in fact, the confidence he projected helped to blunt the sharper edges of his memory. When he relaxed or slowed his mental pace, those sharp memories were there, like swords in the hands of pirates, stabbing their victims on a conquered ship at sea. Sometimes slashes, sometimes deep stabs into his psyche, the pain hovered, never more than a thought away.

Energy and manufactured confidence allowed him to block out his troubles; keeping busy pushed the blues further away. Now, as he entered the building and walked toward his office, he combined the two – energy and a false confidence – which lifted his spirits for the first time in two weeks.

"It's been pretty quiet around here," Donna said, as she failed to conceal sympathy for her boss. Her voice and facial expressions told him how much she cared about him. She left her chair to stand before him.

"No breakdowns?"

"No, none. I sat in on a sales meeting Friday so I could brief you today – Dennis had a schedule conflict. They had never seen me in a sales meeting before." She laughed, though she never took her blue eyes off him. "They said everything was going good. I took some notes and I'll give you the sales numbers, and I think you'll be happy with them."

Walt nodded and smiled. "I always told you you'd run this place someday."

They both grew quiet as they considered his words. Walt seemed the more uncomfortable. "I never thought it'd come to this."

Donna reached out and patted his shoulder. "Well, here we are." After a small pause, she tried to liven up the mood. "We'll make do. We grew to this point. We'll just do it again." She flashed what they both knew to be a fake smile. But it helped.

"Yep, we'll just start again."

"Just so you know," Donna carried the conversation back to specifics. "Dennis has been going over the books again with Defense. I'm not sure what's up with that, but I'm sure they had questions or he wouldn't have been doing it."

"I didn't know the DOD was still concerned about financials." Always suspicious, Walt looked across the room, eyes focused on nothing, deep in thought. *What are they up to? Hell, what's he up to? Why is he even in charge? How am I gonna uproot that guy? He's insane. I wouldn't doubt if –*

"Are you taking care of yourself?"

The question interrupted the flow of thoughts, which alternated between the angry and the paranoid. "What's that?"

"I said," Donna said with firmness. "Are you taking care of yourself?"

"Well, I'm not hitting the bar scene or taking a handful of sleeping pills every night," Walt said with a laugh.

"I'm being serious, Walter. I'm really worried about you. I can always look at you and tell when you're not doing well."

"You're the only person in the building who can read me well." He knew anyone could read his pain at the moment. His face transformed from a tough, focused warrior preparing for battle to a kind, grateful gentleman, happy to oblige any request from his longtime friend and leader of the clerical department.

And then the adversary entered.

"Hey Donna, can you – oh! Hi, Walt. Welcome back."

253

"Dennis, isn't it good to see Walt again?"

"Yeah. Of course." Dennis appeared as sincere as ever.

"Did you need something?" Donna stood at the ready.

"No. No, it can wait. Walt and I have some catching up to do. We'll go back to my office." If Dennis felt uncomfortable, he did not show it.

"Okay, well I've got to check in with a contractor and find out why he's been slow on permits." She looked at Walt. "All the leaders have expanded roles, I guess." She gave a nervous laugh, as though she should not be performing such tasks. With that, she headed out of the office, toward the parking lot.

"Donna has been great. She's earned herself a nice little bonus when this is all over with," Dennis said, in command of his surroundings.

"Yeah. She's great." Walt did not show a willingness for small talk.

"Let's go to my office. It's on the way to the elevator for you. I'll keep it brief." Dennis remained in "boss" mode. He displayed a coolness that almost unnerved Walt.

Walt nodded and followed the younger man out the door, into the hallway.

The pair walked together, side-by-side. Neither spoke. With their expressions, they looked as though they were at one of the several recent funerals. With each step, hatred welled up inside Walt's chest, into every molecule of his being. He wanted to grab Dennis by the throat. He wanted to thrash him – throw him onto the floor and pound his face until every portion of the wicked man's face caved in.

His thoughts steered to his darkest wishes. Did those thoughts make him evil like Dennis? *No! No way. No one is that wicked.* His thoughts raced to infamous men of the 20th Century. *How could Stalin or Pol Pot be any more evil?! Are there grades of evil? Is Dennis more like Himmler or Hitler? No. Wait. Those people killed millions. There's gotta be grades of evil, but that doesn't help Bill and Alex any. Maybe he's like Che Guevara and Castro, who killed whoever disagreed. That kind of evil.*

The disjointed thoughts continued until the pair reached Dennis' office. He convinced himself just because Dennis had not earned a dubious spot with wicked creatures like Mao and Amin, evil was still evil. He knew it; he could feel it. There was something familiar about this young man – something he could not quite pinpoint – and yet all he could sense was an evil nature.

"Come on in." There were other people in the hallway, so Dennis maintained a level of deference to the boss.

When they walked into the office, Walt's mind switched from failed philosopher back to successful businessman. While Dennis made his way to the chair behind his desk, Walt surveyed the room. Three posters on the walls conveyed messages of business savvy, including one which carried the simple message "Plan to Succeed."

He certainly plans. The thought caused Walt to smile.

"You like my office?" Dennis caught the smile before a new thought shoved it off Walt's face.

Walt noticed the absence of personal photos. "Yeah. Sure. Just looking around."

"Sit. Please." Dennis motioned with his hand to one of two empty chairs.

Walt closed the door before obliging.

"So far, so good with the DOD. They're still on board, though I do detect some concerns with our company's turmoil."

Walt nodded. His face could have been chiseled from granite.

"Today's Monday," Dennis continued. "I cut you some slack because of Tony's murder."

Walt stiffened. His heart rate increased. He felt his face redden. Breathing quickened.

"But I want you dead by Friday. We've got to get this over with." Dennis looked directly into Walt's eyes as he delivered the ultimatum. His flat tone delivered the message as though announcing the time of the pizza deliveryman's arrival. As cold as a February ski run down the slopes at Big Bear, the date of Walt's death – at least, the latest acceptable date – was chosen.

Walt slowed his breathing down in time to respond. "You're out of your mind." He matched the chill in the air which lingered from Dennis' icy declaration. His voice decayed into a rough, gravelly scraping of vocal chords. "You're not gonna get your way, Fry."

"And don't forget that suicide note. I expect you to say nice things about me to Heidi. Very important." Dennis pursed his lips, as though to stop the haughtiness from leaking out.

Afraid Dennis might be recording the conversation, ready to perform selective editing, Walt did not tell him the depths of his desire to kill the young man. He contained his recent thoughts about evil men and resisted the urge to leap over the desk, gouge out Fry's eyes, and then rip out his throat with his bare hands. He understood such actions could work against him. He was out on bail. Any wrong step and he would spend his days until the trial – and probably for the rest of his life – behind bars.

Walt shook with anger.

Rather than speak, Walter Musgrave took another deep breath, climbed out of the chair, and exited the office. On his walk to his own office, he maintained his calm, subdued state. It was not until he reached his own office, shut the door with a gentle push, and seated himself in his chair that he erupted in a deafening, animalistic scream. The unnatural, guttural outburst was short-lived enough no one pursued the source of the sound.

The end approached. Walt sat and pondered whether this end was that of his own life, that of Triumvirate Technologies, or both. He was certain that Friday would be an eventful, tumultuous day – a day the nightmare might at last reach its conclusion.

Chapter 34

"Thanks for meeting me here. As messed up as he's been lately, I didn't want you to come over to the house."

"What's the difference?" Dennis asked. "I see him at the office every day – every day he shows up."

Heidi considered her words before verbalizing feelings. "I can't keep going through this. I'm gonna move out pretty soon. I mean, what if he's really guilty?" Tears flooded her eyes. "We told the police our concerns, but I'm just – I'm just not sure."

Dennis reached across the table and grabbed her hands. A waiter approached, but Dennis shook him off. The waiter understood the head movement and passed by the table, notepad at the ready for their order. He glanced back as he walked away, in time to see Heidi lower her head.

"Listen, honey." Dennis broke off his words in a show of concern. "Don't worry about his guilt right now. Don't worry about all this split personality stuff. You just keep dealing with your father like normal and we'll get you out of there." He spoke to the top of her head as she continued staring at the table in front of her.

"That's just it. I *can't* act like everything's normal." Heidi stressed "can't" in a way that communicated despair more than fear.

"Look, I've been talking to a psychiatrist friend of mine. Psychiatrists are like psychologists, but they also deal in medicines." He maintained his loose grip on her hands. "Look at me."

She obeyed his soft command. Red eyes dominated her gentle face. She looked away long enough to fetch a tissue from her purse to use on her moist eyes.

"Listen, he's not gonna get help on his own, you agree?"

She nodded, face obscured by the tissue and her hands.

"So, we're gonna get him a medicine that will help him out, normalize him, ease the paranoia."

"You can do that?"

"They make medicines for everything," he explained with a caring smile.

"No. I mean, get a prescription for someone the doctor hasn't seen." Heidi put away the tissue and looked at Dennis.

"Yeah, that's no problem. These guys have extras on hand. No problem."

Dennis' reassuring voice did just that: it reassured Heidi to the point of not probing further. "Okay."

"I'll worry about the details later. For now, I agree it was best for us to meet away from your house. Are you hungry for lunch?" He sat back in the booth.

Heidi smiled. "No. I'm not hungry. I haven't been hungry much lately. I feel like I betrayed my dad."

"You didn't betray him." Dennis added another layer of reassurance to his voice. "Remember, he's been making stuff up. There's this bet thing. There's the power grab at Triumvirate – I mean, if that isn't obvious, I don't know what is. The man killed his business partners – or at least hired someone to. I don't know." He shrugged. "Maybe he participated. But we'll get him straightened out and they'll put him in a nice facility where they'll take good care of him."

The tears returned.

"Oh, I'm sorry. I didn't mean to upset you." The look of pain on Dennis' face transcended words.

"It's okay. It's not your fault. You just hired in at the wrong time." Her voice cracked as she completed her sentences.

259

"Yeah, it seems that way." Dennis smiled. "But look at it another way. Maybe I had good timing. You ever think of that?"

Heidi looked at him and smiled.

"We'll get through this, Heidi. We'll get through this. When this is all over, things are gonna be a lot different." Dennis nodded as he spoke. "I can promise you, things are gonna be a lot different."

• • •

"Thanks for meeting with me in the evening." Walt took in Mel Harvey's spacious yet congested office. Files littered the floor and his desk. A path cleared the way to two separate bookcases – one filled with law books and the other with murder mysteries and detective stories. The carpet needed cleaning – not just vacuuming. The thirty-year-old wallpaper needed to be peeled off (and burned, Walt thought), and who knew what lurked amongst the folders and papers scattered across the floor?

"It's the life of a trial attorney," Harvey said as he watched Walt survey the scene.

"I've never heard of a lawyer having detective novels at his office," Walt snickered. "But as long as it works for you, I guess." He shook his head.

Harvey removed a file from a chair and motioned for Walt to sit. He then made his way to the other side of the desk and sat in his own chair.

"How am I getting out of this mess?" Walt asked as he sat.

"Well, that's a tricky one. You have a serious problem. Three pieces of evidence were found in your house – three substantial pieces of evidence," he added for effect.

Walt tried to interrupt, but Harvey held up a hand – a silent order for him to shut his mouth and listen.

"I told you before, the lead detective has been told you may have something called D.I.D., which is what you and I know as 'split personality.'"

Walt put his elbows on top of his legs and dropped his face into his hands.

"So, we're here to talk about the psych eval they're gonna do. Now, I know enough about split personality to know we've got an uphill battle to prove it."

"Wait a minute," Walt said, a confused look on his face. "We prove it?"

"They're going after you as a sane man – to put you on death row." Harvey leaned forward in his chair, his gray hair dropped to conceal his eyes until he swept away the strands. "You're gonna take my advice on this one and help them prove the split personality."

Walt leaped to his feet. "You're out of your freakin' mind!"

"You wanna go to prison for the rest of your life?" Harvey remained calm. "You told me your side of the story. I've evaluated what we have and what they have. This is my professional opinion."

"I'm not crazy!" Walt's shout could be heard outside the doors of the office.

"Okay. So, you're not crazy. Sit down, by the way." A sweep of the hand toward the chair acted as an invisible guide. "Off to prison you go. For life. If they tie you to Tony Harris, they'll also get you for your two business partners, probably as an accessory somehow. Got that?" Harvey rocked his head forward and back in a quick "yes" motion, underscoring his point of doom. "These are our options. We defend you as sane and we'll lose because of the evidence. We defend you as not guilty because of mental reasons – insanity – and you'll go to a little hospital somewhere and spend your days looking at rolling green hills. Or we figure out how that evidence got in your house."

"I like the third one." Sitting seemed to lower Walt's blood pressure, if only a little.

"I knew you would. Good luck. If the Sheriff's Department's info is right about you, you're not gonna like how that evidence got there." Harvey paused and stared at his client. "Now, I've got an investigator who's gonna check things out, but I gotta tell ya, you're not helping yourself out with all this Dennis Fry stuff – if you're sane, that is. If you're not – perfect."

Walt's rate of breathing increased. The red in his face reflected the level of rage he felt.

"That would look way too convenient to the jury. You hire someone to kill your business partners – or maybe you participate in the killings yourself – you kill the company lawyer, and the one executive who is trying to save the company is now the bad guy." Harvey studied Walt's face. "And the lawyer was your best friend, which makes you look even worse. Your top remaining executive has told the police you're paranoid and you have two or more personalities, and they'll probably drag your daughter deeper into this, based on what the detective told me."

"Dennis has a hold on her!"

"Yes. He does."

"I've had enough!" He leaped to his feet again. "You're out of your mind believing all this crap! This garbage!" The shouts increased in volume. "You've made all these assumptions and you've gone along with the prosecution and the cops or something. This is absurd!" Walt spun and headed toward the door.

"Walt, it takes California a long time, but they do execute people in this state."

Walt paused at the door.

"I'm not siding with the prosecution, I'm just looking at what they've got and I'm plotting to use it against them. They've got evidence, Mister Musgrave. We don't." He waited for Walt to respond. When silence filled the room, the lawyer continued. "Now we can either live in a fantasy world where everything's gonna be all right or we can start plotting how we're gonna keep you off death row and use the whole split personality thing against them." Another pause. "You can walk out that door and be as stubborn as you want, and you can tell the prison guards for the next twenty years how innocent you are, right up until they stick you with needles and put you down like a lame horse."

A quiet filled the room, which seemed all the more vacant of life now that the shouting had ended. Walt took his hand off the door handle, maneuvered around various files and folders spread out on the floor, and found himself in the same chair again.

The two stared at each other until, after a long ten seconds, Walt spoke. "I have a witness. The FBI agent Curtis Bretz was hidden in my house when I had a conversation with Dennis. Fry said he wanted me to commit suicide by Friday."

"Okay. When was this?"

"Yesterday, right after I posted bail." Walt sounded like a worn-out, defeated shell of a man.

"Well, that's a problem."

Walt sat up in the chair. "What do you mean?"

"I talked to Special Agent Bretz yesterday. Today's Monday? Yeah, yesterday. He said he hasn't talked to you or seen you since the day he told you and Tony about the death of the guy they originally believed murdered Yoo and Heil. He said he's been

263

in Riverside the last few weeks, on loan to the FBI office there, working a case."

Walt lacked the energy to explode; anger was inaccessible at this moment. He could only fall into a state of uncontrolled depression. An inconsolable sense of defeat enveloped him. The impossible was happening. He *remembered* events, but they did not – *maybe* they did not – happen.

But I only heard of Norman DeWinter from Bretz. I never met the guy. I couldn't have hired him. I don't have any connection to him. He looked at his legal counsel and realized the man was studying him, as though he could read Walt's mind. *This guy doesn't believe me. My own daughter doesn't believe me. Now Bretz says he was never at my house. I remember it! I remember him being there. We had conversations about Dennis and investigating him and what Tony may have figured out. Dennis left and Bretz stayed. We talked!*

"You all right?" Harvey knew it was a stupid question, but he seemed to feel a need to fill the silence and perhaps to derail whatever dominated Walt's thoughts.

"Of course, I'm all right. My life's hurtling to destruction, but I'm good. How about you? You doing all right?" Had the sarcasm been physical, it would have stained the carpet, the acid burned with such intense heat as it dripped out of Walt's mouth.

"Look, I'm sorry," the lawyer began. "With my clients, my job is to be realistic. I can't sugarcoat things or it's worse for you. Not only do I want you to avoid death row, I want you to avoid prison altogether." It was clear to both men that Harvey was about to deliver a line difficult to utter. "But I want you to consider 'guilty by reason of insanity.' We'll keep you out of prison." Harvey quickened his verbal pace in an obvious attempt to gloss over the difficult request. "We'll lay out a plan to get you help. In the meantime, I'll have my investigator look into everything you say."

Walt replayed the request over and over in his head; he was convinced the pledge to investigate further was wrapped in multiple layers of insincerity.

"I may not have a choice, huh?" Walt tried to force a smile but could not manage it.

"Probably not."

"But you're not gonna investigate anything. You're just trying to make me feel better."

"No! No, really. Look, when you look around my office you see a mess. That's just how my mind works. I know where my files are, and I like to have them available. I stay on top of things."

"I've heard that about trial lawyers. You're the most unorganized people on Earth." Walt looked around the room again.

"Yeah, I've read the best ones are." He smiled. "You hired me for a reason, Walt. You coulda hired an L.A. gun, but you knew I'd get the job done. But there's only so much that can be overcome, you know?" Harvey had the look of a man in search of sympathy.

"I assume I'm here to give you permission to change my plea?"

"Yes. That and to prepare you for your psych eval. We'll change your plea only if we have to. But again, it's 'insanity' or the death penalty."

"Not yet. I'm not pleading insanity just yet." Walt lacked energy, but his brain emerged from its low point of only a minute prior. "Going back to this Bretz thing, what's that have to do with split personality? What's it called now?"

"Dissociated Identity Disorder." Harvey came close to getting the name right.

"Yeah," Walt continued, as though he were waking up from an emotional coma. "This has nothing to do with that. I can see if I'm really somehow connected to DeWinter – which I'm not – but if I am, then there's evidence. Cell phone records. Security cameras somewhere. DeWinter – what was his real name? Bruce Desmond? He was a bad dude, so maybe some law enforcement somewhere was monitoring him and they'd also have me on camera. I'd have to be paying the guy, so check my bank records."

"I want you to see a couple different doctors. We need to cover our bases."

Full of vigor, Walt roared back to life. "If I'm connected to him, there's evidence, somehow, somewhere. We had to meet or speak or something. So that's where your investigator can start. Forget Dennis." Walt paused at the name of the thorn in his side. "I'll check out Dennis."

"You can't be–"

"Don't tell me what I can't do, Mel. It's my life on the line here." The fire burned again. Walt's mental crash and burn had subsided. The flames had licked portions of his psyche, but he emerged ready to fight again. "No one's going to take my life or my business from me, Mel. No one. I know damned well I didn't kill anyone. I'm not going to prison – or the funny farm – just yet."

Walt left his chair as a man on a mission. He extended his hand and the two shook. "I'll chat with you soon." Walt turned to leave. Two steps into the exit, he turned to Harvey and with a forcefulness in his voice that had been absent for weeks, announced, "I'm not crazy. I'm also not a killer. We're gonna figure this out."

Once Walt walked through the doorway and the door closed, Harvey picked up the phone on his desk and punched in

266

numbers. "Carlos, Mel Harvey." He paused. "Looks like I've got some work for you on the Musgrave case after all."

After finishing his instructions, Harvey ended the call and stared toward the door. "That crazy sucker doesn't even know he's crazy. But I guess we'll try it his way. For now."

• • •

The phone rang. Walt looked at the clock to see "2:46." Middle-of-the-night calls had only brought news of death; of the people for whom he cared, only Heidi remained with the living. The rush of adrenaline caused him to lunge to the phone and answer on the second ring. The voice on the other end was disguised, yet the words were clear. Walt thought maybe he was too groggy. "Pardon me?"

The voice repeated the words. "It's playtime, Walter."

Walt did not speak. His head hurt due to being awakened from a deep slumber. The silence did not make the annoying interruption go away.

"Shall we play a game?" The disguised voice asked.

Walt erupted. In his brain, a bomb detonated. Instant fury. "Dennis! If that's you, I'll kill you! Do you hear me? I'll kill you!" He crashed the handset into the telephone's base. The call ended, but the phone tumbled from the nightstand onto the floor, sending the sounds of a second crash through the room.

Unable to return to blissful sleep, Walt got up, turned on a light, picked up the phone, and checked the Caller ID. He wrote down the unfamiliar number, then retraced his steps and returned to bed. His elevated heart rate ensured he would be awake for at least another hour.

He harbored no doubts about the identity of the caller. He understood the game. Dennis planned to drive him crazy. The young man had already convinced the police of Walt's disturbed mental state.

A fact which had gotten lost during the evening visit with his attorney made its way into Walt's mind with a jolt. *Heidi.* Harvey said Heidi would probably get dragged into this. *Dennis.* He had convinced her. *He's been close to her, even before all this started. He's got her on his side.* His blood boiled. *He's turned my own daughter against me.* Never mind she had always felt emotionally detached from her father. *Dennis has her convinced I'm paranoid and I have multiple personalities!*

Walt seethed with hatred for Dennis, more than he had ever felt before – toward Dennis or anyone else.

For the first time he could ever remember, Walt fantasized about ways to commit murder. When the four o'clock hour arrived, murder had given way to the return of slumber. His last conscious thoughts were of guns and knives, aimed at the face of Dennis Fry.

Chapter 35

Bleary-eyed and in need of caffeine, Walt backed out of his garage. A quick tap on the accelerator started the car rolling down the inclined driveway until it reached the street. Just as he reached the street and applied the brake, he saw it. He stopped and stared, hoping his squinting eyes deceived him.

The half-feral, half-tamed cat lay in the front yard with a stake driven through its ribcage. Heidi's cat. The Javanese, unique to the neighborhood, had been claimed by Heidi – perhaps it was the other way around – two years prior when she found it wandering through backyards. Walt installed a 'kitty door' in the wooden garage door for the cat to come and go as it saw fit, while Heidi left food in a bowl near the door. The distinctive-looking creature only showed itself to Heidi once every week or so, but in her mind, it was her cat.

And now it lay dead, a stake pinning it to the grass.

Walt dropped his forehead onto the steering wheel. *She's going to have to accept what Dennis is doing.* He glanced at the time above the radio. Seven o'clock. *No time to remove the cat before she leaves for the office. I gotta go.* A business appointment in Los Angeles. Traffic would be horrible for a 9:00 a.m. downtown L.A. meeting, but he was leaving in plenty of time. A SigAlert or worse than normal traffic could cause him to be late. He preferred to stay and deal with the matter, but the bane of every southern California commuter kept him in his vehicle.

He felt guilty as he drove away. It also occurred to him that his neighbors might complain, but his meeting included three potential customers. He drove down the street, away from his house, with a knot in the pit of his stomach and rage in his heart.

He could not delay, and he could not bear the thought of breaking the news to his daughter.

. . .

The nameplate on the desk read "Russell Hett." The tall, soft carpet; the wood paneling; the five bookcases – Walt counted them – and the high ceiling presented an air of luxury. Nothing in the room was inexpensive. The leather chair in which he sat had to be at least $2,000 by itself, Walt estimated.

Hett was short, with light-brown hair and light-brown eyes. He came across as a little too caring for Walt's tastes.

"I will tell you, Mister Musgrave, it's not often I see murder suspects in my office who aren't chained and accompanied by officers. You must be a respected man."

Walt shrugged.

"The worst ones I have to visit in jails and prisons. I hate that." Even when he complained, Hett's voice carried the effect of the gentle roll of water cascading down a small creek. "I prefer my office."

Walt nodded, but it was apparent to the psychologist his subject remained distant, skeptical.

"Why are you skeptical, Walt? We've been here thirty minutes and we've had a good conversation, and yet you're still almost impenetrable."

"It probably has something to do with the fact that I'm in jeopardy of going to prison for crimes I didn't commit."

Hett nodded. "Yeah, that would make me distant."

"Yeah."

"You realize that I don't hold your life in the balance, Walter."

"Walt. I keep telling you, call me Walt."

"Okay. I'm just going to make an evaluation."

"A recommendation."

"Yes, that's true," Hett admitted. "A recommendation based on my evaluation. But you hold your life in the balance right now, not me."

"Oh yeah? How's that?" Walt took the bait.

"Because you're not cooperating. Just the fact you're free on bail tells me you have hope. Don't blow that chance, Walt." To Walt's fenced-off emotions, the doctor sounded nauseatingly caring.

"Okay. I get it." Walt paused in thought before he continued. "I don't quite believe that, but I'll bite. How about if I give you an example of what I've been dealing with?"

Walt gave a three-minute explanation of the cat staked to the ground in his yard. He finished by telling Hett that his daughter must know by now, and she would be in great distress over the creature.

The longer he stayed in the office, the more Walt opened up – about Dennis; about his friendships with Bill, Alex, and especially Tony; and about how hard he worked with them to build up the company only to see this young, mysterious man come along and tear it down. No subject was taboo for the businessman – except one. He avoided expressing his deep hatred for Dennis. *Maybe he'll figure it out*, Walt reasoned, but he was not going to utter the words. *Maybe he won't. Maybe I'll get out of here unscathed.*

Walt did not appreciate the skill with which the psychologist performed his job. Hett did not have a problem translating evasions into emotions and descriptions into hidden meanings.

• • •

After their second ten-minute break concluded, the men returned to their respective chairs, with Dr. Hett behind his desk and Walt in front of it.

"You hate Fry, don't you?"

"I hate what he's doing to my company."

"You mean, to the company Won Yoo, Alexander Heil, and you built."

"They're dead. I mean *my* company." As soon as he uttered the words, Walt realized he had stressed the word 'my' too much. "We built it together. I miss those guys. But I have to protect what's left. Dennis Fry is a predator and he'll do anything to tear it down."

"Will you do anything to protect it?"

"Anything within the law, sure." Walt recognized the trap. He had failed to recognize every nuance over the past two hours, but this snare was as conspicuous as though it were surrounded by flashing red lights.

"What about illegal?"

Walt leaned forward in his chair. "No."

"Have you ever broken the law, Walt?"

Walt leaned back, relaxed again. "Every day – every day I get on the freeway, anyway."

"I'm not talking about speeding. You know what I mean."

"So, now I'm supposed to know what you mean? Wasn't it you who told me earlier to say exactly what I mean? Works both ways, doc." Walt had grown tired of the long conversation, the examination, and the restating of every statement he made.

"But if you really care about something, you'll do anything to protect it, won't you?"

Walt dropped his arms with a *thud* onto the arms of the chair. He shook his head. "Are we really gonna go down this road,

Doctor Hett? I mean, come on. This is stupid. Quit playing dime-novel detective and get back to psychology."

"Do you think it's a stupid question to ask –"

"Yes, I do!"

The loud growl startled Hett. "Okay. I'll change subjects."

"Thank you," Walt sneered. *If I don't get out of here soon, I really will be crazy.*

"I think we're close to being done. I do want you to know something, though. I think it's important."

Why can't this guy just say what he means instead of making it so dramatic all the time?

"I called your daughter during the first break. She headed home from work a few minutes early. During the second break, I called her back. She was home. Not only was her cat not staked to the ground –"

"Well that's not surprising. That's been how many hours?"

"But her cat is fine. It was in the garage, eating, when she came home."

Walt sat up straight in his chair.

"She said it's a distinctive cat. A what? Javanese?"

"Yeah. Java – What? It's fine? How can that be?" Dr. Hett did not need to be a psychologist to read the expression of incredulity on Walt's face.

"Look at the positive side of this, Walt. If you are suffering from Dissociative Identity Disorder, you didn't kill a cat this morning." The gentle, sincere words of the psychologist danced through the room.

That voice, encountered one too many times by Walt's ears, sounded like jackhammers colliding with steel. "No! It's positive because my daughter isn't upset about losing a cat. Can't you

273

understand that? I know damned well I didn't kill a cat this morning, you idiot! You over-educated fool!"

Walt leaped from his chair. The action caused the doctor to recoil in his chair, rolling it backward several inches, away from the desk and Walt.

"Oh, don't give me that fear crap, either! Don't pretend I'm coming at you. You're a fraud! You hear me? A fraud." Walt turned and stormed away, livid at the doctor's final comment. The back of the proverbial camel had been broken by a melodious voice that portrayed sweetness and gentleness but mutated after a few minutes into the grinding sounds made by a wood chipper.

Walt marched across the tall, soft carpet and out the door.

Dr. Russell Hett shook his head. "Oh, I'm afraid you have some serious issues, Mister Musgrave. Some serious issues."

• • •

Walt kept his eyes focused on the hockey players skating back and forth on the flat-screen television, pursuing the puck. His thoughts could not stay engrossed in the game. When his favorite team scored a goal, he reacted with a muted "Yes!" and stood for a moment, but within a second he returned to his seat on the bed. The L.A. Kings might have found success, but he found only failure. His friends were dead; his daughter had little feelings for him; law enforcement thought he was a murderer; and now, he began to doubt his own sanity.

How was it possible Special Agent Bretz was not at Walt's house that day? He remembered it. He held multiple conversations with the man. Did this make him delusional? Such a diagnosis was inconsistent with doing things he did not recall, Walt reasoned.

Over the past weeks, he thought about Bill and Alex and Tony and Heidi almost without ceasing. Only when he concentrated on his growing hatred – yes, he discovered, it was still possible for him to hate the younger man even more – did he find respite from the torturous thoughts of his dead friends and emotionally disengaged daughter.

All thoughts returned to Dennis – every time. Before Dennis came to work at Triumvirate Technologies, the company found success and Walt's life was filled with relative happiness – relative to the amount he sought. Happiness to Walter Musgrave was not in "the little things," as many people repeatedly told him, or in successful relationships; rather, in successful business plans and ventures. Since Tina's death, he tried not to find happiness through other human beings. People brought only pain.

Since Tina's death ten long years ago – it seemed like many decades– Walt only cared about building his company with his business associates and providing for his daughter. His version of "providing" was material, monetary. The only woman he ever loved with deep passion left him through death. His first wife, Stacy, was a monumental mistake – a half-crazed woman who enjoyed being spiteful in her sane moments. *At least I haven't heard from her in years.*

Walt felt driven to succeed; driven, along with Bill and Alex, to run the best business in their industry. When they realized batteries for various technological devices would provide the ride to the top, they rode the elevator of success skyward. They had not yet reached the apex, but they were speeding upward, on their way.

Until life crashed to the ground. Worse yet, good people – friends – died. Murdered.

His mind slipped back to Bretz. He was there. *I saw him. I shook his hand.* Baffled by the experience – the experience with the psychologist and the non-experience with Special Agent Bretz –

Walt's attention flitted between the television and where his mind might be headed.

If I imagined Bretz, then what else have I imagined? Events of the last two months raced through his mind. There were indeed certain events he wished were products of his imagination. He still did not buy into Dissociative Identity Disorder – for other people that could happen, but Walt knew himself to be a sane, successful man whose flaws were minor in comparison.

I haven't been running around killing people! He punched the mattress to emphasize the thought. *I didn't kill Tony! Or anyone else!* The louder his thoughts became, the faster his heart pumped blood throughout his body. *This is a sham, and I'm gonna prove it.*

Walt finished off his fifth beer and escorted the empty bottle to a trash can across the small, dingy motel room. He failed to notice a cockroach race under the bed for protection. Instead, distraction came in the form of an exciting play on the television.

The fleeting distraction of a goalie's great save failed to divert his dispirited thoughts for more than ten seconds. Back on the bed, he relived the attempts to reach Tony by text and the mysterious indication that Tony was in the process of texting back. *What did that mean? Why didn't I get it? Was he killed in the middle of the text?*

Unable to decipher the mystery of Tony, incapable of explaining the Bretz non-conversation which he remembered so well, and unwilling to accept the diagnosis by amateurs that he had multiple personalities, Walt slid into a brief catatonic state. The opposing team's goal brought him back to a conscious state. "Here come the Oilers," he grumbled at the TV.

So, if I'm not crazy, then that means the murder weapon was planted by Fry. Heidi lets him in all the time. But how can I not be

276

crazy if Bretz really wasn't at my house? And if I'm crazy, maybe I killed Tony. And if I'm crazy, did I kill Bill and Alex? Or just hire it done? Walt's mind sank into a dark place. *But I didn't kill Tony, or anybody else, which means I'm not completely crazy.* He stopped with the 'crazy' thoughts to ponder whether the five beers or the deep thinking hurt his head more.

The night Tony died, Dennis was by himself in my house for at least ten minutes, wasn't he? I don't remember how long. The game again. He let out a muffled "Yes!" when the Kings scored another goal.

One thing of which he was certain: freedom could end at any moment. The prosecution and the Sheriff's Department both wanted him locked up. One more piece of evidence – planted evidence, surely, he reasoned – would mean months behind bars, until the trial. A cold chill enveloped his skin at the thought he was not doing enough to prove his innocence.

The brief moment of coherence slipped away. Depression returned. The meeting with Bretz – or lack of a meeting – dominated his thoughts. In between those thoughts, he thought about the decades of good times with Tony Harris.

He celebrated the outcome of the hockey game by opening beer number six. Sitting on the bedspread, back against the headboard, he was halfway through the drink when the phone rang. It was 10:40. He reached behind the phone and unplugged it. The ringing stopped. He took another sip. He did not have to answer the phone to know the identity of the caller.

What have I done that I don't remember?

Chapter 36

As he walked toward Dennis' office, Walt thought about the cat. Somehow, Dennis had found another Javanese, killed it, put a stake through it overnight, then removed it before Heidi could see it. Nothing else made sense.

Man, that's a lot of work. The thought left him wondering about the number of personalities he possessed – whether the accusation could be true.

The open door beckoned, but Walt resisted the urge to enter. He heard the voice of the young executive. Curious, he stopped close to the doorway and listened as Dennis negotiated with a supplier.

"Yeah, but you're just looking at how much I need it. You're not looking at the long-term good this would be for you. You should know this. You make me happy, I buy more. Happiness seems expensive in the short run, but it's really inexpensive in the long run."

He can be so smooth. Listen to him work that guy.

"But Jerry, think it through. You make me happy, you make more money. You make more money, you get to hire more employees. That's more happy employees, Jer. I mean, we're growing here. Big time. Some people grow up and they forget their roots. I'm telling you, we won't forget our roots. We won't forget." Dennis ignored the fact his last line had a twinge of threat attached. "You make more money, we make more money. We're intertwined, Jerry. If you drop your price by just a hundred dollars per each thousand units, not only do we have a deal, we have a stronger future."

Walt, still in the hallway, hidden from view from the young executive, shook his head in marvel and disbelief. *He'll never bite, Dennis.*

"Great! Awesome. You write up an invoice and I'll have my Purchasing Department get all over this. Thank you, Jerry. You won't regret it."

In the hallway, disbelief overwhelmed Walt. His zeal to confront Dennis about the cat dissipated. Based on what he had just heard, Dennis had lowered the price on the compound used on the exterior of some of their batteries. He knew to whom Dennis was speaking – a tough negotiator – and yet he had just saved the company in the neighborhood of two million dollars for a year's worth of material, provided the contract was of standard size and length.

Walt walked down the hallway toward the elevator, in thought about what he had just heard. Dennis had just tamed a shrewd negotiator. Walt remained shocked. How could this evil man be so good for the company?

• • •

The rest of his Wednesday morning passed without significant developments. Walt spent most of his time signing papers for Donna and others to keep the company moving forward. In a few instances, he learned, Dennis had signed as "Acting Chief Financial Officer." Walt did not know from where the title originated, but at the moment, he did not care. He only knew a permanent title would never be bestowed on the conniving young man.

The only time he saw Dennis was when the latter poked his head in Walt's office, smiled, then continued on his way. The acids

279

in Walt's stomach attacked upward, into Walt's esophagus, at the sight of his tormentor.

The bright spot of the day came when he received a text response from his daughter. Yes, she would meet him for dinner at a local restaurant – alone.

· · ·

"I don't understand. Why are you staying at a hotel?"

"Because I need to."

"That makes no sense." Heidi could not hide her indignation from her father.

"I don't want to go into all of that."

"You mean Dennis. You don't want to go into your paranoia about Dennis." Although he did not wish to admit it, other than the word 'paranoia,' she was right.

"No. I just mean I don't want to argue with you. You're my only child, Heidi. You're all I've got left. I'm losing my company – my livelihood – but I don't want to lose you." Though he meant every word, it was not in his nature to express feelings with the earnest plea most people would have mustered. This flatness was as loving as he could manage, at least since Tina had been killed.

"I don't understand you. I just don't get you."

"Do you remember the day your mother was killed?"

"Of course." An instant sadness permeated her, from head to toe. Her head dropped until her chin came close to her collarbone as she turned her face away. Her shoulders dropped. She exhaled through her nose as though incapable of sucking air into her lungs. Her back slumped and her legs weakened underneath the tablecloth. "I was thirteen years old. I remember when you told me."

Walt observed her as he gave her a few seconds with her memories. He understood his own weaknesses, and to speak now would make himself look colder than he really was.

"I remember every time I saw a truck on the road I was afraid it would kill me, too, until you explained that a car wrecked the semi, and that's why the semi crashed through the center divider." Her somber tone signaled a flood of memories – both difficult and happy.

"It was the deadliest accident on the 101 Freeway in something like eight years," Walt added. He paused as they both recovered from the brief pain. "Well, I never fully recovered from that. It changed your life and mine." He paused again. "Now something's happened that's changed our lives again. This guy Dennis has come around. I don't know why, but he's seen fit to date you and attack me."

Heidi tried to interrupt, but Walt plodded forward.

"Heidi, I'm passionate about my job, about my company. Bill and I built it up from nothing, with Tony's help. Then we added Alex." He paused, reflecting on those years. "There was always some reason to work harder, work longer hours." He paused again. "I've done some thinking, some reflecting. I keep reflecting, every day. I haven't been there enough for you. You've gone through this ordeal almost on your own – growing up without a mother without much help from me."

"Don't do this."

"There were times when I thought aunts or the girls' schools would help, so you went through some important years without a mother or a father. I'm truly, truly sorry for that."

"Dad."

"I'm still learning, Heidi. But I can't let go of the only person I have left. You. I've never been as good of a father as I should've been. I'm trying, Heidi, I'm really trying. But what kind of father would I be if I saw danger and didn't warn you?"

Heidi sighed and shook her head.

"You've inherited too much of my lack of emotions and not enough of your mother's tenderness." Walt meant it as a statement of fact, but Heidi winced at the perceived insult. "I didn't mean –"

"I'm fine," Heidi responded. "You don't have to protect me anymore. I'm not a little girl."

"You obviously don't understand men enough yet. Most of them are animals."

Heidi laughed. "You're probably right about that."

"I met with my attorney, and we've made a lot of ground toward exposing this guy – some things in his past. So just be aware. You're a big girl. I'm not gonna try to stop you, but just know The Law is gonna turn his life upside down real soon." The way Walt emphasized 'The Law' made it seem like a hairy monster, hiding under the bed at night. "In the short run, I'm in trouble, but my lawyer assured me we can stretch this out and close the trap on this guy," Walt lied to his daughter with a straight face. "I don't want you caught up in it," Walt returned to the truth.

"I don't understand your problem with Dennis. He's doing a good job at the company – at least that's what I've heard from Donna and the guys I know there. He's watching out for the company, which means watching out for you. I just don't get it." Energy returned to her body as she spoke. "And what's this about my cat?"

"Yeah, so the prosecution's psychologist called you." It was less question and more statement. Walt already knew the answer.

"Yes, he did. And Dennis."

"Wait a minute." The baffled look on Walt's face presaged his questions. "How did Dennis know? When did he tell you?"

"When the psychologist called me, I was at work. I left for home and called him on the way. He said you had mentioned it to some people at work. Word got around. It's a small company, dad." The sarcastic comment was designed to bite, but Walt sat fixated on the explanation itself. "When I got home the cat happened to be there, at our back door – you know how it is, it's gone for a week at a time, sometimes. So, then he called me back and –"

"Who? Who called you back?"

"The psychologist. I told him the cat was there and it was fine. I told him somebody was playing a joke. I was thinking that maybe somebody was hallucinating. We all know who that would be." Another jab; another miss.

Walt thought the matter through before he spoke. "So, I saw the cat staked to the ground yesterday morning –"

"Oh geez!" Heidi appeared tired of the entire conversation.

"I didn't tell anyone until later in the day, when I told the shrink, and yet Dennis knew. You get home and there's no evidence of any of it, leaving you and the shrink to think I was making it up or imagining it." He allowed his words to drift through the quiet restaurant. No one sat in the booths on either side of them, so the tranquil setting allowed Walt's thoughts to drift along with his words.

"You really believe Dennis killed somebody's cat?" Although it was worded as a question, it came out more an indictment.

"There's an old story about a guy who had one of his cows disappear," Walt responded. "He didn't tell anyone about it.

Finally, one day one of the neighboring farmers asked him, 'Did you ever figure out who stole your cow?' The old farmer said, "Yep. Just now."

Heidi laughed. "I'll give you credit – I've always liked your stories. They pretty much stopped after Mom died."

"Thank you. That's the nicest thing you've said about me in a while."

"But I still think you're imagining the cat. And I'm really, really afraid you've done some things you don't realize you've done." Heidi looked at her father with an icy stare.

"How can you say that?" His voice became a growl. He detested the accusation, particularly from his own daughter.

"My cat's fine, dad. It's the only one around like that. You *had* to imagine it." Her emphasis on 'had' made it clear she thought he was out-of-his-mind mad.

"You think that cat is the only one in the world that looks like that?" His voice rose by several decibels, then rose further the longer he spoke. "You think it's the only Javanese in the world? Think about it. What are the odds your cat comes back just at the perfect time for you to know it wasn't your cat on the lawn, convincing you the whole thing didn't even happen? What are the odds it shows up yesterday morning, after I see a dead Javanese that morning? Hmm? You think maybe the whole point of all this is to make me *look* insane?" The word 'look' was uttered at a volume level high enough to gain the attention of other patrons. "I didn't go into the office, Heidi. I didn't tell anyone except the shrink about the cat."

Heidi squirmed in her seat at the sudden rush of anger she witnessed from her father. "Hold it down, please, or you're going to prove everyone's point."

284

"Everyone's point?" His voice remained loud. "You mean yours and Dennis' point. And you convinced the cops, who planted the seed with my lawyer. Then that psychologist, who saw what he wanted to see, was more of an advocate than anything. It was ridiculous." By his last word, he was again too loud for Heidi's comfort level.

"All right. All right. That's enough. Keep it down or I'm out," she hissed through clenched teeth.

"You've never even tried to be on my side." Walt's accusation stung her.

"I can't help it. I don't think you're acting rationally." She fought back tears.

"Try having your best friend and your two business partners murdered, then be accused of killing your best friend, if not all three. Try it some time. It's a real blast, Heidi. And you're siding with my main accuser." The realization hit Walt that he was attacking his daughter; this was not his intention. "I'm sorry, Heidi. I truly am. I'm just deeply hurt you're siding with this guy. He's made it clear I have to commit suicide by Friday or – well, he hasn't said it, but he's implied that he'll kill me."

"Are we back to that? Your paranoia? Your obsession with Dennis and some mythical bet? Then I'm done with you! You're *insane!*" She did not utter another word. She threw down her napkin in disgust and stormed out of the restaurant in an emotional mish-mash of anger, frustration, and resignation. Tears filled her eyes and ran down her cheeks, but Walt could only see her backside as she fled the eating establishment. The waitress managed to dodge the speeding Heidi just enough to avoid being bowled over.

"Is everything okay, sir?" the young waitress inquired.

"No. Not really," Walt answered in the typical flat tone he used when emotions confronted him. "I don't think she's coming back. Let's start with your beers. What do you have?"

• • •

I've got to be insane. That's got to be the answer! Walt yelled at himself in his thoughts. *Nothing else makes – well, if it wasn't for Bretz and that whole thing, I wouldn't think so. But I* remember *him being there. I* remember *that cat. I remember!*

Walt looked around the small, dumpy motel room. Another night, a different fleabag motel. The time arrived to have a conversation with himself – a time which seemed to occur on a regular basis. *But I couldn't have killed Bill and Alex! I couldn't have killed Tony! Maybe Troy.* He laughed out loud at his quasi-joke. Within a half-second, the laughter flitted away like a butterfly in the wind and the angry, confused man grabbed the thin, worn comforter off the bed and slung it against the wall. The quiet temper tantrum did nothing to assuage the pressure building in his head.

Think this through, he yelled in his thoughts again. *Forget Bretz. Something's wrong there. What about Bill. The cops woke me up. That's the first I knew about it.* He flung the television remote against the far wall, which was only a few feet away. The battery fell out and lay on the floor. A crack extended across the plastic remote control to both ends of the device. *There's no hockey on tonight, anyway.*

He paused his thoughts to redirect them, then continued with his self-flagellation and attempt at self-analysis. *I would never kill Bill or Alex. There's nothing inside me capable of that. Nothing!* A distraction entered his mind. *It's Dennis. Everyone warns me about Dennis. Hell, Dennis warns me about Dennis. He's out of his mind crazy! And he must have had help! That DeWinters guy! Dennis hired him. He must have!*

Walt rose from his seat on the bed. He grabbed a lamp next to the bed and smashed it with all his might into the carpeted floor. *And that's how Dennis is going to get away with it. He's probably hired somebody else now! He's going to get away with all these murders!*

Plastic and metal sprayed the room. The lack of a crashing sound surprised the mentally deteriorating man, yet he felt better after the release of adrenaline. He looked down at his hand and saw what remained of the mangled appliance formerly recognizable as a lamp. He sucked in a deep breath, realizing he had just pulled off the quietest outburst of anger in his life.

Yet the same problems remained.

Scattered on the floor lay an assortment of sharp objects which could come back to haunt Walt if he chose to leave his bed before daylight returned. He walked to the small, flimsy table at the end of the room where he had set his wallet. He pulled out a one-hundred-dollar bill and then scribbled out a note of apology to the proprietor of the motel. After a scan of the room, he returned the hundred to his wallet and set down a twenty.

Chapter 37

Walt turned the key to the ignition and backed out of his parking space. The little dump of a motel in Simi Valley served its purpose. Despite not knowing Simi very well, and after recovering from his little outburst, which included the highlight of breaking a ten-dollar lamp, Walt felt refreshed from a good night of sleep.

Thursday morning; he felt strong. Two nights in cheap motels, but two nights of good sleep. No bed bugs; no noisy neighbors; he was two-for-two when it came to dives to rest his head. He never saw bugs, and at the moment he did not care either way.

As he prepared to pull onto Cochran Street he put on his turn signal. The small *clicking* sound was replaced as a distraction within a quarter of a second by the blue powder that shot upward from his feet and out of the air conditioner vents. In another two seconds the entire driver's compartment filled with fine, blue chalk.

Choking and unable to see, Walt was fortunate his car sat stationary at the time of the mini-explosion.

He thought by parking his car in the back of the motel, away from the main street, no one would find him. With the great number of small motels throughout southern California, he believed 25 miles would be far enough to travel. He was mistaken. His adversary had found him – and had won another mental victory.

• • •

When Walt received the call at his office, he felt dazed by the request. Special Agent Bretz wanted to speak with him in the Ventura office, but no one else should know about the meeting or the call. His first reaction was to imagine walking into Dennis'

288

office to announce that he had an errand to run, just to gauge Dennis' reaction. Would Fry be surprised to not see blue powder all over the elder executive? *No, he'll know I went home and cleaned up*. Fearing his BMW Z4 Roadster was also booby-trapped, Walt had called Uber for a ride to work.

After nixing the idea of going to Dennis' office, Walt let Donna know of his departure and ventured out, into the unknown. Was it a trap? Was it good news? Was there hope?

He called his mechanic, who was still at Walt's house wrapping up work. The mechanic confirmed the BMW was free from blue chalk or other surprises and it would be driven to the office forthwith. Cleaning the Lexus was already underway by an auto detailer. *I'm resourceful, Dennis, don't you forget it*, he told himself. *And I'm not telling anybody about this.*

• • •

Walt drove his BMW north on the 101 Freeway with the same questions from the office, and more, on his mind. If this was a trap, what did it matter? *Once the FBI is after you, it's over. What good news could they possibly give me, unless they have something on Dennis?* At this point, he was unwilling to hold out hope.

After his arrival and subsequent audience in front of three federal agents, he took the time to review his surroundings. The conference room was not as posh as those at Triumvirate. In fact, everything he encountered in the building seemed rather plain. He found himself in an old, low-back wheeled chair, across from Bretz and two serious-looking agents. The old carpet did not look terrible, but it did not look impressive, either.

Walt's dazed mental state was at the top of the agenda.

"First," the high-pitched voice said with all sincerity, "I apologize that I lied to your attorney." Bretz grimaced. "It's not what I normally do, but we're in a situation here. We think we've got some information that'll help us with Fry's whereabouts on the night of Tony's murder, but we're afraid he'll be tipped off, even if by accident."

"You don't trust my attorney?" Walt asked.

"Mel Harvey? He's okay. He's not a bad attorney. I was kinda surprised you went with him, but hey, that's not my area." Bretz laughed. "He looks like a slob and acts like a slob until he puts on that Superman cape in court. Then I hear he's pretty good. He's just got a big mouth. Then there's Encarnacion. A good cop. Helluva detective. But he's always under-staffed, so he'll take shortcuts, including relying too much on anyone who comes to him. I don't want Fry going to him again and Rob slips and says something he shouldn't. Better he doesn't know."

Bretz looked at his fellow agents. "Oh. I'm sorry. This is Agent Bauml. This is Agent Boles. They're on the Fry case. Well, technically it's the Harris case, but like you, Tony and I were good friends, so I don't like to think about the fact that he's dead." Bretz grimaced again.

"I have a question," the dark-haired, mustached Agent Bauml announced, his voice deeper than what would be expected of his average size.

"Wait a minute, wait a minute," Walt interrupted. A prior statement from Bretz just now made it to the part of Walt's brain that interpreted language. "You lied to my attorney. About what?"

"That our meeting at your house never took place," Bretz responded. He looked surprised Walt missed the reference.

Walt felt his shoulders and back lighten. Having felt as though a Mini-Cooper were strapped to his back every waking minute, the weight now disappeared. He fought the urge to cry – until recent events, something he had not done since Tina's death.

"You're saying you were there? At my house?" His voice fell to almost a whisper. Amazement and relief combined to leap out of every pore.

Bretz glanced at his cohorts. "Man, they have you messed up in the head, don't they?"

Hands shaking, Walt dropped his head and looked at the table in front of him. He sucked in a loud, long breath. "Yes." The response was quiet. Heart-felt. Painful. He stroked his beard once before tremors of relief hit him.

The hardened agents were also human. They let the moment last so Walt could feel it, savor it. They understood his need for recovery and quiet celebration.

Twenty seconds passed. "You okay, Walt?"

The proud, battered businessman lifted his head. His eyes were red and moist. "Yes." His voice cracked. His spirits lifted. For the first time since Bill's murder, hope dripped into his heart and flowed into his arteries. "Yes." Stronger. Clearer. "I'm fine. A little stunned. Relieved – big-time. I'm fine." *I don't have split personalities! Damn right!*

Bretz looked at his partners. "Agent Bauml?"

In a softer tone, Bauml asked, "What's the worst threat Dennis Fry's made against you?"

"That I'd better commit suicide, or else."

"Or else?" Bauml followed up.

"He didn't say. He just implied he'd kill me."

Bauml nodded.

"Boles?" Bretz asked.

291

"We've run current information: criminal history – he has none; financial records; the like." The tall, bulky agent had a voice to match. Large hands, large ears, and a deep voice made the man with African roots a formidable sight. "I'm charged with researching his past. We have a good lay of the land, but I'll be digging deeper. Much deeper. I'll be starting that later today. We're just wrapping up a case in the Inland Empire and I have to tie up a few loose ends."

"I heard you guys were in Riverside. I'm glad you're back." Walt let out a quiet chuckle. The relief he felt lingered. The news about the meeting at his house altered his outlook. "But I do have a serious concern. Today's Thursday." To Walt, the statement carried significant meaning. To the agents, he stated an obvious observation about the calendar. "Tomorrow is the day I'm supposed to commit suicide. Tomorrow is the deadline. He says he's serious about it. We don't have a lot of time."

"I'll make this a priority," Agent Boles reassured him.

"Here's my hunch," Bretz offered. "This guy didn't materialize out of thin air, and everyone has a motive." Despite having met multiple times, Bretz was in his "serious FBI agent" mode. "Sometimes they're sociopaths or psychopaths, but there's always a reason, or a catalyst. We already started on his criminal history, thanks to Tony's prodding." He motioned to Boles. "Agent Boles took care of that at the time, but we got extremely busy. I fell down on my end of the bargain, and I'm sorry."

"What matters is we get it done," Walt volunteered, returning the sympathetic courtesy he had received moments ago.

"Tony told me he was looking into Fry's history, but now he's dead. That may not mean anything," Bretz continued. "But it might. So, now we can focus on this – now that this is a full-blown case for us – it wasn't before – we can get it done right." Bretz looked at his counterparts for backup.

"My job is to provide surveillance," Bauml said. "Apparently, I have one of those faces. I just blend in." The agents laughed.

Walt studied Bauml's face and judged the pronouncement to be correct.

"I'm going to surveil Fry," Bauml continued. "I'll be switching up vehicles and looks, and I'll keep an eye on him. Who knows? Maybe at some point I won't care whether he sees me – maybe it'll suit my needs that he sees me; but for now, I'll lay low."

"As I said, I'll be digging deeper into his past," Boles jumped in. "That may send me across the country, but I'll tap into our records and track down his family, his history, and do some interviews. I'll figure out what drives this guy."

"And I'll coordinate these two," Bretz added. "And I'll stay in touch with you, let you know what you need to know for your safety."

"And deny our meetings?" Musgrave said with a laugh.

"Only if necessary," Bretz laughed. "They really messed you up."

"I had a psychologist telling me certain things didn't happen. My lawyer's telling me I need to plead 'guilty by reason of insanity' because our meeting didn't happen. Yeah, I'm a bit messed up." Musgrave displayed a lack of bitterness.

"I am sorry," Bretz said in a slow cadence, his sincerity evident. "But I did what was necessary."

Walt sighed. "I understand. And I'll keep my mouth shut. In the meantime, we gotta keep me out of jail. Apparently, the only reason I'm not in jail is because of the judge I drew."

The agents smiled. "You're not in jail because Boles here made a couple of calls and called in some favors. That's how you got the judge, and how the judge heard from us before the hearing," Bretz explained.

Walt's eyebrows shot toward his hairline. "Are you kidding?"

"No." The emphatic answer by Bretz left no doubt. "We knew. We understood. We just didn't know this would mess with your mind so bad."

Walt laughed. "My life is so insane right now." He cocked his head. "Maybe I ought not use that word."

They all laughed. Walt felt a rush of satisfaction just by having the ability to laugh, yet tears again filled his eyes.

"Okay, listen," Bretz said, bringing the conversation back on course. "Because of the secrecy we want about Fry, don't talk about this meeting to anyone. Not anyone. Your daughter. Rose Bakkeby. Anyone."

"Rose? How do you know about Rose?!" Walt looked at each agent, dumbfounded.

Bauml grinned. "We're the FBI. We know everything. Well, almost everything."

"Almost," Boles chimed in. "And what we don't know, we learn – if we need to."

"I'm glad you're on my side," Walt chuckled, still amazed at the revelation.

"We're glad you're innocent," Bretz said, no humor in his voice.

• • •

During his drive back to the office, Walt rejoiced in the knowledge he was sane, after all. His mind slipped back to the beer-induced thoughts during the televised hockey game. *If I'm not crazy, the evidence in the house had to be planted by someone. That someone must – must! – be Dennis Fry! Pretty soon the police and the Prosecution will know I didn't kill Tony. The conversation* did *take place. I'm sane. I am* sane*!* The repetitious thoughts bounced around in the elated man's head.

One problem existed: the matter of multiple personalities. To the psychologist and prosecution, Walt still could have carried out the murders, even after the existence of the conversation with Bretz would be made known during the trial.

Despite his concerns, Walt's brain felt a newfound freedom. Sanity was real, not imagined; however, a paradox arose when sadness overcame him. This knowledge of sanity gave him time to focus on other thoughts, which provided the freedom to further grieve the loss of his dear friend, Tony.

•   •   •

"You shouldn't be here, you shouldn't be talking to me, and I resent the fact you've accosted me in public." Angela Rosario made her points with a firm and harsh crispness which Walt could not miss.

"I'm terribly sorry," Walt said. "But you have to hear me out."

"No I don't!" Rosario quickened her pace in a bid to distance herself from her adversary. The short, thin woman's steps clicked on the concrete, her high heels protesting the pace. Her business suit and heavy briefcase also fought the speed of her steps.

"But Ms. Rosario, I –"

"I don't care what you have to say." She stopped to face her pursuer. "You are represented by legal counsel. I will not speak to you. End of story." Her emphasis on 'will not' failed to sway Walt.

"I'll sign a waiver. I don't care. I care about justice. This is not a game to me!" One block from the courthouse, most people in the area were coming and going to that building. "I'm an innocent man, Ms. Rosario."

Had the reserved parking lot not been full at the moment, Rosario would not have found herself in this situation; she would have been able to park in the courthouse parking lot. Instead, the long walk played into Walt's hands. "That's for a court of law to decide, not a conversation on the sidewalk." Her brown eyes cut like razor blades into Walt's eyes. She resumed her stride, confident she had made her point.

To Walt, she had not. Within seconds, he was again at her shoulder. "I'm not here to argue the case."

"I'm not speaking to you, Mister Musgrave."

"That's fine. But you'll listen." Walt's indignant tone, though strong, meant nothing to the prosecutor. She was seasoned enough to have experienced most of the uncomfortable situations one could imagine.

She reached for her purse. "I'm calling Mel Harvey."

"Screw Mel Harvey. All I'm here to tell you is you're going about this the wrong way. Watch me. I don't care. But watch my house, even when I'm not there."

She persisted in digging through her phone contact list in an effort to reach Walt's attorney.

"Watch my house and you'll start catching on."

She stopped again. "Tell that to the Sheriff's Department."

"They won't talk to me, either, but I know you're in control. You can make it happen. So, do it. Forget winning or losing a case. Let's find out who killed my business partners and attorney. Watch my house."

Rosario resumed her angry walk toward the courthouse, cell phone against her cheek. "Mel. This is Angela Rosario. We need to talk. I'm going into court for a Motion to Compel on another case, but your guy Musgrave is harassing me on my way to the courthouse. I'm trying to get rid of him and he won't –" She turned to look. Walt was not in sight. "I'm trying to get rid of him. He's gone now. This is ridiculous. Call me. This can't happen again."

Chapter 38

At another low-budget motel, another hockey game graced the television screen. The play-by-play piped out of the speaker at a low volume. The light over the dresser filled the room. Southern California's other hockey team skated across the screen – a team Walt loved to hate.

The phone on the nightstand rang out its relatively quiet electronic tone, announcing a caller. No one should know about this motel; Walt had been meticulous in not only maintaining his privacy, but in taking a tortured, zig-zag route to the seedy Van Nuys location.

The ringing continued. The Anaheim Ducks scored a goal, but no one was in the room to notice. None of Walt's possessions was in the room. The ringing stopped.

Thirty minutes later, the phone rang, again to no response. Walt, at long last, had managed to advance one step ahead of his pursuer.

• • •

"You okay?"

Walt failed to notice he was staring off into space – he stared at the wall across the room, which included family photographs, but he did not focus on any particular item. "Yeah, I'm fine. It's been a good day, overall."

His cell phone rang. "Oh. Shoot. Forgot to silence it. I'm sorry."

"Don't worry about it," Rose said, her concern evident. "That's quite a story about the FBI. What do you think will happen next?"

"I don't have a feel for it either way," Walt said, thinking back to what he had just relayed to Rose. "I'm the prime suspect in Tony's murder. Dennis made up some cockamamie story about me having multiple personalities and all of a sudden you'd think he's Sigmund Freakin' Freud. This is crazy." He shook his head in disgust. "If it wasn't for that judge, I wouldn't be a free man right now." He had left her uninformed of certain details concerning the FBI.

Rose climbed out of her chair and joined Walt on the couch. She sat next to him and slid her arm around his waist. After a brief time with her head on his shoulder, she pulled back and looked at him with an expression of someone just hit with an epiphany. "Who would've thought, thirty years or so ago, that we'd be together again without us fighting all the time? I mean, I know we're not *together* together, but you know what I mean."

Walt cackled as though she told a classic joke. "Yes, I know what you mean. And no, I wouldn't have believed it, either."

Neither hesitated. The stoic, exhausted man and the jaded, neglected woman flowed together like two forks of a river coming together to make one. The long, passionate kiss was interrupted by the announcement from Walt's cell phone of a voicemail message. With the deftness of a teenager with his girlfriend, he reached into his pocket and tossed the phone onto a distant chair. The phone bounced off the chair and made a small *thud* onto the floor.

"Sorry. I still didn't silence it."

Rose pulled back. "It's your attorney, isn't it?"

"Probably."

"You should answer it."

"No, I shouldn't." Walt moved his face to hers and kissed her again.

Again, she pulled back. "Walter, you're going to be staying here for as long as necessary. I'll be here. Listen to your voicemail in case it's important. It's after ten o'clock, for Pete's sake."

Perplexed, Walt argued as he rolled off the couch and onto the floor. "This is at least the third message he's left." He climbed to his feet. "He just wants to chew me out for talking to that prosecutor."

"But what if it's something else? What if he has important news?" Rose did not hide her serious tone. "I mean it, Walt. You need to make sure."

Walt picked up the iPhone and used the touch screen until he found the message. Phone to ear, he listened. Within seconds, he moved the phone away.

"I only listened to the third one. He's lecturing. He's pissed. I don't care."

"I know that look," Rose said with a smirk. "You're gonna do what Walt wants to do."

"It's my life on the line."

"But you have the FBI on your side," she pleaded for reasonableness. "You don't have to worry."

"Rose." He walked toward the couch. "Rose darling, you always were the optimist, but a little naïve." He sat next to her. "Tomorrow's Friday. Tomorrow's the day. THE day."

She understood, even without his dramatic delivery.

"So how come he never calls your cell phone?" she asked.

"I've thought about that. I think he wants me to know that he knows where I am by calling the landline wherever I am. Plus, it might have something to do with tracking calls. I don't know."

"That makes no sense. Landlines can be tracked by the authorities."

"Yeah, I don't know. I guess he wants me to know the call isn't random. I guess."

Rose's face showed she did not know what to make of his answers.

He looked at the floor.

"What is it?"

"Oh, it keeps popping into my mind what a lousy father I am."

"No! Why? Because of how Heidi acted in the restaurant?" They were both secretly amused by the defensiveness for Walt in Rose's voice.

"How else can I spin it? I can't. I failed." The melancholy delivery matched Walt's mood.

"Do you ever wonder," it was apparent Rose was thinking out loud. "About other people? About how they got the way they are? Do you ever wonder what made Dennis Fry, Dennis? Do you ever wonder what his family was like?"

Walt looked at her as though she were an alien announcing its arrival. "No." The laconic answer summed up the entire subject, in Walt's mind.

"No. I'm serious. What drives a guy like him to be this way? We don't know he was behind that other guy killing Bill and Alex, but you're pretty sure he killed Tony. Why? What makes somebody do that?" Rose crinkled her nose, in thought. "I mean, I get – it's not right, but I get it – I get killing someone because you hate them because you think they killed a loved one or something, but what did Tony do to Dennis? What did you do to Dennis? He's obviously torturing you. Why? Why would someone do that? I just don't get it."

301

Walt shook his head as he looked up at her. "He's an adult. That's all that matters. Besides, tomorrow's the day," Walt said, repeating his earlier thought. "That's all that matters right now."

She inhaled a nervous breath. "Do you really believe he's serious?"

"Rose." He gazed into her eyes as memories flashed by before he continued. "Bill, Alex, and Tony are all dead. I'm next. Their deaths aren't coincidence. You said it yourself. You understand. He's the guy."

A tear ran down her left cheek. He leaned over and kissed it. Walt's gentleness had been missing since Tina's passing. Only Rose could resurrect that side of him. "Rose, do you know how much I loved you when we were young? But we just couldn't be together, in the same room, for very long. After this is all over, let's try to overcome that. Can we? We're adults now."

She leaned into him and resumed the passion they had shared before the cell phone had uttered its rude interruption. She held a tight grip on one arm and on his shoulder blade. He understood her fears; he understood that grip.

A phone rang with the loud, piercing ring of a 1970s-era telephone. Startled, Walt jerked away from Rose enough for her to notice.

Laughing as she climbed to her feet, Rose let out a gentle rebuke. "It's my home phone, silly." She laughed again as she scampered across the room and answered it.

While Walt did not share in the amusement to the same degree Rose did, he felt a slight embarrassment about his reaction. *I'm getting too jumpy,* he thought. *Tomorrow's* the *day, and I'm letting that dirtbag get to me.* He ignored Rose's end of the brief exchange until he heard one word.

302

"Flowers?"

That's what I should've done. I should've sent her flowers. Well, too late now.

"Walter, did you send me flowers? There's flowers at the front gate."

He shook his head for her to see. Then, a switch moved in Walt's brain. He leaped from the couch and hurried to Rose's side, shaking his head back and forth as he hustled over.

"Hang on just one moment, please," Rose spoke into the phone before dropping it to her side and covering the mouthpiece with her hip. "If you didn't, I don't know who did. I guess we're about to find out."

Before she could remove the phone's handset from her hip, Walt cried out a sharp, "No!"

A baffled look came over Rose's face.

Walt's brain and mouth synchronized. "It's him. It's Dennis. He's figured out I'm here – or at least he's fishing. If you don't think there's anyone else who'd send you flowers, that means it's him. And besides, who delivers flowers this late?" A seriousness took hold of Walt and his demeanor changed from a concerned man to someone who knew the *appointed hour* approached.

Rose had never seen him with such a look in his eyes. Without looking away from him, she put the phone to her jaw and conveyed her verdict to the delivery man. "Uh. Sir." She could not hide the fear. Words seemed to escape her. "Uh, we uh. I can't take them. Sorry. Can you, uh, can you send them back to where they came from, please?"

"Is there a note?" Walt inquired.

"Is there a note?" Rose repeated. After a brief delay, she continued. "No. That's okay. Leave it sealed, please. Thank you." In embarrassment she added, "I'm so sorry." Without hesitation, she returned the handset to its cradle. "Oh God, Walt. You seriously think it's him?"

"Yeah, I do. He finds me wherever I go. It's him."

After a slow stroll to the couch, which felt like a death march to both, they sat together again. This time, Rose left space between them and studied her old flame.

"You seem to be scared and angry. But there's this determination, isn't there?" Rose's gaze did not break away.

Walt's eyes met hers as he responded. "I've run the gamut emotionally, but I've decided although I may go down, I'll go down fighting."

The couple spent the next several hours conversing as Walt laid out his thoughts. Walt did most of the talking, but he valued Rose's input and gained ideas. As the night wore on, the words were repeated multiple times: "But I'll go down fighting."

• • •

The motel's design allowed for outside access to each room. The old building did not have interior hallways; patrons parked in front of their rooms if they so desired. Walt's blue Lexus GS 300 sat in front of Room 113 – a ground-floor room. The expensive car stood out like a purple penguin in Antarctica.

A silhouette on foot entered the parking lot. The appearance was that of a person on a casual stroll, despite the late hour. The man looked around for witnesses, then stopped in front of Room 113. He moved around in an attempt to peer through or around the blinds. No matter where he positioned himself, he seemed to fail at gaining a desirable view.

After two minutes of effort, the man stepped between two cars. The light of a cell phone glowed like a torch in the darkened lot. The phone in the room rang until the figure tapped the screen and walked away. Confirmation of the correct room had been made.

At 3:04 a.m., the man crossed the parking lot and disappeared past a few trees which separated the motel from a lot belonging to a small strip mall. He would have gone undetected if not for the large camera and night-vision equipment in the possession of Agent Bauml, who sat in his car, parked in the perfect position to witness the entire episode.

Agent Bauml drove onto the road in time to see a car ahead do the same. His shadowy figure, no doubt. He gunned the engine in an attempt to close the distance, but a quick turn by the unknown vehicle onto a perpendicular street followed by an immediate right-hand turn onto the 101 Freeway left the FBI agent's car alone on the dark street. He followed the same path but realized Walt Musgrave's pursuer had vanished into the night.

The agent drove around for several minutes, in case the individual returned or parked nearby. He knew pursuing on the freeway would have been pointless – while the streets sat empty at that late hour, enough cars and trucks utilized the freeway to cause confusion about which taillights he should have been following.

Agent Bauml returned to Walt's car and began the search for a GPS tracking device. He started with the rear bumper. With the aid of a flashlight, he immediately found the device.

Chapter 39

He stared straight ahead; he did not know what to do. He knew this was the day. THE day. Dennis had not dropped by Walt's office to drive home the point – a dearth of conversation which made the bearded man all the more uptight. The phone rang, causing Walt to jump like a nervous teenage girl watching a slasher movie.

"Walt Musgrave." He paused to hear the Department of Defense official identify himself, then throw in a nicety about his return to the office. "Yeah, this is my first week back. I was off for two weeks. I just had to get away for a while."

The voice on the other end reached its limit of small talk. He gave Walt the news, followed by a brief explanation.

"Yeah, after all my company's been through, I expected you'd reject the contract." He paused as his brain raced through a checklist of emotions, ensuring they were all below expected limits. "We would've made a great partner with DOD, so I hate to hear it, but we'll get our house in order and work with you guys in the future." Walt did not have to put on an act; he accepted – even welcomed – the decision.

The call concluded after the brief exchange. The receiver landed with an easy drop into its cradle. A sardonic smile – almost a sneer – decorated his face. Despite the loss of the contract, Walt felt a sense of peace flood his frame. The negotiations, the audits, the headaches – they were over. Relief. Finality.

Then a thought – an inescapable, persistent germ of a thought – mushroomed from a tiny seed into an urgent directive that must be handled immediately.

He could not wait. Within five seconds, the original thought grew to maturation and propelled him to his feet. Into the hallway, down the elevator, and down another hallway. Before he thought through the complexities of the matter, he stood outside Dennis' office and rapped on the open door. No matter Dennis sat only a few feet away; this was official business.

"Are you aware of DOD's decision regarding our contract with them?" Walt asked, curious whether Dennis had been alerted first.

"Decision? I thought this was a done deal. The IRS stuff was just a formality, right?" Dennis had the look of a serious businessman, buried in his work.

"They declined to proceed with our contract. They said we had too many problems. They said with all the deaths of our top people, we weren't in a position to move forward at a professional level." Walt paused as he considered that last statement. "I hate the sound of that, but I'm inclined to agree."

Dennis stood. "But Walt. This company can handle it. We *need* that contract." His emphasis on 'need' struck Walt as though Dennis flirted with desperation. "We're fine. We've had some adversity – we'll be okay."

"Even if you lost the final top executive?" He raised his eyebrows. His tone scraped at Dennis' ears. The point hit home.

Dennis glared at the final member of the triumvirate. "Even if we lost our final top executive." His eyes narrowed. Dennis the Businessman mentally exited; Dennis the Menace to Society stood in defiance. "We still have three junior executives, counting myself."

"Yeah, but the other two only recently received real responsibilities." Walt saw Dennis about to argue. "Don't worry about it, Dennis." Walt's voice sounded reassuring.

A quizzical look crossed the younger man's face. During the brief silence, Dennis relaxed. "Okay," he responded, his facial expression telegraphed he did not know what to make of the momentary truce.

But the truce, a fleeting respite between two combatants, indeed slipped away. "There's no need for you to worry, Dennis." A haughty expression and firm voice backed Walt's words. "You don't work here anymore. You're fired, effective immediately. You have twenty minutes to be off the property, and you will not be allowed back." Walt paused for effect. "Ever."

Before Dennis could respond, the doorway stood empty. By the time the doorway was filled again, with Dennis' frame, Walt had disappeared from sight, on his way to alert security of the ejection of one Dennis Fry.

After notifying security, Walt walked to the break room, where a muted television broadcast images of sports action from the previous night. He stopped at two different tables to engage in small talk with his employees. They appreciated his care and concern for them, unaware his real motivation was the need for witnesses in case Dennis found him and uttered threats.

Dennis left the building, unnoticed and without incident. Within the hour, Walt sent an email to the employees announcing the departure as a "change in direction."

Ah, freedom. First the excessive weight of the federal government disappeared from his back and shoulders; now someone whom he believed to be a killer had left the scene. He felt invigorated. Alive. He thought back to Special Agent Bretz's admission he was indeed present at Walt's house, hiding in the shadows, taking in the threats of Dennis Fry.

Former employee Dennis Fry.

• • •

'FBI Bretz' showed up on Walt's cell phone while the theme to the old TV show *Dragnet* blared and filled his den.

"Curtis, how are ya?" He placed the call on "speaker" and rested the phone on his desk.

"Never better, Walt. Never better," came the disembodied reply. "How about you?"

"I'm happy – just a little concerned." Walt took stock of THE day, as it had progressed thus far. "Not bad for a guy who just fired the guy who wants me dead today."

"This will cheer you up even more," Bretz offered. "My team has been a little busy. Fry has 40 bank accounts – 40 on the dot – under various names in order to dodge the IRS and to throw off, he thinks, anyone who investigates him." He chuckled as he delivered the news. "It seems that Movie Man mostly watched older movies. Had he watched newer ones, maybe newer TV shows, he would've better understood how things work. I predicted this to Detective Encarnacion. I called this one."

Walt raised an eyebrow. "What do you mean?"

"Fry paid Bruce Ellis Desmond a day after Bill was killed and again after Alex was killed, and there are a couple of people who were around Fry who were murdered before he came here. We're looking at one now while he was at UC Davis. A person with information says he's Troy Gustafson's cousin. He steered us in the right direction." Bretz paused. Noises over the phone sounded like pages turning. "We're still trying to piece it all together. It's separate from you; apparently, some people who crossed him."

Walt sat up straighter in his chair and looked toward the entrance of the den, hoping no one else could hear, even though he knew he was alone in the house.

"I suspect he may have killed Desmond to tie off the loose end," Bretz added. "Things are looking up. The proof is piling up that Fry is a bad actor."

"Wow! So, you think he really did murder someone?!" Walt asked with amazement. He could not disguise his hope.

"I'm not prepared to go that far yet. We're still working," Bretz said. "Even if he didn't, we're building circumstantial evidence that he paid someone to kill for him."

Walt smiled until Bretz continued. "But don't forget, we have to convince a DA to press charges. No guarantees with that; it's still just circumstantial. At least for now."

"Well," Walt said, looking for the positive. "It's better than nothing. I guess."

"Oh, big time. It's better than what we knew yesterday," Bretz's cheerful voice pitched higher as he spoke. "We'll keep digging, but things are looking up."

"Sounds good to me," Walt agreed. "I like good news."

"Oh. Another thing," the FBI agent interjected, his energy still high. "There was a tracking device on the rear bumper of your Lexus. The person who scoped out your motel room last night slipped away before Agent Bauml could identify him. Whoever it was tried to see into your room. Anyway, Agent Bauml found the GPS tracking device and we're tracing that now through the manufacturer to see who purchased it."

Walt smiled. A feeling of warmth – genuine happiness – welled up inside his gut and spread throughout his body.

"You there?" Bretz called out.

"I'm here. Just happy and weighing it all out," Walt answered, an excitement in his voice which neither man missed.

"I have a little more," Bretz added. "A stolen car was recovered outside Palmdale, in the desert. The Sheriff's Department up there checked it out and found traces of blood in the trunk. Long story short, it was Troy Gustafson's blood. The car was wiped clean, except the trunk, like someone wanted us to find out Troy had been in it." Bretz paused.

Oh boy. Here it comes. Every muscle in Walt's body tensed up.

"The car was a 2010 Mercedes that belonged to a Garrett Teasdale. Ever heard of him?"

"Not that I know of," Walt answered.

"He bought that Mercedes used from a dealership," Bretz continued the story. "It was your old Mercedes, stolen off the street from Teasdale. You sold it to the dealership and they turned around and sold it to Teasdale. Somebody stole the car, then transported Gustafson, whether dead or alive at the time we still don't know, and wanted us – wanted you – to know about the connection to you. Weird. Very weird."

"Very Dennis." Walt felt relief at the knowledge Bretz could not see his red face or trembling hands. *He just tries to get to me any way he can.*

"Don't worry about it," Bretz counseled, although the reassurance of his voice was lost over the cell phone. "But I did want you to know. Whoever it is – Dennis, I assume – is just messing with your mind. That's all."

Oh, that's all! Walt's emotions crashed into a heap of convulsing contradictions. Fury. Fear. Relief. Frustration. Happiness. And the desire to commit murder.

"All right, well, I just wanted to give you an update," Bretz added. "I got into a bad habit with Tony. I'm not supposed to be giving these updates, but I figured you could use the peace of mind."

Walt heard the door to the garage open. "Yes. Thank you. I better go. We'll chat later."

"Sounds good," the disembodied voice responded.

Walt pushed the button to end the call. Just as he did, Heidi entered the den.

"I'm sorry I lost it at the restaurant."

Warmth and encouragement flooded Walt, but he knew his daughter enough to know a 'but' was coming. "It's okay, honey. What matters to me is our relationship." The concern of the father flowed like a river, swollen after a strong thunderstorm.

"But I still don't understand you and Dennis. Why did you fire him?" Her face pulsated with anger. Her narrowed eyes and clenched teeth made clear her question was a statement – a declaration.

"I've always made it a habit not to discuss business with you. Nothing against you, it's just that –"

"Don't give me that," Heidi hissed. "You're dodging the question. You didn't have a problem telling me about the so-called 'bet.'" Her face appeared innocent enough when she had apologized, but now she stood in the den, at the end of Walt's desk, looking down at him in anger. The apology was long-forgotten. She now lapsed into the rage displayed at the restaurant. She had not wasted time switching emotions from the doorway to the brief walk to the edge of his desk. Her face now appeared as that of a woman scorned.

Walt tensed up as he rose from the chair. "Do you know why I never knocked you around or abused you? Respect." Walt was just getting started. "Do you know why I've worked hard and why I've provided for you every way I know? Love." He stepped toward his daughter, which caused her to take a step backward, a frightened look on her face. "Do you know why I've informed you about Dennis and what he's done to me? Or at least tried to do to me? Caring. I care about your well-being and I'm concerned about his motives."

She gulped, anger still plastered across her face, yet unable to retaliate with words.

"I'm not always right, Heidi," Walt said, a firmness in his voice. "But I have your best interest in mind. You know why I think Dennis doesn't? Because he doesn't have my best interest in mind." He stepped back and sat down in his chair. "Think about that, Heidi. Think about what that means. Think about what I've been through – what my friends have been through – and then think about how concerned I am for your safety."

Heidi let out a loud sigh. She took another step back. "Okay, fine." Neither seemed to understand what the statement meant, but Walt considered it a minor victory. "I'll talk to you more about Dennis later, but I still think it's unfair that you fired him."

"Okay." Walt had no desire to prolong the conversation. If anything, he failed to understand her weak attack. *She just gave up*.

"Aunt Jean messaged me on Facebook. Did you know your ex-wife, Stacy, died?"

With abrupt force, Walt stood up again. "Stacy died?! When? I didn't know that. When did this happen?" The excitement in his voice was not of happiness, rather of surprise. He despised the woman, but did not wish her demise.

"Does that make you happy?" Heidi teased, a brutal harshness in her voice.

"No. Not at all. I'm just shocked. I thought she'd live forever. She was too hateful and spiteful to die." Multiple memories – mostly bad ones – slipped in and out of his mind. There was a brief period, perhaps six or eight months, when he thought he loved her. Instead, he discovered her manipulative powers and false charm. Once they were married, it were as though a switch had been thrown. She became a different person. A difficult person. A vicious, demanding, unlovable demon seemed to possess her.

"You all right?" Heidi observed his eye movements and motionless body.

"Yeah. I'm just glad we didn't have any children. Geez! Then I'd have to deal with all that visitation crap and I'd be seeing her every week or month or whatever. Holy crap!"

Heidi laughed. "You married her."

"Yeah, but I was young, dumb, and ugly," Walt replied, no humor in his tone. "I – it's a long story. It doesn't matter now. The only person in that family who was any good was your aunt, Jean – and she's not really your aunt, anyway, because Stacy's not – wasn't – your mother. That's it. The rest were the type of people you try to avoid in life." Walt began reflecting the moment his words ended. He popped out of a memory long enough to give a command to his daughter. "Get the information from Jean and we'll send flowers to the funeral."

"She's been dead over eight months."

"What? How come we're just finding out now?" Walt's surprise continued.

"She hunted me down on one of my social media accounts. She searched, but couldn't find you," Heidi explained. "She said she got busy with other things, then remembered to look me up."

"Wow. Eight months, huh?"

"Yeah. I'll tell her you send your condolences."

"To her. Only to Jean." Walt's mood changed from reflective to bitter. "I don't care about the rest of her family. Mention her specifically."

"Okay."

"Wow." Walt sat in his chair and faced his desk. With hands stretched wide on the desk, he looked like a schoolboy waiting for the teacher's instructions.

"I'll be right back. I have something for you." Heidi hurried out of the room.

Alone, and thus alone with his thoughts, Walt attempted to remember the good in Stacy. The task challenged his mind.

Within a minute, Heidi returned. She clutched a small bottle of water in one hand and something unseen in the other. "I have something I want you to try for me."

With a quizzical look, Walt examined his daughter. Satisfied she looked sincere, he took the bait. "What is it?"

"I talked to somebody knowledgeable about medicines and he told me this would help relax you."

"'Somebody' recommended this. Not a doctor. Not a pharmacist. 'Somebody.'" Walt's skepticism peaked.

Heidi's cheeks turned red for a brief few seconds. "Trust me. For once, please trust me. Remember how you just want what's best for me? Well, I just want what's best for you."

"May I ask who made the recommendation? It wasn't Dennis, was it?" As playful as he could make the accusation sound, he meant every word.

"Dad!"

Walt shook his head 'no' but reached for the pills in her now-opened hand. "Why do I listen to you sometimes? What do they do?"

"They just calm your nerves, that's all," Heidi explained. "You've been through a lot. A whole lot. I can't imagine going through what you've gone through." She put a reassuring hand on his shoulder. "Just take both these pills and chill for the evening. Based on what I've been told, you'll probably want more later."

Walt started to speak, but Heidi lifted her hand.

"Ah! Trust me. They're legal. They're helpful. You need it."

Walt tried not to change the expression on his face, but she reminded him of Tina. The way she could take control and convince him to relax or take a vacation while work circled overhead always amazed him. He took a deep breath. "Okay."

He put his left hand, with the two yellow-and-white pills, to his mouth and tilted his head back. He then used his now-empty left hand to unscrew the top of the bottle of water. A quick gulp of the clear liquid satisfied his daughter.

"Thank you, Daddy. I appreciate it." She leaned over and kissed Walt on the cheek, just above his beard. "I will try to learn to trust you again," she whispered.

Walt stopped himself; he knew any words he offered up would only serve to shatter the positive moment.

When she walked out of the room, Walt's brain succumbed to two thoughts; while divergent in content, they were actually quite similar. First, he found it odd she referred to him as 'Daddy.' He knew she only did so when nervous or afraid. Second, he did not take pills: vitamins, medication, or otherwise. This night would not change his approach against ingesting drugs for what he could fix naturally. He understood someday he might wind up on heart medication or some other life-prolonging drug, but something to help him 'chill,' as she put it, for the evening, was not in the cards. Not tonight; not any night.

His sleight of hand successful, he put the two pills in his desk drawer. He thought about Tony's gold watch, which had somehow found a home in this same drawer. Curious, he pulled the drawer open wider to search for other surprises. Finding none, he picked up the novel he had been reading the night Tony was murdered and attempted to read again.

His mind wandered too often to read. Stacy was dead – was everyone dead except Heidi and himself?

• • •

"He took the pills." Cell phone in hand, Heidi waited for a response, then replied, "Okay. I'll see you then."

Chapter 40

The novel was but a prop in Walt's hands. He could not bring himself to focus on the problems and misadventures of the characters while focused on his own circumstances – circumstances which propelled him closer to Death's door. Tired of re-reading the same sentences and paragraphs, he set the book down, off to one side of his desk.

"Tony is not a threat to me." Dennis' words rang in his ears. The delivery, tone, and expression amplified in Walt's mind now that Tony was gone. "It won't happen," Dennis had snapped about the possibility of Tony stopping the takeover scheme. Walt could hear the words as though Dennis stood in the den at that very moment.

Bill. His mind wandered. The man's personality. His sense of humor. The way he thought as he spoke, yet after a few seconds the words absorbed the thoughts and brilliance spilled out of his mouth. It were as though a thousand memories crashed into Walt's mind at once. He missed Bill's friendship and what he meant to the rise of Triumvirate.

His thoughts of Alex were just as complimentary, though Walt had not known him as long. Then his thoughts jumped to Tony. As he allowed his emotions to bog down in a swamp of happy times and pain, the face of Dennis Fry popped into his mind. He toyed with the mental image. Something bothered him.

He doesn't want to destroy the company, just everyone in it. Why?! His thoughts raced like a rodent fleeing a hawk. *He was upset about losing the DOD contract, even though he caused the loss.* Walt shook his head, perplexed.

The cat; dead, but not Heidi's. *Of course, not Heidi's; he wouldn't harm her. Just me. Just Triumvirate. Why?*

That face.

"I'm not worried about Alex," Dennis had said while they drank in *Sonny's*. Walt recalled thinking about the arrogance of the young man. *He knew Alex was going to die, now the FBI knows it. He paid that DeWinter-Desmond guy the next day. He needed a sidekick. An alibi. He hired one.*

Even Orion the Hunter had a sidekick – his trusty dog. *Dennis had a dirty dog, getting down and dirty for him.*

The square jaw. The brown hair. Walt sat up, as though pushed from behind. "It's those eyes," Walt blurted. No one shared the room to hear what bothered him.

He tried to relax in his chair but could not. He searched his mind for any clue. He thought back to conversations with Bill, Alex, Tony, Special Agent Bretz, Detective Encarnacion, and everyone else who came to mind. He convinced himself a clue lay in conversations or memories, waiting to be discovered.

He let his thoughts interrupt each other and soon was back to considering what bothered him about Dennis. Something that was always there. Something that bugged him, just under the surface. Something he always ignored.

His eyes.

"Those green eyes. Brilliant green." He stopped. "Green," he focused on each word. "Eyes." He stared into nothing.

A loud *pop* from in front of the house ended his trance for a brief moment.

A look of horror invaded his face. He stood up, a wild look in his own eyes, and looked around the room.

He knew. It all made sense. Everything made sense, in a sick, warped way.

The doorbell rang.

With frantic strides, Walt reached the front window and looked out, cell phone in hand. The car in the driveway confirmed his fears. He thought about his plan: *Go through the garage door and get to Agent Boles' car for protection.*

Agent Boles had the evening shift, staking out Walt's house, waiting for what Walt believed to be the inevitable visit from Dennis.

As he ran past the front door the doorbell rang a second time. Out of the corner of his eye, he caught a glance of Heidi, about to descend the stairs. *The two pills. That's why he's here.*

As Walt entered the garage, the thought crossed his mind that he possessed an unhealthy level of paranoia. *What if there's a rational explanation for all this?* The thought failed to slow him, and as the large garage door clunked upward, he raced underneath and into the driveway. *He didn't block my cars because he thinks I'm unconscious.*

Then he stopped. He felt his skin turn cold. He put his hand on his chest and struggled to breathe. He thought he might have a heart attack at the end of his driveway.

Agent Boles lay in the middle of the street, a pool of blood steadily growing, flowing from his ear.

Walt took an additional step forward to see a second, smaller pool forming under Agent Boles' mouth. The motionless man was either dead or would be in minutes.

Walt's knees buckled. He grabbed each with a hand to support himself and fought the urge to vomit. After a deep breath, his wits returned.

Walter Musgrave felt more alone than at any point in his life. He looked around, tempted to run; he was physically unprepared for such over-exertion. Armed only with his cell phone, if discovered away from his car, he would not survive against the younger, leaner, better-conditioned Dennis Fry.

Dennis made a mistake by failing to block in Walt's cars. That was the opening.

• • •

Heidi and Dennis stood in Walt's den. "He took the pills, right?" Dennis asked. They heard the engine of Walt's orange BMW Z4 fire up in the garage. "What the hell?! He should be unconscious by now! Stay here!" The final two words were delivered with a harsh expectation of obedience.

Unhappy at the command, Heidi watched Dennis rush out the front door, then followed him outside. She reached the driveway in time to see her father's car race away and Dennis hop into his Audi and make the same mad dash. She could not see the dead body in the street from her vantage point.

Heidi returned to the den and looked in the partially opened desk drawer. Her face expressed bewilderment her father had not swallowed the two yellow-and-white pills. "Well, so much for trusting my father." Bewilderment then extended to Dennis' angry reaction about the discovery. She looked down at the pills again and back toward the closed front door, as though she could find answers by staring at the inanimate objects. It was apparent she did not understand what was happening, but a sense of foreboding overtook her. "Oh, dear God," she muttered. "What is my dad up to now?"

Chapter 41

"Was that Agent Boles in front of my house?" Walt did not wait for a response. "He's dead!" Walt shouted every word. He had routed the call through his car's stereo system in order to avoid interfering with his driving. The passenger compartment could not contain the booming voice and gushing emotions.

"Where are you now?" Bretz asked. Before Walt could answer, a degree of emotion leaked into the FBI agent's voice. "Are you sure he's dead?"

"Pretty sure. There was a big pool of blood by his head." Walt stopped speaking. The last three words cracked, delivered by a troubled voice. He did not wish to remember what he had just witnessed.

"I'm sending messages now. We'll have an army of cops and agents there in a few minutes." Despite the ordeal, Bretz and his stoic manner provided a small piece of comfort to the frantic, fleeing man. "Is Heidi safe?"

"I doubt she's in the car."

"Wait a minute. What car?" Bretz asked. "She's not in the car with you?"

"I mean in Dennis' car. He's gaining on me now."

"Where are you headed?"

"I made a wrong turn!" Every word came out of Walt's mouth as though on fire.

"Okay, but where are you headed?"

"I'm headed south on the 23."

"Okay, get on the 101 north," Bretz ordered.

A pause in the conversation resulted as Walt's maneuvered his sporty orange car. He was in the fast lane, traveling at too high of a speed to dodge cars and get to the right lane in time.

"You didn't tell me in time!" Walt shouted. "I'm on the 101 South ramp." Where Highway 23 ended, Walt had the option of north or south on the 101 Freeway and chose incorrectly, according to Bretz's wishes. After another pause from the play-by-play of his reckless drive, Walt announced, "I'm getting off the 101. I'll turn around."

"No! Walt, no. You don't want him to get to you in traffic. Fry is dangerous." Bretz did not attempt to hide his concern. After a few seconds of silence, Bretz followed up. "Walt?"

Walt broke the silence. "I'm on Westlake Boulevard."

"Westlake Boulevard?" Bretz's displeasure came through the phone. "Make sure you cut over and get back on the 101. Go north. If you go south on Westlake, you might lose cell coverage."

There was another pause as Walt zig-zagged through traffic. He ran a red light without incident, then watched in his mirror as Dennis' Audi did the same. Despite two lanes of road meant for his direction, keeping his distance from Dennis remained difficult. Every move he wished to make seemed blocked by cars.

Continuing his frantic, ill-planned drive, Walt's BMW cut between cars, causing frightened drivers to swerve, honk, and gesture. Streetlights illuminated his path and allowed him to see the pursuing vehicle. As he left the populated area, the street dropped to one lane in each direction, and he steered through oncoming traffic. Now he saw only headlights and taillights.

"I'm out of Westlake, headed toward the coast," Walt cried out, his arms, chest, and legs tense. Highway 23 had transformed from a freeway, jogged onto the 101 Freeway, then cut south as part of Westlake Boulevard. At Walt's location it transformed again, this time to a mountainous roadway with sharp curves.

"Okay," came the soft response.

In his mind, Walt could see Bretz shake his head.

The voice again came through the speakers. "Listen, when you get to PCH, head north, up the coast toward Oxnard. We'll be waiting for you. Got it? In the meantime, I'll try to get police to the intersection of PCH and 23 to stop you there."

"Okay."

"Listen, Walt," Bretz said. "He's gonna ram you. He's gonna try to take you off a cliff. It's really easy to do. It doesn't take much to wreck another car like that. If you can't drive away from him, in a straight section slam on your brakes, okay? It'll mess up his car and yours, but the damage to his front end might make the car undriveable. You got that?"

"Got it."

"And Walt, we have evidence – Tony – for – found – Dennis – the –"

"Curtis, you're breaking up. I can't hear you. But I think I know who Dennis is." Walt glanced at his phone on the center console next to him. "Curtis! I know who he is! I know why this is happening!"

The phone squawked three sharp beeps. The cell connection, lost. The call, dropped.

"Damn it!" Walt slapped his dashboard. "Damn it, I screwed up!"

Anger, interrupted by the car which closed behind him, still lingered as Walt worked the steering wheel, gas pedal, gear shift, and brakes along the mountainous roadway. His fixation with the rear-view mirror proved near-fatal when he failed to notice a pickup truck ahead of him, going in the same direction. He slammed on his brakes and skidded, nearly out of control. Seconds later, he saw the headlamps of an approaching vehicle light up the guard rail ahead. He timed the pass perfectly.

The pass on the curve complete, he jerked the car back into his rightful lane, prompting an angry honk from the pickup truck driver. The darkness concealed the one-finger salute which followed the horn blast.

Two additional cars in quick succession prevented Dennis from duplicating the pass. Now angry, the driver of the pickup sped up at an inconvenient moment for the pursuer, delaying further the latter's meeting with Walt.

Walt used the interference from the pickup to his advantage. As he pulled farther ahead, he toyed with ideas about how to trick his nemesis. He reached the unfortunate conclusion nothing would work better than getting off Highway 23 as soon as possible. No adequate turns were available, and if he made the attempt – and Dennis discovered him – Walt would be trapped, unprepared for the maniacal man.

The road never seemed to straighten out. The switchbacks enhanced the intimidating heights of the cliffs – some of which reached 100 feet, but darkness concealed that which should frighten the panicked driver. Each time he thought a passing opportunity awaited, the next curve robbed him of hope. By the time he approached the bottom of the mountains, Walt felt as though he and his car had survived a slalom course.

Through the darkness, he could not see the Pacific Ocean, but he could see the darkened void left by the absence of light, which he had grown accustomed to seeing from Tony's hillside house. As his Z4 slowed to make the turn at the approaching intersection with Pacific Coast Highway, the seemingly menacing headlights threatened only 200 yards behind.

No police; no roadblock; no joyful ending to this miserable months-long battle with his former employee. Walt pointed his car "up" PCH, as the locals say, and headed toward the town of Oxnard. Before him lay a long 15 miles of what should be pleasant coastline driving, but Walt would not notice the nighttime sights and sounds or have time to visit any of the darkened beaches which zoomed by his windows.

Walt glanced down at his phone; no service. For the first three miles, he enjoyed the luxury of two lanes for cars traveling in his direction, but twice he resorted to passing cars, which traveled side-by-side, on the right shoulder. On both occasions, however, Dennis met the traffic with propitious timing, the faster of the two cars having completed its pass. The drivers on PCH certainly thought the nuts were out that Friday night.

Walt checked his rearview mirror twice every five seconds. He saw the ominous lights, gaining on him, promising to deliver death. For a moment, he felt ready to give up. Down to one northbound lane, his only solace lay in the frequently wide right shoulder in which to pass other cars. The only danger he faced on the shoulder were the endless white concrete barriers – parallel to the road – which stopped minor rock slides from reaching the highway.

Back to two northbound lanes, Dennis again hit traffic at a perfect time. Sharp turns followed by long straightaways followed by sharp turns turned PCH into a road course for the two drivers.

Walt felt a twinge of optimism as he closed within three miles of Point Magu Naval Air Station. *They've gotta be set up*

close to the air station or we'll be in town. They don't want that.
He reasoned with himself safety beckoned a few turns away.

The car rocked hard. Shocked, Walt whipped the wheel around to avoid colliding with an oncoming SUV. The straight stretch of roadway included a subtle climb. Dennis had not waited for a curve; he attacked at his first opportunity. Walt heard his left rear tire rub against metal. Another crash clipped the Z4's left side and spun the rear end of the vehicle to the right. The car launched to the left, but a highway scenic turnout saved him from plunging downward, onto the shoreline rocks.

Walt fought the wheel and stomped on the brakes. He slid on the dirt past where cars normally parked during daylight hours. Dennis and his damaged car followed into the turnout.

Walt's car plowed to a stop with the passenger side facing Dennis' car. Dennis managed to stop his vehicle before another collision ensued.

The crazed man climbed out of his car. He looked back to see that two cars behind them did not turn in, and no other cars sat in the turnout. They were alone. "Walt, let's go. Get out. We have some unfinished business." He approached the BMW but took time to notice the stone wall which prevented vehicles from driving off the cliff and into the ocean. At an elevation of roughly 30 feet – and two miles from town – Dennis knew he owned the advantage. Although motorists passed by on the highway, Walt would not be able to get close enough to the road to flag them down.

Walt's driver's-side door was opened.

"Walter Musgrave!" Dennis's throaty shout pierced the darkness. "I know you're here. Stop running." He paused to listen, but the passing cars and the ocean waves crashing against the rocks below worked against him. Dennis gave a quick scan of the area, then pursued what appeared to be the easiest way around the rock parking wall. A short-lived search led to the fleeing man. Dennis yelled at the top of his lungs, waving like a girl excited to see her boyfriend arriving at the airport. "Over here! Hi, Walt, over here!"

Exhausted, Walt turned to face his tormentor. A quick glance revealed his inferior position. Unfamiliar with this turnout, he had run into a trap. He could climb, but the rocky hill near the road led to nowhere. He could clamber the 30 feet down to the water's edge or jump, but either move would be suicidal. He could confront Dennis or go through him. The odds of success were low, but the last option was the only reasonable one. He looked back to Dennis, who walked toward him.

Two police cars sped south on PCH, heading toward the direction from which Walt and Dennis had just come, their lights and sirens announcing an emergency. They passed the turnout without seeing the BMW and Audi, which were sufficiently hidden from view.

Dennis grinned as he watched the police cars race away from them, then turned his attention back to the matter at hand. "I'm not here to kill you. I'm here to watch you kill yourself." Dennis paused for effect. "Dad." He paused again before concluding his thought. "Or did you figure that out already?"

Chapter 42

"They're out looking for them now," Agent Bauml explained to Special Agent Bretz. "The Sheriff's Department said they might be able to get us a chopper within the hour."

"Musgrave will be dead within the hour," Bretz responded, his even tone obvious over the cell phone's speaker.

"I put a call out, but they only sent one squad car at first, and it did a drive-by at the 23-PCH intersection. They only have two choppers available at the moment, and they're in Santa Barbara County, helping with a search and rescue in some canyons. Lost hikers. One of the choppers is on its way back now, apparently." He paused to change subjects to the urgency at hand. "I think they turned south on PCH," Bauml announced, unaware of his factual error. "The county sent two cars down Pacific Coast Highway, then north on Highway 23 and they didn't see anything. They're making their way back toward us, checking cliffs and turnouts," Bauml paused to see whether his boss had lost the cellular connection.

"What about south?" Bretz inquired.

"On PCH? They sent two more cars south. They're past 23 now, and they're checking turnouts and beaches and cliffs."

The unhappiness in Bretz's voice came through the speaker. "This guy Fry's been good at destroying and concealing evidence, so we have to get this figured out ASAP. We need as much evidence against Fry as possible and, of course, we have to protect Musgrave from him."

"Copy that." Bauml paused before asking the question. "Is he dead?"

"Yes," came the flat response. "Boles never drew his gun. He got out of his car for some reason, gun holstered." He paused. "I'm on my way to join you."

"Copy that. I'll keep you informed," Bauml responded. He ended the call, then punched another number into the phone and resumed his efforts to find Walt and Dennis. Surrounded by a sea of twenty police officers, he turned to a captain and urged a course of action involving a partial dispersal of the deputies.

• • •

"I thought you were dead."

"What?" Walt's confusion from the remark fused with his anger at the entire situation, sending his adrenaline levels higher.

"Oh now, don't tell me you don't watch John Wayne movies? Or maybe, *Escape from New York*? Although I don't suppose you saw that one." Dennis yelled his words to make up for the distance and the sounds of the nighttime coastline.

"The cops will be here any minute, Dennis. Get out of here while you can," Walt ordered.

"You still don't understand who I am, do you?" The flat ground, away from where daytime tourists and locals walked, was strewn with rocks – some as small as pebbles, others larger than basketballs. Traversing the area in darkness required deft footwork.

"I figured it out tonight." Still 100 feet apart, that Walt and Dennis had to yell every word to hear one another gave the conversation an almost comedic touch, but neither noticed the opportunity for humor.

Dennis began a methodical approach, careful to avoid a tumble on the large rocks spread out in the darkness. "Walter, this wasn't a mystery. Don't you understand that? It was obvious. Everyone tells me I look a lot like my mother. I have traits similar

330

to you. The whole timing of my arrival. You should've figured it out long ago." He paused as he stepped around a rock the size of a basketball, lit just in time by the faint headlamps of a car passing by on Pacific Coast Highway. "What's my motive? I mean, come on! I don't have an obvious motive unless you combine it with everything else. Then it's obvious, Dad. All of it."

When Walt elected to not respond, Dennis lashed out with one more verbal jab: "And you're a businessman, supposedly able to see the big picture? Pathetic."

"Give it up, Dennis. You've lost your mind. All these killings! You're insane!"

Continuing his mocking approach, Dennis responded with an acerbic bite. "Pretty sad a man doesn't recognize his own son." While dodging another large rock, he continued. "But, I guess that's what happens when you walk out on a pregnant wife."

Fifty feet apart.

"I didn't walk out on anybody!" Walt snapped.

"Oh yeah? Did you just forget how to get back to your own house? You couldn't find a map?"

"We split up. We shouldn't have even married each other."

"So, you walked out. Nice. Tells me what kind of man you really are."

Twenty-five feet.

Walt chose not to reply to the latest insult. His thoughts floated to Stacy and their rocky relationship; to the way their marriage ended; to the way she tormented him until he paid her over a million dollars to leave him alone, forever. Even at the time, he doubted the pay-off would work – that she would abide by the written agreement – but indeed, she went away.

Dennis continued to walk forward. He did not appreciate the silence. "You're not gonna dodge this one, old man!" he bellowed. "Look at me!"

Face-to-face.

Dennis stopped directly in front of his father and poked him in the chest. "Look at me. You're not going to ignore my existence anymore." Yelling was now by choice rather than necessity.

The cold breeze sent a shiver through Walt's frame. The moist air left a trail out of both men's mouths until the words dissipated into the night air. The only consistent light beamed from the rising Moon; facial expressions proved difficult to distinguish. Walt took in every detail. The poke to his chest ushered in his hour of death on THE day. He wanted to see, hear, know, feel everything. He wanted to experience his last moments rather than have them rush by, a crazed blur.

"If it's me you hate," Walt began, sadness escaping his mouth with the moisture. "Why kill Bill and Alex? Why kill Tony?"

Dennis grabbed Walt by the throat. "Don't change the subject," he hissed. The moonlight caught enough of Dennis' eyes for Walt to see the frightening sight of smoldering rage about to ignite the air.

Walt pushed him away. Dennis relented, released his throat. Walt turned his head to one side and cleared his throat in an attempt to drive away the mild pain. "I don't even know you're my son. I figured out you're Stacy's son, but that doesn't mean you're mine."

Dennis threw up his hands in disgust and laughed. "Search your feelings, Luke." He laughed again, but this time the laugh morphed into that of a wicked, deranged man. "You must be out of your mind. What are you talking about? Are you gonna tell me about a virgin birth next? Are you just crazy? Are you an idiot?"

His disgust grew with each word. "I've known my whole life that you're my father, and now you want to deny me?"

Walt could not see the back of Dennis' hand in the darkness. When it struck his face, the collision and pain surprised him. He staggered backward.

"Don't ever deny me again." In the darkness, he peered past Walt. "You're twenty feet from the cliff you're going to leap off of. Before you jump, you will not deny me again. Understood?" The words were like a growl from a wild beast, out of its den to feast on human flesh.

"I didn't know you existed, Dennis!" Walt cried out with a mixture of pain and frustration. "I'm not making it up!" Desperation joined the blend. "I don't know what she told you, but I didn't know you existed." Resignation entered the fray.

"When I was a boy," Dennis said, calm voice meeting the ocean breeze. "I used to write you letters. Mom used to mail those letters – dozens of them – but you never bothered to write back."

Walt's laugh was one of frustration, but before he could comment, Dennis delivered a straight-right punch to Walt's stomach. Walt's brain had not processed what happened when his knees dropped to the dirt, followed by his hands. He tried to shake the feeling he would never breathe again.

Dennis walked a small circle, away from his adversary, to let him recover. No one could see them. They were blocked from the highway by a large, rocky hill. The headlights of passing cars did not point toward them and cast only minimal, indirect light. Dennis appeared to not be rushed.

After what seemed ten minutes to Walt, he reached his feet in sixty seconds.

"You ran away, Walter. You just couldn't handle it, could you?" Dennis' mocking tone was designed to cut. "Some man you are." Dennis laughed an over-the-top, snarling laugh that sounded like a character out of a 1950s mad-scientist movie. "You ruined my life, now I'm gonna make you pay." He laughed again.

Walt felt little, emotionally; Dennis' words failed to wound him. His cheek hurt; his stomach and lower torso sent signals to his brain that he might vomit at any moment; he felt the cold of the ocean air pressing down on his skin; and he held on to the gnawing thought he could not physically stop this young man. Words were now meaningless to him. He retreated two steps, toward the cliff.

As he gathered himself physically, he also allowed his mind to clear. He worked the math in his head. He had reviewed Dennis' personnel file enough times to remember his birthday; the timing made sense. It was reasonable to Walt that he had unknowingly left Stacy when she was pregnant with Dennis.

"And I see you were all broken up by my mom's death," Dennis hissed, sarcasm almost visible in the darkness.

"I just found out tonight. Heidi received a message from your Aunt Jean."

"Oh, isn't that convenient. Everything's 'tonight,'" Dennis continued his exhibition of mockery. "You find out about Mom tonight. You figure out who I am tonight. Did you also grow a conscience tonight?" He rushed forward and put his nose inches from Walt's nose. "Or is that too much to ask of a great businessman like you?"

Fearing another punch, Walt stepped backward. "You went to business school and then got a job at Triumvirate, just to get to me." What started out as a question ended as a statement of fact. Walt took another step back.

"Yes. Exactly." Dennis remained in physical control, but he sent signals that emotional control slipped perilously close to the edge of mental mayhem. "At first I just wanted to prove myself, show you what I accomplished despite you – despite your denying my existence. When I got my first good job, I wasn't satisfied. It wasn't enough. I wanted to destroy you." Dennis paused his tirade for a moment and threw back his head, looking upward at the glow in the sky from the area's city lights along the coastline, which highlighted the clouds and washed out the stars.

Walt used the break to look around, to check his surroundings. He saw the impossibility of escape.

Dennis continued with his verbal attack. "Oh, I decided a long time ago you weren't getting away with what you've done to me, but then I got to Triumvirate and I decided I wanted to take over. *That* would show you." Dennis took a step forward, making up for Walt's retreat. "But I still didn't find the idea fulfilling. I wanted more. I started hating you so bad – I just couldn't find satisfaction – I wanted to kill you. But then I finally decided you'd kill yourself. That *does* satisfy me." A wicked laugh pierced the darkness. "That makes me feel real good. *Then* I take the company."

Walt took a step backward, away from his antagonistic offspring. He had to find reason to hope. His thoughts dwelled on escape or fighting back while the man before him raged on.

"Killing made me feel better," Dennis added. "It empowered me – and I've done it before, so it was no big deal." Dennis paused before adding, "I liked that killing gave me the power to hurt you, to wound you, to make you afraid. I liked that power. And the power to kill – the rush I got – made it all the more rewarding. I should've done all the killing myself. If that idiot

DeWinter hadn't gotten himself mixed up with drugs, I wouldn't have experienced the exhilaration of killing Tony and Troy."

Walt took a step toward their cars, despite the distance to his BMW.

Dennis took note of the movement. "Just so you know, I want this moment to last as long as possible. They're not gonna find us, Walter." He pronounced his father's name with disdain sharp enough to slice through any father's heart – even one who just discovered his parentage. "I'm enjoying torturing you. I want you to know that; but if you think you can make it to your car, I'll show you what real torture feels like."

Walt did not doubt the threat.

"I envy Heidi," Dennis switched thoughts. "She had a father and mother who loved her. I was going to destroy her, just to hurt you, but I realized she's a good person. She's not a monster like you." Dennis glared at his father. "I made sure I took good care of her."

"*I'm* a monster?" Walt noted the irony.

"I had a psycho of a stepdad who beat me and cursed me and criticized everything I ever tried." The rage which built as Dennis spoke subsided again. "But Heidi, oh, she had a dad who didn't pay attention to her enough – I get that. But he was kind to her. Was. She'll cry at your funeral. She had a dad who loved her mom." He hesitated, as though remembering his childhood. "I can't imagine what that would've been like." He paused before snarling again. "But you walked out. You denied my existence."

In no danger of being seen, Walt reached into his pants pocket and pulled out a pocketknife. In the darkness, neither man could see the wood handle of the unopened knife. The three-inch blade was not much of a weapon, but it would have to suffice. He

336

retreated two more steps, toward the cliff's edge. He now stood on a piece of land which jutted toward the water, too close to the edge to advance to his right, toward his car.

"Nothing to say to that, huh?" Dennis challenged.

"You're a madman, Dennis. You've been living your whole life based on a lie. A lie!" He shouted the last two words to make his point. "I never received any letters. Your mother never told me she was pregnant when I left. Your mother was crazy and a liar." To Walt's surprise, the assault on Stacy's character did not invite another punch or slap. "This is all news to me, Dennis. All of it! You come here, bent on revenge. You wage death and destruction on my business and friends and you expect me to feel sympathy for you?!" Walt's shouts reflected the return of his energy.

Dennis stepped forward, causing Walt to step backward. "I can do whatever I want, old man. You can spin it all you want, make yourself sound so innocent, but I lived the life. I know. Now, you're at my mercy. I can do anything!" His last words flew out more roar than statement. "I got traces of explosives from DeWinter and put them in the G&S guy's trunk. It worked! The FBI was thrown off track. Don't you see, Walter? I can do whatever I want and you can't stop me! So, spin tales all you want. It doesn't matter. You can't stop me."

"You've. Lived. A. Lie." Walt's staccato delivery emphasized every word before he returned to raw anger and let his words flow naturally again. "You hate me because of what your mother told you. She was deranged, Dennis. Don't you understand? I left her because we couldn't get along. I made a mistake marrying her. She was manipulative. She was a liar. She was devious." He paused, again waiting for blows which never came. "She finally went away when I paid her one-point-two million dollars to leave

337

me alone. I heard she remarried – I assume that's the stepdad you're referring to – and my life was peaceful again. But all this, this anger, this hatred. It's based on a lie. This is all a waste of time and energy."

"That's what you want me to believe," Dennis responded in an unrecognizable voice, the hatred dripping off every word.

Walt sensed doubt. He rushed for the opening. "Don't you find it odd, Dennis, that just a couple years later I wasn't afraid to raise a child?" He pleaded, though he attempted to disguise the tone. "Have you not thought that maybe I would've liked to have had a son, too?" Walt waited for a response but did not receive one. "This whole pursuit is built on nothing but bitterness – yours and Stacy's. She turned you into a bitter child. You grew up into a bitter man. And it's all a lie."

"Liar!" Dennis shouted.

"If I'd known I had a son, I would've tried to get custody of you, to get you away from her. I know how manipulative she is – was. I know what she was like. I wouldn't want you to grow up in that environment."

As Dennis repeated his charge against Walt, the elder man advanced toward the younger. "Listen to me, Dennis," Walt begged. "If I'd known about you, I would've done everything possible to raise you, to rescue you from her clutches. I wanted out for my sanity, Dennis. I would've wanted you out for yours!" Walt punctuated his last sentence with such ferocity his voice cracked as he yelled.

"I've known my whole life what you're really like, Dad." Dennis stressed 'Dad' with such disdain, Walt dropped his shoulders.

"I guess you're gonna believe whatever you want."

"Well guess what, old man," Dennis' attitude changed again, unfazed by Walt's words. "I take it you didn't write your suicide note like I asked you to, but I have a story for the cops and Heidi, all clean and shiny and ready to go. You chased me out here, told me how you hired that idiot DeWinter lowlife to kill your business partners, and oh yeah, you were going to kill me, even though I'm the father of your grandchild." Dennis laughed. It were as though Hell itself opened up and taught Dennis the nastiest laugh imaginable.

Dennis could not see Walt's reaction. Physically beaten and emotionally exhausted, Walt was not ready to take on the smallest of adversaries. He felt as though he lacked the strength to lift a puppy off the ground. He was beaten. Until Dennis' last statement.

Inside Walt's brain, something snapped. It were as though a valve released several deadly emotions and chemicals, brewing a fearsome concoction. Blood rushed to his muscles and face. Rage arrived. Anger was but a frivolous emotion compared to the wrath which boiled over.

In one motion, Walt opened the pocketknife and rushed forward.

Dennis heard the metallic *pop* as the knife clicked into a locked position, giving him a split-second notice of the attack. He stepped aside to avoid the onrushing man.

Enough light infiltrated the top of the cliff for Walt to see Dennis' reaction and adjust. He changed his path to crash his arm – and the knife blade – forward, into Dennis' upper chest, just above his heart. The blade entered close to the shoulder, between the top two ribs.

A high-pitched scream, which lasted only a second, split the chilled Pacific breeze. Lying on his back, Dennis could feel the blade leave his body. The father lifted the small knife to plunge it again, to strike a death blow, but the son struck back with a punch to the throat.

With Walt's grip lost, the pocketknife disappeared into the night.

"Police! Get away from each other!" Bobbing beams of light cut through the damp air. Light from the powerful flashlights danced onto the subjects, then off, repeating the cycle.

Walt paused to look at the oncoming lights. His averted attention came to a crashing end as he felt his body flying backward. Dennis had hurtled into Walt in an attempt to carry the elder man toward the cliff's edge. When the younger man stumbled on a rock, both crashed to the ground. Walt delivered a blow to Dennis' face before he realized they were three feet from the cliff. He could hear the waves colliding with rocks 30 feet below.

One of the flashlight beams disappeared.

"Dawson!" the more distant voice shouted. Confused, the sheriff's deputy called for his partner again. His beam searched the ground until he saw the deputy, prone and motionless. Crossing the flat but black ground with confidence came with a price.

"This is 857, Martinez. We found your guys. Dawson is down. He took a header. We need that chopper at the turnout south of Point Magu Beach." Deputy Martinez changed his focus to the fighting men who were 40 yards away. "Stand down," he shouted. The confusion from the sudden loss of his partner dominated his voice. "Separate yourselves now!"

Unfazed, Dennis rose to his feet and let loose a painful groan audible over a gust of wind and the violent surf not far away. "Are you telling me the truth? You really didn't receive those letters? You really didn't know?" Dennis demanded, the pain from the knife wound evident in his voice.

With a weak "yes," Walt nodded. He tried to climb to his feet. "I really didn't know about you." He struggled to speak. "And the FBI knows you're connected to that hitman. They know about the 40 bank accounts. They know what you've done."

"You really didn't know you had a son?" Dennis asked the same question in a different way.

"No! I didn't know," came the answer.

"Then you can live." The pronouncement communicated the intended sincerity. Dennis hesitated. "I've lost, Walter. I've lost. If you know about my past crimes, then I know where you got the information." Dennis paused. Neither man moved. "But you're still gonna pay a price. You ruined my life; now I'm gonna ruin yours." Dennis replied.

To Walt's shock, Dennis pulled him to his feet.

"Separate from each other," Deputy Martinez ordered, now 60 feet away. He looked back in the direction of his fallen partner, and the beam of his flashlight followed. The level of uncertainty which plagued Deputy Martinez's mind was clear, even in the darkness.

"Help me!" Dennis shouted. He grabbed Walt's left arm with his right hand and lifted them up, standing side-by-side, like a referee declaring a winner after a boxing match. Dennis pulled the pair backward a step. The flashlight beam again found the combatants.

"Separate!" came the repeated command, the officer yelling at the top of his lungs.

"He's gonna kill me!" Dennis cried out above the sounds of the coastline.

Confused and exhausted, Walt did not move. Too afraid to fight Dennis so close to the cliff's edge, too engrossed in a thousand thoughts that crashed into his mind, Walt kept his feet planted in their current location and felt no urge to do anything except wait for the deputy to resolve the madness.

Dennis dropped their arms to waist level. He turned to his father and looked him in the eye. The brilliant beam of the powerful flashlight lit their faces. "Your turn to be ruined," he stated in a flat, gruff voice.

Before Walt could react, or even process what was happening, Dennis leaped backward. He held Walt's arm long enough to spin him around. Walt lurched toward the edge of the cliff, then shifted his weight and staggered parallel to the cliff in a desperate attempt to avoid following Dennis over the side.

To Walt, the impact below occurred in silence – the wind and sea conspired to conceal the sound of bone striking rock, 30 feet down. His first thought was one of puzzlement – why would Dennis kill himself to spite Walt? The two deputies' reactions provided the answer. The spin; the upraised arm; the timing of the fall. Dennis had given up only to make it look as though Walt had knocked his long-lost son over the cliff.

The deputy screamed profanities and irate questions as he walked forward with a renewed vigor and a drawn gun. From behind him, a dazed voice added to the commotion. "I saw it," a weak Deputy Dawson called out, unseen blood dripping from his cheek and forehead. "I saw what he did. I saw him push him."

Walt wailed – in anger, in sadness, and at insanity's door. On hands and knees, Walt wept – he wept for the son he never knew; for what his daughter would think of him; for himself. The deputy put his foot in the middle of Walt's back and pushed. The businessman collapsed, as though he were a weed in the ground.

Cuffed. Humiliated. Prisoner.

The Pyrrhic victory had been won: nothing was left but his life, his daughter, and his house, and the latter two would not be his for long, he reasoned. But he was alive.

"Your turn to be ruined." The words echoed through his brain as Deputy Martinez read him his Miranda rights and shouted words of amazement and disbelief such a wicked crime could be perpetrated in full view of an officer of the law.

Only 30 feet below, the body lay on the rocks, motionless. Ocean water licked the carcass. The moonlight cast a pale glow over what had been Dennis Fry.

He lay dead, but the nightmare of Dennis Fry continued.

• • •

A helicopter hovered overhead, its floodlight providing illumination for the deputies to escort their prisoner away when ready. FBI agents toured the scene, flashlights in hand. Inconsolable, the broken businessman trembled, babbled, repeated his story to anyone who would listen, and trembled and babbled more. None of the deputies wanted to believe the tale of Dennis' bizarre suicide. Meanwhile, Deputies Martinez and Dawson relayed the story of Walt's brazen murder, committed within full view of the officers.

The two FBI agents at the scene offered no opinions, no backgrounds of the men involved, or explanations of the situation beyond the initial briefing the deputies had received earlier in the evening. The agents listened, nodded, shook their heads, then departed.

The weight of the damp ocean air on Walt's shoulders could not compare to the weight on his mind. Too much information, sorrow, and pain passed through his brain to process. The defeated man hung his head as the police car hauled him away.

Chapter 43

His haggard face, his unkempt hair, his defeated demeanor – all were amplified by the orange jumpsuit. The bruises on his cheeks and jaw were noticeable without close inspection. His swollen lower lip showed evidence of a cut on the mend; overnight, the healing process had begun. On the opposite side of a table from her, separated by an almost impenetrable wall and thick Lexan, Walt found it difficult to look his daughter in the eyes as he related his story into the phone handset. He fought to lift his head and peer at her as he explained his long-lost son's irrational leap.

"I don't buy a word of it," Heidi scolded in a voice as though speaking to a small-time conman scheming to obtain bus money to Riverside. "Dennis was here to help you, and yet you say all this crazy stuff about him." Incredulity dripping from every word, she succeeded at letting him know her level of disgust through the telephone in her hand. "And I cannot believe." She threw her head back as she emphasized every word. "I just cannot believe he told you this whole ridiculous story about me being pregnant. He never even kissed me good night!"

Walt's eyebrows lifted in surprise.

"Yeah. See what your paranoid fantasies caused? He never laid a hand on me. I don't even know if I believe he's your son. I think you're out of your mind. I'm sorry, but you're nuts!" Her anger continued to rise as she spoke. "I sat here and listened to your stupid paranoid story without saying a word, but I think it reflects on what you think of me, too. Just disgusting!" She slapped the table in front of her.

Walt attempted a defense. "Heidi, he was trying to destroy me because of the garbage my ex-wife put in his head." Despite the passion the words should have carried, Walt was emotionless, bordering on monotone. Speaking into the phone only enhanced the cold, disconnected feel of the conversation. Despite sitting three feet apart, they were worlds away from each other.

"Are you sure you aren't confused about who filled who's mind with what?" Heidi did not give an inch.

"Heidi. Sweetheart. You're all I've got. Listen to me," Walt begged. "I've been working with the FBI on all this. They know. Ask Agent Bretz. Curtis Bretz. I'll put him in touch with you. He'll tell you. He knows I –"

"He knows what? Your stories? Your wild paranoid fantasies?" She motioned to the guard. "I can't take this anymore. You murdered my boyfriend! He was a good man!" She burst into tears as the sheriff's deputy on jail duty stopped next to her, ready to usher her away. "You murdered my boyfriend," she repeated. Tears streamed. She stood and shot daggers from her eyes. "They emailed and upped their offer in Dallas. I'm accepting it today." The shattered young woman walked away, flanked by the officer. The tears increased, from a stream to a swollen river.

Walt wanted to be left alone. He had not cried in years, but of late it had become a habit. At this moment, he wished to cry, but his tear ducts were empty. His broken heart could not pump enough blood to energize the production of tears. Pain gave way to a numb emptiness. Misery and surrender danced over his hollowed shell.

The deputy on his side of the impenetrable wall shook his head when Walt tried to stand. Before Walt could protest, the deputy's hand pressed on his shoulder, a firmness which told him to sit still. His mind remained with Heidi. Nothing else mattered.

Walt never completely grasped the importance of the concepts of empathy and setting aside time for others. He did manage to serve Tina's needs to a tolerable level, but she loved him all the same – the type of woman he needed. She understood him. The only other people to understand him to a large degree were Tony and Rose. To everyone else, his drive for business success was extreme. His relationships were cold. His interactions were unusual.

Now, when it was too late, he understood he had failed his daughter. She needed him – had always needed him – but he remained emotionally absent.

While these contrite reflections bounced through his brain, he came to the realization his attorney, Mel Harvey, and Special Agent Curtis Bretz sat on the other side of the window. He recalled he had previously consented to more visitors. In no mood to speak to anyone, Walt frowned but did not voice his unhappiness. He needed to speak to the two men, but Heidi – Heidi clouded his thoughts. Heidi gnawed at his soul. His only child.

Only hours prior, he learned he had a son, and then he did not – the son he never knew was gone. He could not fathom losing Heidi.

Walt stared into Harvey's eyes.

"Walt, I'm sorry," Harvey began, phone in hand. "But I object to meeting you with anyone else present. I don't understand your demand. We should be in the private room for attorney-client conversations." Harvey looked at Bretz. "No offense personally." He looked back at Walt, through the glass. "We can't discuss matters with him, or any other member of law enforcement, present. I've worked on a plea deal and I think we need to discuss it alone."

No answer from the client.

"Excuse me, Mister Harvey," Bretz interjected. "But do you understand what Walt and I have accomplished together over the last –"

"You shouldn't be here," the lawyer interrupted, his voice louder. "This man has serious psychological problems and you want to –"

"Psychological problems? Are you kidding me? Did you not talk to Detective Encarnacion about what the FBI uncovered about Dennis? Are you kidding me?"

Harvey turned his attention to Walt, who could only hear the lawyer's portion of the conversation. "I talked to Detective Rob, Walt. He says you're being accused of murdering Dennis. We know about your split personality and it doesn't look good, Walt." Harvey seemed perplexed at Walt's silence. "I was thinking about some important points that will support my plea plan that can spare you the death –"

Walt held up his hand; the lawyer obeyed the silent command to stop speaking.

"I've got nothing to defend, nothing to plead," Walt began. "My daughter hates me, my only son is dead – suicide, right there at my side – and my company is in tatters." Walt stared into space, between the shoulders of the two men. After a long five seconds, he continued. "There's nothing left to defend. I don't care. Let 'em do what they will. It doesn't matter."

"Walt, what I was thinking was you could plead guilty to manslaughter and –"

"Uh, excuse me," Bretz interrupted. "I can't hear him, but I have something to contribute here."

"I told you, I don't even like your presence here. This is ridiculous," Harvey protested. "Walt," he turned his attention back to his client. "Why did you tell the deputies you'd only talk to me with him present? I don't understand this?"

"Because," Walt began with a slow, deliberate delivery. He gripped the phone tighter. "I didn't feel like getting ushered all the way back to my cell and then called back here again. It's just easier to fire you now, then talk to Bretz."

With an embarrassed look, Harvey looked at the FBI agent, as though Bretz could hear his client's words, then back to Walt. "You're firing me?"

Walt nodded. His slow movements were that of a man who just survived a medieval torture chamber. "Your advice sucks. If not for Bretz and his men, I'd be headed to prison for God knows how many murders, or maybe the funny farm for life. If I need an attorney, I'll call anybody but you."

Walt did not speak another word until Harvey disappeared beyond the door, escorted by the sheriff's deputy.

A broad smile crossed Bretz's face as he grabbed the phone's receiver. "Well, you still got it. You're still the tough businessman. Glad to see it." Bretz laughed.

The laugh failed to bring a smile to the face of the accused.

"You don't need to plead to anything," Bretz assured the prisoner. "I've got lots of information, but I'll keep it to the essentials. The Sheriff's Department confirmed your cell phone never left your house the night Tony was murdered, but here's the interesting thing." Stepping outside his normal stoicism, Bretz became excited as he explained the situation. "Neither did Fry's. He left his phone at your house."

"Is that good?"

"It shows me he understood how his phone could rat him out, but not his car."

Walt flashed a confused look.

"He had *OnStar*. We were able to trace his path that night. Agent Bauml got a subpoena and we looked at the records last night. That's what he was reviewing when I sent him to Oxnard to stop you and Fry."

Walt's broad smile signaled his rising interest.

"We know for a fact Fry parked a few hundred yards from Tony's house around the time he was murdered. He was there for 15 or 16 minutes, then his car left. If Fry were alive, he'd be under arrest right now."

"That means he came back to my house and planted the watch and that club," Walt added.

"And Troy Gustafson's keys, although that'll take more proof – we haven't found his body yet. And because Heidi let him in whenever he came over, he didn't necessarily plant those items immediately."

Walt thought for a few seconds before the smile deflated. "I still don't have anything to live for. I'm sure my company will go bankrupt. Heidi still hates me."

"I'll explain things to Heidi when she's ready to listen to reason," Bretz said. "I got enough on Fry. Don't worry. You're not getting charged for murder. Fry was crazy. All capital letters. Bona fide. I've already talked to the two deputies on-scene and they say it could've happened the way you said. No jury's gonna buy murder; Harvey hasn't talked to everyone yet at the Sheriff's Department. Oh!" Bretz remembered a key point. "Rose Bakkeby says she quitting her job as CEO where she works and she's going to become the interim boss at Triumvirate. Some of your junior executives – all two of them, apparently – approved it. It'll be fine."

Bretz noticed the smile come and go at the mention of Rose's name. When Walt looked away, an evil grin appeared as Bretz narrowed his eyes. "I'm sure they'll take the company public. But at least you'll have something to come back to."

Bretz lost the grin as Walt's fiery eyes met his.

Walt leaned forward and growled his response. "They're not taking my company public. I can tell you that right now."

"You can't stop it from prison. You can't stop it if you give up." With that, Bretz stood and nodded to the deputy on duty. "You'll be in prison forever if you give up. You're the only one who knows what really happened out there last night."

"I won't allow it!" Walt snarled. "They're not gonna do that! They're not taking Triumvirate public!"

The FBI special agent looked down at the face of the accused, phone still in hand. "I'll do some talking and you'll be out of here later today, maybe tomorrow – if you have something to live for, of course." He disappeared through the doorway.

Walt's snarl twisted into a smile. He realized he now had something to live for. Bretz knew that was all Walter Musgrave needed.

About the Author

Brian W. Peterson was born and raised in Missouri and has lived in Oklahoma, California, and his current home of Kansas, where he resides with his wife, Mindy. He leads a dull life (according to others) because all he does is read and write.

Brian's intense dreams and overactive imagination have always compelled him to write. As a child, he would imagine bad and weird things happening to him, then would write down the ideas so he could someday have material to write novels. He has written the sci-fi adventure Children of the Sun and the psychological thriller Dead Dreams. This is Novel Number Three.

Whatever you do, don't ask him about his sleepwalking.

You can contact Brian through:

His website: WrittenByBWP.com
Twitter: @WrittenByBWP
Facebook: /WrittenByBWP

Made in the USA
Columbia, SC
11 January 2020

86482063R00214